This Time
Justice

This Time Justice

Liz Roadifer

Liz Roadifer Books

Published by Liz Roadifer Books
P.O. Box 22
Pine Bluffs, WY 82082-0022

LizRoadiferBooks.com

Cover art by Duvall Design
Edited by Final Eyes Editing

ISBN 978-1-942335-02-3

"It is better that ten guilty persons escape than that one innocent suffer."

~~~ Sir William Blackstone, jurist, 1897

Chapter One

Vermin live underground. Skunks. Roaches. Rats.

People.

One of the reasons Gillian Dohr hated taking the subway whenever she came to New York. It was always safer to be on top of Mother Earth and feel the wind and sun on her face. To breathe real air.

To have more than one means of escape.

She slid slick palms down the skirt of her hunter green dress, then peeked carefully at the man seated far to the right. He was still there after the previous stop, dressed like other white-collar workers in the crowded New York subway car, in an overcoat and suit. But, unlike them, he didn't act bored or in need of caffeine. He sat hunched over. Head tucked in. Body tight like a coiled spring—except for one fist pounding his thigh. Like a clock ticking down, it struck his leg. Relentless. Urgent.

Pound. Pound. Pound.

Gillian closed her eyes and turned away.

Oh God, I should have taken a taxi or a bus.

Waiting out the traffic jam in the safety of her hotel would have been the smart thing to do, but she desperately needed to get to court on time. After a three-year hiatus as a jury consultant, she was struggling to get back on her feet and prove to herself she was once again professional and dependable. Trustworthy.

In control.

Sweat slithered down her back, and she shivered. She clasped her shaking hands and ordered herself to sit still. Not the type to give up, nor the type to give in, she scanned her fellow passengers, seeking help. But no one else noticed the man. Or no one cared. Everyone in their own little world, blissfully ignorant of the tell-tale signs.

But she knew.

Don't look again. Don't look.

She tried to focus on something else. The two women grumbling about the unfair advantage of male execs taking clients to strip joints. The teen lovers snuggling. But not even the tabloid article read by the man next to her about UFOs snatching people off the streets of Manhattan could keep her distracted. Resistance was futile. Morbid fascination seized her and she had to peek again.

Pound. Pound. Pound.

If her brother Wyatt was here, he'd be whispering out the side of his mouth, growling, "Don't be stupid, sis. Get out. Go into the next car. When the train stops, run." And he'd be right, damn him. It was the smart thing to do, practical and sane. The kind of thing which would put her back in control of her life.

But she couldn't leave. Though every one of her people-reading skills screamed at her to flee, she would not desert the man pounding his thigh.

"Home sweet home," Detective Samson Brankowski said as he exited the precinct station and looked around. No wonder his partner was late. Morning traffic was tied up in all directions. Out-of-state drivers honked and swore, but the locals didn't. After the horror of 9/11, most knew when to keep quiet, be patient, and let the authorities handle things.

"I'll never get to court on time." Assistant District Attorney Stephanie London glanced at her slim gold watch as she followed him outside. "Can't you do anything about this?"

"Yeah, sure. Like I expected a suicide bomber to whack himself on 43rd this morning." The idiot just had to do it in public where even the smallest bomb turns into shrapnel.

Sam shrugged, trying to dismiss his unease, but even from here the distant sirens grated on his nerves. The terrors of WTC had left scars on everyone's soul.

"It'll be hours before the bomb squad and forensics pick up all the pieces," he added. "Parts of the bomber and his victims tagged both sides of the street. No way this'll thin out before noon. You're stuck unless you have a horse or a chopper available. Or Spidey fluid on your wrists."

Stephanie stormed down the stairs of the police station, a black cape draped over the arm holding a briefcase. Her thin high heels clicked angrily on the stone steps. Sam paused to enjoy her movements. He loved the way her tight ass shifted back and forth beneath the professional cut of her suit. A shame to waste all that energy on anger.

She reached the sidewalk. Hands on her hips, she glared at all the vehicles jamming the street, then turned to look up at Sam and grumbled, "What are you smiling about?"

"After all the high profile cases you've been taking on, you're back to being a normal, angry commuter." He winked knowingly at her. "I like the old you."

Stephanie scowled. "Priorities, Sam. When are you going to stick to priorities? I have to get to court, and you're thinking about sex?" She raised her hands in exasperation and shouted, "Do something!"

He ambled down the stairs and led her up the street. "Come on. I've got an idea."

"Thank God. I knew I could count on you." Stephanie fell in step beside him, head high, her strawberry blonde hair in a tight French twist, not a strand giving way to the breeze. Her posture was perfect, her stride as long and sure as his. She smiled at him, confident, trusting . . . until he placed a hand on the small of her back and circled her around a railing to a set of stairs leading down below the sidewalk. She stopped in her tracks. "You can't be serious."

"The trains are still running. View's not great but it'll get you where you want to go."

She wrinkled her nose in distaste. "I'm not *that* desperate."

But others were. Commuters who normally traveled by bus or taxi opted to ride underground. As they rushed down the stairs, one pushed Stephanie aside and into Sam's arms. Sam snuggled her close, loving the feel of her, and frowned when she pulled away.

"Sam, he stole my briefcase!" Stephanie pointed to the man who had bumped into her, swiftly snaking through the flow of commuters into the subway. "He's got my laptop! Do something!"

"Stay here." Sam ran after him. The thief had a good head start but Sam kept him in view. Caucasian with kinky brown hair. About five-eight, early twenties, hundred forty pounds. Red loop earrings in both ears. Wearing a satin, embroidered Yankees jacket, black sneakers, and jeans.

The man swiped his way in so as not to attract the attention of the transit cop.

"Hey, you! Stop!" Sam jumped the turnstile. He pulled his leather jacket aside to flash the shield on his belt at the cop on duty, shouting he was after a snatcher. Usually the officer would follow or radio for assistance, but the bomb had altered everyone's routine. All MTA cops had been ordered to stay by entrances to provide security. After 9/11, everyone took bombs seriously, even the small one used today that had killed three people. Petty theft was trivial in comparison.

The thief shoved people aside as he sprinted to the stairs that would take him deeper underground.

Sam grunted. Vermin always took to ground when running. Fortunately, the path the cockroach created through the crowd helped him close in. Soon Sam was at the top of the stairs, the thief at the bottom, scurrying across the platform and into a subway car. By the time Sam got to the bottom of the stairs, the doors on the cars were shutting.

It was close. At the last second Sam wedged his hand between the doors. The sensors automatically reopened them, and he eased inside. He quickly scanned the interior. Four male teens were bunched together. All wore the same gang jackets and hats. The Blue Warriors. Potential trouble but not today. Too many commuters to be able to pick on anyone and get away with it.

His eyes met theirs in challenge. They looked away.

The train built up speed, rumbling with power. Sam studied the passengers. Eight women dressed like office workers, some wearing sneakers. Probably change into dress shoes when they got to their desks. One with frizzy hair was trying to use her phone, but the tunnels blocked signals. There were bunches of guys in suits, some standing, some sitting. One of the stupid ones trying to use a smartphone.

A bum in the corner stashed what looked like a bottle in a brown paper bag inside his filthy jacket. Five blue collars with dark circles under their eyes on their way home from the graveyard shift, three waitresses wearing name tags, and a grandmother with two preschoolers on her lap.

It had only taken five seconds for his perusal.

Not here.

Sam shouldered his way to the rear of the car, scanning all the riders, then headed for the next car in line, hoping, as he went, that he'd find the thief before they reached the next stop. He didn't dare let the creep escape. He could just hear Stephanie's high-pitched whine if he didn't get her briefcase back. "Oh, Sam. Can't you do anything right?"

Lately, she could be such a bitch, but in bed she more than made up for it.

Gillian's gaze shifted to the young man who had rushed into the car just minutes ago. The last one to get on. He'd elbowed his way into a group of commuters and now sat hidden in their midst, hugging something under his satin Yankees jacket. His glances flipped through the crowd, never pausing long enough to meet anyone's eye. He reminded her of Scrounger whenever she caught the golden retriever in the horses' feed. Nervous. Guilt ridden. Tail between his legs afraid. Who was this guy so afraid of?

She heard the door between the cars open. The man stiffened. Curious, her gaze shifted to the person entering. White, male, thirtyish, clean-shaven, rugged-looking, short black wavy hair, brown leather jacket, cream shirt tucked into belted brown trousers. Laced brown Hush Puppies, the city version of running shoes. Large hands, old scars on the back of them.

The jaw was tight, eyes always moving—fast but not darting. Observing—quick, deliberate, with a sharp attention to detail. A lean, energetic hunter after its prey.

He prowled steadily closer, and she caught the glimmer of metal by the waist. A gold shield. A detective. Yeah, that fit. And he was after the man who was now slinking lower in the seat, hoping to disappear from view.

The cop's eyes had already assessed her and moved on to the other commuters. He would soon find the hidden man. Her gut churned. New York cops were notorious for having egos the size of the Empire State Building. Flexibility was not one of their redeeming qualities, and on the tolerance meter they usually scored lower than this subway.

The last thing she needed was a hard-nosed, in-your-face, obey me or else cop to deal with.

She used to be famous for making the best of a bad situation. Almost always she came out on top. After three years out of the game, Gillian hoped her skills would reappear on demand.

If not, deep underground they were hurtling straight for disaster.

There he is.

Sam weaved around the people hanging onto the metal poles for support, balancing like a seasoned sailor with the shift of the car as it rounded a curve. His eyes never left the snatcher even though the jerk refused to look at him. Like a kid who believes if you can't see them, they can't see you. It never worked.

The car momentarily darkened, the lights cut out as the train crossed a relay. When the lights flickered back on, Sam found himself face to face with a woman barring his way. She was in her late twenties, brown hair long and stylish, wearing a dark green dress and matching sneakers. Not an office worker; they didn't coordinate sneakers to outfits. An out-of-towner?

With his standard, monotone, don't-mess-with-me, I'm-a-cop voice, he said, "Miss, please get back to your seat."

He stepped toward her, expecting her to yield and retake her seat. Instead, he came up short, directly in front of her, surprised she refused to move.

Definitely an out-of-towner.

In a low voice, he said rapidly, "Miss, I'm a cop, and you're interfering in a police matter. Please sit down. Now."

The woman stood her ground. She stared him straight in the eyes, and said, "Fools rush in where angels fear to tread."

Crap. An out-of-town religious freak.

"Miss, if you don't step aside, I'll have to arrest you for interfering with a police officer. Take your seat."

The car suddenly shifted. She reached out and grabbed his shoulder. At the same time, he automatically caught her around the waist to steady her. With a grateful smile, she said, "We'll dance later."

At least the religious freak has a sense of humor.

"Miss, I—"

She leaned lightly into him, like a lover about to bestow a kiss on his cheek. Her breath was warm, her scent slightly floral, as her lips softly brushed his ear. He assumed she was a freakin' police groupie who got turned on by men in blue, or, in his case, a plainclothes cop, until he heard her whisper, "He's not the one you want."

The car trembled again, and he hugged her closer. "I don't?" he whispered back. It occurred to him the snatcher and this woman were working together: her job to distract any pursuer long enough for her partner to get away, though she didn't seem like the type. Didn't feel like the type, either—at least his arm around her didn't think so. But experience reminded him that prostitutes came in all shapes and sizes.

"He's not as dangerous as the man behind you to your right." With that, the woman stepped away, out of his arm, and retook her seat. Her light brown eyes shifted slowly to the snatcher, then to Sam, and then to someone behind and to the right of him.

She was letting him choose. Stephanie would be yakking a mile a minute, pointing with her long manicured nails and insisting he do something. But this lady was content to let him decide what was best. And because of that, Sam heeded her suggestion.

He casually turned to brush an imaginary speck of lint off his right shoulder and spied a man sitting with his back to him. Yuppie type. Short blond hair moussed to keep all the strands in place. Tan raincoat. One hand was on his navy polyester-clad thigh, clenched in a fist, the thumb firmly plugged inside the grip. He was hitting his thigh with the fist. Steady. Rhythmic.

The hair on the back of Sam's neck rose in warning. His gut tightened. Months ago he had faced another man with a thumb held within a fist. A man in an apartment, sitting at his kitchen table, wife on the floor with a knife in her chest, a gun in his hand pointed, not at Sam or his partner Tony, but at the guy's own head. A hopeless look in his dark eyes, his face a sheen of nervous sweat, the room sour with fear—and one dark fist pounding on the kitchen table, slow and rhythmic, with the thumb clenched inside the massive fingers.

A sign of insecurity, the cop shrink told him over a beer later that same night after Sam finished washing the blood and brains out of his hair. A physical manifestation of feeling worthless. Helpless. She'd suggested visiting a local school some time and notice how many students sat at their desks with thumbs inside their hands. Low self-esteem was rampant in the population. A feeling of being no better than trash. The warning signs were there if you knew how to read them.

The subway car continued to rumble, the sound vibrating up Sam's legs as he eased back, away from the man with the pounding fist. The snatcher was predictable. Nine out of ten ran, hid, surrendered when caught, claiming innocence or acting like what they did was no big deal. Getting caught was no big deal. Doing time was no big deal. But the man seated with his back to him was an unknown. No criminal classification to help Sam judge how he would react to a confrontation with a cop. Was he armed? Was he crazy? High? Drunk? Suicidal? A threat to himself or others or both?

Too many unknowns. Sam didn't like it.

His training insisted that officer safety came first. A no-brainer. He'd be no use to anyone if he was injured or killed. The only way to guarantee his own safety and that of everyone else in the car was to lower the odds of damage. And quickly. Before they reached the next stop and he had a jumble of people exiting and entering the car who would block his line of sight to the potential danger.

With a nod to the woman in green, he hustled to the back of the car where the thief sat partially hidden, all the while aware of the man who kept hitting his thigh. Easing in among the suits, he motioned to the one sitting next to the thief to move. He stared until the suit shifted away.

People hate confrontation.

Sam sat down next to the thief. The guy was younger than he first thought. College age but not a student. Didn't have that tired someday-I'll-be-rich look about him that college students have. A drop-out desperate for cash? Or part of a well-organized team of snatchers with a good fence, an operation that netted $200,000 or more a year, tax free?

Didn't matter. The man on the other side of the car mattered more.

Sam glanced at the thief. He made sure their eyes met for an instant, long enough for the jerk to see his flat determination and tacit message: I'm going to get my way, so you better listen or else.

In a low voice, Sam revealed his rank and precinct, and what would happen to the guy once he was placed under arrest. The creep didn't blink. A professional snatcher. Good. The odds were better already.

Sam kept talking. "Or you can hand over the 'case, nice and easy, and leave. You hear me? Give and go. No arrest, and no mountain of paperwork for me to do."

The man raised his brow in suspicion.

"One condition," Sam added.

The thief sighed, smart enough to know nothing was as simple as it seemed.

"After you give me the 'case, get up real casual-like and go into the car behind us. Got it?"

The man nodded slowly, as if unsure whether that really was all that was expected of him. He slipped the briefcase to Sam, then got up, straightened his fancy satin jacket as though he had all the time in the world, and strutted to the back of the car, through the door, into the next one.

Sam put Stephanie's briefcase on the seat and stood. In a firm but hushed voice, he told all the suits in his vicinity he was a cop, holding up his shield for the disbelievers. He ordered them to quietly exit the car to the rear. Some grumbled but they all left.

Suits knew to respect authority.

As for the clueless kid singing off-key to himself, Sam popped the earbuds out of his ears and told him to get lost. The kid muttered something ranker than the obscenity on his shirt and left.

The desk jockey women also obeyed but had a tougher time keeping quiet. Gabbers. Social animals. Their yammering would give away the stealthy evacuation. Sam pulled his gun out of his shoulder holster, almost certain the man making his gut clench would glance around at the exiting noisy women to see what was going on. He didn't. That scared Sam almost as much as if he had.

Barrel pointed up, he motioned to the rest of the people situated behind the unknown threat that they were to move into the car behind him, quickly and, with a finger on his lips, quietly. No one argued with the gun. By now even the dead could detect the tension rising in the car. And still the guy with his back to him hadn't moved. Except for the fist pounding his thigh.

With the rear of the car now empty, Sam motioned to the people in front of the seated man to move into the car ahead. Those who didn't notice him, noticed the others leaving. They turned and saw him waving at them to go. They complied, some with fear on their faces, some with a just-another-day-in-the-subway look about them. And still the man with his back to him didn't move.

Whatever happened, at least there'd be only two bleeding all over the car.

Make that three. To Sam's annoyance, the woman who'd precipitated the whole situation was still seated. He angrily motioned for her to leave.

The woman in dark green firmly shook her head no.

Was she connected to the guy? Is that how she knew he was dangerous? Because they were related? Partners? Or was the freakin' out-of-town, religious cop-groupie turned on by watching a cop in action?

Lights flashing outside the car indicated they were quickly approaching a station.

The freaky lady would have to take her chances. They were out of time.

Sam moved fast. He snapped around in front of the man, knees bent in a modified crouch, gun pointed at the guy's chest. "FREEZE!"

Light blue eyes stared at the gun. Wide, bloodshot, and dilated. Forehead was covered in perspiration. Nose running. Snot on the cranberry tie and blue shirt. The guy hadn't even made an effort to wipe his nose.

Cokehead?

The fist pounding on the man's thigh froze in midair. His other hand was inside the tan raincoat, arm bent at a right angle as if he was holding or hiding something. Could be a gun. A knife. Or drugs.

"Don't move," Sam warned.

The man's pale eyes blinked once in acknowledgment. His Adam's apple bobbed as he swallowed in gulps. Death a palpable certainty in the sweaty heat oozing from the stranger.

Sam glanced at the hand under the coat. "Whatcha got there, buddy?"

The man opened his lips, but no sound came out.

"Talk to me," Sam said.

The man blinked rapidly. The fist above the leg moved toward the torso.

Sam stiffened, crouched lower, clenched the gun tighter. He was ready to shoot if the hand went anywhere near what was under the coat. It didn't. It rose chest high and reached for the second button down on his shirt. The man's fingers were shaking violently, but somehow he managed to unfasten the button. He pulled the shirt open as far as the unfastened button would let him, drawing aside the tie with it. Below the throat, a flat small round object was taped to his skin. What looked like a wire ran down from it inside the shirt toward his waist.

"What the f—"

As soon as Sam began to curse, the man let go of his shirt and sliced a finger across his own throat. Sam cut off his remark.

Shut up, stupid. He's wired. But why? What the hell's going on?

Slowly, the hand hidden inside the coat moved. Sam held his breath, his gun trained on the wrist, not sure what to expect. It seemed to take an eternity for the hand to come into view.

Jesus Christ!

The guy had a bomb!

Small. Plastic explosive the size of a large crayon box, but a bomb nonetheless, with colored wires on the sides of it, and nails wrapped around to add to the damage. A sure bet if it went off, everyone in the car would be dead. The concussion might blow the car off the tracks, injuring those in the cars in front and behind them. Maybe the other cars, too. He had a thousand people on this train to protect.

His basic training said to radio for help, get backup. But terrorist training countermanded standard procedure. In the last years he'd been taught radio waves, even cell phone signals, could inadvertently activate a bomb. He sure as hell wished Tony was here to provide more options. But wishing was like buying a lotto ticket. Everyone made their own luck. He was on his own.

Sam glanced sideways out the windows as the train shuddered past a station, and thanked his lucky stars they were on an express. He glanced up at the route map. He had a few more minutes to neutralize the situation before a whole new bunch of commuters got on the car.

The hand that had opened the shirt, returned to the thigh. It tightened into a fist, the thumb once again inside. The fist hit the thigh. Hit. Hit. Hit. But the hand holding the bomb remained deathly still. The man was breathing rapidly, but his lips barely parted as he whispered, "I can't move. Not until we reach Union Square."

"What's at Union Square?" Sam whispered back.

"Life." The man's eyes grew watery. "I don't want to die."

"Neither do I, buddy, so let's just put that thing on the seat next to you, and we'll both walk away. Okay? You and me, we'll go to Di Martino's and have a coupla beers. What do you say? Give it up, and I let you walk."

The man smiled thinly at the thought, and a tear escaped one eye, trickling down his cheek. His mouth flinched. "If you don't let me reach Union Square, I'll trigger the bomb."

The index finger holding the device moved. Sam could see the arming button revealed beneath it. If Sam shot him, the guy might have time to set off the bomb before the shock and pain disabled him. Even if shot in the head, the finger might flinch enough to set it off.

But why was he wired? Was someone listening in, someone who could also set off the bomb? Or was it a bluff so no one would shoot him?

Too many variables. Not enough time.

Sam backed off. He stood up straight but kept his gun pointed at the bomber's heart. "Okay. We'll play it your way."

Up until now, the bomber had been staring solely at the gun. Now he looked around. As his gaze took in all the empty seats, his shoulders slumped as if they carried a weight too heavy for them to bear. The fist pounding on the leg slowed and slackened. "Everyone's gone."

"I'm here," said the woman in dark green.

The bomber froze, spooked by the unexpected voice. His finger hovered threateningly close to the trigger button as he glanced at the woman. "Who's that?" he asked Sam.

Sam scowled. He'd been watching the finger over the trigger start to relax, hoping it would move away far enough to risk a shot.

"Some freakin' out-of-towner," Sam said. Who was going to screw everything up. Why the hell didn't she leave?

"Gosh, it's hot in here." The woman got up and walked toward them, opening the matching jacket to her dress. She didn't stop walking until she stood near him and the bomber. Both men looked at her. The bomber's fist was back to hitting his leg.

"You guys hot? I am."

Sam opened his mouth to tell her to clear out. But she spoke first.

"They really should put better ventilation in these cars." She slipped out of her jacket and tossed it onto the seat on the other side of the bomber. The bomber's eyes followed it. Sam's eyes didn't. They watched the bomber's.

Smart chick.

The bomber tilted his head at the woman, puzzled.

She ran her hand up and down her neck, slinky, seductive. "So hot." She unbuttoned the top button of her dress. "Real hot."

The bomber's eyes were riveted as the buttons opened to reveal an inviting show of cleavage. He licked his lips. His fist stopped pounding. The trigger finger moved slightly away from the button. Sam saw it all. He didn't move. A single shift and the guy's attention would be back on him. Back to the bomb.

By now the dress spread open to below the woman's waist. She was out of buttons.

"Do these windows open?" the woman asked in a sultry tone. Her voice shook on the last word, telling Sam she wasn't as confident as her actions indicated. He'd give odds she was sweating bullets like him, and not because of the temperature.

"I'm so hot." She moved to the window by Sam. With an exaggerated swing of her hips, she pushed him aside—shifting him closer to the bomber—and reached up to the latches. She opened the window as far as she could, which, for reasons of liability, was a scant few inches.

"That's better," the woman said as she turned back to the bomber. "But not much."

To Sam's and the bomber's amazement, she began to slip out of her dress.

"What's with her?" the bomber asked Sam, licking his lips even more while he watched her undress.

"Freakin' out-of-towner," Sam muttered. He tried to sound like they were old drinking buddies taking in the view at the local strip joint, establishing a rapport no matter how tenuous in order to get him to lower his guard even more.

The bomber glanced at Sam with a frown, perhaps dissatisfied that when at last the dress was removed, the woman's most alluring parts were still modestly covered by a matching dark green slip.

Sam frowned, too.

The woman caught his eye and noticed his disappointment. Not enough skin showing.

She closed her eyes and clenched her hands, and for a moment he thought the woman was going to turn tail and run. He wouldn't blame her if she did. Duty insisted he stay. As a civilian, she was free to go.

But then her jaw firmed, her hands unclenched, and she plastered a smile on her face that made it seem like the sun was shining on them all the way down here in the subway. She offered the bomber a long, flirtatious wink as her hand reached down to the hem of her slip. Her shaking fingers were a dead giveaway, and Sam hoped the bomber was too busy lusting to notice. In a flash, she yanked the slip up and off.

Anywhere else, Sam would have whistled in appreciation.

The bomber stared, entranced, surprised, shocked by the woman's shameless audacity, and mesmerized by her dark green bra and matching high-cut panties, and sheer thigh-high stockings. His trigger finger hung loose. Looser still as the woman unhooked her bra and tossed it toward him. The fist on his thigh sprang open, reached up to grab it. At the same time, Sam snatched the bomb away.

"No!" The bomber lunged towards Sam, clawing Sam's back as Sam shoved the bomb out the opened window. "My family!" he screamed.

"Get down!" Sam tackled the bare-breasted woman to the floor. An instant later, the bomb exploded, blowing the car sideways off the tracks, plunging them into darkness as the three tumbled together. A terrifying screech filled the air, mixing with the acrid scent of scorched metal as the top edge of the car scraped against the tunnel wall until the car finally came to rest against the wall at a steep angle. The car shifted and settled into its new position, its shell emitting a vulgar structural groan that resonated deep within Sam's bones.

Dust settled, and the emergency lights came on. Sam heard the bomber moan beneath him in pain . . . and saw a great pair of breasts poised in front of his face. 36Cs that had saved his life. Beautiful. Absolutely beautiful.

His arms gripped her tight. He could have mumbled his thanks to her for saving all their lives. He could have cursed her all the way to Jersey for pulling a lame-brained stunt that might have gotten them all killed. Or he could have asked if she was all right, if she was hurt.

Instead, he looked at the two luscious mounds, so close his tongue could reach out and lick them, and said, "You've got great tits, lady."

Chapter Two

Torture comes in different forms, Gillian thought as the door to the interrogation room opened. She raised her head. The simple gesture shook loose the pungent scents of concrete dust, scorched metal, stale vomit, freshly pissed urine, and smoke embedded in her hair from the explosion in the subway. She couldn't wait to take a shower.

She recognized her visitor. The hunter cop, Detective Samson Brankowski. He carried her leather satchel in one hand, a folder in the other, and he didn't look happy. No doubt he'd been told who she was. All the bonus points for what she'd done in the subway had been deleted.

For a good second, his gaze dropped to her chest before rising to fix on her face. Her cheeks burned. Even with her dress on, she felt mortified. She knew exactly what he was thinking, what he was seeing. Every cop who came in the room had done the same. Except for one. Detective Stetson, her main interrogator, had stared at her breasts for a good five minutes to let her know what he and everyone else in the NYPD thought about her. So she was surprised when Brankowski's face suddenly turned a shade darker, and he averted his gaze. If she didn't know better, she might believe he was embarrassed.

She fingered the bandage over the cut on her forehead and wished the EMS had left extra painkillers for her throbbing headache. "May I go?" she asked, her voice neutral, refusing to give him the satisfaction of hearing her beg. Yet in her mind, she pleaded: *Please say yes.*

After six hours of false imprisonment, she hated this place. One couldn't actually see the blood of the criminals and victims, the accumulated tears of pain, fear, and lost hope, but they were present. Ghosts in the scratches on the table, on the washed spots on the walls, in the tired eyes of the cops who came to sneer at her. How many had gawked at her from the other side of the two-way mirror, she couldn't say. Maybe it was fortunate she hadn't been able to see them. But she had felt their hate.

"We need to talk." He glanced at the two-way mirror. "Not here."

"Sure." *Anything to get out of this place.*

Another man came into the room. "*His Excellency* wants to see us."

Detective Brankowski grimaced. "I'll be right there." He glanced her way and said, "I'll be back," then left, locking the door behind him.

With a bleak sigh, she crossed her arms on the table and laid her aching head down. In cop talk, being right back could mean ten minutes or ten hours.

The last time good news came from the lieutenant's office was two years ago when *His Excellency* announced he was taking a two-week vacation for a triple by-pass. Outside the interview room, Sam eyed his partner Tony's grimace with joyless expectation.

Anthony Torelli was a good fourth-generation cop. His Italian-American heritage insured a stable Catholic morality and delicious meals whenever Sam ate at his home. His wife, momma, and grandmama doted on Tony. He was always fighting thirty extra pounds of pasta around his belly. Sam had goaded him for the past five years to join his health club, but the most exercise Tony got was running after one of the city's rats.

Tony handed him a folder. "Here's her updated file. G.S. Dohr, a.k.a. The Oracle. The devil incarnate herself, in person and in our custody. Too bad you didn't know it at the time, huh? You'd have thrown her out the window with the bomb."

"Yeah, right out the window," Sam echoed. Yet he was having a difficult time reconciling the woman's scorching reputation with what she had done in the subway. The two didn't fit. Not at all. He wanted to find out why, and not just because she looked great without any clothes on. He asked Tony, "Anything we can keep her on?"

"Littering. Heard she threw her bra away. Absolutely no regard for the local statutes about cluttering our beautiful subways."

Sam caught the licentious twinkle in his partner's eyes. By now every cop in the city knew how she had distracted the bomber. Good news travels fast. "Can't bust her till the evidence shows up."

"Bust." Tony laughed at the pun.

Sam grinned. He wouldn't put it past Tony to be in possession of the bra. Then he heard the clatter of high heeled shoes.

Stephanie rushed toward him. "Darling, are you all right?"

Sam winced as bony arms encircled his bruised ribs. "I'm fine," he said, though her painful hug almost brought him to his knees. He was tempted to ask why she was only showing up now—the bombing had been seven long hours ago—then thought better of it. With her skyrocketing career, being late was the new norm for her. At least when it came to him.

"I was so worried." She gave him a long kiss. "Did you get my briefcase?"

"On my desk." He eased her arms from around his aching ribs.

She kissed him again. "You sure you're okay?"

"Nothing worth complaining about."

She studied him, noting the small bruise on his cheek. As if satisfied he was telling the truth, she shifted her interest to the door of the interview room. Her lips twisted into a malicious smile. "Is she still here?"

He nodded.

Stephanie hurried into the viewing room. Sam followed.

Stephanie smirked. "Doesn't look so formidable, does she?"

Through the two-way mirror, he watched the woman in dark green yawn tiredly. Dust from the explosion formed a soft halo on her brown hair. A red abrasion on her calf would evolve into a purplish-yellow bruise during the coming days. It had taken a lot of guts for her to strip in front of two strangers in order to provide a distraction. Most women he knew would never have gotten involved in a showdown between a cop and a perp. But she had stayed.

Her long sigh reminded him of how she had purred warmly into his ear, "He's not the one you want." She had paired an intimate gesture with a dangerous warning to keep him from reacting rashly. The lady was a curious mixture of moxie and smarts.

Stephanie snorted in derision. "The smart-assed bitch has freed more criminals than an appeals court. Because of her and the bombings, the trial was postponed a day."

Sam scrutinized the woman with bitter resentment. The Oracle was every cop's worst enemy in court, a jury consultant who knew which jurors to pick in order to secure her client a not-guilty verdict. After six frustrating hours with the bomber, he'd been surprised to learn she was still being held for questioning. It might explain why she hadn't been released. Cops got even with enemies any way they could, especially within the gray areas of the law.

"You never mentioned she was connected to your case," he said.

"She's a late addition. The defense flew her in a few days ago to help with jury selection after firing their original consultant. He was good but not half as good as The Oracle. Word is Gillian Dohr can see into a prospective juror's soul, find the saps who'll take pity on the defendants no matter what they're guilty of. Just looking at her gives me the creeps."

"You think she uses a crystal ball?" he asked sarcastically.

Stephanie scowled. "Doesn't matter how she does it. My concern is she'll tip the scales of justice in her clients' favor . . . unless you find a reason to keep her here. Any chance she's connected to the subway bomber, even remotely?"

He shook his head. "I was just told to let her go before her lawyer shows up and demands to know why we're detaining the city's latest heroine. The news jackals out front are clamoring for an interview with her."

"I heard she undressed during the incident. How about indecent exposure?"

Nothing indecent about it, Sam thought. Every time he looked at Dohr, he pictured her half-naked: buxom breasts accenting the sleek curves that sloped in and out of her waist. The lady must work out. Definitely no flab on her. At least not what he had held. "She saved my life."

Stephanie thrust out one of her famous pouts. "Her stupid interference in the subway has resulted in at least a million dollars worth of free publicity for the defense team. Hell, every time the jurors look over at her clients, they'll see the stripper heroine of New York sitting behind them. The psychological advantage will blind any chance at justice."

"Justice is already blind," he said, referring to how American artists depict the female icon as blindfolded.

She noticed the scratched leather satchel his hand. "Is that hers?"

"Yeah."

Lieutenant Winslow yelled from his office, "Brankowski and Torelli, get in here!"

Sam rolled his eyes. "Back to work." He led the way out of the viewing room and dropped The Oracle's satchel on his desk next to Stephanie's briefcase.

Sam and Tony eased into the chairs in front of Lieutenant Winslow's wooden desk. Automatically, their eyes counted the notches carved into the edge on the visitor's side. Eight. One for every officer killed on duty in this precinct. Everyone who came in here counted them. Counted them in their sleep, each a stark reminder of what happened when stupidity, recklessness, and plain damn bad luck turned against an officer of the law. Which was why *His Excellency* had carved them into the desk. To keep his people on their toes. Remind them to act smart. Not take any chances.

"I've been warned that within the next twenty-four hours we'll have more Feds in Manhattan than cockroaches. FBI. ATF. Homeland Security. Everybody wants in on these two bombings. FBI wants the bomber from the subway handed over ASAP."

Sam opened his mouth to protest but was silenced by a stern look from the lieutenant.

"Nothing you or I can do about it. Everyone's nervous. The First Deputy Mayor keeps telling me what these bombs will do to our economy. Scare away tourists. Turn the city's budget into a sieve. Orders are to cooperate with the Feds. Fully. But that doesn't mean we can't be a fly on the wall. Brankowski, I've got you designated NYPD's official liaison with the Feds. Torelli can assist, but I'm counting on you not to let them make us look like a bunch of nincompoops. This is our city. I want a New York cop arresting the wacko who wired the bomber in the subway. Got that?"

Sam grimaced. He hated working with Feds. But if it meant getting info to nail the suspect still at large, he could play dumb cop for a while.

"Pick up a copy of the witnesses' statements from Stetson on your way out. Scour them for anything that helps. In the meantime, in gratitude for our wholehearted cooperation, my counterpart in the FBI let me in on a piece of evidence not known to the press. And it's not going to be known unless I say so. Got it?"

Sam and Tony nodded obediently.

"They've already identified the source of the explosive used in both bombs. Came from a batch stolen from a corporate ranch in Wyoming two years ago."

"Wyoming?" Tony said in surprise.

"Yeah," Lieutenant Winslow grumbled. "Cowboy country. And home state of The Oracle. I'd say that's quite a coincidence."

"Shit," Sam muttered under his breath.

"Cowpie is what they call it out west, and I don't like it in my city. If there's a connection, I want to know about it yesterday. Brankowski, when you're not screwin' with the Feds, I want you keeping tabs on that Oracle bitch. After what happened this morning, you two now have a history. Capitalize on it. Be her friend, her confidant, find out how she's connected with whoever is making these bombs. I want her tailed twenty-four hours a day until we find out what the hell is going on. Got it?"

"We'll stay on her." Sam stood up to leave but not before he glanced one last time at the notches. They reminded him of how close he'd been to the bomb that morning. He swore he wouldn't be the next scar carved into the desk.

He left the office and noticed Stephanie at the copy machine.

* * *

Gillian had promised to talk with Detective Brankowski as a reward for getting her away from the police station, and she always kept her promises, including those she hated. Even so, she grudgingly gave the detective credit for being discreet. The restaurant he took her to wasn't a cop hangout. Not a lawyer hangout either. Samson Brankowski had picked the most neutral territory for their talk, a yuppie sports bar. Mid-afternoon, not many customers, yet the air was filled with the aromas of bratwurst, beer, illegal trans fats, and a trace of banned tobacco. HDTVs were on all sides. Four were showing baseball games, one a tennis match, another golf.

Except for their waiter, no one paid them any attention as they sat semi-isolated in a dark red vinyl booth. The local stimulant was sports, and everyone watched the monitors with more interest than most men give their wives.

As they waited to order, Gillian ran her fingers over the worn oak table polished smooth by ages of use. She loved the triangles and squares of inlaid cherry wood along the edges, a comfort to touch the work of someone who appreciated the rustic arts, especially when surrounded by the steel and concrete of the ultra-urban city.

After tossing back three aspirin with a chaser of water, she ordered a club sandwich and iced tea. The detective decided on a cheeseburger, fries with ranch dressing on the side, and a Coke. As soon as the waiter left, Gillian spoke up. After her ridiculously long incarceration in the interrogation room, she wasn't in any mood to be questioned. Figuring only the setting and interrogator had changed, she decided to seize the bull by the horns and be the one asking questions.

She glanced at the files on the table by Sam. "Are those about me?"

"That's what I'm here to find out."

She blinked in surprise. "You haven't read them?"

"I like to form my own opinion first."

"Careful, Detective. You almost sound impartial."

"Strange talk considering it's from The Oracle. I may not have read your file, lady, but I know you. You're a jury consultant who hires herself out to killers, then finds wimpy jurors who'll let 'em go free."

"That's not true."

He lifted both brows in exaggerated surprise. "Really. Remember Ray Andrew Follett?"

He might as well have slapped her. Her head jerked. Her vision clouded with nails and blood and small young bodies. Bitter cold crept over her heart and squeezed it, sending an icy shudder rippling deep inside.

Beneath the table, both hands clenched into fists. You can handle this, she tried to convince herself. You knew when you decided to come out of hibernation someone would eventually bring it up. Deal with it. Acknowledge it. Then let it go, and maybe it won't come up again.

She stared into his hard eyes and said, "That was a mistake."

"A mistake?" The detective leaned across the table, his voice an angry whisper. "Good old Ray. On trial for slaughtering three children, all under the age of five. And the jury—the jury you helped pick in favor of your client—decided he couldn't possibly have killed those kids. So your carefully selected bleeding hearts found him not guilty. NOT GUILTY."

A collage of images filled her mind, nightmares she thought exorcized long ago. Of Ray looking at her with gentleness in his eyes while proclaiming his innocence. Of children drained of blood through the gaping wounds in their palms and feet. Of grieving parents cursing her name. Of reporters hounding her day and night: in her face, on the phone, at the ranch, peering through the windows of her home.

But worse than the images was the voice which filled her head, one that sounded a lot like her own. It yelled she was just as guilty as Ray Follett.

Guilty. Guilty. Guilty.

She could barely breathe. Instinctively, she wanted to flee. The detective's words had ripped open old wounds.

God, even hell must be better than sitting here, facing the truth one more time.

In a pitiful voice she barely recognized as her own, she whispered, "Please."

But the detective refused to stop. "Within six months, he slaughtered five more children. FIVE. Only this time the cops made sure Ray Andrew Follett wouldn't have a chance to face any more of your personally hand-picked jurors."

She glanced at him, startled, not certain she had correctly understood his insinuation, and afraid that she had. "He was killed while resisting arrest," she reminded him.

"That's *the story.*" He leaned further over the table, inches away from her, his voice raw and sharp. "But the real honest-to-God truth is Ray Andrew Follett was executed on the spot for his crimes. Like he should have been the first time he went to trial."

Gillian shivered, more from the vehemence in Sam's voice than the atrocities committed against Ray Follett. "I'm glad he's dead."

The detective leaned back, a look of surprise on his face. "You are?"

"I'm glad he can't harm anyone else." She glared fiercely at him. "But nothing justifies how he was killed."

Detective Brankowski opened his mouth in what she was sure would be a biting rebuttal when she cut him off. "Why did you bring me here? You could have said all of this back at the station. I'm sure your fellow 'finest' would have applauded. Or do you get a kick out of verbally abusing people in private?" She gathered her belongings and got up to leave. "I don't have to take this."

He stood up as well. His voice returned to being neutral and polite. "I want to talk to you about what happened in the subway this morning."

Gillian glanced at the unopened folders. "You've got hours of testimony there. More than enough to satisfy even a cop's mentality."

"And colored by the investigators' take on your reputation. I want to hear your version, personally, privately. As if I don't know a damn thing about you."

Gillian studied him in the dim lighting of the restaurant. He sounded sincere. To his credit, not once since the interrogation room had his eyes drifted to her chest. Dare she give him a second chance?

Fool me once, shame on you. Fool me twice, shame on me.

And yet, Gillian reasoned, if anything they talked about could prevent another bombing, another victim, a few more minutes might be worth it.

She offered him her hand. "Hello, I'm Gillian S. Dohr. Gillian to my friends."

He shook it firmly. "Samson L. Brankowski, Detective, Homicide. My friends—and enemies—call me Sam. Care to eat with me?"

They both sat back down. The waiter brought their drinks. After he left, she asked, "So, what do you want to know, Sam?"

"How'd you know about the bomber?"

"As you may have heard, I'm a professional people reader."

"Body language expert."

"Uh-uh. That alone doesn't work. Never has. I look at patterns of behavior: actions, personal appearance, what a person says. I use all of it to devise probable responses to potential situations."

"How jurors will evaluate certain types of testimony. Evidence."

Gillian nodded. "Not a perfect science, but statistically valid."

Except where it concerned Ray Follett. She could see Sam thinking the same as his eyes momentarily turned cold, his face rigid. She couldn't blame him. The only one she kept blaming for that was herself.

She continued. "But I also look for discrepancies. Extreme discrepancies. Like the bomber this morning."

Their meals arrived. Sam grabbed a French fry, dunked it in the little steel bowl of ranch dressing, and munched on it. The intensity of his interest showed on his face. Though repulsed by her profession and talent, he was intrigued by it, too. "What in particular did you notice about the bomber?" he asked as he grabbed another fry.

"On first appearance, most would assess him to be a white-collar family man. Clean cut, in need of sleep, dedicated to work and family. Typical middle class goals and morality—if anyone is really 'typical.' He had a wedding band on his left love finger."

She paused to glance at the same finger on Sam. Bare. But that didn't mean he wasn't married. She noticed him scan her finger. It, too, was bare. "Single," she told him.

"Divorced but dating," he replied.

Gillian returned to her assessment. "There was a peanut butter and jelly splotch on his right coat sleeve—probably from one of his kids. A trace of lipstick on the edge of his lips. Scuffed shoes. Clean but not ironed clothes. Wife probably works outside the home. Shaving nick on his face might mean he was rushed while getting himself and the kids ready to leave on time."

"Roger T. Walgood is an accountant for Market Economies. Has a wife, three kids. Claims he loves them more than life itself. Would do anything for them."

"Really? So why the bomb?"

"You finish telling me what red flags you picked up, then I'll tell you his motivation. We'll see if they match."

"Testing me?"

"Just trying to get a handle on what happened. And how to keep it from happening again."

"You think there'll be another bombing?"

"Two on the same day, in the same city, on the same morning is too much a coincidence for me."

She put down her sandwich. "They're related?"

He shrugged. "What else about Mr. Family Man?"

"Most white-collar workers on the subway seemed harried, tired, but indifferent to their surroundings. Roger Walgood was anything but. Yet he should have been. He was in a familiar environment on a routine workday. He should have been fairly calm, at ease, a little put out if he was more used to taking a bus or taxi. But he was sweating, anxious, fearful, almost scared to death. It seemed to take everything he had to will himself onto that car. Like a twenty-point deer caught in the sights of a trophy hunter's rifle, he should've turned tail and run."

Sam chewed on another fry. "Why didn't he?"

"I assume because of the man who came into the car with him."

Sam stopped eating. "Go on."

"Do you know about him?"

"Only what Roger T. Walgood said. I want to hear your version."

She nervously sipped the iced tea. Sam had a way of looking at her that made her believe she was the one under investigation. He was being extremely patient, attentive and nonthreatening. Yet she could easily imagine that, if he wanted to, he could make her feel like a bug under a microscope.

"A Caucasian, somewhere between twenty-five and forty. Ash blond hair, brown eyes. Five eight, on the heavy side of two hundred plus pounds. Authoritative. He had a tight hold on Roger's arm. Must have been for quite a while because when he let go, the wrinkles on the sleeve of Roger's coat where the man had gripped were deep and sharp.

"He pulled Roger onto the car and sat him down. He pointed a finger at him, stiff, straight, maybe threatening, then touched the finger to Roger's chest, then pointed to his own ear and said something. Roger nodded. Roger started to look around when the other man suddenly grabbed his chin and jerked it back to the front. He said something, snarling—I could see his canines. Then he left. Roger never turned his head again. He just sat there."

She paused. "There's something else that's been bothering me. The man with Roger displayed faint traces of feminine mannerisms."

"You think he's gay?"

"Could be. The train was filling up fast, and I only caught glimpses at a time. Just something odd about it, but I can't put my finger on it."

"Was Roger holding the bomb when he was escorted onto the car?"

"I assume so. The entire time Roger's arm was bent at the elbow, the hand inside his partially-opened overcoat."

"Did you describe the stranger to Detective Stetson?"

She nodded. "I'd be interested in knowing how close the sketch matches the one Roger gave you."

Sam pulled out a paper from one of the files and handed it across to her. "Two hours into questioning, Roger gave us that."

It was a crude, almost childlike, drawing done in pencil of a tall stick figure wearing a huge hat and coat. Flames came out of the circular face where the mouth should have been. The fire shot across the page, curving down to a small stick figure drawn in the bottom corner. Huge tears dripped from its tiny dot-like eyes. Gillian studied it in fascination. "Roger Walgood drew this?"

"Yeah, he did. Then shut up like a clam for about an hour. Just sat there and rocked back and forth. Must have finally occurred to him how close he came to being killed. We tried bribing him with coffee and doughnuts—"

"And threats."

"Those, too. Nothing worked until my partner Tony offered him a candy bar. Settled down real nice after that."

"Sugar-addict?"

"Or hypoglycemic. After that he got more talkative. But he refused to give us a physical description. Every time we asked, he closed in on himself and started rocking."

Gillian handed back the drawing, and Sam slipped it into the file. She said, "You know, some therapists have patients draw as a way of dealing with their emotions. If Roger has a previous history of counseling, he might have resorted to the technique as a way of coping."

"I don't see you doing any drawings."

"We all handle stress differently."

Sam dunked another fry in the ranch dressing. "Getting back to the subway, did you know there was a bomb under Roger's coat?"

"No."

"But you knew something was up. Something was wrong. You saw all those—what did you call them?"

"Extreme discrepancies."

"Yeah. Red flags. So why, if all your talent was honking at you that something bad was going down, why didn't you get off the train and simply wait for the next one?"

Gillian bit her lower lip. She'd asked herself the same question at the time—and a hundred times since. "I don't know."

The dubious look Sam gave her indicated he didn't buy it. Not for a second. Neither did she. But if she couldn't admit the truth to herself, she definitely couldn't reveal it to Samson Brankowski.

She took a sudden interest in eating her sandwich.

Sam asked, "Do you think I'm good looking?"

Startled by the absurd question, she looked across the table at him. "Excuse me?"

"Do you think I'm good looking? Or maybe what I should've said is do you think I'm good looking for a cop?"

Gillian laughed softly.

"Good. It's good to laugh." His mouth curved into an easy smile, causing two matching arcs to form vertically on each side of his mouth. Triple smiles, her grandfather used to call them. An indication of a person with a good heart.

Sam continued. "Seemed like you needed a break. When you get too serious you lose perspective. Forget things." He said the next sentence slowly and deliberately. "Hide things."

"So, you're a people reader, too."

"Sort of. But I only work for the good guys."

She grumbled in annoyance. "I don't—"

Sam raised a hand to halt her rebuttal. "That was a low blow. Sorry. Just sneaked out. Won't happen again."

I bet, Gillian decided. He'd pushed her emotional buttons first one way, then the other. And he thought what she did was merciless.

"I think I've done enough talking," she said. "Now it's your turn. Why did Roger Walgood, average commuter and family man, suddenly turn into a bomber this morning?"

"Coercion. A guy hands him a bomb, orders him to Union Square station where he's to hand it over to another guy. If he doesn't caddie the bomb as ordered, an accomplice will kill Walgood's kids. Same thing will happen if Walgood doesn't blow himself up if anyone interferes, or if he tells anyone who gave him the bomb."

"Sounds contrived."

"Tell me about it." Sam took a drink of his Coke. "It's looking more and more like Walgood was a bomb hostage."

"I thought bomb hostages usually have a metal collar locked to their necks and attached to the bomb."

Sam shrugged. "Threats against his family were a good enough yoke."

She nodded in agreement. If her own brothers' lives were threatened, how much of her soul would she be willing to sell? Hopefully, she'd never have to find out. "Why Union Square?"

"Only the bomber knows. The thing is, Walgood had a wire on his chest. The bomber probably told Walgood he was listening in. If he didn't like what he was hearing, he could detonate the bomb remotely, which he must've done when I threw it out the window."

"Shit," Gillian said under her breath. Sam's brow rose in surprise, and she added, "Sorry. It just never occurred to me until now how little control we had over the whole situation."

"You mean if you had known, you wouldn't have stripped?"

She covered her face with her hands. Did he have to keep reminding her of that?

Sam laughed at her embarrassment, which made her even more embarrassed. But then she felt his fingers on hers, gently drawing her hands down. His fingers were calloused but the touch was tender and warm, and his expressive dark blue eyes showed a hint of admiration for what she had done to save their lives. He held her hands for several seconds longer than necessary, then let go.

A spell of mutual attraction settled over them. A common side-effect, she told herself, when two people share the threat of death and survive. It had nothing to do with the fact she was getting to like the way Sam's left brow rose into a roguish slant whenever he was intrigued by a piece of information. After all, he was a cop. He was gleaning information, nothing more.

"I, uh, didn't know something like a wire could work so well in the subway," she managed to say. The words came out slow and rough as his eyes continued to convey a personal interest in her. "You know, with all those tunnels and electrical connections, and the solid rock it's built into."

"Wires don't." Sam glanced down at his plate of food. He took a deep breath. When he looked her way again, his eyes were cool and calculating. Professional. Back to being one hundred percent cop. "The experts are testing it, but my guess is the bomb-giver had to be in one of the other cars of our train in order to stay in contact with Walgood and detonate the bomb."

She leaned forward, astonished. "If that's true, wasn't he taking a big chance? He could have been killed in the blast. At the very least injured."

"Maybe the wacko gets his kicks out of cheating death." Sam's broad shoulders rose up and down with uncertainty. "It was a *small* bomb. Everyone two cars away from the one we were in are fine. I think he knew the odds and played them like a violin.

"We're checking the background of everyone on the train, but from the list I've seen, it's incomplete, missing some gang members I saw. The bomb-giver probably just walked away in the confusion. We're looking over the security tapes, maybe got him on video."

He shook his head as if regretting the lost opportunity to catch the real bomber while on the train. Grabbing a few French fries, he kept dunking them in the ranch dressing but didn't eat them. "Let's get back to the yoke. This guy literally handed Walgood a terrible dilemma. Walgood had to choose between his own life, the innocent lives of everyone on that train, and those of his family."

"How are his children? Did the accomplice—"

Sam waved away her fears. "They're fine. Wife is fine. No indication there ever was a shooter staked out at the school or their apartment. We've got people with them just in case."

She breathed a sigh of relief. "Thank goodness." Her fingers rubbed the inlaid squares in the table while her mind sorted the myriad possibilities begging to be analyzed. "You know, this is interesting, in a macabre sort of way. Somehow the bomb-giver knew Roger was the type of person to sacrifice himself in order to save those he loved the most. You know what this means?"

"That Roger T. Walgood doesn't have any balls?"

She raised a brow. "Heavens, no. It takes more than *balls* to sacrifice your own life."

"What about all the other people in the car with him? You. Me. The other commuters. We could've all been killed. The guy's a wimp."

"We'll argue about how stress undermines ethics another time. The important thing is the bomb-giver knew, almost without a shadow of a doubt, that Roger would do what was asked of him. He knew." She gestured with her hands in amazement. "To be able to pick someone out of a crowd and expect them to cave in like that . . . well, the odds are too astronomical to believe."

"But *you* could," Sam said. "You had him pegged pretty good when he got on the train."

"Only the basics. Surmising Roger is a family man and a white-collar worker didn't tell me how much he cared about his family. For all I knew, his wife could be the bitch from hell and the children not biologically his. Maybe stepchildren, the worst brats on the planet. Threaten to kill them with that kind of background and Roger would have thought, 'Good riddance. Go ahead. Make my day.'"

Sam pushed his plate of food aside. "What are you saying? This bomb-giver knows Roger. They're friends? Relatives? Best buds?"

"More like he shadowed Roger for quite a while. Weeks. Listened in on conversations. Tapped his phone. Got a good feel for how Roger felt about life and his family. Or . . ."

"Or?"

"Or he did what I do. Find someone statistically similar to a potential juror and ask how she feels when given the same pertinent information that will be discussed during a trial."

Sam grimaced and threw his napkin on the table. "You mean a mock trial with a mock jury that resembles all the jurors called-in for a particular case?"

"Sure. Don't look so surprised. It's done more often than you think, in both criminal and civil trials. Big corporations do it all the time when faced with a lawsuit."

"And you would know," Sam said tightly.

Oracle. He hadn't said it out loud, but his eyes burned dark with it. He hated what she did. Maybe even hated her.

"Both sides do it," she replied.

"Prosecutors don't have the budget. Taxpayers gripe enough about a D.A.'s pay. In criminal cases, only the defendant can afford the luxury of having you and your kind on their side."

Your kind. Two simple words, yet they conveyed the feeling she was slime.

"We're getting off topic." She rubbed her temple. Her headache was returning.

"You're tired." Sam frowned, giving the impression he was actually concerned about her. He glanced at his watch. "I should take you back to your hotel."

"Just call me a taxi."

"Nah. A gentleman always sees a lady home, even if he's pissed her off."

She smiled wanly. "If another cop sees us, it might tarnish your reputation."

He smirked. "Let me worry about that."

* * *

At the hotel, Sam insisted on seeing Gillian to her room. After all, it was New York. Muggers and rapists weren't afraid to strike in the fanciest halls of the best hotels. Who wouldn't be glad to accept a police escort?

At the front desk, Gillian was handed a large stack of messages. Most were from the media asking for interviews. She read one business card twice. He sneaked a glance.

Jacob Miller, Ph.D. MPD/DID.

The name didn't register, and he didn't have a clue as to what MPD/DID might refer to. He was about to declare Dr. Miller unimportant and trash the name from his memory when Gillian tore the card in half. She handed it and the messages to the desk clerk and told him to throw them all away.

Upstairs, Gillian stood in the doorway of her room, making it clear she wasn't going to invite him in. He didn't expect her to. He'd purposely seen her all the way to her room to put her at ease before he asked the last question on his list.

They'd said their good-byes, and he was turning to leave when he suddenly turned back and in an unassuming voice said, "Gillian, do you mind? I gotta ask you this. It'll bug me all night if I don't. Just between you and me, why didn't you leave the car when everyone else did? I was there. I'd taken control of the situation—as much as anyone could. Why risk your life and stay?"

"And strip?"

For a split second, his gaze dropped to her breasts. He couldn't help it, not after she reminded him of what she'd exposed to view. He looked back up and expected to see her face flushed in embarrassment or outraged at his quick assessment. Instead, she chuckled as though they were sharing a private joke.

This was one classy lady. He chuckled too. "Yeah. And strip."

"Actually, I didn't expect it to go that far." She smiled for another second, then suddenly sobered. "Years ago someone in my family committed suicide because he didn't believe anyone could help him. Since then I've always taken that extra step to save a life."

He grinned. "Mine."

Gillian shook her head. "Roger Walgood's." She closed the door.

Surprise turned to anger. He spat, "Oracle," and headed for the elevator. Leave it to The Oracle to think a cop's life wasn't worth saving. As he stomped down the hall, he exchanged glances with Detective Fran Horowitz, part of the surveillance team, camouflaged in a white housekeeper's dress.

Before leaving the hotel, Sam flashed his shield at the desk clerk and rummaged through the garbage. He retrieved Dohr's messages, including the business card she'd torn in half, and headed back to the station, intent on finding out why The Oracle didn't want anything to do with Dr. Jacob Miller. It might work to his advantage. Way back in kindergarten he had learned "the enemy of my enemy is my friend" usually turned out to be true.

Chapter Three

In the courtroom, whispers behind Gillian repeated the morning headlines.

Oracle Strips For Bomber

Will Oracle Bare All To Save Clients?

Gillian cringed, remembering how the on-camera interviews of "eyewitnesses" who falsely claimed to have seen her disrobe had grown increasingly lewd with each telling. Before she had turned off the TV in disgust, the final account had characterized her as a licentious whore rather than a quick-thinking bystander.

Her boss Calvin Moore hadn't been pleased, but he wasn't about to cull her when things got rough, though he did warn her to keep a low profile for the remainder of the trial. Not easy to do. This morning, reporters had been prowling outside the hotel when Calvin rushed her into a taxi. And the pack had been even larger at the courthouse.

She now sat in the row behind the defense table, trying to ignore the painful injuries from yesterday's violent tossing in the subway. Her entire body felt like one massive bruise.

"Gillian!"

Calvin's harsh whisper drew her back to the proceedings. He stared at her, his dark brown complexion deepening with apparent irritation. He shifted back around in his chair and asked the prosecutor to repeat the question she'd posed to the current potential juror.

ADA Stephanie London smiled politely and repeated her question.

Gillian's jaw dropped, stunned. The wording was different, but for all intents and purposes it was the same question she had in her notes for Calvin to ask this juror. As was the next question Stephanie asked.

Calvin turned to her, his eyes demanding an explanation.

She whispered rapidly, "The police had my satchel yesterday." For up to six hours after her rescue from the subway. *Damn.* Enough time to print copies for the entire police force. "Can you request a recess to give me time to come up with new questions?"

"Not a chance," he whispered back. "The judge didn't like postponing until today, bomb or no bomb. I'm not going to antagonize him further by asking for another delay."

She caught Stephanie glancing slyly at her. Gillian lifted her middle finger against the pen she was holding and subtly flipped her off, smiling sweetly as Stephanie noticed and scowled.

Two young Puerto Rican males were on trial for the robbery, aggravated assault and battery, and felony murder of a well-respected member of the Jewish community. They admitted to the mugging—some of the victim's items had been found in their possession—yet both insisted they'd left their victim alive. Bleeding from a cut lip—that's how César got the victim's blood on his sleeve, or so he claimed—but definitely alive.

Usually these two losers would have no choice but to accept a public defender and cut a deal, even if it meant admitting to manslaughter. But, thanks to the local media, this wasn't a typical case. Inflammatory questions raised by reporters in the Jewish and Puerto Rican communities had stirred up old prejudices and ethnic hubris, escalating into Puerto Rican pride marches and shouting matches with their counterparts in the Jewish enclaves.

To counter what they thought would be a strong Jewish influence in the city courts, a Puerto Rican Justice Fund had been started to hire the best lawyer the fund could afford— Calvin Moore. Not pricey or prestigious, but a good man with a dependable reputation and a favorable percentage of wins. Whether they had hired him because he was a man of color was another matter.

Calvin had convinced her to come out of retirement. He needed her skills—his clients needed them—to insure as fair a trial as possible. He couldn't pay her much, but more than money, he was offering her a chance to get back on the horse and do what she did best.

And to forgive and forget.

He, too, was connected to the Follett tragedy. But Calvin hadn't gone into hibernation like she had. He'd kept working—overworking—to compensate. Everyone had their own way of outrunning the demons of the past. But then her ties to Ray Follett ran deeper than his.

With the added nudging of her brother Wyatt, who thought three years of isolation was enough penance for what had happened, she'd agreed to come to New York. She'd hoped to slip in, do her job, then quickly retreat home. The last thing she'd expected was to have her face plastered all over the newspapers, TV, and Internet.

Wait! What did that juror just say? He used to be a Mets fan but now he's a Yankees fan? Gillian tilted her head in confusion. Die-hard sports fans don't change loyalties. Once a Mets fan, always a Mets fan. Why the change?

She checked her notes on the juror's profile. His attributes made him a favorable candidate: fairly unbiased, Baptist, African-American, open-minded to a certain extent, fireman, family man, four daughters. Wife works part-time at a daycare.

She chewed the end of her pen. Why did he switch teams?

Stephanie had already moved on to ask the fireman what he thought about the crime rate in the city, but Gillian stuck with the sports question. The only reason it was on her list in the first place was to put the man at ease. Most men relax when they talk about sports. It opens them up for the tougher, more personal questions that usually reveal personal biases in relation to the defendants or the charges. But this juror hadn't relaxed when he said he was now a Yankees fan. He'd stiffened, shifted in his seat, rubbed his nose, averted his eyes momentarily. Though he had tried to sound casual when he answered, he'd stumbled when he said Mets. She could still hear the slight stutter when she replayed his answer in her mind.

A red flag, Sam Brankowski would call it.

On a slip of paper, she wrote: Find out WHY he switched team loyalties. Specifics. What made him change from Mets to Yankees?

She slipped the note to Calvin. He read it twice, then turned his head and lowered his brow as if to say: *You can't be serious.*

She nodded firmly. As much as she trusted her instincts, Calvin would have to trust her. By the time it was his turn, she'd managed to supply him with a few pertinent queries.

Considering they hadn't had time to discuss the reasons for each question, Calvin did well, and elaborated on a couple of them when he rightly assessed what she was looking for in the man's background. Everything was going fine. The fireman seemed to be a promising juror. The only question left was the sports one.

Calvin paused. He glanced at Gillian. She nodded and mouthed, "Go for it."

Cal skirted the issue like a wolf circling its prey, asking about football first, not baseball, about the man's own background in sports while growing up. Did he play any sports in school? On a city team? On his firehouse team?

Yeah, the man loved baseball. Played it in some form or another all his life.

Calvin then discussed the Mets: past teams, favorite old time players, working up to the most recent teams, the newest players. That's when the man started to stumble and hesitate. He didn't exactly disagree with Calvin's estimation of the present day players, but he didn't agree either. He gave a lot of iffy, noncommittal answers.

Calvin asked who his favorite players were on the Yankees' roster. The man rattled off a bunch of names, none familiar to Gillian—baseball wasn't her game—yet she noted his tone was confident, his words sure and relaxed, as was his posture. She inferred he was being honest. At the very least, he believed what he was saying.

Calvin thanked the man for his time, then told the judge he wanted the man excused from the jury selection, utilizing a "peremptory" challenge to empower the request.

Stephanie stared at Calvin, clearly bewildered by the attorney's request. So was Gillian. Stephanie must have known from her stolen notes that she and Calvin were originally leaning toward having the fireman in the final jury pool. For the life of her, Gillian couldn't figure out why Cal had rejected the man.

Calvin sat back down and turned to her as the judge excused the juror and asked for the next one to be interviewed.

"What's going on?" she asked in a hushed voice so as not to draw the judge's attention. "Why didn't we keep him?"

Calvin smiled, his large, straight white teeth beaming in satisfaction. "Because I found out why he switched teams. All the Yankees he named—they're either white or black players. The Yanks have exceptional Hispanic players, but he never mentioned one."

"I don't understand. Don't the Mets have Hispanic players, too?"

"Of course. And that's why I think this guy switched. This year they acquired two Cubans, a Haitian, and a Puerto Rican.

Their roster is almost fifty percent Hispanic. The Yanks are only at thirty-three percent, and most of them aren't starters. The guy may not even realize it himself, but subconsciously he's prejudiced against anyone with a Hispanic background. We definitely don't want him on our jury. Good job, Gillian. Now, let's try to keep our heads above water until lunch, and maybe, just maybe we can get a fair trial."

She sighed in relief. One bad juror had been cut. After three years, her instincts were still good.

When the judge declared lunch recess, seven jurors had been selected from the pool of candidates. Three of them Gillian had a good feeling about. Three were questionable. Not a bad trade-off considering the prosecution had plagiarized her notes.

She was packing her satchel when, out the corner of her eye, she saw Detective Sam Brankowski enter the back of the courtroom. Yesterday she hadn't answered his question about whether she thought he was good looking. She did now.

Absolutely. He was loaded with animal magnetism. Strong jaw. Strong chin. A slight shadow of a beard even at midday, which made her wonder if he had a luxurious dark pelt of hair on his chest, the type women like to run their fingers through before and after sex. His eyes were blue-grey, the dangerous color of the sky during a storm. Quick on his feet and with his hands. Well muscled but not excessive. Sure of himself but not conceited. Well, maybe a little conceited. What else could one expect of a man who grew up with the name Samson? What had his parents been thinking? That he'd be a lineman for the Jets?

Gillian shook her head at how fate had thrown them together, literally. Though he had probably blurted it out in the heat of the moment, she'd never forget him saying she had great tits. Her lips curled into a smile. What woman could resist a good-looking, hero-type man who liked her boobs but also talked to her as an intellectual equal?

He had treated her decently enough yesterday, despite the fact he considered her the enemy. On her own home turf, she would have asked him out on a date. At least dinner and a movie.

He was probably here to discuss yesterday's bombing. Or ask why she had bluntly told him at the hotel that she'd been trying to save Roger Walgood instead of him. Her revelation had shocked him. Big time. Perhaps she should have explained. But she'd been exhausted, not in the mood to have him push any more of her buttons. If anything, it was nice to leave him standing outside her door with *his* buttons pushed.

She stared as he walked over to the prosecution's table. To her astonishment, Stephanie welcomed him with a smile and a peck on the cheek. They talked briefly during which Stephanie frowned and glanced Gillian's way. Sam did, too, then headed toward her.

Shit. Gillian swiftly gathered her things. "Ready, Cal?" she asked.

"In a sec." Calvin was still conferring with his assistant John.

By now, Sam stood at the end of the row she was in. "Hey, Gillian. How's it going?"

"None of your business," she said.

He angled his head back, definitely puzzled by her cool reply. He rolled one shoulder and momentarily grimaced at his own aches and pains. "Sore?"

"At you? Yes."

She started towards him, but Sam refused to move. "You mad at me or something?"

"Gosh, detective. Whatever gave you that impression?"

"Maybe it's because you're all red in the face, eyes aflame, mouth spittin' daggers. What's up? Had a bad morning?"

"Bad morning? Listen here, Detective Brankowski—"

"Sam."

"I only call people I can trust by their first name."

"You can trust me."

"Oh, really? Then tell me you didn't let the ADA see the papers in my satchel yesterday while I was being detained."

For a second, he looked away. His mouth scrunched to the side as well. Then he took a deep breath and shifted his gaze back to her. "I didn't give them to her."

She glared at him and wished her eyes really could throw flames. "Tell me you didn't *know* Stephanie looked at my notes yesterday."

Sam winced. His gaze dropped to his feet. "Gillian, we need to talk about yesterday's bomber."

"Don't you dare change the subject."

"It's important."

"*This* is important." She stepped closer and lowered her voice to a harsh whisper. "Letting the prosecution steal notes from the defense team is a crime. It's illegal and unprofessional. If I didn't need to keep a low profile after what happened yesterday, if I didn't think it would hurt our clients' case, their chance of getting an unbiased trial, and if I could prove it beyond the shadow of a doubt, I would file charges against you and your girlfriend."

Sam didn't back away. Instead, he raised his eyes, their blue-grey hue stormier than ever. A muscle jerked in his jaw. His body was stiff and compact, as though he wrestled some inner demon on her behalf. When at last he spoke, his voice was deep but calm. "It's not what you think."

"It's not?" Gillian hesitated. *Damn.* She was starting to give him the benefit of a doubt when all she wanted to do was yell at him some more. Hands on her hips, she waited to hear him out.

Sam took another deep breath. "She's not my girlfriend. We just sleep together once in a while."

Gillian wanted to scream. The man was insufferable.

Calvin asked, "Gillian, you ready?"

Bristling with indignation, she managed to say in a cool voice, "Cal, this is Detective Samson Brankowski, the officer who subdued the bomb hostage in the subway yesterday."

"Nice to meet you." Calvin said, cordial but hurried. "If you'll excuse us, we have a lot of work to do over lunch."

"Sure. No problem. Mind if I tag along? Gillian and I have some things to go over about yesterday's bombing. You understand."

"I'm sure it can wait until we're finished for the day." Calvin walked around Sam, but as Gillian tried to follow, the detective shot out his arm to bar her way.

Gillian glared at him. First, he lets his lover steal her notes, now he won't let her work on the damage. "Look, detective, I spent hours yesterday repeatedly giving my statement, looking at photo lineups, working with the computer sketch artist. I've told you all I know. Except for this."

She got in his face and said, "The ADA is asking the same questions I had in my satchel yesterday. Now we have to come up with a whole new batch so we don't look like fools and our clients aren't hung out to dry. There's nothing more to say. In fact, I never want to talk to you again."

She moved to get by him, daring him to stop her, especially with Calvin present. The last thing she expected was for Sam to place a hand on her arm to restrain her.

With a troubled frown, Sam glanced over at the ADA. Then he looked Gillian in the eyes, telling her something she couldn't quite fathom. His touch was firm, insistent, but his voice was tender. "I'm sorry about Stephanie—I'll get her to use different questions, I promise—but you and I need to talk. Like it or not, I'm not letting you out of my sight."

"See here, detective—" Calvin started to say.

Sam kept his gaze steady on Gillian. "I wanted you to hear this from me, before you got outside and the media threw it in your face. Roger T. Walgood was found in his cell this morning, hanging from his BVDs."

"Ohmigod!" She staggered to the side. Sam put a hand on her shoulder to steady her, but she was barely aware of it. *Not again.* She closed her eyes. *Oh, Jayson, it's happened again.* Shock spiraled into despair, and she followed it down as Sam eased her into a chair. She took a deep breath, then another. *Stay calm. Stay centered. You can handle it. You can. You barely knew Roger Walgood. He was a stranger. Not like Jayson.*

Sam squatted down in front of her so they could be face to face, eye to eye. The tempest in his dark blue gaze boiled even more. She cringed inwardly, knowing she wasn't going to like what he was about to say.

His voice was eerily calm. "With Walgood dead, you're the only one left who can identify the man who gave him the bomb. Until we find the bastard, you're gonna have a guard stuck to you like shit on a shoe, twenty-four hours a day, starting with me."

Chapter Four

"Food here any good?" Tony asked as he plopped into the chair next to Sam.

"Beats me." Sam had been so busy keeping an eye on Gillian, he hadn't paid much attention to what he was putting in his mouth. Any male here might want her dead: the man in the overcoat with a bulge in his right pocket, the heavyset man on his fourth trip to the restroom, the waiters and busboys—everyone was suspect.

At Gillian's insistence, he sat entrenched two tables from where she and Calvin Moore huddled over a tablet. She looked far too cozy with the lawyer, and Sam wondered if more than a professional relationship simmered between the two. The lawyer was rawboned, like a castaway two meals short of dying. He was also flashy, with gold rings on his right hand, a possible wedding band on the left, and a gold watch to match. His brown Armani-clone suit might be considered sophisticated, the strands of gray among the short black kinks distinguished looking, but did The Oracle really go for his type?

Sam glanced down at himself. His brown leather jacket was overdue for a trip to the cleaners, his hands bare and scarred from handling felons, and he'd meant to get a haircut last month. Compared to the likes of a high-class lawyer, he was definitely in the minor leagues.

Tony handed him a file. "You look at that, and I'll let you know how the food tastes." He grabbed Sam's plate and chowed down on the Reuben and cheese fries, acting like he hadn't eaten all week. He licked his lips and muttered, "Not bad. I wonder if they'd give me the recipe for my wife."

Tony rambled on about food and his wife's cooking while Sam studied the contents of the file. For some reason, Roger Timothy Walgood—accountant, family man, Lutheran, scoutmaster, Lions Club member—had thrown away all his conservative, middle class values of selflessness to commit the ultimate selfish act—suicide. Out of shame because he couldn't face his family and friends? Or to spare his family the anguish of trial and prison, thinking his death would be an easier agony to bear?

Maybe Walgood had hoped killing himself with his own soiled briefs would keep his wife and kids' reputations relatively clean. If so, then suicide had been his last and most selfless act after all.

Sam looked over at Gillian. He'd like her take on the matter. See what she thought about Walgood's final motivation.

Yeah, when hell freezes over.

If he was into yoga, he'd kick his own ass. Stephanie was a piranha when on a case. But he never thought she'd stoop so low as to steal Gillian's questions verbatim. Stupid, plain and simple, and he'd told Steph as much before he left the courtroom. Now he needed to do damage control with Gillian, but that wasn't about to happen until he could talk with her, alone.

He settled for Tony. "Says here Walgood never had any visitors, but he did make one phone call. To his lawyer?"

"Nah. His wife. We've got someone over there now, questioning her."

Sam glanced at Gillian. She was staring at him and the folder in his hand, undisguised curiosity in her eyes. She wore dark blue sneakers that matched her dark blue suit. He filed away her propensity for wearing sneakers instead of heels or dress flats as a form of eccentricity, maybe a Wyoming thing—

modern-day moccasins—and fantasized about whether she wore matching dark blue undies, owing to the fact that yesterday her bra, slip, and panties had matched her green shoes and dress. The memory of Gillian removing the selfsame slip and bra popped into his head. He shifted in his seat, annoyed at how often the lustful image kept showing up. At least five times last night.

Sam pointed a finger at her, then himself, and made his thumb and finger mimic a mouth opening and closing. *We need to talk.*

She shook her head and returned her attention to Calvin Moore.

Tony noted the silent exchange between his partner and the woman. "Why are you so interested in her?"

"Just doing what the lieutenant said, getting cozy with her. The thing is the lady's got her head screwed on right when it comes to reading people. I want her input on a few things I got swimming around in my brain."

"About this Walgood guy?"

"Yeah. And the man who supposedly gave him the bomb."

"Well, shit, you don't need to talk to no bitchy Oracle. She's nothing but crap with boobs. You want to find out something, go see the FBI profiler. That's why I'm here. He wants to meet with you ASAP."

"ASAP?" Sam grumbled under his breath. Leave it to Tony to wait until he finished eating before getting down to business. "That reminds me, you got anything on Jacob Miller yet?" They'd checked the notes and other business cards Gillian had thrown away. All from national and local newshounds and bloggers.

"Working on it. There's a lot of Millers, both here and Jersey. So far none of them have a Ph.D. or know Gillian Dohr."

"What about the print forensics lifted from the torn business card?"

"Nada. Too smudged to even get a partial. Why don't we just haul in The Oracle and make her tell us who Miller is?"

"'Cause I don't want her to know we've been going through her garbage. At least not yet." Sam got up to leave. "Keep a good eye on her till I get back."

"Yeah. Whatever."

Sam's voice hardened. "I mean it. No matter what she is, she's more valuable to us alive than dead."

"I know some people who'd disagree with you on that."

"But not you."

Tony waved him off. "I'll take care of her like she's my own baby sister."

"You can't stand your baby sister."

"Yeah, but she's still my sister."

He patted Tony on the back and noticed Gillian look up. She seemed surprised, maybe interested, hopefully disappointed that he was leaving. Good.

He gave her a parting nod and left to go talk with the FBI profiler.

Special Agent Regis Van Decker was your stereotypical Bureau poster boy. Clean cut. Styled short brown hair. Average height, average-looking Caucasian, in average shape for being in his early forties. A man who actually looked good in the nondescript black suit that was the standard uniform of a Fed. If not for the tell-tale sign of a tiny hole in his left earlobe, Sam might have thought the guy didn't have a life outside The Bureau.

Van Decker sat behind a desk the New York office had granted him, the surface arrayed with photos of both of yesterday's bombings plus numerous stacks of reports. Next to the desk were freestanding cork boards and a marker board. Several 3 x 5 index cards were pinned to the cork boards, a pertinent fact scribbled on each. As Gillian had pointed out yesterday, find each person's distinctive pattern and you can predict their behavior. All the cards fastened to the board with red pushpins had to do with the bombs: the explosive agent, wires, fuses, triggering devices, the container. There were two plastic bags, each one holding a nail from the bombs, and a small map of the western United States. The northeast corner of the state of Wyoming was marked by a red star, with the words Rocking Llewan Ranch written in red: the source of the plastic explosive. He smirked. The Fed was as eccentric as Gillian when it came to colors.

Red was for boom.

According to The Oracle's file, she lived on the family ranch. With both parents dead, she shared the place with one brother and his family. He searched the map for Cheyenne, the nearest city to the Dohr-Chester Ranch, in the southeast corner of the state, about three hundred miles from where the explosive material had been stolen. Maybe significant. Maybe not.

Green pushpins were for the person holding the bomb, possible accomplices, and anything in the medical examiner's area of expertise. Walgood's mugshot was there. As for the bomber on Broadway and 43rd Street . . . well, it was the Humpty Dumpty scenario. The ME was still trying to put his pieces back together in order to ID him.

Blue pins held up a map of NYC, the two bombing sites marked in red. Circled in orange was Union Square Station, Walgood's alleged destination.

Sam guessed blue pins indicated the sky's the limit. The next bomb could go off anywhere, maybe even outside the city, though he hoped it wouldn't get that crazy. No bomb had gone off this morning. Maybe the bomb-giver had made his point, whatever it was. Sam frowned. Or was busy constructing the next device.

Yellow pins held data cards on everything that was in the vicinity of the bombs. Anything that might have been the target of the bomber had its own index card. A business. A locale. People, victims—alive, injured, or dead. Sam's name was there as well as Gillian's, plus everyone who had been on the train. Yellow signified targets, possible motives for the explosions, including a card with Union Square station.

The sketch of the supposed bomb-giver had been put up with white pins. If this was the bastard responsible for death and mayhem, Sam would have expected the pins to be an inky, stygian black.

White was for . . . ?

He'd figure it out later.

Two photos were tacked up next to the sketch, blowups from security cameras in the subway. In spite of the grainy texture, he recognized Walgood, but the face of the man gripping his arm was obscured by the brim of a hat pulled down low.

He studied the slightly pudgy, ordinary looking face in the sketch. Penciled underneath was the moniker the Feds had given the suspect.

"The Carpenter?" Sam asked, questioning the nickname.

"The team thought it apropos," Van Decker said. "He uses bombs to hammer nails into his victims."

Sam appreciated Van Decker giving him time to peruse the board before getting down to business, a good way of dispensing with mundane social pleasantries, which Sam hated. This might be the first Fan Belt Inspector in all of history that he could get along with. Time would tell.

He sat down. "As I understand it, profilers are called in as a last resort, after the major investigation is over and the regulars have exhausted all other means of discovering who the criminal is. So how come you're in on this already?"

Van Decker narrowed his gaze and studied Sam in turn. "I could ask you the same. According to your file, you're not an explosives expert. You're homicide."

Sam leaned back in his chair. "My presence at one of the bombings gives me first-hand experience. And you?"

"When I noticed a close friend was involved, I wanted in, more as a forensic psychologist than a profiler. Now, if you're done playing twenty questions, let's get down to business."

Usually the FBI gave only rudimentary information to the local authorities, enough to give the appearance that the locals were in the loop when actually what they received were pigeon scraps. Van Decker seemed willing to provide whatever facts Sam requested, but verbally, nothing in hard copy to keep for his own files. Some traditions were hard to break.

On Broadway and 43rd, three people had been killed—the man holding the bomb, a pedestrian close by, and a customer in a local bakery who had the artery in her neck severed by flying glass. Eight had been injured, most by the nails attached to the bomb. All were expected to recover.

A plastic explosive about the same size as the one in the subway had been used. Five storefronts were damaged: a bakery, tux rental, pizza and coffee shops, and a used-book store with marijuana plants hidden in back to offset falling book sales. Several cars and cabs were in need of a body shop, and the sidewalk where the bomber had been standing now had pockmarks. Sam figured the department of public works would get around to it in a year.

As for the subway, the bomb had damaged two cars, bent the tracks, and did some minor damage to the walls of the tunnel and the lighting system. The tracks had already been repaired, as were the thirty-one people who claimed to be injured—Gillian being one.

Eleven of the injured had been herded together by a lawyer and were suing the city, claiming Sam was responsible for their injuries, not the bomb or bomber. No doubt they would've preferred he kept the bomb and been blown to smithereens rather than chuck it out the window and save all their lives. Go figure.

"Your board says the guy who set off the bomb on Broadway was a suit in an overcoat. Sort of like Walgood."

Van Decker nodded in agreement. "That's about all we have on him. One witness remembers him pacing back and forth in front of the bakery as if waiting for someone."

"You think he was a suicide bomber? Or a bomb hostage like Walgood?"

"We're leaning toward hostage." Van Decker handed him a photo. "Just got this from the bomb unit. Looks like pieces of a remote triggering device."

Sam raised his brow in interest. "Was this guy wired like Walgood?"

"Might have been. Bomb was snug against his chest when it blew. They're still sorting through his remains, digging out whatever they can find from what's left."

"So there's a possibility this first guy was given a bomb like Walgood." He crooked a thumb toward the photos from the subway. "Maybe even by this Carpenter."

"Or an accomplice."

"Why not a group of wackos?" Just what the city didn't need, a gang that used bombs. Great way to circumvent the new gun-control laws.

"Anything's possible," Van Decker said. "There's at least twenty security cameras on every street block in Manhattan. That's a lot of video to dig through. Hell, it might take weeks just to track down where the exchange took place. For now, we're concentrating on the guy who gave the bomb to Walgood."

Sam looked up at the sketch Gillian had provided. A cold-blooded terrorist who went around making an innocent person part of his bomb. And yet, could Walgood be considered so innocent? Despite Gillian's opinion, Walgood could have refused to obey the stranger and found another way to keep everyone safe.

He turned to Van Decker. "It'll be interesting to see if the first bomber was a middle class family man, your average everyday conformist with kids and a good home life like Walgood."

Van Decker eyed him dubiously. "You think they knew each other? Belonged to a militia group of disgruntled white-collar workers who wanted to make a statement?" He snickered. "Maybe taxes too high? Stocks too low? Too much traffic and commute time? Downsized once too often?"

Sam shifted forward. "I'm thinking more along the lines of what it would take to make a man who left his home with the sole purpose of going to work, to suddenly do an about-face on his morals and have him walk down a busy street or enter a crowded subway with a bomb in his hand."

Van Decker shook his head. "Still too many unknowns." His fist pounded the desk twice. A chill ran up Sam's spine. It reminded him too much of Walgood pounding his fist in the subway. The thumb was outside the fist, not inside like it had been with Walgood, and yet the basic gesture meant the same: frustration.

Far into the night, Sam had thought about what he would have done if he'd been in Walgood's place. At first it was a no-brainer. If the Carpenter threatened to shoot his ex-wife, Sam would tell him to go ahead. The cheating bitch deserved it. But later, when the darkness of night remained endless, and life seemed as fragile and rare as a Manhattan rainbow, Sam softened his resolve and decided not even his ex deserved to be killed.

In the end, the one thought that allowed Sam to finally get some sleep was his firm belief that he wouldn't have agreed to the Carpenter's terms. He would have disabled the terrorist with a bullet or two, called in the bomb squad, then have the lieutenant put a guard detail on his widower dad, two brothers, and his sister and their families just in case there was an accomplice.

Victims usually died. Not a doubt in Sam's mind that he'd never be a victim. He'd fight to the last second of his life in order to keep a creep from getting the better of him. Maybe it was his cop mentality. If so, he could sympathize with Walgood's dilemma. The guy just hadn't had enough experience dealing with life and death situations that cops face every day.

"Suppose the guy giving out the bombs did his homework," he said to Van Decker. "Practiced on a variety of people to figure out what type would be most likely to accept the do-or-die situation, the patsies who would take the bomb and do whatever the bomb-giver said." Gillian's theory, but he didn't mention her. He figured the Fed wouldn't take it seriously if he knew the idea came from The Oracle.

"Hmm." Van Decker's damn fist started pounding again. Sam snatched a pencil on the desk and rolled it across to the drumming fist. Automatically, Van Decker grabbed the pencil, just like Walgood had caught Gillian's bra. The similarities kept getting worse and worse. Sam wished he was back guarding the people reader. Her presence stirred up a lot more pleasurable emotions.

"That's a very interesting theory you have," Van Decker said in a slightly condescending tone, as if surprised a New York cop was capable of any kind of intellectual savvy.

"Thanks, but it's not mine." He was a firm believer in giving credit where credit is due. Now that the possibility had been accepted on its own merit, he could reveal its true source. "G. S. Dohr came up with it."

"Really?" Van Decker put the eraser end of the pencil in his mouth, alternately drawing it in and out, a slight smile on his face. "Not a bad theory."

Sam shrugged. "The more I think about it, the more it seems a surveillance job would take a lot of time. And for what? The Carpenter could just leave the bomb near his target, walk away, and detonate it by remote. That'd be easier. Less complicated."

"Could be the person holding the bomb is the primary target."

"According to Walgood's wife, he didn't have an enemy in the world. A mild-mannered sort of guy."

"Then maybe that's who the primary target is. A metaphor. A stereotype that Walgood fit." Regis leaned back in his chair. "Too bad he committed suicide while *you* had him in custody. Now we'll have to wait until the guy on 43rd is identified before we can get a better feel about who or what the target is."

Sam agreed. Yet something nagged at him. Something that wouldn't go away. "Gillian said if this Carpenter already has a good idea about what personalities are suckers for his threats, then he wouldn't have had to surveil Walgood for long. Just needed to know a few pertinent facts about the guy."

Van Decker's eyes widened. "If that's true, maybe there's something else we should check." The Fed headed to a glass-partitioned office where two men and a woman were in conference. Whatever he said caused the woman and one of the men to stop what they were doing and head for a couple of computers. It could only mean one thing.

When Van Decker returned to his desk, Sam asked him straight out, "Gillian Dohr—she's the 'close friend' who brought you here, isn't she?"

Van Decker nodded. "Tried to recruit her a few years back, have her come work for the Bureau. Figured since her brother's a deputy sheriff, she might make law enforcement a family tradition. Surprisingly, she nixed the offer without a second thought."

Sam was startled to hear The Oracle, the antithesis of every cop's sense of justice, had a brother who wore a badge. It wasn't in her file. Yet he knew right away why Gillian hadn't accepted Van Decker's offer. And that meant Van Decker didn't know her as well as he thought.

Sam sat back in his chair, feeling smug. "Gillian's not very good at taking orders," he said.

Van Decker chuckled in agreement. "She does have a mind of her own. Maybe that's one of the things that makes her so good at what she does."

"Except for the Follett case." Sam brought it up on purpose, interested to hear the profiler's take on one of the court system's worst tragedies.

Van Decker grimaced. "Follett. What a mess—on all sides. Not a case Gillian ordinarily would have taken. Did it as a favor for a colleague who had to back out at the last minute for some family emergency."

Sam was surprised at how cozy Van Decker talked about Gillian's past history. He studied the agent. "You two friends?"

"We keep in touch. I see her once in a while at one of my lectures. Whenever I'm in the Denver area, I make it a point to stop by and take her out to dinner."

Sam tried to sound indifferent. "Just dinner?"

Van Decker looked at Sam with the sudden comprehension at what the detective was really asking. He smiled evenly. "We're *very* good friends."

His eyes met Sam's. Neither one blinked. The silent message Van Decker sent was as clear as a dog marking territory. *Stay away from her. She's mine.*

The woman on the computer called to Regis. He went to take a look and waved Sam over. "We share a database with Homeland Security. Any type of bomb or threat of a bomb on a local, state, or national level, no matter how insignificant, is recorded and sent on to Homeland for review.

"Three months ago in Connecticut a man fitting Walgood's background filed a police report. Claimed he was injured in the stomach by a bomb given to him by a male Caucasian, late twenties, early thirties, about five eight, one hundred fifty pounds. No discernible facial characteristics. Average. The bomb went off, but its explosive agent was nothing more than a firecracker. Burnt his skin and clothes by the waist. Never found the guy who gave him the device."

Sam asked, "Gotta sketch of the suspect?"

Van Decker shook his head. "Since it seemed more like a minor prank than an actual bomb threat, the locals never did more than write down the basic description. But look at this." He had the woman go to the other file she had up. "A similar incident in Boston a month later. Same MO. Another average-looking male Caucasian, but heavier, a hundred seventy. The bomb was a dud."

The man at the other computer called Van Decker. Sam followed him over to see what he had found.

"Shit," Van Decker said under his breath. "Gillian was right. Four months ago, the suspect threatened to harm a teacher's girlfriend if he didn't take the bomb and do what he said. The guy refused, thought it a joke, tossed it back to him, and told him to get lost. When his girlfriend found out, she talked him into reporting it to the police."

Minutes later, two more incidents had been found. One victim was a priest, the other a blue-collar worker with a family. Both had refused the bomb.

"I don't get it," Sam said. "Those three gave him the brush-off. You'd think at least the priest would have played along if someone's life was threatened if he didn't deliver it. Don't they vow to be martyrs or something when they're ordained?"

"Not exactly. Though I agree a priest is more likely to sacrifice his own life, I don't think he'd ever barter one life for another. Not in his constitution. All life is sacred. Until I get a chance to talk with him, I can't say for sure."

"What about the middle-income guy, the teacher with the girlfriend?"

"Could be a lot of things. I'd lean toward the fact their emotional ties hadn't grown strong enough to elevate her classification to wife. He may like her almost to the verge of it being love, or he just may be keeping her around for the sex. Neither provides enough of a bond to exchange his life for hers."

Sam nodded. Gillian had mentioned something similar yesterday.

"What about the blue collar?" he asked. "I know a lot of blue collars who'd risk heaven and hell to protect their families."

"You're right, but there's another factor that may come into play. I'm just guessing, but I'd say people who are physically active in their jobs tend to use physical action in their lives. Work hard, play hard, fuck hard. Point is, when threatened, a blue-collar worker wouldn't just stand there and accept the fact his kids are going to be blown away if he doesn't caddie the bomb as ordered. He'd balk, maybe get physical, at the very least put up a verbal fight before accepting the bomb."

Sam thought back over his years of experience with criminals and the public. "The Carpenter, like most people, probably wants to avoid any type of confrontation aimed at himself."

"Could be. Also, you have to take into account other factors in a person's socioeconomic background, things that might make the victim think of another way to handle the situation. The victim might not go where he's supposed to go. Might even decide to find out if there really is someone threatening to kill his kids or wife. Maybe wave down the nearest cop for help, but wouldn't be so blatant as to walk into a police station." Van Decker shook his head. "There's just too many damn variables to make anyone a dependable delivery boy."

"Maybe that's why the Carpenter puts a wire on the victim," Sam said. "Lets 'em know he's listening and will carry out the threat if he hears the caddie ask for help. Gillian said she saw the Carpenter point to his own ear. Maybe he had a listening device in it."

Van Decker sat on the edge of a desk. "If he does wear a listening device, he could be doing so, not to whack the carrier's family if he disobeys his orders, but to detonate the bomb if it sounds like the caddie is messing up. As far as we can tell, there was no shooter staked out at Walgood's children's school."

"But you don't know that for sure."

"No, but bombers usually work alone."

"Unless they're part of a terrorist group."

"No signs of that, though Homeland Security thinks otherwise. At present, no group is claiming responsibility."

Sam raked his fingers through his black wavy hair. "So what does that leave us with?"

"Nothing until we get more evidence, more clues, someone takes credit, or another bomb goes off."

An agent handed Van Decker a file. Regis read it and frowned. "They've identified the bomber on 43rd and Broadway. Vincent Ragino, insurance adjuster, lived on Staten Island. Was engaged to be married in a month. Fiancé is divorced with three children." He looked up at Sam. "Marriage would have made him an instant middle-income family man."

"Like Roger T. Walgood."

"There were pieces in his chest from a microphone." Van Decker put up a photo of Vincent Ragino with green push pins. "Looking more like he was a caddie like Walgood instead of a bomber."

"Why only men?" Sam asked.

"Know any women who can keep a secret? Give one a bomb and odds are they've got to tell somebody about it."

Sam nodded. "Group-oriented."

"Safety in numbers. Could also be men are picked because the bomber's got a grudge against men, or one man in particular that all the men he gives the bomb to represents."

Someone yelled. On the other side of the room, an agent held up a phone. By the desperate look in his eyes, Sam could conclude only one thing.

"Number three," Van Decker hissed and reached for his overcoat. "Where?"

The agent rattled off an address. Sam's heart skipped a beat. "Fuck! The courthouse!" He checked his watch. Lunchtime was over. Gillian was back at work. And Tony was there with her. Heart pounding, Sam raced to the elevator.

Chapter Five

A bloody scrap of flesh clung to the outside windowpane by Gillian's face. At first, she refused to acknowledge that the stringy mass used to be part of a human being. Someone who, only minutes ago, had been living, breathing, thinking, fearing, panicking, maybe wishing to God that God would help save him from being blown into pieces, only to end up splattered on the side of a building like bird poop.

But reality can be denied for only so long before it smacks you in the face. The human tissue slid slowly down the glass, yielding to gravity, leaving a faint red streak to mark its path. Gillian shuddered in horror. In morbid fascination, her eyes followed its passage, her gaze dropping down with it to the street below where the bomb had gone off. She noticed Detective Tony Torelli, her bodyguard, helping victims. Apparently, he had decided the dead needed more protection than she. More than The Oracle.

She sighed in resignation.

So be it.

She could see Calvin down below as well, off to the side, helping the injured. After the bomb halted jury selection, Cal had made her promise to stay up here in one of the conference rooms, certain she would be safe in a building where security made everyone walk through metal detectors.

But there's only so much society could protect against.

"How many are dead?" the other person in the room asked.

She scanned the area and numbered the bodies whose heads were covered. "Five."

She said a silent prayer for their souls, and added a prayer for their families who would grieve for years to come. Then said a prayer for herself.

"And injured?"

Gillian searched among all the people, trying to determine who was being attended to and who were the attendants. "Sixteen."

She stiffly turned to the person asking the questions. "You used more explosives this time, didn't you?"

The man Gillian had seen with Roger Walgood in the subway stood a few feet away, far enough from the window so he wouldn't be spotted. He was dressed the same as yesterday: tan fedora, coat, trousers, but this time she noticed his shoes. They had two-inch heels on them, which meant her description to the police was wrong. He was five-six without them, her own height. The shorter stature also meant he was no longer moderately overweight but obese.

One arm was bent, the hand concealed in the opening of his coat. Just like Roger Walgood when he held the bomb in the subway.

"I miscalculated with the first two jailors," he said, raising his chin defensively. "Not enough explosive. But this one . . . I saw it in his eyes. He was starting to withdraw, let go, yield to the stronger. This time it almost worked."

"Almost?" she shrieked. "You just murdered five people!"

He shrugged with indifference.

That did it. Five lives should elicit more than lukewarm apathy from their murderer. Bristling with righteous indignation, she clenched her hands into fists and asked, "Why are you killing people?"

The vehemence of her question seemed to catch him by surprise, and he took a step back. "Because they're fools. They always put the meekest ones in charge. But put death in their hands, let them face their Maker, and their true self comes out. That's when you separate the women from the men."

I'm dealing with a maniac, she realized. And for the umpteenth time since he had walked in on her, Gillian glanced at the door. It was directly behind him, with no chance for escape. Her only hope was to try to talk her way out. To reason with a madman.

"Is that why you gave Roger Walgood the bomb? Because you thought he was too meek to refuse?"

He looked at her. He tilted his head in puzzlement. "Who?"

"Roger Walgood. The man you gave the bomb to in the subway." Gillian noted the blank look on his face. She couldn't believe what she was seeing. It was worse than she expected. "You don't know who your victims are, do you? You pick them at random."

"Of course not. I know exactly who I'm after. The uptight bastard hiding the bitch."

"You mean you were after Roger's wife?"

"What would I want with her? Roger was the jailor, the messenger, and a bad one at that. He never got to his destination, never let his true self out. If he had, I wouldn't have killed him permanently."

Gillian rubbed her forehead, struggling to make sense out of what she was hearing. "But you didn't kill him. Roger committed suicide in his jail cell."

"Did he?" The man cackled in glee. "Maybe the prisoner killed the jailor. It'd only be fitting, don't you think? You of all people should realize that. If anything, you should be out there helping me."

Confused, she stared into his brown eyes, trying to see into the crazed workings of his mind. "What in heaven's name would make you think I'd want to kill anyone?" She shook her head. "I don't understand any of this."

"Listen, Gillian Dohr. Don't analyze what I'm saying while I'm saying it. *Listen.* I've already told you why I'm doing this.

The lesson is in the learning, the learning in the motivation. Cause and effect. To keep mistakes from happening again. To punish the jailor and set the prisoner free."

He moved toward her, a malicious twinkle in his eyes. "Here's a lesson for you."

He approached, and she retreated, loathed to be touched by the cold-hearted killer. But as she stepped back, her shoulders hit the window. She glanced at the hand inside his coat. Was he holding a bomb? Maybe a gun this time. She hoped so. Dying from a bullet had to be better than being blown into a hundred bloody pieces.

He stopped in front of her. His breath was even, his brow smooth except for a slight crescent scar above the left eyebrow. His dirty brown eyes were steady, and very aware of how much she feared him.

In a voice so monstrously deep it almost seem disguised, he asked, "Why don't you scream, Gillian? Why didn't you call for help when I found you alone without your police escort?"

She tried to sound brave, but the words came out strained. "You tell me."

"Compassion," he sneered. "Your biggest weakness. Afraid of what might happen, what I might do, to the fool who answers your cry for help. And, if I know you as well as I think I do, you also don't want the police coming in and shooting me down without giving me a decent chance to live, do you? Just like when you tried to help the man in the subway." He snarled, "Only you ruined everything."

Gillian shrank back to avoid him. A futile effort. His plump belly pressed into her, followed by the rest of him until the length of their bodies touched, chest against breast, loin against loin, thighs against thighs. She squirmed against the overpowering weight pressing her against the window and turned her face aside to escape his sour breath.

"Now for *your* lesson." He pulled his hand from within the coat and shoved something up between her breasts.

She looked down. A bomb! Just like the one Roger Walgood had but without the nails, a small block of plastic explosive connected to colored wires and a button trigger.

She swallowed hard. Sweat saturated her blouse, and the fabric stuck to her body like a decaying shroud. She could smell her own fear. All she was, all she ever would be, would end in seconds. Her knees shook, threatening to give way. Yet somehow she willed herself to face the bomb . . . and the bomber.

He smiled serenely. "I would never pick you to give a bomb to. Do you know why?"

Gillian shook her head, afraid to speak, not wanting to antagonize him further.

"Come on. Give a guess."

She stiffened, then cringed as he slowly rubbed it between her breasts. The bomber stroked her with it, up and down, a rapist trying to arouse his victim into accepting the inevitable violation, when all it did was make her skin crawl in revulsion

"Why wouldn't it do me any good to give you this bomb?" he asked in a voice so calm and sweet it made her want to puke. "I could threaten to kill Wyatt and his family, and Cody and his, but it would be a waste of time. Do you know why?"

"No," she whispered, her throat tight and dry, unable to swallow, constantly aware of the bomb molesting her through her blouse. She fought back a whimper, aghast the bomber knew about her brothers. In spite of all the publicity about her during the Follett trial, that information had been kept out of the press.

He knows their names. Knows they have families.

If he could get to her, he could get to them. Her heart ached, thinking of her nieces and nephews and the scrap of flesh that had been on the window behind her. For their sakes, she couldn't give up. Wouldn't. No matter what.

Her tongue was thick, cottony, but she managed to say, "Why *not* choose me to carry a bomb?"

The bomber clicked his tongue in disappointment. "You're not listening to yourself. Oh, Gillian, it's the same reason you're not resisting my advances." He leaned into her, the bomb between them. "The same reason you wouldn't do a thing if I slipped my hand up your skirt, between your legs, and fondled you until you got hot and juicy and wet."

He pressed her further back against the glass. Her body quivered uncontrollably, dreading the lurid image he had sown in her mind. Every nerve was on edge, every muscle trembled. A dark, lonely void seeped into her heart. She suffered through the humiliation, terrified that if she cried out for help, anyone coming to her rescue might be killed in the blast.

He scowled impatiently and said, "If you insist on playing this out, there's only one thing left to do." He grabbed one of her hands and thrust it between their chests, forcing her fingers around the bomb until it was grasped securely in her grip.

His hand stayed clenched around hers. Around the bomb. "Feel that button under your thumb? It's on top of a pressure plate. Loosen your hold or remove your thumb, the bomb will go off. Bang. You're dead."

He grabbed her chin and kissed her, possessively, his fat, fleshy mouth slobbering over hers as his tongue slithered between her trembling lips, slinking deep inside where it probed and invaded at will, tasting her while leaving his own taste behind, minty and sour and alcoholic. All the while his weight kept her pressed painfully against the window.

She twisted her lips in disgust.

"Good-bye," he whispered, like a lover not wanting to leave but knowing he must. Yet the absence of any emotion in his unblinking eyes marked him as cold and predatory as a lizard.

He removed his hand from the bomb and took a step back . . . and waited to see what she would do next. With the back of her hand, she wiped his saliva off her mouth. She glanced out the window to the carnage below, then back at him . . . and caught him smiling. The bastard was smiling at her.

Fear dissolved into anger, anger into determination.

No longer afraid, she squared her shoulders, her mind set. Wyatt and Cody and their families would be safe. No one else would have to die. No more innocent victims to feed this madman's plans.

She took a deep breath and lifted her thumb from the button.

Chapter Six

Nothing happened. Gillian stared down at the bomb.

The bomber laughed. "Now you know why I would never give you a bomb."

He laughed again and headed to the door.

"Wait!" She ran after him, determined to stop him. He turned and punched her in the face, knocking her to the floor.

"Stupid bitch," he sneered. "How could I get a real bomb in here with all the metal detectors?"

Dazed, she looked up at him. "Why?" she asked, tasting blood in her mouth. "Of all the people here, why come to me? Because I stopped you from killing Roger in the subway?"

Like a grape shriveling in the sun, his head sagged, his shoulders drooped, and he said, "Haven't you learned anything from Ray Follett?"

Stunned, her mouth dropped open. "What does this have to do with Ray?"

He gestured limply with one hand. "Motivation. Cause and effect. Jailor and prisoner. If Ray hadn't been such a weak bastard, they never would have killed him." Tears came to his eyes.

Puzzled, she peered at him, studying his features: the eyes, the mouth, the nose, the chin, the crescent scar above the brow, searching her memory of all the friends and fellow employees who had testified during Ray's trial. "Do I know you?"

He quickly averted his face. "Later, bitch." He dashed out the door.

Taken aback, she stared after him for several seconds before scrambling to her feet. She ran into the hall. *Damn. He's gone.*

Sam raced up the stairs and spotted her down the hallway. "Gillian!"

"Sam! You're just in time! The bomber's here! You've got to find him before he gets away!"

"You're bleeding." Sam rushed to her. But then he noticed what she held in her hand, and he stopped. It looked exactly like the bomb he'd taken away from Roger T. Walgood, the one that had knocked a car off its track. And she was carrying it around like it was a teddy bear or something. "For Chrissakes, Gillian, what the hell are you doing with that?"

She followed his line of sight to her hand. "Oh, this." She started toward him, holding the bomb out as if she were offering him a beer. "It's a fake. At least I think it's a fake."

He raised his hand and backed away to the stairs. "Stop right where you are."

"It's all right," she said, heading straight for him. "It doesn't go off when I take my finger from the button. See?"

Sam was beside himself. He couldn't believe what she was doing. As she repeatedly took her finger off the triggering device, he backed away and shouted, "Let's not do that, okay? Stay right where you are—now—stop—don't get any closer! And, for Chrissakes, don't take your finger off that! Wait for the bomb squad!"

Sam couldn't believe it. She looked more bothered that he was yelling at her than by the bomb in her hand. No doubt she was pumped full of adrenaline. Who wouldn't be with a bomb in their hand? He had to calm her down, make her realize the danger she was in.

Except she kept coming closer, fast.

Out of desperation, he pulled out his gun. She stopped. He kept the safety on, the barrel pointed down, but, thank God, it had the desired effect.

"Sam," she said in a placating tone that irritated the hell out of him. "This isn't the danger. The man who gave it to me is. While you insist on following procedure, the bomber is getting away."

"First things first." Afraid his transceiver might set off the bomb, Sam yelled down the stairs to a fellow officer and asked for the bomb squad to be sent up. While Sam shouted out instructions, Gillian started pacing back and forth. Sam watched her, his gut tight as she absently passed the bomb back and forth in her hands. Jeez! Any second it could go off.

Gillian raised her hands and shrieked with impatience. "He's getting away!"

Sam holstered his weapon. "Gillian, please stand still. Help is coming."

"It'll be too late!"

Moments later, three heavily padded people wearing metal helmets and thick clear shields in front of their faces lumbered up the stairs behind Sam. Two uniformed cops trailed behind at a cautious distance. Tony Torelli raced past them to join his partner but stopped short when he saw Gillian and the bomb in her hand.

"Take it easy, miss," one of the padded experts advised Gillian. He raised one hand in a "halt" gesture. "You shouldn't be moving. Please slow your movements to a gradual stop. For the love of God, please stop swinging the bomb around!"

Gillian grumbled, "You guys are too much." She spun on her heel and walked back to where Sam had first seen her. While everyone screamed and shouted "No!" "Don't do that!" "Shit, no!" "She's crazy!" Gillian tossed the bomb into a room as if she were throwing away trash.

A collective gasp of doom belched from the onlookers. Everyone cringed, crouching in protective fetal positions, expecting an explosion—everyone except Gillian, Sam noted as he peeked up at her.

She stood in the doorway of the room, hands on her hips, glaring at him. "Satisfied?" she asked. "Now can we address the real problem? The man who gave it to me might still be in the building. Maybe with another bomb. One that works!"

Her comments barely registered. Everyone knew the explosive device she had thrown away was their number one priority. The bomb experts slowly inched toward the room. Dud or no dud, they weren't taking any chances. One muttered under his breath, "Stupid civilian."

Sam headed for Gillian. He grabbed her by the arm and hauled her toward the stairs. "He's right, you know. How could you be so stupid? You could have gotten yourself killed." They came to a stop at the top of the stairs. Sam asked her, "Who gave you the bomb?"

"The same man from the subway. He was right here in that room, talking and, uh, talking to me." She looked away and coughed. "I got a good look at him this time."

She seemed nervous. Jeez, who wouldn't be after being hit and handed a bomb, dud or not. His gaze swept the hall, noting all the doors and elevators. "Where'd he go?"

"I don't know."

"How was he dressed?"

"Same as yesterday."

One of the members of the bomb squad came over to talk to Sam and Tony. "We've screened the bomb to minimize damage if it blows, but let's not take any chances. I want you and your men to evacuate all the floors of this building. If this has a remote detonator like the other bombs, it could be triggered at any moment."

"But I already told you, it's a fake," Gillian said. "You should be searching for the bomber."

By the look on his face, the bomb expert was about to tell her what he thought about her, when Sam told him, "It's okay.

I'll handle it. You do your job, I'll do mine. That includes this woman."

Still too risky to use transmitters, the expert tromped downstairs to relay information to the rest of his squad. Sam turned to her. "Stay put. Don't move until we've secured this floor."

He described the suspect to the two uniformed cops, sending one up the stairs to make sure no one came down from the upper levels before they were searched, and the other down to get backup teams to search all the floors and evacuate everyone.

He motioned to Tony. Both drew their weapons and headed for the first door on the floor. As they worked in unison, checking out each room, Gillian could hear Sam say to his partner, "I thought I told you to keep an eye on her."

"I did till the bomb went off. As your bun warmer would say, 'Priorities, Sam. Priorities.'"

"Gillian was your first priority."

"Yeah, right. Like The Oracle's more important than people with nails sticking out of them."

Gillian winced. She'd never get used to the way people sneered her nickname. Sam glanced her way and frowned. Was that an apology she saw on his face?

They exited yet another room, their movements taut and efficient. The possibility of coming face to face with the Carpenter grew with each room they entered.

Sam kicked open the door to the men's room. Tony whipped around the edge of the doorframe, crouched low, gun pointed low, while Sam pointed high.

"Tan trench coat on the floor," Tony said.

"Got it. Going in."

"Watch it. Could be in a stall."

Sam yelled, "This is the police! Put your hands up and don't move!"

Tony stayed in the doorway as Sam went in. Gillian held her breath, not sure what to expect: a gun going off, an explosion. The tension was maddening, and it didn't let up after Sam came out a moment later shaking his head.

They repeated the process with the ladies room. Sam kicked the door open. A chorus of women's voices shrieked in alarm.

"Police! Everyone out nice and slow!"

Sam backed away as five women filed into the hall. While Tony asked if they had seen the man he began describing, Sam cautiously entered the facility.

The women were nervous, jumpy. One kept smoothing her long, frizzy red hair as she and the others repeatedly told him they hadn't seen anyone fitting the bomber's description. Gillian assessed the hair-touching gesture as a defensive form of preening, an instinctive means of getting a protective male's attention so he would keep her safe. Three were huddled together: safety in numbers. One tossed the dark cornrows out of her face to the side, yet another preening gesture.

Sam exited the restroom. "Nothing." He dismissed the five and told them to use the stairs. As they scurried in Gillian's direction, Sam wiped the bottom of one shoe on the floor.

"What's that?" Tony asked.

"Sand. Someone must have spilt one of those desk Zen gardens in there. Hey!" he yelled to a group of officers headed up the stairs behind Gillian to search the upper floors. "Suspect may not be wearing a tan trench coat anymore. Look for tan pants and brown shoes."

The police nodded and continued up.

By now the women from the restroom had reached Gillian. They hurried by her and down the stairs. Some clutched the hobo bags now back in fashion, some laptops. Most talked in high-pitched voices to each other about what was going on.

Only the one with the frizzy hair thought to give Gillian a passing glance.

Gillian accepted their lack of interest as typical survival reaction. At a time like this, most people thought of their own safety, so she understood why no one paid her much attention, even when Sam sent a second group—court employees he and Tony had found in another room—hurrying down the stairs as well.

Sam and Tony finished checking all the rooms on the floor. No sign of the bomber or anything that might resemble a bomb. The two talked with one of the bomb experts waiting in the hall for more protective gear to be sent up. In unison, all three turned to look at Gillian.

Now what had she done wrong?

Sam shouted to her. "Did the bomber wear gloves?"

"No!" she yelled back.

That seemed to excite them. Snatches of conversation filtered down to her. Fingerprints. A chance to ID the bomber. Sam wanted to keep the bomb intact. The bomb squad wanted to detonate it. After a short argument, Sam and Tony returned to where Gillian waited. Another group arrived with FBI and ATF on their jackets, plus two bomb-sniffing dogs. They started going through the rooms searching—not for the bomber—the entire building had already been evacuated, one agent told Sam. Their job was to make sure another bomb hadn't been planted in the courthouse. Already, another team was checking the elevators and shafts.

Tony asked Gillian, "The man who gave you the bomb, did he wipe it off before he gave it to you, try to clean off his prints, or did he just hand it to you?"

She glanced down at her blouse, and her face burned in embarrassment. Yesterday she'd used her breasts to distract Roger and foil the bomber's plans. Today the bomber had used them to wipe his fingerprints off the bomb. And here she had thought he was coming on to her.

Damn. She was an experienced people reader. Now she felt like a rookie. She was never going to live this down, especially when the press got wind of it. And she thought the headlines in the papers this morning had been bad.

Gillian lowered her head and asked God to open a hole at her feet so she could escape the humiliation looming on the horizon. But no welcoming hole appeared. The only thing she saw was a trail of glistening sand leading to the stairs.

Calvin Moore stormed out of the elevator at FBI headquarters, intent on rescuing Gillian from the bad guys. At least that's the impression Sam got as the lawyer scrutinized the floor of desks and corner offices with a scowling righteousness that any circuit-riding, revivalist preacher would envy.

Gillian sat in a glass-walled booth, a clear cage but a cage nonetheless. No one was more aware of that than her. Every time she'd looked at Sam during the past seven hours and silently pleaded with him to set her free, he'd looked the other way and allowed her to remain a prisoner.

Normally, she would have been let go after three hours, tops. After all, she was as much a victim of the day's bombing as those outside the courthouse. But as soon as she told everyone what the Carpenter said in parting, everything changed. The reference to Ray Andrew Follett had transformed Gillian from a victim to a person of interest.

Sam was outside the glass prison, taking a breather, stretching his legs, and trying to avoid Gillian's desperate eyes. Just before Calvin arrived, he'd noticed the photo of the courthouse bomb caddie Omar Shattalah on Van Decker's boards. Yet another middle-income male, an assistant project manager, with a wife and one kid. Next to it was a second copy of Gillian's photo, this one tacked on with green pushpins, the color Regis used to denote the person holding the bomb or a possible accomplice.

The way Van Decker had been laying into Gillian all night, pretty soon the Fed would have her sharing white pins with the Carpenter.

Sam glanced at the profiler sitting inside the interrogation room with Gillian. He looked as worn out as she did. Maybe more. Something was bothering the agent. Something that made him keep lashing her with questions. Endlessly. Wearing her down. Wearing them all down.

Van Decker was after something. Maybe an important piece of information he suspected Gillian had floating around in her subconscious. The right word, the right emotion, might bring it to the surface.

Or maybe something she actually did know but refused to tell.

Van Decker and his team were still grilling her, trying to force her to come up with a reason why the bombing incidents might be related to the Follett case when Calvin arrived. Not exactly a knight in shining armor but her rescuer none the less. Sam was almost as glad to see him as Gillian was. Her eyes brightened when she caught sight of her employer through the glass wall. A hopeful smile broke through her fatigue.

Calvin paused where Sam sat on the edge of Van Decker's desk. "How could you let them do this to her? Look at her. She looks terrible."

"I've no jurisdiction, the FBI has full control. I'm an observer, a token liaison of the local police. The most I can do is hold her hand."

"Then why aren't you doing at least that?"

"I did better than that." He turned his head to stare at Gillian. "I called you."

What good would it do to reveal how often during the last seven hours he had wanted to snatch her away, at gunpoint if he had to, and stash her in his apartment. Keep her there until this whole incident with the bomber blew over and the world forgot about Gillian Dohr and her relationship to the Follett case. *Shit.* Every time Van Decker or one of his inquisitors brought up Follett's name, he could see the pain in her eyes. She'd even winced a few times. Hell, slicing her with a razor probably would have been less painful.

He told Calvin. "I can't get her out of there. But you can."

"Damn right. And I will."

Moore did just that. He stormed into Gillian's transparent cell and stated his intent, rattling off all her legal rights to leave. As the room rang with half-hearted objections, Calvin grabbed her hand and led her out. Not until they got to where Sam still sat on Van Decker's desk did Calvin realize what she was wearing: a grey t-shirt with FBI emblazoned across the chest and a frumpy pair of black sweat pants.

"Where are your clothes?" Calvin asked in surprise.

Gillian's face turned a mortified shade of red. She glanced anxiously at Sam, her eyes begging him to help. He answered for her. "They were confiscated as evidence. The bomber, uh, brushed against her outfit."

Don't look at where the Carpenter touched her, Sam ordered himself. For chrissakes, keep your eyes above the neck. No point in explaining to Calvin exactly where and why the bomber had touched her, or that the latest quip going around was: Tittie towels foil forensics.

"He might have left trace evidence," Sam added.

His simple whitewashed explanation made Gillian's eyes sparkle with moisture. Tears of gratitude were ready to pour out.

Shit, Sam thought. This was going to make things worse.

Quickly he said, "Gillian, can I see you for a minute?" At the same time he put a hand on her back and turned her sideways so the lawyer couldn't see the tears overflowing. "Alone," he told Calvin, who seemed ready to object. "A minute. No more. We'll be right over there in full view."

"Gillian," Calvin said, "you don't have to do this."

Her face averted, she waved a hand to let him know it was all right with her.

"One minute," Calvin called after them as Sam led her off to the side.

Chapter Seven

Sam made certain Gillian stood facing away from the interested glances of all the people on the floor and far from the glass room, which had too many microphones for his liking. As tears dribbled down her face, he pulled out a handkerchief.

"Thanks." Gillian took the cloth and started dabbing her cheeks.

"Hey, it's nothing," he replied. "You're tired. Must be. Don't see you as the type who wants to be seen bawling in front of a bunch of guys."

She sniffed. "You like tough women?"

"Not particularly. Not biker tough, I mean. I just don't like seeing a woman taken advantage of, that's all." Her watery eyes stared up at him with sudden warmth, making what he had to say next all the more difficult. But it had to be said.

"Gillian, I know the guys were pretty rough on you in there."

She spoke bitterly. "Tell me about it."

"But something's been bothering me. Something personal that I wanted to discuss with you, alone."

By the puzzled look in her eyes, she didn't have a clue to what he was going to ask. His thoughtfulness in taking her aside to cry, his good deed for the day in giving her a hankie, made it safe for her to lower her defenses and open up, like a lamb meeting its first wolf and thinking it's some other species of sheep. *Shit.*

He ground his teeth. No two ways about it, he was going to take advantage of her trust, and hate himself later for doing it.

Sam kept his voice low so only Gillian could hear. "You told the others you didn't think the Carpenter was sexually aroused when he stood close to you."

Sam saw the warmth in her eyes flicker. She stiffened slightly. But she still was open to him, still allowed his kindness to make her gullible.

"At first I thought so," she said, "but looking back, knowing why he really assaulted my chest with the bomb, I see it as a ploy. A distraction."

"And the kiss? Frenching you?"

Her lips twisted in revulsion. "Another distraction to keep me off balance. Playing with my emotions in prelude to leaving me alone with the bomb. A test to see how I would react."

"Gillian!"

Both Sam and Gillian looked toward Calvin. He was holding up his wrist and pointing to the gold watch. Sam's minute was up.

"Be right there!" Sam yelled with a false smile. He quickly drew Gillian's attention back to him. "Ms. Dohr, you're a good-looking woman. Any man standing that close to you, this close to you," he said as he moved within touching distance of her—and noted she didn't withdraw—"would have to fight like the devil not to show any reaction to having a beautiful woman's body so close to his. Are you sure you didn't feel him? Not even a slight pressure?"

"No," Gillian whispered. She was breathing fast, whether because of the topic or his nearness, Sam wasn't sure.

He lowered his mouth to hers. He didn't allow their lips to touch, but the intimacy was just as real. Just as potent.

She breathed heavier. Faster.

So did he.

"When he kissed you, did you feel him then? Even a little?"

"No," she whispered hotly into his mouth. Her earthy brown eyes were riveted on his. He could swear her pupils were dilating.

"Did he move into you, press hard and stiff against you, even for a second during the kiss?"

She gasped breathlessly as Sam moved closer and brushed against her body.

She licked her lips. "No, not at all."

He stepped back, away from the heat rising between them—and something else he didn't want her to feel.

Gillian blinked. She took a deep breath and ran a hand through her hair. She looked all around at everything, anything but Sam. She appeared disconcerted. Uncertain. Maybe ashamed.

Sam refused to let it be the last emotion they would share before she left.

"If we were alone, I'd hug you."

Caught off guard by his remark, she jerked her face up to look at him.

"Not passionately," he added. "But a hug. A real, honest to goodness hug. I'd hold you in my arms, lay your head against my shoulder, and tell you everything was going to be all right. I'm not going to let the Carpenter get anywhere near you again."

Gillian had the same look on her face as Wendy Steiner did in eighth grade when he'd asked her if she wanted to go out with him. All warm and cuddly while nervous at the same time, clearly wondering what she was getting into if she said yes. Wendy had said yes—his first girlfriend, his first love, or what young teens thought was love. It had been good while it lasted.

But the full-blooded, mature woman who was searching his eyes, looking for an ulterior motive to what he was saying, expected a lot more from him than Wendy ever had. Gillian wanted a friend. Someone she could trust. A man she could accept a hug from without any fear of reprisals or ridicule.

"That's what I feel like doing," Sam said with all sincerity. He glanced around. "But I can't. We have an audience. They wouldn't understand." He looked back at her. "Hell, I don't even understand. The thing is, it would ruin my objectivity. Let's just call it a night, okay? I hear they've assigned a Fed to guard you. You'll be safe from now on, so there's need to worry. I'll return you to Calvin. He looks like he wants to take me down some dark alley for a few minutes and let me have it, but he seems like a decent guy."

Gillian laughed softly. All the tension between them had been melted away by his plain-spoken honesty. Sam smiled, glad to have made a difference. "We better go." He gestured with one hand for her to lead the way to the waiting attorney.

"Wait, I think I owe you an explanation," Gillian said.

"Oh? About what?"

"About why I told you I was trying to save Roger Walgood in the subway instead of you."

He shoved his hands in his pockets and leaned back, not sure he wanted to hear her explanation. "I'm listening."

She glanced at the hands firmly entrenched in his pants and fought hard to stifle a laugh. "The first time I saw you, I knew you could handle anything. A bit cocky and hardheaded, but confident. Tough. Experienced."

She glanced at his hands again as he withdrew them from his pockets. He said, "Really? You could tell all that just by looking at me?"

She nodded, and one side of his mouth tilted into a lopsided smile.

"How you talked, what you said when you tried to get me out of your way, confirmed my assumptions. You could stand on your own. But Roger couldn't. I could tell by his voice and gestures that he was giving up. No matter what you said to him, he was getting ready to end it. He needed an ally.

Someone to give him another option so he wouldn't detonate the bomb."

Sam's eyes blazed in sudden understanding. "By saving Roger's life, you saved mine."

She lightly chucked him under the chin, "What goes around comes around, detective." Calvin called again. "I better go."

A moment later, Calvin Moore had an arm protectively around her shoulders as they headed to the elevators. Gillian mouthed a silent "Thank you" before the doors closed.

Sam winked in reply.

Van Decker approached. The other agents were packing it in for the night. "She looks a helluva lot better," Regis said. "What did you say to her?"

"I reminded her she wasn't alone. Which she needed to hear after what you and your team did to her tonight. I thought you two were friends. How could you be such a prick with her?"

Van Decker frowned. "Because *I am* her friend. And I didn't like what I was hearing."

"And what's that?"

Van Decker glanced at his wallboards of facts. "It's late. Go home, detective. Get some sleep."

"You gotta be kidding." Sam shifted closer and got in his face. "Look, there's a crazy bomber running around loose in this city who feels connected to Gillian over what happened to Ray Andrew Follett. He may try to see her again, get to her, maybe with a real bomb next time. Hell, the Carpenter mentioned he was aware of her having a 'police escort.' Means he's been watching her. Keeping tabs. Since I'm part of this case, I have the right to know anything that might help me protect her the next time this wacko tries to get near her."

The argument was valid, but Van Decker still hesitated.

"This is not the time to be coy," Sam growled.

At that, the profiler smiled wryly. He took a step back, yielding to the detective, giving each of them some space. "Did you notice Gillian said she smelled Illusion on the Carpenter?"

"Yeah. Pretty average cologne for a not-so-average guy. Supermarket stuff."

"True. What I'm getting at is the moment she detected it."

"When the creep kissed her."

"Exactly. Not before, not after, only during the kiss."

"So? She was probably so shocked at being alone with him, what he did to her with the bomb, that she didn't notice it before then."

Van Decker shook his head. "Illusion is distinctive, hard to miss. And what could be more distracting than having a mass murderer French-kiss you?"

"What's your point?"

"It's been recorded in thousands of cases on file that when a human being is in a life-and-death situation, as Gillian was when she thought the bomb was real, that a person's senses automatically go on alert. Anything and everything gets noticed. An odd-colored thread on a piece of clothing, a crooked fingernail, the difference between a rasp and a wheeze, whether a clock chimed two or three at the time of an attack, the skitter of a cockroach crossing the floor."

"Again, what's your point?"

"She didn't detect Illusion until the guy was mashing into her face. That meant he only had it on his face. Probably a small area. Why?"

"The guy's frugal?"

"That's one explanation."

"But you don't buy it."

Van Decker shrugged. "It's just something worth noting."

Yeah. The Fed likes notes. That's why the pattern boards now had a list of all the forensic evidence found in the Carpenter's trench coat posted with white pins. A couple of breath mints, a facial tissue, traces of explosive residue—probably from carrying bombs around in his pockets—and a strand of hair with glue on one end, which meant the guy's wearing a toupee or wig. Next to the list was a card with Illusion written on it, and another that reminded the Fed no fingerprints were found on the bomb he gave Gillian except her prints.

"Gillian told me she didn't think the guy got turned on by kissing her. Kept his Johnson at rest. You think that means he's gay? Women don't excite him?"

"Or he gets aroused only when he's blowing up people."

"Like foreplay." Sam nodded. "Then wouldn't he have gotten turned on when he rubbed the bomb between her breasts? If he gets his jollies from explosions, the anticipation of giving the bomb to Gillian should have made his Johnson salute her. Better than staring at a centerfold."

"I've considered all that."

"And?"

"Maybe he's gay."

"Then why French her?" Sam asked.

"To see how she would react. Could be tied in with the reason he gives the bomb to some poor innocent slob instead of just placing it somewhere and letting it go off. He enjoys watching all the emotions a caddie goes through when confronted by the horrifying fact he's holding his own death in his hand. In Gillian's case, the Carpenter seemed to deliberately provoke a lot of emotions when he was with her."

"Yet even then he didn't get turned on."

Van Decker shrugged and looked at his watch. "It's way past my bedtime."

"Mine, too," Sam said with a hard voice. "But we're not going anywhere until you tell me what you were trying to get Gillian to say. Illusion, my ass. I know a detour when I hear one. Talk, Van Decker, or we stay and watch the sun come up."

The profiler didn't look pleased. In fact, he looked downright uncomfortable. But he managed to plaster a genial mask on his face when he waved a cordial good-night to the other agents as they left. No one questioned his staying a while longer with the New York cop. Probably appreciated him doing the grunt work of keeping the local liaison off their backs.

In a short while they were alone with only the irritating hum of the fluorescent lights to keep them company. Van Decker pulled out the nearest chair and plopped into it. The furrows on his brow and around the edges of his mouth seemed to deepen with each passing second. Sam thought he looked worse than Gillian, and yet Van Decker had been the one hammering into her for most of the night.

Sam waited. Whatever was bugging the shrink was itching to come to the surface. He could see it working its way up as the man shifted and grumbled and held his head in both hands.

It took a good two minutes, but a deep sigh signaled its release.

Van Decker talked slowly, as if the weight of each word made it difficult to speak. "Gillian took her finger off the bomb's pressure plate."

"Yeah?"

"She said she did it because she knew it was a fake. She wanted to call the bomber's bluff."

Sam watched Van Decker struggling with himself, fighting to reveal what had been torturing him for the past few hours. As Van Decker grew more agitated, Sam tried to remember the last time he had performed CPR. The agent might need it before this conversation was over.

Van Decker shouted, "How thick-headed are you? Don't you get it?"

Sam shook his head.

Van Decker rushed over to the files of transcripts, pulled out a sheet, and thrust it in front of Sam's face. "Here! Read your own report of what you remembered Gillian saying when you first saw her in the hall and asked what she was doing with a bomb in her hand!"

Sam read it aloud, calmly, not certain why Van Decker was so upset. "She said the bomb was a fake. Said she thought it was probably a fake. That she already knew that for a fact because it didn't go off when she took her finger off the button." He looked at Van Decker. The guy's face was awash with emotions, all of them ugly. "Am I missing something?"

Van Decker laughed dryly. "Only the obvious. You thought it was a bomb. The clay and cardboard made it look and weigh the same as if it was. The wires were accurately placed but hollowed out to keep the metal from setting off the courthouse's metal detectors. The pressure plate was real but plastic, again to get it through the metal detectors. All it lacked was an explosive element and an ignitor. Even the experts weren't sure it wasn't real until they destroyed it."

Sam tensed. A dark, terrible thought had scurried into his mind. He didn't want to acknowledge it. Denied it. Screamed at it to go away.

He read the transcript, his own words, and refused to believe them. He shut his eyes tightly to the truth.

But Van Decker made him face it. "Probably—she said. Probably a fake. Even she wasn't a hundred percent sure. And yet she admitted taking her finger off the pressure plate before you got there—while the Carpenter was still with her. Why? Not to call his bluff. To call hers. It must have been in her mind for the last three years, festering, waiting for a catalyst to set it free. Any excuse to give in to it, to obey the urge, to escape from all the guilt she's still carrying around about Ray Andrew Follett.

"And then the Carpenter literally hands her the means to act upon it. He gave her a reason, which no one would question, to do what she hasn't had the nerve or guts or weakness to do for three years. Oh, she probably told herself it was to save others. It sounded good. Heroic. Courageous. Compassionate. But the bottom line is Gillian Dohr tried to commit suicide today. She just used the bomber as an excuse."

Chapter Eight

Sam repeatedly shook his head, refusing to believe Gillian had tried to kill herself. Yet in his heart he knew. His hands balled into fists so tight the knuckles turned white. White like the pushpins holding up the sketch of the Carpenter.

White pushpins.

Of course.

After spending so much time with Van Decker, he was getting to know how the profiler thought. Regis considered serial killers bloodless, anemic, cold-hearted garbage, lacking any compassion. To the unsuspecting eye, they were whitewashed evil.

Sam opened his fists. He also now realized Regis considered Gillian weak and malleable.

But Sam didn't. Gillian was smart and tough. After all, she was The Oracle. Everyone always said what a steel-assed bitch she was. Easy to think of her that way. Harder to take a step back and believe The Oracle was as vulnerable and scared as everyone else. And so terribly fragile.

And what Van Decker said next chilled Sam to the bone.

"What's had my stomach in knots all night," the profiler said as he stared at Gillian's picture on his boards, "is that the Carpenter now knows she's suicidal, too."

Across the street from the hotel, in the dreary gloom of metropolitan shadows, Dr. Jacob Miller waited for Gillian Dohr.

His body swayed back and forth, matching the intensity of his appeal to the Most High that the woman would appear soon. He had been waiting for hours. He was cold, tired, and scared. Above all, he was afraid of what Michelle might do when she discovered he was out past his allotted time. A strict jailor, everyone had to comply with her schedule. Michelle came first. Always first. It wasn't fair.

"As if the Creator had promised life would be fair," he murmured to himself.

He glanced at his watch. Almost midnight. He shuddered in dread; when Michelle found out what he was doing, she would make his life hell. She might not let him out again for days. Maybe weeks. Being confined with everyone else stifled his academic studies. As it was, his brief daily furloughs provided little time for research.

He glanced at his watch again. Michelle was definitely going to throw a conniption.

And yet he was breaking curfew not only for her benefit but for all the inmates of her prison. In the end, the others would thank him, Michelle would forgive him, he hoped.

Hope. His only consolation.

Squeals erupted from the nearby alley, and he cringed. Rats were scavenging among the garbage—skittering, fighting, mating, dying—a reminder that evil was upon the face of the city. His heart pounded. Death kept striking at his heels. If only he could make it stop, go away, give the others a fighting chance to live.

Vengeance and recompense should be left to the Holy One—words Jacob tried to live by. Always he waited on the Almighty to exact justice. It was difficult. Had always been so. But with the specter of his own mortality suddenly haunting his life, Jacob now yearned to believe the Holy One sometimes used people to work His vengeance. With all his heart he wanted to believe people got their comeuppance now, while they were still on earth.

A black car stopped in front of the hotel. A uniformed doorman approached, then hesitated and hung back as two men in dark topcoats exited the car and scanned the perimeter.

Jacob stood frozen in the shadows, watching, waiting to discover who the two men guarded so zealously.

One of them opened the passenger door facing the hotel. A thin black man got out. He reached a hand into the car and helped a young white woman to her feet. Though she wore frowzy sweats, Jacob recognized her immediately.

"Gillian! Ms. Gillian Dohr!"

He was so happy she had finally come, he ignored the impropriety of shouting out her name with such emotion. Nor did he realize how startled everyone was by the unexpected appearance of a small, black Hasidic Jew as he darted out of the shadows and rushed across the street to her. Until he saw a gun pointed in his face.

"Don't move," said the man holding the gun.

Jacob complied. With downcast eyes, he suffered the humiliation of being frisked by the other guard. No one had ever touched him so crudely. Not for many years, at least. It seemed to be his fate. Yet, as long as he kept reminding himself that the Most High would seek vengeance on his behalf, he could suffer anything.

Except Michelle's wrath. If she found out about this, she might try to kill him. Like she had tried before.

The man who frisked him said, "He's clean," but his voice sounded disappointed.

The agent lowered his gun but kept it out. "Who the hell are you?"

Jacob straightened his black wool coat and flat-brimmed black hat. The long dark sidecurls—glued onto the brim by his temples because Michelle refused to allow him to have true payos—swayed with his movements. He lifted his head high, yet everyone else was still at least a head taller.

He fished around in one pocket and retrieved a business card, which he handed to the agent. "I am Dr. Jacob Miller, a friend of Gillian Dohr. I need to speak with her. It's urgent."

The agent studied the card. "Ms. Dohr, do you know this *gentleman?*"

Gillian approached, Calvin Moore by her side. She stopped next to the agent holding the gun. The other agent constantly swept the perimeter with his eyes, obviously not comfortable with how open and vulnerable their position had been made by this unexpected delay. He was clearly anxious to get her inside the hotel.

Jacob tensed as she looked down at him. He kept his gaze respectfully averted to just above her shoulder.

Gillian sighed wearily. "Oh, Jacob, what are you doing here? I told you a year ago I never wanted to talk to you again."

She turned to Calvin. "I don't need this. Not tonight. I'm too tired." She headed for the hotel. The doorman opened one of the huge brass doors.

"Wait!" Jacob yelled. "It's about Follett! I must speak with you before it's too late!"

Gillian ignored him and hurried inside. One of the agents followed her in.

Calvin stepped towards Jacob. "Follett," he seethed through taut lips. "Always Follett. He's dead. Why doesn't everyone let him stay dead?" He pointed a long finger at Jacob, his arm shaking. "You stay away from Gillian or I'll have a restraining order issued against you by morning. Got it?"

Jacob nodded. What else could he do? His shoulders sagged. After risking everything, he had failed. Already, he could hear the nagging voices in his head.

"Told you so. Outsiders don't understand."

"Contacting my companions would prove more constructive."

"Jacob, when will you ever learn to mind your own business?"

"What a schmuck."

"I want to go home."

As he trudged down the street to catch a bus, his shoulders drooped even more. A failure, and he still had Michelle to face.

Chapter Nine

In the family's ranch house in Wyoming, Gillian stood in front of her bedroom mirror trying on hats. With almost girlish anticipation, she carefully arranged a bridal veil over her face. She tilted her head from side to side, admiring how she looked, then blinked as the pure white color morphed into a black mesh that completely obscured her face. A funeral veil. Repulsed, she tore it off and threw it away.

She grabbed another hat, a pink cowgirl hat. The western style brought a smile to her face and a mischievous sparkle to her eyes. As she positioned it on her head, warm childhood memories filled her with happiness. She took it off and lovingly set it aside.

The next hat she put on was black with a flat brim and curlicues of hair pasted on either side by the ears. Jacob Miller's hat. She grimaced in distaste. Too many painful memories were associated with the all-around pest, and she flung the hat away.

A forest ranger's hat, one of the many hats Ray Follett had worn, sat heavy on her head. Tears fell from the brim but none from her eyes. With a long sigh that seemed to go on for hours, she sadly set it aside.

The Carpenter's fedora felt even heavier. She looked at her image in the mirror. Something wasn't right. She reached for a tube of lipstick and painted her lips bright red—blood red—the color of the flesh that had stuck to the courthouse window.

Slanting the fedora in a jaunty dip over one eye, she placed her hands on her hips and admired the results. With a satisfied smile, she leaned towards the mirror and kissed her own reflection. The mirror exploded. Silver shards sliced into her, shredding her flesh, splattering the room with blood like rain. She screamed and screamed in pain.

In her dark hotel room, Gillian woke up screaming from the searing pain rippling through her. She shot up and frantically searched her body for cuts and blood. A dream, yet a nightmare so real she could still feel the hot streams of blood. Her hands reached out and touched her covers, expecting them to be wet with blood, then jumped, startled, as someone pounded on the door.

Her guard.

He asked if she was all right; he had heard her scream. She yelled back that everything was fine, just a bad dream. When he questioned her again and asked to come in and check the room, she assured him once more that she was all right. He grumbled a good night, and silence filled the room.

Gillian hugged herself tight, feeling alone, insecure, and terribly homesick. She must have been deluding herself. She was never going to be able to reclaim her life and her career. Not after Ray Follett. None of this would be happening if she had stayed in Wyoming and taken up ranching. Raising cows and pigs didn't produce nightmares of exploding mirrors and splashing blood.

She looked around. The red numbers on the radio alarm clock revealed four in the morning. The color reminded her too much of the red lipstick in her dream. She turned the clock toward the wall, and tried to go to sleep. But it was useless.

She stared up at the ceiling. During the past three years, she'd learned to use logic to dispel nightmares, analyze the most disturbing symbols and find a rationale for why her mind had conjured them up. Determined to exorcise her demons, she put her hands behind her head and set her mind to the task.

Okay. Jacob's hat was in the dream because she had seen him right before going to bed—as if she hadn't suffered enough yesterday. The fact that both he and the bomber had mentioned Follett was probably the reason for Ray's hat in the dream. Likewise, the Carpenter's hat had appeared because she had seen him yesterday. The cowgirl hat was probably her inner longing to run away, back to the ranch, and let someone else deal with the trial, the bombings, and the victims of both.

No doubt the wedding-funeral veil was also related to Ray.

Kissing herself in the mirror—that didn't make any sense. Not at all. Could she be subconsciously narcissistic? The possibility made her squirm, as did the memory of the exploding mirror cutting into her body. What was that all about? She wished she had someone to talk to.

In the dreary darkness, she noticed a stream of light sneaking through a gap in the curtains. It cut across the room to the dresser where it reflected off the gold frame of one of the three photos that always traveled with her. Her security blankets, so to speak. One was of Wyatt, his wife, and their three kids sitting on a rail fence at the ranch. All had broad smiles and matching cowboy hats. The photo of Cody and his wife and two children showed them dressed up in their Sunday finest, posing by a white column with green ferns in the background. A studio portrait, yet in this one, too, all the smiles were genuine.

The third photo was of her family who had passed on yet still remained close at heart: her mom and dad, who had died about five years ago, and Jayson, who had left while in his teens.

She studied the two photos of her brothers. She'd already talked with both of them, a conference call as soon as she got to the hotel last night, to warn them about the bomber's threats. Cody had been ready to blow it off—he doubted a bomber in New York City would suddenly dash out to Oregon to kill them. Besides, if the authorities didn't catch him soon, he had a gun cabinet full of protection. He wasn't about to let a vague threat interfere with his daily routine.

Wyatt, on the other hand, had been in law enforcement too long not to take any threat idly. Though he himself wouldn't be leaving, he was already planning to send Sue and the children on an impromptu vacation until the Carpenter was caught. But not to Sue's folks. Too easy to track relatives through public records. He'd send them someplace they'd never been before.

After ten minutes of arguing, Wyatt finally got Cody to see reason. Unlike Wyatt, whose wife and children had probably left within an hour of the call, Cody and his family wouldn't get organized until after lunch, but he promised his brother they'd be out of the house before the day was out.

Gillian apologized profusely for disrupting their lives. She didn't know how many times she'd said "I'm sorry" until Wyatt told her to stop blaming herself, like victims often do. With gentle firmness, he reminded her the bomber was the only one to blame.

When it came to heart-to-heart, bare-one's-soul talking, Wyatt was the brother of choice. She'd love to talk to him about her dream. But it was two in the morning in Wyoming, and he needed his sleep after staying up late to pack and send his family away. It would be selfish to bother him just because she'd had a bad dream.

Calvin?

No. He was a man who worked with facts. Analyzing dreams were for psychologists and New Agers, not lawyers.

Gillian glanced at the phone, almost desperate enough to try a psychic hotline. Except the psychic, if she really got a psychic this time, might tell her something she didn't want to hear. Gillian wasn't after the truth. She just wanted someone to ease her mind enough so she could get back to sleep.

Regis?

After the way he'd interrogated her, the last thing she wanted was to talk to him.

Sam?

Interesting possibility. But she didn't have his number. Besides, after what he'd told her in the courtroom, he probably was in bed with Stephanie.

The image of the ADA snuggled up next to the detective made her flinch in revulsion. Talk about a nightmare. A really bad one. So bad that Gillian suddenly realized it had erased her own nightmare. The sensation of having her body sliced and diced by an exploding mirror was gone. Relieved, she snuggled under the covers and decided maybe Sam and Stephanie weren't sleeping together tonight after all. Sam had still been in the federal building when Gillian left. Even then it had been late. Perhaps too late for him to call on the ADA.

Gillian turned over. She settled into the lumpy mattress and remembered the warm, fuzzy feeling when Sam had said he wanted to hug her. She could do with a long, loving, masculine hug. Just imagining Sam giving her one, with Stephanie watching from somewhere in the background, cartoon smoke coming out of her ears as she fumed with envy, was enough to lull her back to sleep, a smile on her lips.

When Gillian woke again, someone was talking faintly in her room. She struggled awake and vaguely realized the voice was coming from the clock radio. As she fought to open her eyes, the radio declared it had just received word of a bombing.

She covered her heart with a hand. At least one death was being reported.

The newscaster talked incessantly about how many more might be dead and injured, the volume of morning commuters who would be inconvenienced, followed by a tirade about the local police and federal agents "ineffectual" efforts to catch the Carpenter.

She closed her eyes in dismay. His use of "the Carpenter" meant someone must have leaked the FBI's moniker to the media. Idiots. For some serial killers, having an official nickname fueled their egos, inspiring them to kill more often. More creatively. If the Carpenter was after a fan base, this would lay the foundation.

The newscaster jabbered on. Conflicting reports fueled speculation, quickly turning what should be news into an emotionally provocative broadcast. Gillian grumbled in anger. After spending years in courtrooms across the country, she had developed a loathing for conjecture. Opinions without facts to back them up were like Frisbees made out of cowpies. No matter what the shape and form, no matter how eloquently conveyed, shit was still shit. She reached over and slammed her fist on the off button.

A fourth bombing!

She rocked nervously back and forth on the edge of the bed. After yesterday's confrontation, she could easily imagine the pompous smirk on the Carpenter's face as he handed over the bomb. Her skin crawled just thinking about him.

At least her brothers and their families were safe. Though he had elected to stay home, Wyatt could take care of himself. While traveling vast stretches of southeastern Wyoming alone, a deputy sheriff literally learned to spot trouble a mile away. He knew when to call for help.

She glanced across the room at the television. They probably already had live coverage of the bombing. She had no interest in seeing it. Yesterday at the courthouse had been enough. She hated to think she was already becoming desensitized to the tragedy. Truthfully, she felt no compassion for the victims. No tears to shed. No desire to sympathize.

Perhaps because she finally realized nothing could prevent it from happening again.

Why care?

Her gaze flicked to the photo of Jayson, and she squeezed her eyes shut. Caring hurt like hell. Better to stand back and be as disinterested as anyone could be. That's how one survived in a violent world. Emotionally and mentally removed. Safe in one's own little sphere of life. That's what she had learned from the horror of Ray Follett. Exactly what she had done for the past three years, secluded on the ranch.

Gillian gasped in horror.

She had just answered the Carpenter's question: *Haven't you learned anything from Ray Follett?*

With all that had happened with Ray—the accusations, the blame for setting him free to murder more children—she had learned to be as cold and calculating as the bomber.

Oh, God!

Wave after wave of self-loathing roiled through her stomach. As the nausea thickened and churned, she raced to the toilet.

Sam and Tony raced to the location of the latest bombing before the Feds, a Starbucks, a cozy, high-priced coffee hangout which Sam and Stephanie had been to just last week. All the windows were blown out, the victims of the flying shards bleeding all over the sidewalks and street. Most were in a state of shock. Sam caught one pedestrian walking away in a daze, a zombie holding a cell phone to her ear with her mouth slack and open, oblivious to the glass splinters that had hit her and were striping her brown face with rivulets of blood. He handed her over to one of the paramedics now on the scene, then joined his partner inside.

Immediately, the stench of charred flesh assaulted his senses. Sam dipped a finger in the Mentholatum Tony held out to him and stuck it up each nostril to quell the gagging reflex. As added insurance, he popped a breath mint in his mouth and sucked on it greedily. He didn't know anyone who wasn't affected by the scent of roast human.

Taking shallow breaths, he gazed at the remains of the poor wretch who had been holding the bomb. It didn't get much worse. Male, by what was left of his suit. The body gutted, burned, and torn into two parts, upper and lower. Vomit rose in his throat. Sam looked away, but the damage had already been done. The gruesome scene was now socked away into his subconscious. It would come back later. The dead always did. His dreams were saturated with victims of vicious crimes, looking the same as when they had died, with gaping wounds or part of their heads blown off or their crotch bleeding from rape.

The nightmarish images always crept into his dreamscape the night after their killer walked out of a courtroom free or with a sickeningly light sentence, as if the ghostly victims blamed him for what the courts did. A savage side-effect of his profession, the main reason so many of his fellow officers turned to booze and drugs. He'd give his pension if someone could mute the voices screaming for justice that haunted his nights. Hell. He'd even submit to a shrink if he could find one who could actually help.

He clenched his jaw in determination. He had to find the Carpenter, make him pay, or he'd have the charred, gutted body added to the other ghosts moaning for vengeance. Sam turned his back on the corpse. The ME would scavenge the gruesome pieces to determine his identity, the Feds would reassemble pieces of the bomb to see if it matched the previous ones. He had other things to do.

As he moved away from the victim, the distinctive scents of the crime scene blended together. Among the odor of burnt human hair and flesh, he could detect the smell of bitter, roasted coffee and the metallic trace of blood.

From past experience, he knew it'd be months before he could step inside another Starbucks without remembering the scents surrounding him today, if ever. Like Roma's Pizza Palace. He still couldn't go into a pizza place without automatically sniffing for gasoline. Small consolation the arsonist who had torched the eatery had another eight years in prison, barring good behavior.

He shifted out of the way as the paramedics escorted the last of the injured customers outside to waiting ambulances. From what Sam could tell, the caddie was the sole fatality. The relatively minor injuries of everyone inside the place plus the shards of glass blown out of the building indicated the victim had been standing by the windows or seated at a table near them, facing away from the interior.

What had he been doing? Waiting for whoever he was supposed to deliver the bomb to?

The stupid fool. Did he really think he'd be allowed to get away scot free after delivering the bomb? Hadn't he been reading the news and watching TV? The populace had been warned not to accept any device from a stranger and call *911* for help when approached by anyone resembling the man in the police artist's sketch. Why hadn't he?

Tony called his attention to the floor. Sam looked down. Among the debris was a scattered assortment of iPods, laptops, tablets, and phones.

"You think we should push all the redials?" Tony asked.

"Find out if one of them belongs to him?" Sam said, his thumb pointing back over his shoulder at the corpse.

"If one does, he might've been checking in with his significant other just in case the bomb did go off. A last farewell. That's what I'd do. Call my wife one last time."

"Tempting idea." Sam surveyed the phones. The Feds would have a spaz attack if he and Tony did some investigating of their own. As if he cared.

But if he got caught, the Feds might remove him as liaison, and then he'd be stuck on the sidelines. That didn't sit well with him. Sam considered this *his* case. He was there during the second bombing and had talked with the caddie, Roger T. Walgood. He felt obligated to stick with it until the Carpenter was caught.

"If he was wired like the others," Tony said while he squatted down in front of a glowing neon green phone, "talking on his cell might have caused the Carpenter to detonate the bomb." His fingers flickered above the phone, itching to check out his theory. "Maybe the Carpenter didn't want to take any chances. Even hearing the tones as the caddie punched in the numbers might have alerted him."

"Hold that thought," Sam said as his partner reached for the phone. "Better let the Feds take a video of the crime scene first." He looked to the right where a woman in an FBI jacket was using a camcorder. "They've already started. In the meantime, I'd like you to interview the customers and employees before the FBI hauls them away for questioning. Ask if they remember seeing anyone who might have been holding a bomb or a package the size of a bomb before it went off. You know, someone acting nervous by the window. Maybe fidgeting in his seat."

Tony looked outside to where the EMS were treating superficial cuts and abrasions. "Can do. But what's the point?"

"I'd like verification this guy decided to call for help. Maybe someone remembers seeing him use a phone. With just cause, we can bag this techie litter without getting into too much hot water."

"I'll get on it." Tony left to canvass the injured.

Sam stepped outside, away from the FBI and ATF bomb experts swarming all over the place, and took out his phone. He made sure he was faced away from the TV cameras—some of the networks employed lip-readers to get illegal exclusives on police investigations—and called *911*. He supplied his name and shield number, then asked to speak with the supervisor on duty. When she came on, he asked if anyone had called in about the time of the bombing and didn't complete the call. Maybe got cut off all of a sudden. She promised to check and put Sam on hold.

While waiting, he observed the hustle and bustle around him. He smiled in approval as he watched Tony work his special charm on the people he was talking with, getting them to remember stuff not even the devil knew. But as Sam shifted the phone to the other ear, doubts settled in. Why was he bothering with this? The caddie was dead. It didn't matter. It wouldn't change what had happened.

Like it wouldn't change what Regis had revealed about Gillian last night.

She wanted to die.

She had tried to use the bomb to commit suicide.

She'd given up.

Maybe that's why he was going after this worthless piece of info. Unlike Gillian, he was hoping this guy had made an effort to live. To survive. To not go down without a fight.

Shit! How could she not want to live?

As he continued to wait, Sam wondered how long it had been since Gillian had sex. He thought of Regis and the Fed's remark about visiting Gillian whenever he was in her neck of the woods, and Sam amended the thought to wondering how long it had been since she'd had great sex.

The supervisor came on. Sam turned his back on the news jackals.

"We had one waster at the time you indicated," the supervisor said. "A young kid, fooling around like kids do, dialing 911 'cause they got nothing better to do."

"A kid?" Sam said in surprise. "Are you sure it was a child? Could it have been a man with a high-pitched voice?"

"Hold on. I'll let you talk to the dispatcher who took the call."

A few seconds later, the dispatcher came on. Sam asked about the waster.

"Definitely not a man," the dispatcher said. "Sounded like a little girl. Four . . . five years of age."

Sam shook his head. Talk about a dead end. Yet something nagged at him, and he asked, "Do you remember what she said?"

"Sure. It was my last one before the place was flooded with calls about the bombing. She said: 'I don't like it here. I hate my present. I hate it. I wanna go home to Rachel. Please take me—' and then nothing. I figured whoever was taking care of her caught her playing on the phone and hung up without an apology for wasting my time. Happens a lot. Parents teach their kids to call 911 in an emergency. But kids, they think dropping their stuffed animal in the toilet is an emergency, you know what I mean?"

Sam could only imagine. He and his ex never got around to having children.

"I'd like a copy of that kid's call," Sam said.

"Sure, but what for?"

"I got this thing about coincidences. More often, they're not."

Sam worked out the details of where to deliver the copy. Shit, he hated coincidences. Farts from Fate, his philosophy teacher had called them. And though he had hated the inexactitude of philosophy—it was the last class he took before he dropped out of college and entered the police academy—in almost every case what his teacher had said turned out to be true.

He'd been hoping the caddie had decided not to handle the situation on his own and phoned for help. But the only call at the time was from a little girl who wanted to go home. Coincidence?

Both the little waster and the poor schmuck were away from home. Coincidence?

The girl had a present she didn't like. The victim definitely must have hated the bomb in his hands. Yet another coincidence?

Farts from Fate. He hated them.

He still wanted to believe the victim had tried to get help. Maybe he had, but the little waster had tied up the line, not letting him get through to the dispatcher before the bomb went off.

He noticed the Feds had finished taking the crime scene photos and videos. A woman was sketching the interior: placement of body, placement of body parts, tables, chairs, etc. He got out a large evidence bag from the trunk of his car, slipped on gloves, and headed back inside to collect the phones. The victim's phone was probably in pieces since it would have been close to the blast, but maybe, just maybe, he could find it and prove Tony's theory that the caddie had been trying his damnedest to get help before he died.

"What are you doing, Detective Brankowski?"

Chapter Ten

Regis Van Decker stood before Sam.

"I said, what are you doing, Detective Brankowski?"

Sam casually looked around at the debris on the floor. "Just helping out."

With a raised brow, Regis eyed the bag of phones. "What are you going to do with all those? Call a porn line?"

"Funny. No, I'm, uh, retrieving property. That's it, retrieving private property. After the shock wears off, a lot of the owners are going to want these back. Don't want any looters getting their hands on them, know what I mean?"

"Yeah," Van Decker said sarcastically. "You're a boy scout."

"Just doing my job. By the way, there's a severed finger near your left foot. Might want to avoid stepping on that. Forensics would be pissed."

As if convinced the local cop was playing a joke on him, like being told his shoe is untied when it's not, Van Decker scowled. Then he looked down. His frown went limp, and he visibly paled. The torn, bloody digit was a scant centimeter from his sole.

Van Decker placed a red marker by the human remains. Sam saw the Fed's hand tremble. Profilers usually were assigned to a case long after all the evidence was collected. The Fed was rusty. Probably hadn't been in the field for years. Seeing the victims fresh was a whole new ball game for the desk jockey.

"By the way," Sam said, "do you know whether the caddie has both hands intact?"

"The left is gone. Right hand and forearm are also missing."

"Both hands gone? What was the guy doing, hugging the bomb?"

Regis shrugged. "Why do you ask?"

"Might explain the finger."

Van Decker watched Sam sift through the wreckage and retrieve phones until his hand stopped shaking, then withdrew to where the medical examiner was conducting an initial examination of what was left of the caddie.

Sam worked faster, afraid Van Decker might have second thoughts and impound his "collection" on a matter of principle: a power play about who had jurisdiction over who.

He returned to the severed finger. Near it, behind a coffee cup, he found a smartphone with a nail sticking out of it. His neck prickled with an unearthly chill. Could be the victim's phone. Blown away by the blast along with the finger. Where the rest of the hand was now was anybody's guess.

Gently, he picked up the phone. With what came close to being a prayer, Sam hoped it had at least one good print on it.

He placed the phone in its own small paper bag, keeping it separate from the bigger bag with the other phones, hoping an electronics expert at forensics could download the phone's memory and see what number was in the redial file.

On the way out, he informed the woman sketching the scene about the finger on the floor. She thanked him and made a notation on her map. He hurried out to his car and put the bags in the trunk before Van Decker thought to confiscate them. Sam smirked. Out of sight, out of mind.

Tony joined him. None of the witnesses could remember the person holding the bomb. Chances were the people closest to him might remember, but they were also the most likely to have been seriously injured in the explosion and were already en route to hospitals.

"I also talked with the manager," Tony said. "The place has a security camera, more for catching employee theft behind the counter than keeping an eye on the customers."

"Great," Sam said. Maybe it got the caddie on tape. Maybe even the person who gave him the bomb.

"Not so great. The system's on the blink. Been waiting three days for a repairman."

"Damn."

"Now what?"

"We drop our bag of goodies off with forensics," Sam said as they got into the car, "then go talk to the injured at the hospital before the Feds get to them."

Van Decker knocked on the driver's window. Just to let him know they weren't taking orders from a Fed, Sam started the car first. Then he rolled down the window, but only halfway.

"Going somewhere?" Van Decker asked.

"Just wanna check out some things," Sam replied casually.

"Uh-huh. Like what?"

"Oh, this and that."

"You wouldn't be jerking me around?"

"Wouldn't think of it. You're not my type."

With one hand on the roof of the car, Van Decker leaned down to the window. "Sam, you can't hold back. Not on something like this. If the Carpenter repeats his pattern from yesterday, there's a good chance he'll give another bomb away before the end of the day. Maybe even before lunch."

Sam looked Van Decker in the eye. "I know."

"Anything, I mean anything you get on him, you've got to let me know. For the sake of his next victims. And Gillian."

He stared at Regis. This wasn't a jurisdictional battle over who collared the Carpenter and got the recognition. No, it was a basic primitive struggle over territory, and Gillian was the territory they each wanted to protect. Maybe possess. She was the key. To make matters worse, they both had competition from the Carpenter. In his own sick way, he wanted her, too.

Sam took a deep breath and let it out. "If I find anything, I'll contact you—but only because of Gillian."

Regis straightened up. He patted the top of the car, then turned and walked away.

Tony eyed his partner as they pulled out. "So, you and Van Decker think the Carpenter will go after The Oracle again?"

"Let's just say I'm starting to think there may be a reason why the bombings didn't begin until after she came to town."

"Yeah. I've been thinking about that myself. Thing is, the lieutenant told us the Feds claim the plastic explosive was stolen two years ago. You think the Carpenter waited two years for The Oracle to come out of retirement?"

"I don't know what this guy thinks or why he's doing this. All I know is I hate that he's doing it in our city. To our people. And Tony," Sam paused to look at him, "her name's Gillian Dohr. Not The Oracle."

"Whatever you say," Tony replied. But he didn't look pleased. And the second glance he gave Sam indicated he didn't like what might be causing his partner's change of attitude about the infamous people reader.

Jury selection had ended by lunch, and the trial was finally under way.

The courtroom was packed. The family of the victim filled the three rows behind the prosecution's table. Behind them were members of the Jewish community, mostly men, seeking justice for what they thought was an anti-Semitic crime. Though Stephanie London hadn't referred to the aggravated assault and murder as a hate crime, if she thought the jury might be favoring the defendants, she'd undoubtedly whip out the emotionally charged "hate" designation to get their sympathies back to the victim. Gillian had seen it done before and effectively.

The seats on the other side of the room were primarily filled with the defendants' families and people who were noticeably of Puerto Rican descent. All the trustees of the Puerto Rican Justice Fund were present, wearing large buttons with the initials PRJ on them, plus ribbons pinned to their outfits in the commonwealth colors of Puerto Rico: blue, red, and white.

Representatives of the major news networks were seeded throughout the gallery. A sketch artist sat a few chairs away from Gillian, working on portraits of the defendants for the news media since no cameras were permitted in the courtroom.

Security at the courthouse was tight. Metal detectors were supplemented with body searches: brief but thorough pat-downs of everyone who entered the building. No one was taking any chances. Calvin had wanted her to sit at the defense table, but Gillian had refused. She felt safe enough in the gallery. Plus, with all the unwanted publicity she'd been generating, she'd rather stay out of the spotlight and sit inconspicuously in the first row behind the defense.

In Calvin's opening remarks, he counseled the jurors not to make assumptions or insinuations, to solely look at the facts of the case. They would be presented with circumstantial evidence but none of it would prove his clients were murderers. Almost as an aside, he implied the real perpetrator was still on the street, maybe even in their own neighborhoods, on the prowl for the next victim.

Usually Calvin wouldn't have brought up the possibility that a murderer was still at large, which implied police incompetence. Not a good tactic at this early stage, but he had done so at her request. There were three jurors she wasn't sure of, three with large question marks by their names.

If she went solely by body language—and that's all Gillian had to go on until the end of the trial, when she would try to interview the jurors—she would say the majority of them were starting out with fairly open minds: good eye contact with the attorneys, no restless movements. Most sat back in their chairs and remained fairly still, alert, and interested.

What Gillian kept looking for was the exception to the norm. And there it was. Two of the three jurors she was uncertain about had just displayed contrary actions. When Calvin suggested the real killer was not in the courtroom, that the police needed to find the true perpetrator, both had crossed their arms in front of their chests and tightened their lips. One had even looked away from Calvin.

She made a note of it. Where these two jurors were concerned, something in their mental makeup made them averse to believing police could make mistakes. Perhaps a conservative respect for law and order, or a relative or friend in law enforcement, although checking her notes, neither one claimed to have any personal or casual relationship with a cop.

Gillian tapped her pencil pensively against her notepad. They might like viewing the world as an orderly place: predictable, manageable. Bad guys steal. Cops catch them. Courts send the bad guys away. Admitting that police were ineffectual would erode their perfectly ordered world. They'd have to start thinking outside the lines and concede the possibility that some cops are bad and some criminals have good in them.

She ground her teeth in frustration. Without being able to talk with the jurors, it was all speculation. Just in case, she'd suggest that Calvin forego any insinuation that the police had screwed up. Instead, he should stress all the reasons why the defendants didn't have killer mentalities. Thieves are thieves. Killers are killers. If the two jurors preferred the world in black and white, they might be predisposed into believing thieves don't turn into killers on the spur of the moment.

As the opening remarks concluded, she handed her initial observations and suggestions to Calvin's junior partner John, who made his own notes before handing them to Cal.

The prosecution called their first witness, and Gillian took a few seconds to scan the courtroom. Since her terrifying encounter yesterday, she was constantly on the lookout for the Carpenter. In the halls of her hotel, on the street, in the restaurant, she defensively searched for any tell-tale sign of him: anyone who seemed to move like him, dress like him, or look like him. Even with a federal bodyguard, she didn't feel safe.

As her gaze slowly returned to the front of the courtroom, her mind strayed to thoughts of Sam Brankowski. Last night he had spared her the humiliation of telling Cal that the Carpenter had molested her and used her blouse to wipe his fingerprints off the bomb.

And yet Sam had used her, too. It took her a long time to figure that one out—early that morning at breakfast while she was trying to get her stomach to accept a few bites of toast. Sam had done her a favor with Calvin, but then had seduced her into reliving her intimate encounter with the bomber. The detective's one redeeming trait was that he hadn't asked the disturbingly personal questions in front of anyone else.

Sometimes she liked Sam. Sometimes she didn't. And then there were the times when she remembered Sam's lips, so close to hers last night that even his breath was like a kiss. Warm and caressing. Beckoning. Asking for something beyond the words of his questions. His dark blue eyes had continually searched her face, eyes the color of the sky when a summer storm is approaching the ranch, his emotions shifting, intensifying, yet held in check. Did he still dislike her for being a jury consultant? Or was he disappointed she hadn't found a way to keep the Carpenter with her long enough for Sam to catch him?

In retrospect, she should have taken care of the Carpenter herself. Bit his tongue off while he Frenched her. Kneed him in the groin. Kicked him in the knee before he had a chance to punch her. Wrestled him to the ground like she did calves during branding time. She doubted he weighed more than a young steer.

Instead, she'd let the situation and the bomber get the best of her, and had accepted the role of victim. A harsh self-judgment, but true. She wasn't an aggressive person by nature. Reacting to the Carpenter in a violent manner would have been categorized as abnormal behavior on her part. No one would have been more surprised than she would if she had attacked her attacker. Even at the cost of her own life, it wasn't in her to do it.

Exactly the point Calvin would make in defense of his clients, she thought as her attention returned to the trial. Murder is atypical behavior for common thieves. She straightened in her seat and assessed the body language, words, and tonal quality of each witness so she could alert the defense team when a certain mannerism, choice of word, or a deviation in vocalization indicated the witness might be lying or stretching the truth to fit the prosecution's case, as when a piece of evidence was not as conclusive as the witness claimed it to be. So far everything the witness had said was matter-of-fact and spoken in a monotone. The only one raising her voice was Stephanie when she wanted to stress a particular fact, like a talk show host trying to steer the audience into her way of thinking.

Gillian glanced at her watch. Only three, yet already her eyes ached from fatigue. A headache was coming on as her body demanded more caffeine to keep her sharp-eyed and awake. Times like these she regretted not staying closer to home and choosing a different career. But then she would hear the echo of a promise she had made long ago on the high plains of Wyoming with her tears swept away by the hot wind as she stood alone at Jayson's grave and vowed to do something to make the justice system fairer for all.

It had always seemed ironic that the U.S. has Lady Justice wearing a blindfold as a symbol of fair play when, in the 18th century, political cartoonists placed the blindfold on Justice to depict the corruption of the judicial system. The original representation of the Greek goddess Themis has her eyes wide open, able to see clearly who and what stood before.

The American judicial system was long overdue for sweeping changes. With all her heart, Gillian fought to remove Justice's blindfold. Until then, her skills would lift the cloth and give Justice a peek at whatever was placed on the scales. After all, a sack of garbage can weigh just as much as a sack of untainted evidence. Her job was to make sure only what was true and free of prejudice was placed before a jury.

A noble goal worth any discomfort, any fatigue, or so she told herself as she looked at her watch again and sighed. This was going to be a long afternoon.

Stephanie saluted Calvin right after the judge left the bench for his chambers. Gillian noticed Cal nod his head ever so slightly toward the ADA in acknowledgment. Though adversaries, attorneys usually recognized each other's talents. Cal had done a superb job of manipulating the time in order to prevent the medical examiner from being the final witness of the day.

It was bad enough the arresting officers had confirmed finding blood on one of the defendants' clothes. DNA testing indicated the blood belonged to the victim. Having the ME display photos of the victim's naked and brutalized body right before the day's adjournment could have been even more detrimental to the defense.

Cal didn't want the jury stalked by the gruesome images all night long. Too often they produced nightmares about the murder, nightmares that might include their clients. From previous post-trial jury interviews, they knew how often dream content affected a juror's perspective on a case, overriding common sense and the facts.

Cal would rather have the jury see the photos first thing in the morning, then distract the jury as quickly as possible with the more mundane facts and witnesses in the case. To that end, he had asked an abundance of cross-examination questions of the first witnesses to testify.

The courtroom emptied quickly. Gillian, Calvin, and John were the last to leave as she briefed them with her final notes. They exited the courtroom into the hallway, accompanied by her federal guard. Calvin offered to pick her up later for dinner. She was about to decline—she had a date with a tub full of soothing hot water—when she caught Sam Brankowski's eye. He was down the hall, a file folder in his hand, talking with Stephanie. And yet he repeatedly glanced her way. After the prosecutor entered an elevator, Sam headed toward her.

Calvin saw him. He muttered in Gillian's ear, "Here comes trouble."

"Heard things went well for your side today," Sam said as he stopped in front of them.

"If you're referring to the side of justice," Calvin said, "then I would agree with you. I hear the same can't be said for you. Still haven't caught the Carpenter?"

"We're getting closer. That's why I'm here." He lifted the folder in his hand. "I need to talk with Gillian."

Calvin scowled, about to say something, when Gillian quickly said, "It's all right, Cal. I'll only be a few minutes. I'll meet you by the elevators." To her relief, Calvin and John left, as did her bodyguard after an affirming nod from Sam that the detective would keep an eye on her.

When they were alone, Sam asked, "Have you been able to come up with anything new about the Carpenter, any particulars that came to mind during the night?"

She thought of her horrific dream, and of her reaction to the bombing that morning. Neither would help find the bomber, though both were caused by him. None were Sam's business.

She shook her head and looked down at the folder in his hand. "What's in there?"

"Regis found reports from around the country of someone handing out fake bombs. All to men. All given out by a man—dressed differently each time and with different colored hair. Only vague descriptions of how he looked, but one interesting thing. Over time, the suspect gained weight. Started out about one hundred thirty. Then a hundred fifty. The last time, he weighed closer to two hundred, if we're talking about the same guy. The thing is, if it is the same guy, the Carpenter, why would he be gaining weight?"

"Have you asked Regis what he thinks about it?"

"Yeah. Claims the entire country has a weight problem. Which is why I want your take on it."

"I could throw out a few possibilities but without more information, they'd be guesses."

"Let's hear 'em."

"Okay. Could be symptomatic of a medical problem. Could be the side effect of medication. Then there's depression, boredom, dissatisfaction, a need for protection, a need for comfort, low self-esteem—there are a lot of possible reasons."

Sam slapped the file against his leg in frustration. "Van Decker was right. It's a dead end."

She studied his face with concern and softened her voice. "You look tired. Were you at the Starbucks bombing?"

"Yeah. For most of the morning. Not a pretty sight. A simple routine like stopping for coffee shouldn't end in death."

She shuddered in understanding. After yesterday's bombing at the courthouse, it was far too easy for her to imagine how grisly the coffee shop must look.

"Tony found two people at the hospital who think they saw the person holding the bomb right before it went off," Sam said. "He was hunched over, whimpering like a little kid. One definitely saw a phone in his hand, the other saw something in his lap. Probably the bomb, but with the victim sitting curled up tight, nothing specific could be seen. Neither witness thought much of it. Figured he had a fight with his wife or girlfriend and was probably calling to patch things up. Then all hell broke loose."

His dark blue eyes seemed to reflect the carnage, weary of death yet also hardened to withstand the emotional drain. Impulsively, Gillian raised her hand to touch his cheek in sympathy. He tensed warily in anticipation, and she stopped. She withdrew her hand. They didn't have a relationship that warranted such intimacy.

Embarrassed, her gaze fell to the floor. Sam turned his head to look at the nearby wall. Both shifted uncomfortably but neither moved away.

She could smell Sam's distinctive scent, gritty and masculine. It reminded her of the good, rich soil on her ranch, a place she always felt safe. Strange that in a city of millions she had found someone who made her feel the same.

"How do you handle it?" she asked.

"I don't. Not really. I guess I distract myself. I only think about getting the bastard who keeps doing this, imagining the pleasure I'll get meeting him face to face, beating him to a pulp on behalf of his victims." He shrugged dismissively. "It helps blur the images of the bodies. For a while, anyway."

Gillian glanced up. As Sam talked, the horror of what he had witnessed at the coffee shop had again filled his eyes with cold weariness. It hurt to see him tortured by the memory. This time she didn't stop as her hand rose to his face and touched it tenderly. The coarse whiskers growing on his cheek gently prickled her palm, yet the muscles along his jaw softened beneath her caress. She picked one hell of a time to start caring about a man.

He turned his head into her touch and looked at her. The coolness in his eyes thawed into warmth, and the wariness in his face eased.

She kept her hand on his cheek and said, "Quite a job you picked for a career: finding and catching people who do monstrously evil things. I wish there was some way to make it easier on you."

Sam reached up and covered her hand with his. In a rough voice filled with emotion, he said, "Don't worry about me. Most of what I go through will disappear as soon as the Carpenter is taken into custody. Or killed."

"Killing: the preferred solution of cops." She lowered her hand.

"Let me put it this way," he replied, his voice as stone hard as his features. "If I spot the Carpenter within ten feet of you, I'm going to shoot first and ask questions later. I'm worried about you, Gillian. Worried sick he'll get near you again, the next time with a real bomb."

The vehemence of his caring touched her. Such vows of protection seemed outdated in the modern age. Almost romantically chivalrous. Even more startling, she never would have expected a cop to take her welfare to heart. But here he was, standing strong and steady before her, looking into her face as if she was the most fragile and important person in his life.

He was a cop. She was The Oracle. He the champion of the victim, she the paladin of the accused. Oil and water. Chocolate and fish. He should have welcomed the possibility the Carpenter might want to kill her. Most cops would.

Instead, he wanted to kill to protect her. But she didn't want any more people killed, good or bad. As an adamant opponent of capital punishment, it felt wrong.

With Sam, killing was part of life. Part of his job. Kill to protect. And because of that, because he'd meant it as a compliment, she raised herself on tiptoe and kissed him on the cheek.

The look of surprise on his face was almost comical. Yet the modest kiss put a sparkle in his eyes. It burned bright with the promise of something more developing between them.

He glanced down the hall to where three people were waiting for them. "Guess we better go."

"I suppose so." Though what she really wanted to do was stretch out the moment, make it last for hours, and ignore the rest of the world.

When they reached the elevators, Calvin was frowning.

"I want to talk with you," Calvin told Sam in a tone he usually reserved for unruly clients, then said to Gillian and his assistant, "I'll meet you two back at the hotel."

Accompanied by her federal escort, she and John got on the elevator.

Calvin waited until the doors shut. Then he tightened his grip on his briefcase and turned to Sam. "Stay away from her."

"Can't do that. She's met the Carpenter up close and personal, and, since the bombings have something to do with the Ray Andrew Follett case, in which she was involved, she's part of this investigation. Whether you like it or not, I'll talk with her anytime, anywhere."

"You do and I'll file harassment charges."

Sam snorted. He wasn't going to let any lawyer push him around. "On what basis?"

"That getting her further involved with this terrorist bomber will kill her. You saw how she looked just now. She's worn out. Exhausted. Gillian takes everything to heart. Everything is personal. Long after Stephanie and I have forgotten this trial and moved on to the next, Gillian will still be reliving it, questioning herself, wondering if she could have done better. She's a bleeder with a heart as big as Texas.

Someone with her personality shouldn't do this type of work, and yet, despite the cost to herself, she's still doing it. And she's damn good at it."

"But she helped free Ray Andrew Follett."

Calvin's dark face appeared to blanch. The lawyer recovered fast and stuck a finger in Sam's face.

"Listen here, detective. What happened with Follett wasn't Gillian's fault. She thinks it was, but it wasn't. A whole lot of people share responsibility and guilt over that. If one person other than Gillian had done their job better, Follett and those five kids would still be alive today. No one went untouched by Ray Follett. No one."

Calvin reached into the inner pocket of his suit jacket and took out his wallet. He opened it and removed a nail hidden inside.

"Even I carry around a piece of Ray." He held the nail up. "Sent to me anonymously after Ray was killed, probably someone in the police department or FBI; they're the only ones who had access to the evidence. Gillian got one, too. So did Dr. Newhall, the psychiatrist who treated Ray, and Cliff Jackson, Ray's lead attorney. Hell, Jackson just got out of rehab. About half the jurors from the trial were treated for clinical depression. Two tried to commit suicide. One succeeded. Three others were so traumatized their spouses filed for divorce. As for the prosecutor, she decided our judicial system was hopelessly flawed and ran off and joined a religious commune in Arizona."

Sam was stunned into silence. The cruel gesture of sending nails to everyone on Follett's defense team disgusted him. Amazing how one person named Ray Andrew Follett could wreck so many lives beyond those of the victims and their families.

Yet sympathy was a luxury he couldn't afford.

"Everyone is still being touched by him," Sam told Calvin. "Everyone in New York. The Carpenter is making sure of that."

Calvin nodded in assent and put the nail back in the wallet. Sam noticed he looked as drawn and exhausted as Gillian.

"You're right," Sam said. "This guy *is* my problem, not Gillian's." He rubbed his hand over his face in frustration. "I've been burning my brains out, trying to figure out what the Carpenter has to do with Follett. If I can discover the link, I might have a better chance at stopping him before he kills again. What's got me is Follett went after kids. This guy doesn't. So what's the connection?"

Calvin looked away, avoiding eye contact. He checked the hallways, as if hoping someone would come along to interrupt their conversation. But the hall was empty. He jabbed the down button for the elevator.

On instinct, Sam asked, "Do *you* know what motivated Ray Andrew Follett to kill those kids?"

To Sam's surprise, Calvin let out a maniacal chortle. Eyes big and wild, he whispered, "Some would say Ray didn't kill any of them."

"But he was caught with the kids—right there, he'd just done it. Their blood was still on his hands. The bodies nailed to the walls."

Calvin's voice turned to ice. "No one ever said Follett didn't kill them."

"But you just said Ray Follett *didn't* kill them."

"Did I?" Again, Calvin hit the button for the elevator. And again. With each passing second, he jabbed it with his finger. "I find it insanely ironic that a cop wants to know Follett's motivation when it was cops who gunned him down—killed an unarmed murderer—and thus prevented the world from discovering what motivated Follett. The old dictum is true: what you do to others is done to you. In an act of vengeance, those cops killed the one person who might be able to stop your avenging bomber."

Calvin's finger kept stabbing the down button.

The frenzied gesture was driving Sam nuts. He grabbed the lawyer's wrist to make him stop. "Doesn't anyone know why Follett killed those kids?"

Calvin stared at him. "I'd say maybe three people in the entire world know. One is your bomber."

The elevator arrived. Calvin shook free of Sam's hold and rushed inside. He turned and held up a hand. "Take the stairs, detective. I'm in no mood for company."

The doors began to close.

"Wait." Sam held open the doors, but didn't try to get on. Something told him that in Calvin's present state of mind, the lawyer might physically try to keep him out. "You said there are three who might know Follett's motivation. The bomber may be one. At least he thinks he knows. Who are the other two?"

Calvin shifted his briefcase from one hand to the other. "Ray Follett had a psychiatrist. He may know but he'll never tell now that Follett's dead. He's too decent a person to let fame and greed break his professional ethics. That's why all the books on the case were duds. All filled with baseless speculation. No one had proof of what was in Follett's mind."

Calvin pressed the lobby button. The doors started to close but Sam insisted on keeping them open.

Sam asked, "Who's the third person? Van Decker—the guy who profiled Follett?"

Calvin kept stabbing the lobby button. The guy obviously felt cornered. Desperate. Maybe even scared. Sam knew how to use all three to his advantage.

"Tell me who the third person is, and I'll let you go."

Calvin's finger paused, ready to hit the button again. His finger shook. The lawyer's entire arm shook. He gazed at Sam, like a man drowning who has just realized the hand reaching out to help him is too far away to grab.

His shoulders slumped. His lips hardly moved as he spoke two words. Shocked, Sam stepped back and let the doors close.

Chapter Eleven

"Gillian Dohr?" Sam whispered in disbelief.

It couldn't be. Last night Regis and his inquisitors had repeatedly asked her what motivation the Carpenter and Ray Andrew Follett had in common. And she repeatedly denied knowing. Hadn't a clue. She was as baffled as they were.

Why had she lied?

To protect the Carpenter?

Or to protect herself?

He was tempted to race down the stairs to the lobby, grab the lawyer by his thousand-dollar lapels and throw him up against the nearest wall, and demand that he tell him how and why Gillian would know what had motivated Ray Andrew Follett, and what was now motivating the Carpenter. She might be one of the best people readers in the business, but she was no shrink.

Sam stared at the elevator doors, thinking, trying to make sense of it all. From the first it had been obvious a deep, personal connection existed between Calvin and Gillian. Had to be if he could convince her to come out of her three-year withdrawal and return to work on his behalf.

So how could he imply Gillian was withholding info? The bastard. He had to know Sam could arrest her for that.

So could Van Decker.

How could she have lied to Regis? Weren't they friends? Close friends? Lovers?

And what about himself? How did Gillian view Samson Brankowski? As a tolerable enemy? An acquaintance thrown together by fate and the Carpenter?

Sam headed for the stairs, fuming. Gillian had lied to him. He'd been in the room with Regis and the others when she insisted she didn't know the Carpenter's motivation.

Damn! He didn't want to believe she had lied.

But then he didn't want to believe she had tried to commit suicide either.

He found Tony waiting for him in the lobby.

"Hey!" Tony said. "You're not going to believe this. I was in the john taking a leak and guess who comes in, locks himself in a stall, and starts bawling like a baby?"

"Calvin Moore."

Tony blinked in surprise. "Yeah. How'd you know?"

"Part of the Judas syndrome, a reaction to betraying a close friend. Got any news on a print matching the one taken off the broken phone?"

"Yeah. Belongs to a Christopher Bonaventure. According to forensic, he was holding the bomb when it went off. I got ahold of his wife. Sobbing like there's no tomorrow, but I got her to confirm that that particular Starbucks is where he usually stopped for an Arabian Mocha on the way to work."

"I'd like to talk with Mrs. Bonaventure."

"Not possible until tomorrow," Tony said. "The Feds arrived while I was on the phone with her. Knowing them, by the time they get done, she'll be on tranquilizers for the rest of the night. Her sister came on at the end, a bitchy but protective lady, and said we could see her eight in the morning and not a minute sooner."

"Sounds good. What's the wife's first name?"

"Macie. Macie Marie Bonaventure. Why?"

"Nothing." But it would have been a whole lot of something if it had been Rachel, the name the little waster had used during the bogus 911 call.

"By the way, Van Decker is pissed. When he found out we ran a matching print to a hand found at Starbucks, he called Lieutenant Winslow. We're in deep shit."

"What's new about that?"

Tony chuckled. "Nothin'. Ain't we always? Meanwhile, the FBI and ATF are in a turf war over who gets possession of the phone as evidence. But even that no longer matters 'cause I just got word another bomb went off. A big one. Port Authority. Level One Mobilization."

Shocked, Sam looked at his beeper. Sure enough, he had two messages waiting. One from Lieutenant Winslow, who probably wanted to chew his head off, and the other about the bombing from Tony. He'd been so intent on Calvin, Follett, and Gillian, that he hadn't even noticed his beeper vibrating. This case was getting to him big time.

"Ready?" Tony asked.

"I'll go," Sam said as they headed outside. "You take the car. I need you to get me the Ray Andrew Follett files from California." He checked his watch. "With the three-hour time difference, everyone should still be working out there. Tell them it's high priority. The highest. I want the files faxed within ten minutes of you asking for them. Don't take any crap. Tell 'em anything, but get everything you can. If anyone gives you lip, let 'em know the next person the Carpenter kills will be on *their* conscience. I want this guy dead or behind bars before the morning commute."

"I'm on it."

Tony hurried to the car while Sam jogged to the subway. With all the rush hour traffic at this time of day, even a car with a siren wailing would be slower than going underground. As he raced down the stairs and joined the pack of commuters going home, he wished he could get cloned for the day and send his other self off to talk with Gillian. He'd shake the truth out of her. Yell the truth out of her. Make her scream and cry until she had to tell everything she knew because it would be too painful to keep it all in.

He could force it out of her, break her. He'd done it in the past with other witnesses. It'd be messy because she wouldn't see it coming. Wouldn't expect him, of all people, to use words to torture it out of her.

But he couldn't.

Wouldn't.

He liked her. Liked her a lot. She was gutsy and tender and strong and vulnerable. Unpredictable. Caring. Too caring. Too driven by guilt.

No. He wanted her to tell him because, of all the people in the world, he wanted her to believe he was the only one she could trust with the truth.

Because he cared about her. He had only known her a few days, but he could already guess the one emotion that was making her hold back. Pain. Something was too painful to acknowledge. Hell, she probably didn't even realize she had tried to commit suicide yesterday. Even that was too painful for her to admit to.

He'd go to her. Make it easier for her to release the pain, free her from whatever in the past kept hurting her in the present. He'd do it.

But first, he had to go to Port Authority. With all the people headed home from work, this might be the deadliest bombing yet.

On an average weekday, the Port Authority Bus Terminal hosts two hundred thousand travelers and commuters on more than seven thousand buses. With its own post office, bank, restaurants, shops, pharmacy, blood bank, art exhibits, and bowling alley, it's a city within a city. Into that mass of people and acres of glass-walled shops, someone had delivered a bomb.

Taking a deep breath, Sam braced himself and entered the south wing of the main floor.

Kill one or two people, and everyone's heart weeps. But blow up a large number of people and the mind numbs the emotions. There's no time to be angry. There's too much to deal with, too many people who need help. Too many bodies to be disposed of.

Anger seeps up slowly, surfacing hours to days later. Most departments have shrinks on contract to help diffuse post-traumatic stress. Unfortunately, most responders consider yakking about their emotions a sign of weakness. Definitely not a tough-guy solution. They find their own ways of purging themselves of the horror. Some choose alcohol or drugs. After all, you can't blame a guy for crying in his drink or shooting off his mouth if he's drunk or high or both.

Some go home to their spouses, girlfriends, or boyfriends, and fuck 'em like crazy, replacing pain with pleasure.

Some eat until they vomit—another form of purging.

Some work out at a gym, replacing one pain with another.

Some go to church more frequently.

Some start idiotic fights.

Some just keep it balled-up tight inside where it slowly rots the soul.

Some just kill themselves and get it over with, permanently. The ultimate catharsis.

Each of his fellow officers, along with the EMS, firemen, and Feds who were working amid the splattered flesh and blood, would be making choices later as to how to cleanse themselves of the hellish emotions held in check. He hated to think what his choice would be. But it would come. And soon. He could feel it eating away at him, the frustration building. Just one more horrendous thing would set it loose.

God, he hoped he was alone when it happened.

Sometimes he thought the victims had it the easiest.

It was the Carpenter's biggest explosion yet. A crater in the tiled floor near a set of escalators marked the spot where the caddie had last stood in one piece. Surrounding the jagged pit were ten covered bodies.

The next circle of people had already been taken away by ambulances. Trauma units would have their work cut out for them with that batch.

The next ring of injured were being treated by the EMS until more ambulances arrived to transport them to the hospitals.

The outer circle of victims sat bleeding from superficial wounds, waiting their turn, quiet for the most part, a few sobbing, some moaning, all in the throes of shock. Uniformed officers kept an eye on them, assuring them they weren't alone but mostly reminding them that they were still alive.

Sam blinked. He'd been standing by a rack of emergency lights illuminating the area, absently watching searchers going through the debris. Only now did he realize what they were doing. He took deep breaths to hold down the bile. Body pieces were being photographed, their locations marked before being picked up, a ghoulish task the Feds had bequeathed to those deemed on the lowest rung of the investigation, the NYPD.

A second set of searchers—the ATF and Homeland Security—searched for bomb fragments. And nails. As one ATF woman said to another who was marking where a nail was embedded in a book, "Bombs seem to have a life of their own."

He noted a security camera. With about forty in the complex, at least one must have recorded the caddie before the bomb went off. Maybe the Carpenter, too.

On the far side, he found Van Decker with the newest head of the multi-agency task force. According to the chatter, Captain Lewis Freeman had arrived hours ago from Utah where he had recently wrapped up the capture of a bomber who'd been targeting all the Mormon temples in the western part of the U.S.

Van Decker and Captain Freeman stood a short distance away from a bunch of figureheads: the police commissioner, the Assistant Director in Charge of the NYC field office of the FBI, the Deputy Mayor of New York, the assistant director of Homeland Security, and the ATF division leader.

When Van Decker saw Sam, he waved him over and made the introductions.

Sam had heard about Captain Freeman. The standing joke was Freeman had nitro in his veins. Must have, because when he retired from the Army, instead of counting himself lucky that he had survived as the military's leading demolitions expert for twenty years, he'd turned around after one month of boredom and gotten hired as ATF's chief bomb expert.

Sam couldn't understand how anyone could face a bomb exploding in his face at work every day. The one in the subway had been enough for him. Scared him so bad that the next morning a gray hair had shown up. Might explain why Captain Freeman had a whole head of kinky white hair.

"Heard about your work in the subway," Captain Freeman said as they shook hands. "Snatching a bomb. Stupid, but you got the job done. Saved lives. Don't do it again."

"I don't intend to." Sam looked over at the crater in the floor of the cavernous room. "A lot bigger this time."

"A lot more nails, too," Regis said. "Either we're not getting the message fast enough or he's angry about something."

"Or he got a fresh supply of explosives that he wants to try out," Sam said.

"Don't think so," Captain Freeman said. "Tags in the plastic from all the other bombs were traced to a large ranching operation in northeast Wyoming. Reported a break-in twenty-five months ago. Never recovered the explosives. Whoever has them has enough from the original theft to make ten more bombs of this magnitude. Thirty if he goes back to the small ones."

"Thirty more bombs." Sam grimaced. If they didn't catch him soon, at least that many more people were going to die before he ran out.

"My bet is on fewer but bigger bombs," Van Decker said. "The initial thrill of killing a few at a time has worn off. Now he has to kill in quantity to get the same rush."

"I want this one to be the final one," Captain Freeman said. "Got that, gentleman? I don't care how we do it, but we're gonna sack or kill this terrorist before he hands out any more bombs."

Sam expected a salute in dismissal. Instead, Captain Freeman pivoted smartly on his heel and joined the search with the other ATF agents.

Sam glanced at Van Decker. "He thinks we're dealing with a terrorist? I thought we had a serial killer on our hands."

"We get more funding if we label him a terrorist." Van Decker stared out over the vast floor of the station at all the people working the scene and attending the wounded. Particulates from the blasted ceiling, walls, and floor were still sifting down through the air, creating a ghastly pall on everyone and everything, including a cluster of Hasidic Jews over by the main ticket plaza whose dusted black garb made them look like ghosts. They, along with other bus riders, were being interviewed as witnesses.

Sam asked, "Do you think it's a coincidence the explosives were stolen from the same state where Gillian lives?"

"Unlike a lot of conspiracy theorists, *I believe in coincidences*. Did a paper on it just last year. I don't think the Carpenter waited two years for Gillian to come out of retirement. He'd have to be psychic to know she would get back in the business when everyone else thought she was out for good."

"Calvin didn't think so."

Van Decker frowned. "Calvin should have left her alone."

"Gillian doesn't strike me as the type of woman who lets someone else make up her mind for her."

"Given the right circumstances, anyone can be swayed into doing anything."

The cool certainty of the agent's words bothered Sam, and the smirk that accompanied it made him wonder if the FBI agent had profiled one too many serial killers. At what point does someone stop questioning killers and starts thinking like them, and believes their reasons for killing are valid?

Sam thought back to Roger T. Walgood, who had taken a bomb into the subway, not to save his own life, but his family's. "In my experience, only the threat of death can make someone do something against their will."

"If that's what you want to believe."

Van Decker's flippant reply irritated him even more. Change the subject, Sam told himself. More important things to do than argue with a stuck-up Fed who keeps talking down to you.

He inclined his head towards a security camera. "Anyone check the tapes to ID the caddie, maybe get a good shot of the Carpenter?"

"Already on it. But I doubt if we see a caddie this time. Did you notice the crater in the floor?"

"Yeah. Pretty big."

"And deep. The experts think this one was near or on the floor when it went off, not in someone's hands."

"No caddie?"

"Several witnesses reported an object hurtling through the air and landing in the vicinity of where the bomb went off. The Carpenter changed his MO and threw this one."

"Are you sure? Maybe it's a copycat bomber. Or the caddie panicked and threw the bomb away."

"From the description of the eyewitnesses, I'd say it's the Carpenter who tossed the bomb."

"But why change his pattern? Why not use a caddie this time?"

"Perhaps spontaneous rage."

"It doesn't feel right," Sam said, looking around. "What would set him off? Things not going according to plan? Someone not where he's supposed to be? Desperation?" He shook his head, trying to make sense of it all. "I'd like to get a look at the security video."

"Not going to happen." Van Decker turned to face him. "I don't share with someone who withholds evidence from a case."

Sam grinned. "Still pissed about the cell phone."

"No, I'm not. We would have caught it, eventually. No, the problem, detective, is that maybe if you had clued me in sooner, this . . ." he swept his hand toward the carnage, "might have been prevented."

Sam folded his arms against his chest. "I don't see how."

"That's the problem, detective. You're not trained to understand how everything is related. That's *my* job. *Your* job was to make sure I was provided with every goddamn piece of information the NYPD could find about the bomber and his victims, and what happened before, during, and after the bomb blew up. It's not a question about jurisdiction, or stepping on each other's toes, or who bags the Carpenter first. That's one of the things that went wrong in the Follett case. Too many agencies involved, each too full of their own goddamn pride to cooperate and share. Well, it's not going to happen again. You're off the case. I've already talked with your lieutenant. He's made arrangements for someone to take your place."

Sam fisted his hands, furious. "You can't do that. This is my city. These victims are my people, my responsibility. What's more, Gillian is still at risk."

"She's not your concern. The Carpenter is no longer your concern. Go back to investigating your petty little homicides, detective. You're no longer wanted." With his imperious chin leading the way, Van Decker turned and walked away.

Sam fumed. No one took him off a case. No one.

But he was also furious at himself. Van Decker was right. He had withheld info on the cell phone. Sure, pride in his own department was involved. But he'd also done it because he believed the FBI and ATF weren't giving him all the facts either.

He should tell Regis Van Decker to go screw himself. Let him and his fellow suits find the Carpenter. The case was such a mess of inconsistencies.

But then who would keep Gillian safe? Not Regis. The Fed hadn't done a good job so far.

Swallowing his anger, Sam called Lieutenant Winslow and dutifully kept his mouth shut as his superior blasted him for failing to cooperate with the Feds. Sam knew when to play timid, but the verbal thrashing was a little too fire and brimstone even for *His Excellency.* He was starting to believe he really was going to be taken off the case when the lieutenant happened to mention the first deputy mayor was in his office.

That explained everything. The lieutenant was on the hot seat, picked to be the mayor's scapegoat because it was *his* officer who was working with the Feds. Shifting the blame was not above the lieutenant; sometimes it was the only way to navigate the mud of city politics. Sam understood, but he was in no mood to play the game today.

When the lieutenant paused to take a breath before he resumed bawling him out, Sam cut in quickly. "Sir, may I make a suggestion? Tony and I have reason to believe the caddie at the Starbucks was calling *911* for help when the bomb went off. If we could provide a way for the next caddie to get help without alerting the Carpenter, we might be able to save the next victim. Here's what I suggest . . . ."

It was the longest the lieutenant had gone without interrupting him. Hopefully, a good sign. When Sam finished, he held his breath and crossed his fingers. He could hear Lieutenant Winslow tell the first deputy mayor that he had some ideas on how to improve the chances of saving lives the next time a bomb was handed out. *He* had some ideas. The lieutenant was taking credit for his suggestions. Sam could handle it if it bought him an extension of his liaison duties.

The lieutenant came back on, told him to keep up the good work and keep him informed, then ended the call.

Yes! He was still on the case.

He went in search of the profiler. Van Decker was looking at overhead photos of the crime scene. Sam tamped down his pride. Being humble to the lieutenant and eating crow was one thing. Doing it with a Fed was like eating glass. His ego would be bleeding for days to come.

In a tone as neutral as he could muster, he said. "You're right. I was wrong."

Van Decker glanced sideways at him. He looked surprised, and suspicious.

"The lieutenant is going to give me one more chance to play nice."

Van Decker rolled his eyes and frowned. Sam kept his face impassive. Inwardly he was grinning from ear to ear. He loved ruffling the agent's feathers.

He added, "Now it's your turn to share. You never told me how the bomber is related to the Follett case and Gillian."

Van Decker's eyes were hooded, his lips tight and thin, not giving anything away.

"If you want me to keep sharing with you, you have to do the same," Sam said. "The ball's in your court."

Van Decker looked out upon the destruction. The EMS who had taken the most severely wounded to the hospitals had returned to load the second batch onto stretchers, sidestepping debris and the slick blood staining the floor.

Sam wondered why Van Decker would rather view the senseless slaughter than admit to what the connection might be? What could be worse than Gillian helping to defend a serial killer or her suicidal tendencies?

The longer Van Decker remained silent, the more Sam's instincts went on alert. This had to be bad. Real bad.

One of the most cunning, effective interrogation techniques is silence, the awkward pause of nothingness that gnaws at each person to say something to fill the void. He'd used it on Regis before, and it had worked. Was the Fed now using it on him, hoping he would say something and change the subject?

Sam widened his stance and clamped his jaws shut.

The groans and pain-filled cries of the victims waiting for the next squad of ambulances to take them away filled the station. The dim roar of distant murmurs added to the discord; commuters were being routed around the scene by the Port Authority police, some cringing in horror at the senseless loss of life. But the most deafening sound was the tense silence filling the space between him and Van Decker.

He continued to wait, not moving, not giving the profiler anything to distract him with, like a teacher who's just called on a student and will wait forever until the student gives an answer. This was a power play ingrained from the public school system. The first one to break the silence loses.

Van Decker was getting restless. He wiped his brow, then ran tense fingers through his hair. The fidgety pattern was played out twice more before the Fed finally turned to him.

"You're not going to like it," Van Decker warned.

"I don't like anything about this case."

"Yes, but this you'll really hate. It'll twist your belly into knots. Make you so sick you can't eat. It'll wake you during the night, not allow you to get back to sleep until the sun comes up."

Sam shrugged indifferently though common sense was now screaming at him to hightail it out of there and not listen any further.

He tried to sound calm. "You don't know my nightmares. I've probably seen worse than you can imagine."

Regis laughed bitterly. "I doubt that, officer. You have no idea." When Sam refused to back off, he said, "Don't say I didn't warn you."

"All right already. I'm warned."

"The bomber kissed Gillian," Van Decker said.

"So?"

"She didn't like it."

"Know that, too."

"But she always liked it when Follett kissed her."

Sam felt like his legs had been kicked out from under him. "I, uh, don't, uh, understand." He shifted uneasily. "You mean Gillian and Ray Andrew Follett . . . the two of them . . . together . . . as . . . ."

"I did warn you." He sounded pleased by Sam's reaction. "If you'll excuse me, I have a bomber to catch."

Van Decker calmly withdrew, leaving Sam standing there, struggling to breathe. Gillian Dohr. The woman who had touched his cheek so tenderly only an hour ago, who he had been fantasizing about getting into bed with. She . . .

Bile rose as his mind grappled with the image of Gillian in the arms of Ray Andrew Follett—the man who had crucified children.

Hundreds of people were all around him, but Sam felt completely alone in his own private hell, a hell created with a few choice words from Regis Van Decker.

Chapter Twelve

On the way to the hotel, Sam cut off four trucks, two buses, and a multitude of honking cabs—normal for when he was in a bad mood. But he was in a dangerously nasty rage, which is why he also ran three red lights and forced a bike messenger onto the sidewalk as he turned a corner too sharply to spare the rider room on the street.

As Sam got out of the car, he savagely gripped the Follett files Tony had gotten him. He'd told Gillian he never actually read files until he talked with the subjects and got their take on what had happened. This was no different. He'd skimmed until one comment, one terse but damning notation by the prosecutor in the Follett case stopped him cold.

He couldn't believe it. Didn't believe it. It had to be a mistake.

But deep in his gut he knew it to be true.

As he walked down the hall to her room, Sam kept telling himself to be calm. Cool. Unemotional. Distant. Professional. But as soon as he told the guard on duty to take a break for a few minutes, his temper unreeled fast.

Gillian opened the door to his knock with a welcoming smile and the words, "I was just thinking about you."

All his pent-up emotions from the Starbucks bombing and the slaughter at Port Authority came blasting out, unleashed in a fury that took even him by surprise. Almost like he was a bystander watching some stranger go berserk.

It happened automatically. He charged into the room and threw the Follett files at her feet.

Gillian jumped back in alarm.

Sam slammed the door and took a step toward her. "You fucking bitch! How could you fall in love with Ray Andrew Follett?"

He stalked towards her, hands clenched into fists, face beet red, his features contorted and ugly in revulsion.

Gillian backed away and wished her hotel room had more than one exit.

Sam moved threateningly closer. "You fell for a serial killer! A man who snatched helpless little children and crucified them on the walls of his bedroom with a hammer and nails!" His lips snarled in disgust. "How could you love such a fucking sadistic monster? How could you even touch someone like that? What are you? Psycho? Perverted? An S&M freak?"

Sam let out a guttural sound of contempt and outrage. He panted, fighting for control. "I liked you. I really liked you. You seemed like a decent person in spite of what everyone said. But this . . . this is too much."

Gillian raised her hands, trying to placate him. "It's not what you think. Let me explain."

"Tell me you weren't in love with Follett," he growled.

She was tempted to cower and ask for forgiveness. She didn't want Sam to hate her. Over the past few days, she had come to respect him. Admire him. She liked having him around, talking with him, being near him when the Carpenter threatened to blow their world to smithereens.

But she was tired of defending herself and Ray. Tired to death of accusations.

It had been foolish to think Sam would like her for herself and ignore the past, forget what happened three years ago, and let them live only in the present. But as righteous indignation continued to burn off Sam in waves of raging heat, she realized she had already lost him. He was a cop. She was The Oracle. Nothing would ever change that. She glanced at the photo of Jayson with her parents. *Nothing.*

"It's true. I fell in love with Ray Follett. But I didn't love a serial killer."

Sam's hands flexed and unflexed. "Son of a bitch! You sound just like Calvin Moore. Follett killed them but he didn't kill them. What is this? Legalese for innocent by reason of insanity?"

Her heart went out to him. The strain of betrayal on his face, the loss of trust, were unmistakable. As bad as finding out your high school sweetheart is sexting your best friend. She bowed her head. Or finding out the man you love turns into a beast that preys on little children.

Nothing could repair such a violation. Forgiveness might dull the pain, but the scar on the heart would never completely heal. Always a reminder, always a warning, that what happened in the past might happen again.

A nightmare she still lived with. And now Sam Brankowski had joined it.

"You talked to Cal about this?" she asked in surprise.

"And Regis. According to the files, he was working you into Follett's profile during the trial. Suspected you of being an accomplice when Follett was acquitted and the next bunch of kids started disappearing."

She nodded, lips trembling, her mind awash with the horrid memories she desperately wanted to forget. Though she fought to maintain her poise, she stumbled over the words. "Regis and I have talked about it . . . at great length. He was just doing his job, trying to make sense out of what Follett was doing. I forgave Regis a long time ago."

"Have you also forgiven Follett?" Sam sneered. "Your lover! The butcher of preschoolers! The man who washed his hands in his victim's blood!"

Gillian pressed her palms together and looked away, wishing Sam's eyes weren't so sharp and painful. "It's not what you think."

"Bitch," Sam said, and Gillian flinched as if she'd been slapped. "You don't know what I'm thinking because if you did you'd be running for your life."

He made a fist, grappling with his darkest emotions, refusing to give in to them.

Knowing he had to put distance between himself and Gillian before he completely lost control, he turned his back on her and said, "You're not worth it. No one is. Everything they say about you is true. You're a two-faced bitch who loves murderers."

"Me? Two-faced?" Gillian let out a shriek of anger. "Why, you stupid, arrogant, pig-headed cop! You think you've got me all figured out, don't you? Well, I've got news for you, detective. You haven't begun to know who or what I am. And you're not leaving until you do."

Surprised by the vehemence in her voice, and uncertain what she meant, he turned to see Gillian rush to a night table where she opened a drawer and pulled out a Glock 9mm. She aimed it at him.

His eyes went wide. His hands came up. "Whoa! Wait a minute. Hold on. You got a permit for that?"

"Damn right I do." The hand holding the gun shook, and she added the other hand to hold it steady. "I know the law. I know the difference between right and wrong. But you don't believe I do. I'm The Oracle. I let criminals go free. I get acquittals for murderers, and I do it all by myself. The defense lawyers don't do it. The prosecutors don't. The judges, the twelve jurors don't. Only me. *Only I'm to blame.* That's what you think. That's what all cops and prosecutors think. I see it every time one of your kind finds out who I am. *Oracle.* You said it right to my face the first day we met. And because of what you think I am, you let your lover, Stephanie, steal my personal notes on the case. And you call me a bitch?"

She saw one of his hands slowly inching down, ready to make a quick move to the gun in the shoulder holster under his leather jacket.

Gillian stiffened her stance. "Don't even think about it. Put those hands up. High!" she yelled when he was slow to respond.

He lifted both hands above his head. "Anything you say."

"Good," she said, her voice quaking angrily in resentment. "At least that time you didn't call me a bitch. Now, move over there." She waved the gun toward the dresser. Above it hung a large mirror in a garish gold frame.

Sam eased over, keeping himself faced toward her. His gaze constantly switched from her eyes to the gun in her hand then back to her eyes. She could see his mind working fast, still amazed she would pull a gun on him while at the same time trying to figure out what she would do next. Shoot him? To kill or to wound?

He glanced at the items on the dresser: her satchel, a pink comb and brush, three photos, and a telephone. She could feel him silently assess what he could use to distract her: divert her attention long enough to pull his own gun. A glance at her, then at the floor, indicated he was judging the distance between them. He might try to jump her. Kick or grab the gun away. Tackle her in hopes she didn't pull the trigger while they fought over the weapon. Maybe throw a punch and knock her out before she could get a shot off. So many possibilities flitted across his face. Through his eyes she could see his mind sort and reject. Then his gaze firmed, and his shoulders tightened ever so slightly. He had decided on the option with the best odds for success.

Gillian took a step away, and removed an outright physical assault from his plans.

"Move back," she said.

Sam looked disappointed, but he readily moved to the far side of the dresser. Once more, his gaze took in everything. He glanced twice at the phone, no doubt thinking of using it either as a diversion or a weapon. In the subway, she had learned Sam was a man of action. He wouldn't stay passive for long. Time to end this.

"You're a bad cop, Samson Brankowski. You hear one damning piece of evidence—that I was in love with Ray Follett—and you judge, convict, and condemn me without hearing my side."

"Maybe I did," Sam said, his tone soft and nonthreatening, and obviously fake.

"Maybe? You can't even admit doing anything wrong, can you? And you call me a bitch, you bastard?"

"Okay. You're right. I jumped to conclusions. Comes with the territory. Sometimes all I have is a split second to decide who's pointing a gun at me and who's holding a phone. The wrong decision and I'm dead. The right one I live a little longer. With you, I was wrong, so why don't you put the gun down and we'll talk."

"Don't patronize me, detective."

"I'm not."

She raised a brow in mocking disbelief.

"Okay, so I am. But you've got a gun pointed at me. What am I supposed to do? Send out for tea?"

"You're supposed to ask me what happened. Offer me the benefit of the doubt. Let me give my side. Well, here's my side."

She swung the gun at the mirror. The end of the grip struck the surface, cracking it. The fractured pieces reflected a multitude of shattered images.

Gillian pointed at the mirror. "That's Follett."

Keeping her gaze and gun aimed at Sam, she grabbed her satchel with the other hand and dug blindly around inside its contents. She didn't dare take her eyes off him. He could be quicker than a rattler when he wanted to be. One second was all he would need.

Gillian took out a lipstick and switched hands with the gun. She removed the top of the lipstick case with her mouth, spit it onto the floor, then wrote a rose red *J* on one of the sections of the broken mirror.

"That's Janeane," she told Sam. "The monster who crucified children."

She wrote two *J*s side by side on another section. "That one's John Jr. He's believed to be the original occupant of Ray's body. What's called the birth person."

She put a rosy *D* on another section. "That's Dragon. One of the core personalities. A tough, streetwise teen who took John Jr.'s place whenever the little boy was threatened. He endured the stepfather's sexual abuse so John Jr. could escape to a secret *nursery* in his mind where he was safe from what was going on."

On the largest fractured piece, she wrote a large *R* with the lipstick. "Eventually, John Jr. refused to leave the *nursery*, so Ray appeared to take his place, to be the normal one in the world. Ray, the gentlest, most caring, most loving man I have ever met."

She raised the lipstick to write another letter, but stopped. She tried again, but every time she began to write, her hand would tremble. "Oh, God. After three years, why does it still hurt so much?"

Gillian stared at her own reflection in the mirror, gazing into her shattered past. She felt Sam's fingers on her other hand gently ease the gun out of her slackened grip and heard him release the clip. He sighed when he discovered it empty.

She did, too. "You believed I was capable of pointing a loaded gun at you. But Ray knew I could never do that. He believed in me. And I in him."

As Sam stood next to her, she glanced at his reflection in the section of the mirror with the *R* written on it. No regret softened his features as he stuck her gun in the back waistband of his pants. Not an ounce of apology. His face neutral, impersonal. A cop's face.

Maybe if she told him everything she knew, she could penetrate that facade and make him grasp what had happened. At the very least, help him comprehend the complexity of Ray Follett's mind.

With renewed determination, she put an *A* on a fifth section of mirror, then a *Y* on another. But just thinking about Ray and Dragon and John Jr., what they had suffered for years without anyone knowing about it—with no one to turn to for help except each other—sapped her strength. She put down the lipstick. "Too late Ray and I discovered he had multiple personality disorder. One of his multiples, his alters, was the killer. He never knew, never suspected, until the trial."

She turned to face Sam. "If Dr. Newhall had been given more time, things might have turned out differently. Ray might still be alive. So would the last five children who were killed."

Sam didn't agree. Every time shrinks were involved with a criminal, they made excuses for their client. Sheesh. Multiple personality. What a load of crap!

Obviously Gillian bought into it lock, stock, and barrel.

Disappointed she was so gullible, not knowing what to say, he walked over to the window and looked down. A thick stream of people were coming and going on the streets below. Traffic was backed up; a truck had double-parked, removing one entire lane from usage. Taxi and car drivers angrily waved their arms, as if obscene gestures and honking horns could move the driverless truck. By the edge of one building, observing all this, a dark-skinned Hasidic Jew shook his head, no doubt at the profanity flowing all too readily. Further down the street, a woman appeared to be screaming, while in the distance he saw a man in a satin Yankees jacket running away with her purse. The same guy who had snatched Stephanie's briefcase. Shit.

Added to it, the Carpenter was out there—God knows where—with up to thirty more bombs.

Who had time to be compassionate in a world like this?

Still facing the window, he said tiredly, "Calvin thinks you might know what motivated Follett to kill children. Do you?" Sam heard her take a deep breath in prelude to answering, but before she did, he added, "And don't give me the standard 'I don't know' that you were giving Regis and the FBI last night. I won't accept it."

He heard her feet shift restlessly on the carpet, then the whisper of fabric on fabric as she sat on the edge of the bed. Her answer was long in coming. "During all the sessions Ray had with Dr. Newhall after the trial, Janeane never came out, so they could never ask her. A lot of supposition, of course. Ray suspected the crucifying of children had something to do with his stepfather using a crucifix to spank all the children in the family when they were bad, or when he thought they were being bad.

"During one session with the psychiatrist, Ray's alter Dragon blurted out that Janeane was a bitch who was always trying to impress the other bitch, but Dr. Newhall could never get Dragon to explain what he meant. In subsequent sessions, Dr. Newhall hoped to discover if another female alter in Ray was Janeane's accomplice." She hung her head sadly. "But there never were any more sessions. Ray abruptly disappeared. Three weeks later on the news I heard he had been found with the missing children. They were already dead, and he was killed by the police."

The mournful sigh which followed had Sam shaking his head in regret. He turned away from the window to face her. "I hate to burst your bubble, but for years defense lawyers have been trying to use multiple personality disorder to get their clients off. It's a load of crap. Frankly, I'm surprised you could be suckered in by someone claiming to have it."

For a second, Gillian seemed taken aback. Then she stood up. "Multiple personality disorder, MPD, is a bona fide psychological disorder."

"It's a mental con job."

She put her hands on her hips. "It's a documented mental escape from trauma."

"It's junk defense. I've seen it before. The perp uses a different voice, alters his mannerism, and claims to be Ivan the Terrible or Darth Vader. He admits to committing the crime, changes back to his normal tone and looks around dumbfounded while his lawyer asks that he be sent to a mental institution for a few months instead of prison—like that will make everything all right. I've never bought into it, and I never will. It's a good acting job, that's all."

"That's not true," she insisted. "MPD is real. It's horribly, hurtfully real. And its victims take years of intensive therapy to recover, if ever."

"Look, if that's what you want to believe, that's your choice. Me, I know better."

"So now you're an expert psychiatrist," Gillian said in a mocking voice. "You think you have everyone and everything figured out, don't you? Not only do you think I'm capable of loving a serial killer, you think I'm stupid, too."

She stepped towards him, fury bristling in every movement. "Well, listen here, Detective Brankowski. I am not so easily duped. I'm a people reader. I know when someone is trying to fool me. Not like you and your black and white world of right and wrong. Sure, some people fake multiple personalities. Some even fake guilt when they're actually innocent out of some bizarre sense of self-hatred. But that doesn't mean you throw them into jail. You certainly shouldn't put the mentally ill in prison."

"Hey, I just call them as I see them."

"Fine. I'm a bitch, and you're a bastard. Now that we have each other neatly pigeon-holed, there's no reason for you to stay."

She yanked open the door, gathered up all the files on the floor, and threw them into the hall. The papers scattered in all directions.

"Okay, maybe I was a little too hasty," Sam said.

Gillian stood by the door, mouth shut, glaring at him, daring him to somehow make amends.

Sam shrugged. "Nobody's perfect, you know. Not even you."

Her lips parted in shock. "Don't you dare try to blame this on me "

"I'm not. I didn't mean that. Jeez. Don't you understand? It's this case. I have to go where the facts lead me."

"No matter what you say or who you hurt along the way?"

The pain in her eyes was unmistakable. If he could just make her see things from his point of view . . . "If I don't do everything in my power to find the truth, more people may die. Whatever the reason you and Follett got it on . . ." he paused as she clearly seethed with resentment, "it might have a connection to why the Carpenter is bombing on behalf of Follett."

"You think my sicko relationship with Ray might be the reason the Carpenter came on to me in the courthouse?" Gillian asked, her voice laden with sarcasm. "Talk about crap. Let me find my boots. This place is filling up fast."

"It's my job to check into everything. I have to follow any possible leads."

"So do I. And if I ever find proof that those cops in California deliberately killed Ray—not in self-defense but out of a warped sense of vigilante justice—I'll . . . I'll . . ."

"Pin 'em to the wall?" Sam interjected when she was too angry and tongue-tied to come up with the rest of the threat.

Gillian blanched, and he instantly regretted his choice of words. A common expression, one he belatedly remembered Ray Andrew Follett had taken to heart. *Damn.* The way she was wincing, he might as well have stuck a knife in her heart.

"I didn't mean it," he started to say.

"Yes, you did." Cold fury coated her words. "Get out."

She refused to look at him as he left her room. In the hall, he turned to say something—anything to repair the damage. But before he could squeak out a sound, the door slammed shut in his face.

He stood there, staring at his feet. From deep in his heart he wished he could recycle the last ten minutes. He'd been a first-class lunatic, ranting and raving at Gillian like an asshole. Like the insane person Follett must have been. He wouldn't be surprised if she never talked to him again. Hell, right now he couldn't even stand to be with himself.

He gathered up the files. Gillian's FBI bodyguard came strolling back. He raised a brow at Sam's menial chore but didn't say a word. Didn't have to. As the guard took up his position by Gillian's door, Sam could detect the Fed's snobbish contempt. And then it hit him like a New York cab. The guard's expression matched the one on Van Decker the last time Sam saw him.

The sewage the Fed had used to poison Sam's mind against Gillian was finally filtered by the truth. Clutching the files, Sam got on the elevator. He slapped his forehead several times and spat, "Stupid! Stupid! Stupid!" Regis might not be a people reader like Gillian, but in his job as profiler he'd learned to figure out what motivated people. Knew what buttons to push to get people to react in certain ways.

What had Van Decker said? Anybody can be swayed into doing anything.

Sam groaned. He felt dirty. Used. Duped. And it didn't set well when he remembered accusing Gillian of the same thing. It made him wonder who was the worst master of deception:

Ray Andrew Follett for making Gillian believe he had MPD, or Van Decker.

When the elevator doors opened, he wasn't surprised to see Van Decker waiting patiently in the lobby, leaning back against one of the columns, hands in his pockets, looking smug.

Sam stomped over and pointed a finger in his face. "Son of a bitch! You set me up!"

Regis smiled thinly in derision. "Gillian's favorite saying is: you can lead a horse to water but you can't make it drink. Face it, detective, you wanted to believe the worst about her. I only provided the direction, but you chose how to react. So, what did you do to her?"

Sam lowered the accusing finger and looked away.

Regis smirked. "You blew it."

"Yeah, I did." He looked back at the Fed. "With your help."

"This was all you. I wasn't there, remember?"

Sam fumed. If ever he wanted to hit someone, this was the person. *Damn this Fed!*

"Gillian believes Ray Andrew Follett had more than one personality living in him. A three-faces-of-Eve type situation, one of whom did the killing. Is that your take on it?"

Van Decker chuckled. "Are you kidding? That's the oldest defense ploy in the book. Unfortunately, Gillian is such an innocent, she bought into it. Wants to believe there's good in everyone. But, no. Even if Ray had been hearing voices, Ray wouldn't kill unless Ray wanted to kill. It's as simple as that. Follett's lawyer would have done him a favor by pleading insanity."

He looked at Van Decker in surprise. "Isn't having multiple personalities considered a form of insanity?"

"I'd say yes. Most shrinks say no, claiming they're just a person with a lot of identities living inside them. Remember that the next time you get on a bus and the guy next to you starts talking to himself in a weird voice. Change your seat or you might wind up carrying on a conversation with a mother, a kid, gang member, nun, family man, and a hooker, all in the same body. Quite a con job, if you ask me. The nucleus is: no matter how good you are at changing your voice or your mannerisms, a killer is a killer."

Van Decker started toward the elevator. "You're in way over your head, detective. Do Gillian a favor and never see her again. The lady's suffered enough."

The one thing that kept Sam from punching the arrogant smile off the profiler's face was the guilt over what he himself had done to Gillian.

He exited the hotel, slapping his forehead one more time and muttering "Fucking bastard" at both himself and Regis Van Decker.

Gillian's hands shook.

How dare Sam accuse her of loving a killer? Samson Brankowski was an oafish brute—jumping to conclusions, thinking she was scum. The whore of scum.

She covered her face with her hands. "I'm not. I know I'm not. But why do I keep feeling like I am?"

Gillian raised her tear-filled eyes and slowly shuffled towards the mirror she had broken. She stared at the red *J*.

"I hate you," she told Janeane, the killer. "I hate you so much." Would always hate her for all the pain she had caused. Was still causing. She, Calvin, the families of the victims, everyone connected to the case, not to mention the surviving members of the Follett family. They were all hurting.

Most of Ray's brothers and sisters had changed their names after his death, hoping to flee the shame and notoriety of being related not only to a serial killer, but a child killer—the worst type of murderer.

Sonya Follett, an up-and-coming actress, found no one would hire her—except for sleazy porn movies—until she started over as Terri Joy, bobbing the distinctive Follett nose and dyeing her hair red.

Jules and Hal's Follett Furniture Warehouse became McMurtry's Homestyle Furnishings.

Jodi, the high school English and drama teacher, was riffed from her position, then floundered in unemployment limbo in spite of the shortage of teachers nationwide until she became Sissy Lang. She, too, dyed her hair. Blonde. All of Ray's siblings divested their ties to the Follett ancestry. Except for Cindy. Cindy, the only family member to attend Ray's funeral.

Wait, that wasn't exactly true. Jodi had been there, a grieving shadow in the background, sobbing, inconsolable. At the cemetery, Cindy insisted she stay in the car to spare her further anguish.

At the gravesite Gillian and Cindy stood side by side, holding hands as the coffin was lowered into the dark ground that accepts all without reservation. With unspoken agreement, they stayed until he was completely entombed. Gillian wasn't sure why. Perhaps they needed closure.

Or maybe it was necessary to have physical confirmation Janeane would never again stalk young innocent lives. Undoubtedly, that was why Regis had been present, standing a few yards away, in attendance in a professional capacity, but also as a comforting friend. The minister had been brief and unsympathetic. Doing his duty but obviously relieved such a monstrous soul had been finally laid to rest. Four people to mark a person's passing, plus a reporter and cameraman in the distance to capture it all for history.

Unlike Gillian, Cindy Follett had withstood the horrendous publicity surrounding the case with her head held high, her back to the wall, defending what was left of the family honor. In the end, though, stress has a way of gouging the best of intentions, and she was forced to leave a prosperous IT career in California and seek obscurity in South Dakota.

The last Christmas card Gillian received from her still had Follett on the return address. A note on the back said she'd started a new career in environmental management, with the hope that one day soon both their lives would return to normal.

Normal. Gillian had always taken solace in the fact that Cindy had been able to survive as a fairly stable person in such an abusive and dysfunctional family. But then, in the majority of situations that produced an MPD, only one child was selected for abuse. The other siblings were usually left alone. Ray had been the sacrificial lamb in the family, offered up without protest to satisfy the stepfather's depraved needs.

Gillian's studied the shattered mirror, taking in all the letters, all the personalities Dr. Newhall had discovered living in Ray's mind.

Her eyes zeroed in on the *D*. Dragon, the survivor. He'd withstood unspeakable abuse to save John Jr.'s life. So had Annabelle, the forty-year-old spinster who wasn't afraid to tell Ray's mother what was going on, even if it meant getting burned with the car's cigarette lighter to make her shut up and keep the family's dirty little secret.

All of it remained hidden from Ray, the dominant personality who emerged after John Jr. went into isolation. Dragon and Annabelle kept Ray out of the loop when either parent was abusive, concealing the memories from him so he could have a normal life. None of the personalities knew about Janeane lurking in the dark recesses of Ray's mind. Not until she started killing.

Gillian's gaze slowly focused on her own reflection. Sections of her face were copied in the fissured pieces. Some showed only her bloodshot eyes, others her mouth.

Her mouth.

Instantly, she recalled the nightmare from last night, the one that made her wake up screaming. How bizarre that the next day she would deliberately break a mirror.

Her gaze circled the mirror again, looking at all the red letters, then at the image of her own mouth, barren of color, the surrounding skin still flushed from the savage confrontation with Sam.

She picked up the lipstick and painted her lips red. From habit, she pressed her lips together, smoothing out the color, then surveyed the result in the mirror. Her red lips were reflected on the pieces with the letters *J* and *R*. Janeane and Ray. Evil and good. Dark and light. With the lipstick, she drew a small circle on the piece with Ray's *R*, then drew another, and another. She started yet another circle when someone knocked on the door.

Regis took in her appearance with a single glance and inwardly smiled. Her eyes were red from crying, her face flushed and drawn. Fingers fluttered with uncertainty along the collar of her blouse. Even with the fresh coat of lipstick on her mouth, she looked terrible.

Good.

He summoned his most authentic frown of concern. "What's wrong?" he asked, while slipping through the doorway before she had a chance to shut him out. On reflex she closed the door. Her eyes were glazed over, her mind preoccupied.

Better and better.

She waved her hands through the air. "Sam was here. He, uh, found out about me and Ray. He was very angry." She wrung her hands in misery and lowered her head. "He hates me."

"Maybe he just doesn't understand everything the way I do."

He moved nearer, and frowned when she shifted away to the mirror. He noticed it was broken.

She gestured at it. "I tried to explain about Ray and his alters. He didn't believe me."

Regis drifted towards her, smooth and unhurried, coming up beside her, barely touching, letting her get used to his closeness. He saw their broken and scattered reflections in the mirror. In some were her image, in some his. In the one with a *J*, he could see both of their reflections side by side. It made him smile.

"It doesn't matter whether he believes you," Regis said. "I'm here."

"But I want him to understand."

"What if he does? In a few more days the trial will be over, and you'll be gone. To him you're just part of this Carpenter case. An eyewitness. Someone to flirt with. Maybe have a little fun with. After the Carpenter is caught, he'll move on. Another case. Another pretty witness to spend time with. Nothing more. Nothing permanent."

She turned to him, her eyes shadowed with doubt. "I suppose you're right."

"Of course I am." He spoke softly, trying to lighten her mood, but not too much. He didn't want her to regain full control of her feelings. Not yet. He put one arm around her waist, a little snug but not tight, conditioning her to his touch. A friendly gesture. "Sam could never fully understand. Not like you and I do."

She closed her eyes, squeezing tears from between the lids. "It meant so much to me for him to finally know." She reopened her eyes and looked at all the letters on the mirror. "I wanted him to appreciate everything that happened."

Slowly, Regis turned her towards him, away from the mirror that stole her attention. He gazed steadily into her eyes, locking her awareness, fixing it solely on him. He moved closer.

"Gillian, everything will be all right. What happened with Ray is in the past. All is forgiven. I've never let it interfere with our relationship, you know that. More than anyone else, I understand. Haven't I always helped to share your pain?"

She nodded.

"Haven't we suffered enough from what happened with Ray?"

Again she nodded.

"And that's why I'll always be here for you. Because I care. Because I'm the only one who will accept what you did and love you anyway. We've talked about this before. You know I don't blame you entirely for what happened. It's all right. It's not important to me. Only you matter."

He lifted a hand to her face and ran a finger possessively along her jaw. Her skin still radiated heat from her confrontation with the detective. He had no qualms about what he was about to do. After seeing the atrocities at the bus station, he needed this. With one lone finger he lifted her chin.

"Regis, I really don't—"

He didn't let her finish. His mouth covered hers, and he drank her in. No protests would be accepted. They would only be half-hearted anyway. She was weak, vulnerable after what Sam had said to her. In need of comfort. Her defenses drained.

The last time they'd gone out, she had mentioned breaking things off. Being together reminded her too much of their mutual past with Ray, she had said. She wanted to let go of painful memories and start over with someone who didn't know about her relationship to Ray Follett.

He smothered a chuckle. How ironic that their link to Follett had her welcoming him into her arms once again. One day she would learn what he already knew. That she would never be free of Ray and so she would never be free of him. Not until he decided to give her up.

He eased a hand from around her waist and slowly moved it up her back. His fingers, agile through the soft material of her blouse, unfastened her bra. As she murmured something about not being in the mood, his other hand reached up between them and fondled the breast loosened from the stricture of the bra, full and beckoning. Ripe for a man's touch. A man who knew her past and accepted it.

She no longer protested. No longer resisted. He knew exactly how long it would take to get her naked and in bed. And how long he would make sure she stayed there until his needs were met.

As he unbuttoned her blouse and slipped it off her shoulders, he murmured a thanks to Sam Brankowski.

Chapter Thirteen

They say misery loves company.

Sam thought otherwise when he got home and found Stephanie in his apartment.

She lounged on his brown leather couch in a scarlet teddy that he swore was the same shade of lipstick Gillian had used to write letters on her cracked mirror. The similarity rattled him. So did the sudden realization of how small Stephanie's breasts were compared to the seductive fullness of Gillian's. And how little warmth Stephanie's perfectly painted smile held for him in contrast to how much was revealed in the people-reader's soft, expressive lips.

"Hi, baby. What kept you?" Stephanie got up and wrapped her long, thin arms around his neck. "You look beat. I guess the P.A. bombing was really bad, huh?"

"Yeah, you could say that."

"Poor guy. I know how you feel. Court today was a bitch. Calvin Moore really knows how to twist the jury around his little finger. Must be getting an inside track from The Oracle on how to win them over. Talk about a gift for gab. I thought he'd never shut up. Thank God, Judge Conway keeps a constant eye on the clock or I'd probably still be there."

She snuggled up and kissed him. But he didn't kiss her back.

Hands still clasped around Sam's neck, Stephanie pulled her head back and looked at him. Her brow wrinkled. "Tired?"

"Yeah, I am."

"That's okay. I've got just what you need."

She rubbed herself playfully against his crotch, but he was dead in the water. He unlocked Stephanie's hands from around his neck and drew them down to her sides. "I'm sorry."

"I understand. You're hungry." She grabbed one hand and tugged him toward the kitchen table. "Come and sit down. I'll take care of you."

He stood wearily by one of the kitchen chairs while Stephanie bustled to the refrigerator. Opening the door, she bent over to reach inside. Sam noticed the skinny strap of her thong. Not a flicker of desire stirred.

"I made a salmon spinach salad with a peanut dressing that you're going to love," Stephanie said as she removed a plastic-wrapped bowl. "And I brewed some of that white iced tea that I've been dying to try. I'm sure you'll feel better after you eat. Go on and sit down. I'll be your waitress." She giggled. "Make that your French maid." She got a frilly white apron that she kept in one of the drawers and put it on. With an exaggerated sway of her hips, she carried the bowl of salad to the table. As she started to take the plastic wrap off, Sam gently grabbed her hand.

"Don't do that."

For the first time since he arrived home, Stephanie took the time to really look at him. "What's wrong?"

He reached behind her and untied the erotic white apron and placed it in her hands. "I'm tired. I need to be alone, sort through stuff." He glanced at the pile of files he had brought with him. "I have to work on the Carpenter case. Find out how the bomber's motivation matches up with Ray Andrew Follett's before he strikes again."

He looked steadily into Stephanie's huge, disappointed eyes. "I need you to go home so I can look at all of this and think things through."

Her bottom lip protruded in a stubborn, scarlet pout. "Are you sure?"

"Positive."

"Maybe we could have a little wine with the salad instead of the white iced tea. That'll get your engine going. Then a quickie before you get down to work, just a little romp, fast and hot like you like it. After that I promise to be good and stay out of your way. What do you say?"

"I say: go home, Stephanie." He went to the coat closet and got her wrap. He held it out to her. "Get dressed and go home."

With a long pout that dropped to her knees, Stephanie snatched her wrap away from him and tramped into the bedroom. She slammed drawers and doors, muttered and grumbled, none of which bothered him, then came storming out in black leotards and an oversized T-shirt that proclaimed I♥NY.

Part of him said he was a fool to give up the beautiful, sophisticated lawyer. The rest of him knew when to call it quits before things got mean and nasty.

He helped her on with the wrap and gave her a parting hug. "Good-bye, Stephanie."

"Good night, Sam." She left in a huff with the salad, dragging her ever-present pout along with her.

From his window, Sam watched until she got safely into a cab. He removed Gillian's gun from his back waistband and locked it in his desk drawer. He'd return it later.

He ordered a large triple-pepperoni pizza and a six-pack of Bud to be delivered, then settled down at the kitchen table with the Follett files. Around one in the morning, he went to the john and vomited. Whether it was because he had eaten too much pizza, drank too much beer, or seen too many photos of the bodies of children nailed to walls didn't matter. He hurled it all away.

Dawn was casting a dirty light over the city when he finished reading the last of the files on Follett. There were photos of Follett: mugshots and body shots, both before and after death, including autopsy photos. A good looking man. Agreeable and pleasant enough not to frighten away young victims until it was too late to flee. Handsome enough to attract a woman like Gillian. The thought made Sam's empty stomach queasy. He forced himself to look dispassionately at the photos and tried hard not to think about Gillian making love to the man they depicted. But it would take two more six-packs to accomplish that, so he gave up trying.

Apparent in all of Follett's photos were small, circular white scars. One on his neck, a few on his back and chest, and a few more on his upper arms above where a short sleeved shirt would hide them. At first Sam was cynical enough to believe each one marked a special occasion, like the notches cut into Lieutenant Winslow's desk. A permanent stamp to remind Follett of each of his victims. But a notation on the back of one photo by the preliminary investigating officer said Ray Andrew Follett claimed the scars were made by a hazing incident at one of his schools.

A serial killer who had been bullied at school.

Yeah, he could believe that. Happened way too often. Killers weren't formed in a vacuum. Something in their environment—family, community, too often school—sparked the need to share the pain and kill, kill, kill.

Not that he had any sympathy for them. Must be tens of thousands of kids subjected to the same kind of abuse and hadn't resorted to murder. Hell, it wasn't his job to figure out the why's and wherefore's. That's what psychologists were for. But every time he saw a corpse, he wished they'd hurry up and find a way to block the evolution of a murderer. Until they did, it was his job to stop the killers from killing again.

To his surprise, only in passing did the files mention the defense's investigation into whether Follett had more than one personality living within his body. The psychiatrist hired by the defense team to do a psychological evaluation of Follett—Dr. David Newhall—had tentatively suggested Follett had Multiple Personality Disorder, MPD. Or DID—dissociative identity disorder, the current politically correct classification.

Newhall. Must be the shrink Gillian and Calvin kept talking about. And Calvin would know because, according to the files, he was the junior defense lawyer on the case. Interesting. He wondered if Calvin believed Follett had multiple personalities. He'd corner the lawyer later and find out.

He scratched his overnight growth of beard. Getting a handle on this whole multiple personality thing was tough. And yet Gillian believed with all her heart that Follett had alternate personalities. And that only one of them—Janeane—had been the crucifier of children.

Could the people reader be right?

He didn't want to think so. Just thinking about prosecuting an MPD made his head hurt. What do you do if it's real? How do you lock up the bad personality while letting the innocent ones go free?

His mind was a trash compactor filled with legal issues, morality, and junk psychiatry. He'd known felons who could look him straight in the eye and lie all the way to Mars about their purported innocence. How easy could it be to dress up weird, fake a voice, kill someone, then go back to your usual mannerisms, clothes, and voice and claim one of your alters committed the murder?

Multiple personality disorder had to be bogus.

Van Decker thought so, and he was the expert profiler.

He was also the sleaziest Fed Sam had ever met. That alone made him want to believe the opposite of whatever Van Decker claimed to be true. Or false for that matter. Which would make MPD/DID a real possibility.

His mind shifted to Gillian and her broken mirror. Is that what MPDs felt like—fissured, cracked, one life broken into many lives, all sharing the same body?

It would drive anyone insane.

But was MPD/DID a valid reason to plead insanity? The defense in the Follett trial had not attempted to use it, in spite of Dr. Newhall's initial assessment. Must have something to do with what Van Decker told him: most psychiatrists don't consider MPD a form of insanity. The files claimed Follett got off because the jury believed there was a lack of irrefutable evidence.

He checked the NY Giants clock above the sink. Closing in on four. He rubbed his dry eyes. He should get some sleep.

Sound advice. Instead, he went to a tiny desk in the corner of his small apartment and removed an old coat and two baseball caps from on top of his laptop. He sat down and searched for "multiple personality disorder," anxious to see what it would find.

Chapter Fourteen

Sam choked in surprise. "Multiple personality disorder" had uncovered over half a million sites, and the very first one—with the stuffy title of *The Official Home for Everyone with Multiple Personality/Dissociative Identity Disorder*—had Dr. Jacob Miller's name right next to it.

He took out the torn business card from his wallet. It'd been right there all along. MPD/DID.

He flexed his fingers over the keyboard. "Okay, Dr. Miller. Tell me something I don't know."

"Children are inherently prone to fantasy. When recurring traumatic events occur in childhood, especially during a developmental stage, a child may create a fantasy personality to take his place, a secret identity to deal with the stress or horrors of the situation. An alter."

Hmm. Kinda made sense.

"A young victim's mind splits into many personalities in order to share the pain, to console and be consoled."

Okay. I might be able to buy into that.

"Each alter, dissociative identity, claims to have its own memories, its own personality, its own goals in life. In one example, an adult body contained a forty-year-old male gynecologist; a twenty-year-old female prostitute who insisted on taking over during certain hours of the night in order to work; an eight-year-old boy who only spoke fluent Spanish; a sixty-year-old coal miner who exhibited symptoms of Black Lung disease but only when his personality was present; and an extremely shy five-year-old girl who wanted to play with dolls whenever she came out."

Sam slumped back in his chair. For one person to have all of those identities hanging out in his head, well, it was downright freaky. Just thinking about it made his skin crawl.

"Some alters may physically exhibit traits distinctive from the dominant personality. One personality may exhibit cancer but when another alter comes forth, the cancer disappears. There may be a different shade of skin tone or a change in hand dominance. Some can actually change the color of their eyes."

He squirmed in his chair. He didn't like the idea any of this might be possible.

"In electroencephalographic studies, brain patterns of alters exhibit differences comparable to that of two separate normal people. Under this type of testing, MPD cannot be faked. A patient either has MPD/DID or does not."

Sheesh. Scientific stuff always made his head swim.

"Some adults may be in their twenties or thirties, married with children, before they are made aware of having dissociative identities."

He rubbed his eyes. This was too much like cramming for finals in college. Dr. Miller had exhaustively compiled every known fact, theory, and treatment for MPD/DID.

He clicked on the site's chat room, curious to see how these people talked to each other, and what they talked about, but discovered the area "temporarily closed."

He tried the *Art Gallery*. The hodgepodge of drawings and sketches, some childlike, ran the gamut of emotions, from rainbows and shooting stars and happy faces to mountains and flames and people crying. And blood. Blood dripping from hands, from knives, from eyes. A lot of anger and pain were depicted.

Better on paper than in real life, Sam decided, and he exited that section, only to return to it a second later. Something about the flames and big tears seemed familiar.

He went to his file on the Carpenter case and found a copy of the drawing Roger T. Walgood had made of the Carpenter.

Damn. Childlike, just like on the website, with flames coming out of the Carpenter's mouth and big tears pouring out of the little figure's eyes. Anger and pain.

A coincidence?

He rubbed his eyes again.

In the area titled *Case Histories,* he scrolled through some of the names listed, looking for anyone familiar. Jack the Ripper had three question marks next to his name. The others didn't ring a bell. Sam was about to call it a night when he saw Ray Andrew Follett's name. He clicked on the link. Dr. Miller had made only one comment. But after reading it, Sam wished he'd never seen it.

It was a quote dated 1897, by Sir William Blackstone, the jurist whose work on English law heavily influenced America's system of criminal jurisprudence. "It is better to let ten guilty persons escape than that one innocent suffer."

Shit. He remembered discussing this during his Academy days.

Blackstone's maxim was a constant source of irritation. Everyone's supposed to be more concerned with protecting the innocent than punishing the guilty. And yet every cop and prosecutor in the country believed punishing the guilty was the best way to protect the innocent. The good of the many outweighing the needs of the one.

No doubt about it, this had something to do with how Gillian felt about Ray Follett.

He no longer wondered whether Gillian knew Dr. Jacob Miller. Now he wanted to know how well Gillian knew him to the point that she had torn up his business card and didn't want to see him.

Maybe he should get Dr. Miller's opinion on what was going on with the Carpenter. He and Tony had never been able to find the doc's phone number or address, but the home page provided an email address.

He sent an email, asking the MPD/DID expert to get in touch with him ASAP, and why, providing his own email address and several phone numbers where he could be reached.

He yawned tiredly. His eyes were having a tough time focusing on the monitor.

Go to bed, his mind nagged.

For once, he listened. He and Tony had an early morning interview with the wife of the Starbucks victim. He hoped to God she'd tell them something that would help them find the Carpenter before he struck again. He was way overdue for luck on solving this case.

Van Decker was right about one thing. When this was all over, investigating simple homicides would seem like a vacation. For the first time ever, he was looking forward to a regular murder.

When Gillian woke the next morning, Regis was gone. His absence made her feel used. Abandoned. Yet she didn't mind. At least the emptiness of the night had been filled with another body to warm the bed. If Sam thought she was a bitch, at least Regis desired her. But not enough to kiss her good-bye.

Maybe she deserved no less.

She dragged herself out of bed, feeling sore and bruised— Regis had been unusually rough last night. Hoping sunlight would dispel her sullen mood, Gillian shuffled to the window and drew back the curtains. She made a face. As far as the eye could see, dreary gray buildings were topped by a dreary gray sky. Added to the gloom, some jerk in the building across the street was jacking off in front of his window.

With a sigh, she shut the curtain. A bucket of coffee might perk her up. At least it would be a start.

Gillian eyed the small carafe of the coffeemaker, then called room service. When assured a gallon of caffeine was on its way, she checked her messages. Besides the ones from the media anxious for a sound bite was a terse message from Calvin. Instead of breakfast with him and John, he would meet her at the courthouse. For a second she wondered why he'd changed their plans, it wasn't like him to alter their daily routine, but then decided it wasn't worth worrying about. It was going to be that kind of day. Fluid, gray, and worthless.

All because Sam Brankowski thought she was a bitch.

Damn, where was that coffee!

She glanced at herself in the cracked mirror—they're going to charge me a small fortune to have it replaced—and reached for a comb to make herself look presentable. As the thin plastic teeth swiftly found every knot in her hair, she happened to see her reflection in the fissured piece labeled *R* for Ray. Her hand stilled. Her image, her face, was covered with the red lipstick circles she had drawn on the mirror last night, making her look like she had contracted supersized chicken pox overnight, except for the one circle she had never finished drawing because Regis had showed up. It was only half done. Half a circle.

It looked familiar Where . . . ?

"Room service."

Gillian let the waiter in and generously tipped him. With a polite "Good morning" to her latest bodyguard from the FBI, she handed him a cup of coffee, which he accepted with a grateful smile, then shut the door and returned to the mirror. She moved her head from side to side, up and down, forward and sideways, this way and that, then stopped when the half circle appeared on her reflection's forehead.

Like the crescent scar on the Carpenter!

Think. Think. What could this mean?

Does it mean anything?

She poured herself a cup of coffee and downed it in one fiery gulp. The hot liquid hit her stomach like a dollop of lava. She gasped.

All right. All right. Think slower.

Gillian poured another cup. This time she sat down and sipped it.

Ray had had small circular scars on his body from a car cigarette lighter: an instrument of torture to keep his alters, mostly Annabelle, from speaking out about the abuse going on in the family. Maybe the Carpenter had fooled around with a lighter as a kid and accidentally burned himself.

Or the scar could have been caused by something else. A cut. A sports injury. Wrestling. Football. Someone's finger grabbing and cutting into his forehead. Maybe a cat or dog had scratched him.

It could be anything.

She took another sip of the caffeine and looked at the mirror.

If the scar on the bomber was from a car cigarette lighter—it was about the same size—then maybe the Carpenter came from an abusive family that also used it as a deterrent.

A crazy thought came to mind that the Carpenter was from the same family as Ray. It certainly would explain his grief over Ray's death.

She poured herself another cup and sipped some more, thinking.

In criminal history, had any family produced multiple serial killers?

Regis would know.

Gillian called him. His phone went directly to voice mail. She left a message saying they needed to talk, but not about last night.

She paced back and forth. Did any of Ray's siblings have scars like his? Other than Ray, the only Folletts that she'd ever seen were Cindy . . . and Jodi, briefly at the funeral and when Cindy had brought her along during one of her visits to the ranch.

Gillian didn't remember scars marring either Cindy or Jodi's face. She distinctly noticed their unblemished skin because it had been such a contrast to Ray's branded arms and torso. But then both sisters wore feathery bangs. Yet if either woman had a circular scar or two that she had been hiding with her hair, maybe their two stepbrothers had some as well. At the first touch of searing heat, one of them might have jerked away and gotten half a circle burned into his forehead.

She drained the cup of coffee, her imagination on full throttle. Could one of Ray's brothers be the Carpenter? Add forty to fifty pounds to Hal Follett and he might look like the Carpenter.

Gillian phoned Cindy. She didn't answer though it was two hours earlier where Cindy lived, certainly too early to be at work. Gillian left a message, saying it was urgent but warning her phone would be off whenever she was in court. No doubt they'd be playing phone tag all day.

Maybe it was a good thing she hadn't been able to talk to her. What would she have said? "Hi. You know how your brother's alter used to kill kids with a hammer and nails? Well, I think maybe one of your stepbrothers is doing the same to adults using bombs."

Sheesh. It was a screwy theory based solely on one little scar.

Maybe she should call Cindy again and tell her to disregard the first message.

She reached for the phone, then noticed the clock and moaned. Court! She hurriedly did her make-up and hair while her stomach growled, asking to be fed, making her wish she had ordered toast to go along with the coffee. Her phone played *Silver Inches*. The caller ID showed Cindy Follett.

"Cindy, I'm so glad you called." Gillian glanced at the clock. She had a scant five minutes to get dressed. Judge Conway was a stickler for punctuality. Stragglers were given an icy stare; sometimes asked to leave. She put the phone on speaker and raced around getting clothes while she talked. "I'm in New York and have a problem. Actually, it's a question, kind of personal—family history—but very important. Do you mind?"

"It depends. What's it about?"

"You know those terrible circular scars Ray had on him? Can you tell me if any of your stepbrothers had similar scars? Maybe on their faces?"

Cindy paused before speaking. "Why do you want to know?"

She told Cindy about the Carpenter and what was happening in New York, adding her suspicions based on the crescent scar she had seen on the bomber's forehead.

"You think Jules or Hal might be the Carpenter?" Cindy laughed. "They don't have half the brains to put together a bomb. Plus they're wimps. One of the reasons I can't stand being around them."

"They don't have any half-circle scars on them?"

Cindy laughed again, this time with a bitter edge to it. "The only scars they have are the ones I gave them when they picked on Ray. Besides, my dear stepdaddy never came near his own kids. He went after Ray. Might have gone after me or Jodi, but Ray took us with him when he left home. I doubt Jules or Hal could be responsible for what's going on where you are. If the Carpenter was an abused kid like Ray, you're going to have to look elsewhere. And good luck to you. There must be a million adults out there who were abused as children."

Gillian slipped on shoes, then grabbed her satchel. If she was going to avoid Judge Conway's wrath, she'd have to leave now. "Cindy, I hate to cut this short, but I'm due in court.

You've been a great help. When all of this is over, I'll give you a call, and we'll talk about normal things: how you're doing; how's your love life. You know, girl talk. It always seems like we end up discussing the past, never the present."

"That's because we can never outrun our past. But if you insist, next time we'll try girl talk. Say, how are you doing on the Capitol? Is it finished?"

"The rotunda and south wing are completely done," Gillian replied, smiling, liking the fact Cindy never failed to mention her hobby. "You should visit some time and help with the north wing."

"The way things are going, I might take you up on that. My current project is a real bitch, and chocolate's become my new best friend. A few days of ranch chores might be just the thing I need to drop a few pounds. I might bring Jodi along. Last time I saw her she was looking as stressed out as me."

"Sure." Gillian headed for the door. "The more the merrier. Right now, I really have to go. Thanks for your help."

She shoved the phone in a pocket, then hurried to the elevators, her bodyguard at her side. Thankfully, Cindy had put her mind at rest about the scar. She could just imagine what Regis would have thought if she had told him her wacky theory about the Carpenter's identity.

Tony was strangely quiet as Sam drove the car down into the Lincoln Tunnel. It would take several minutes to cross under the Hudson to New Jersey. Static came out of the radio, so Sam turned it off. Tony shifted uncomfortably.

"The tunnel is quicker than the bridge," Sam remarked.

"So you said."

"Just close your eyes until we get to the other side."

Tony grumbled miserably, and Sam suppressed a chuckle. Tony hated being underground in any shape or form. He rarely took the subway and knew all the bus routes like the back of his hand. When Tony retired, Sam wouldn't put it past him to get a job with the transit system, routing buses or maybe even driving one.

Tony rapped his fingers on the door handle, restless. He craned his neck forward, searching for any sign of sunlight that would signal the exit, but all they could see was more tunnel. He started whistling.

Some people sing off-key. Tony was one of the few who could make the Guinness Book of World Records by whistling in pitches that made the entire body cringe. Given that Sam's daily supply of tolerance was directly related to how much sleep he got the night before, the ear-splitting trill quickly scraped away what little patience he had.

Three solutions came to mind: doughnuts to stuff Tony's mouth, but the bag was already empty; a fist to his puckered lips, which, though initially satisfying, would cause a shitload of trouble—after all, Tony *was* his best friend—or change the sound coming out of Tony's mouth. Conversation.

Sam asked, "Why do you think there wasn't a bombing this morning?"

"Maybe the big one at the P.A. yesterday sent the Carpenter on such a high he still hasn't come down. Doesn't need a fix yet."

"Sounds logical."

Tony craned his neck forward, still looking for the light at the end of the tunnel. "But then I get to looking at the lanes of traffic heading into the city and you know something isn't kosher. At this time of morning they're usually backed up with commuters. This looks like Sunday morning traffic. Sparse. Mostly buses."

"Maybe there's something blocking traffic into the tunnel from the Jersey side."

"Could be, but the buses aren't packed like usual, either. We'll soon find out," Tony said with an audible sigh of relief as they rounded a bend. The artificial lights were quickly giving way to full-spectrum, smog-filtered sunlight. They exited the tunnel and circled up and around a ramp. Sam kept his eye on traffic, making sure he was headed in the right direction, while Tony observed the lanes headed down into the tunnels to New York.

"Don't see anything unusual," Tony remarked. "You know what I think?"

"No. What do you think?"

"I think people are scared. They want to stay home. Don't want to risk being on the morning news as the next victim. Everyone knows the bomber usually goes after someone during the morning commute.

"I mean look at him." Tony picked up the morning paper he'd brought with him and pointed to the photo on the front page, a frame of video recorded by one of the security cameras at the bus station. It showed the slightly blurry image of a man in an overcoat and hat hurling a bomb into the crowd. The lower half of the bomber's face was visible, the mouth open as if yelling.

Next to the photo was a copy of the sketch made from Gillian's description, revised from the original to show the slight crescent scar above the one brow. "He looks like someone from a low budget horror movie, slinging out death to commuters."

Sam glanced at the picture. It was the clearest one they had of the Carpenter, the only one where he was standing fairly still while facing one of the cameras. "Kind of makes you want to avoid any guy wearing an overcoat and hat."

"You got that right. But every time an Indiana Jones movie comes out, those hats are back in style." Tony looked around at the sparse traffic. "I bet a lot of the middle class guys are staying home today."

"Or going into work late."

"Could be. Now me, if I fit the Carpenter's requirements and had to go to work, I'd dress differently. Forget suits and coats. I'd go in torn jeans, sneakers, and a t-shirt. Yeah. That would fool him into ignoring me."

"Sounds like a plan." They passed a Park & Ride off Route 3. Sam glanced at the people getting on the buses to go into the city. "Look over there. They must have heard you." Most of the male commuters were dressed like they were going to a ball game: sports jackets, jeans, shirts with no ties. Except for one important detail. People, after all, were creatures of habit.

"The briefcases and laptops are dead giveaways," he pointed out.

Tony swore. "People are so stupid."

"Maybe they should go in drag."

Tony laughed. "Or use gym bags."

They got off Route 3 and entered the maze of streets that composed the highly dense suburban confines of northeastern New Jersey. Before Christopher Bonaventure was torn in two by a bomb while visiting his favorite coffee hangout in New York, he had lived in Clifton, one of many commuters from the Garden State who wanted his family to live in a home that had tufts of grass and weeds around the perimeter instead of steel and concrete.

They pulled up to a modest light green split-level home with white shutters. Purple flowers lined the front walkway. As they got out of the car, Tony asked the same question he'd been asking since they first became partners. "You think I should move to Jersey? Give my kids a chance to live normal like? Fresh air. Peace and quiet. Low crime—except for drugs. Drugs are everywhere."

Sam glanced up as a passenger jet roared over the house, going to one of the three busiest airports in the area. Yeah, nice and quiet. As another jet followed it seconds later, he said, "Jersey's a great place to live. Better yet, have all your relatives move here with you. Take over the neighborhood. The deli down the street looks Polish. Might be good to change it to Italian."

"You think?" Tony said. "Of course, I'd take the bridge to work instead of the tunnel."

"Of course."

Another jet flew over as they walked up the steps to the porch. Sam noted the bleached spots on the flower petals in the front window box. Acid rain. "You do know how much lawn mowers cost?"

He pressed the doorbell and knocked. A woman in her mid-thirties, who identified herself as Lynn Russ, the sister of the widow, opened the main door, but kept the storm door closed.

"Are you sure this is necessary?" she said through the screen. "Macie told the FBI everything she knows yesterday. I don't see how repeating the same answers will help things; she'll just start crying again. Can't you guys share information and leave her alone?"

Sam and Tony frowned in sympathy but refused to budge.

Lynn Russ scowled. "She's not taking this well. Not at all. She didn't get much sleep last night. You being here will just make it worse."

"We promise not to stay long," Tony said in his easy-going manner. "This is very important or we wouldn't have come all this way. Just a few questions."

She agreed, albeit reluctantly, and left them in the living room while she went upstairs to fetch her sister. They settled down on a beige couch. A little girl with frizzy brown hair sat on the floor, watching TV. She held a yellow and brown ragged lion tightly to her chest.

"Hi, there," Tony said .

The little girl turned her head to look at him. "Hi," she said softly.

"What's your name?"

"Rachel. Rachel Bonaventure."

Sam and Tony exchanged knowing looks. The little girl who made the 911 call yesterday had mentioned a Rachel.

Tony made conversation while Sam took in the room. Middle class furniture with middle class taste in paintings, family photos, and knickknacks. Carpet was a bit beaten down. Could use a new one. Nothing out of the ordinary.

But then that's who the Carpenter picked: ordinary middle class guys who didn't threaten anyone—until they had a bomb in their hands.

"Shouldn't you be in school?" Tony asked.

"Mommy said I didn't have to go. My daddy died."

Again Tony and Sam exchanged glances. Leave it to children to reduce reality to its simplest components.

"Yes, we know," Tony said. "That's why we're here."

"Are you going to make Mommy cry like they did yesterday?"

"Not if we can help it. Say, that's a nice lion you got there. What's his name?"

"Samson."

"That's my name," Sam said.

"Really?" The little girl turned completely around to look at him. "I always thought it was a funny name. But Adam liked it. He said it made him feel strong. That's why he wanted to grow long hair, to be really strong like the man in the Bible. But Daddy wouldn't let him, so he had to settle for having a lion with long hair."

"Is Adam your brother?" Sam asked.

She sadly shook her head. "Pete's my brother. He went to school today. He told Mommy he could handle it. I think he lied. I think he's going to miss Adam as much as I do. That's why Mommy gave me Samson to hold. It helps."

Sam scratched his head in confusion. "If Pete's your brother, who's Adam?"

"He's my friend." Her eyes looked down at the floor. "He *was* my friend. Mommy said I'll never see him again. I liked him. We played together a lot. He was really good at drawing. Do you want to see some of his pictures?"

"Sure," Tony said. With a firm grip on the lion, the little girl ran up the stairs. Tony told Sam, "Kids love to share. At this age, they're all artists. You should see what my little Tina brought home from school the other day. She's going to be another Michelangelo, you wait and see."

The little girl came hurrying down the stairs. "Here they are." She handed the drawings to Tony.

As Tony looked through them, he handed them one by one to Sam. "These are real nice. I like the sun in this one. And, let's see, what's that, the lion, Samson, in the other. Adam was a good artist. You should be very happy he left these for you to keep."

"I am."

"Where did Adam go?" Sam asked.

"Away." She turned her body from side to side, then shrugged in uncertainty. "I guess to heaven. That's where my Daddy is. They're together like they were here."

Sam looked over the drawings. Definitely kid's stuff. Some stick figures with large heads. A generic four-legged animal with lots of yellow hair—must be the lion. Colorful flowers with no leaves. Nothing unusual except for two drawings that showed a boy—or was it a man?—with huge teardrops falling from his face. And frowns that evoked a matching sadness in Sam over what he had said to Gillian last night.

Sam held up the two drawings of someone crying. "Was Adam a sad boy?" he asked the girl.

"Sometimes." Rachel's frown matched the ones in the drawings. "Sometimes he would sit very still and not talk at all. Sometimes, if you asked him a question, he'd just keep shaking his head." She imitated the gesture with her own head.

"Mommy said it was okay for him not to talk. In his own good time, that's what she said. He'd talk in his own good time. Once in a while when we drew together I could get him to talk." She smiled. "I taught Adam how to laugh. I'm going to miss him. But not Gerta. Gerta took my dolls without asking. I didn't like her."

"That's enough, honey. Don't bother the officers." A woman in her early thirties entered the room. She had the same frizzy brown hair as the little girl, but much longer, and held back with a plastic clip. She looked worn out, yet she smiled pleasantly, given the circumstances. The dark eyes were deep and hollowed with grief.

"It's all right," Tony said as he and Sam stood up. "She was just keeping us company."

"Yeah. She was telling us about Adam," Sam said. He had mentioned it to put the mother at ease. The last thing he expected was to see her turn even paler.

In a sudden sharp voice, she told the little girl to turn off the TV and go to her room. "Now, Rachel," she added sternly when the girl started to protest. "Don't make me tell you twice."

Rachel's quivering chin indicated she wasn't used to being yelled at. She shut the TV off and ran out of the room, hugging the lion to her chest.

With her back ramrod straight, Macie Bonaventure sat on the edge of an upholstered chair.

Sam and Tony retook their seats on the couch. Tony brought out his notebook and started asking the list of questions he and Sam had come up with on their drive over. None of the answers interested Sam. He felt tingly. Hair-standing-up-on-the-back-of-the-neck kind of tingly. He'd felt it before, usually when he entered a room or hallway, searching for a perp, able to sense his presence yet without knowing from which direction.

He stared at the drawings, at the big tears falling from a face.

Tony asked, "Mrs. Bonaventure, did your husband—"

"Who's Adam?" Sam interrupted, still staring at the drawings.

The woman looked from one detective to the other, not sure who to answer.

Sam made the decision for her. "Who is Adam?"

The woman crossed her arms against her stomach and looked down. "A playmate of Rachel's." She looked at Tony. "You were saying?"

Sam solemnly raised his gaze from the drawings to her. "Mrs. Bonaventure, is Adam dead?"

She hesitated before answering. "Uh, yes. Yes, he is."

"When did he die?"

"Recently." She looked at Tony, as if silently begging him to return to the original line of questioning. But Tony, from past experience, knew better than to interrupt when Sam was zeroing in on an important piece of information.

Sam said, "Your daughter seems more upset about Adam's death than her own father's. Why is that?"

"You know children."

"No, I don't. I don't have any of my own, so please tell me why the death of a playmate would be as tough on her as her own father's death?"

"Death is hard on everyone." She stood up. Sam and Tony stood as well.

She turned away. "I'm sorry. I really can't handle this right now. If you'll excuse me, Lynn will show you out."

Sam took a step toward her. "Mrs. Bonaventure, was Adam and your husband the same person?"

Her back stiffened. "No."

"But they were in the same body, weren't they?"

Macie Bonaventure turned to face him. Her eyes were wide and filled with tears. "How did you know?"

Sam held up the drawings. "He had Dissociative Identity Disorder, MPD, didn't he? Just last night I saw drawings like these on an MPD/DID website."

She raised her hands to her mouth, as if afraid to speak, and nodded.

Sam led her to the couch and sat down next to her. He held her hands, trying to impart comfort while needing to keep her talking. "Mrs. Bonaventure, did your husband also have a little girl personality in him? Someone like Adam who played with Rachel?"

"Gerta. Her name was Gerta. When she could be coaxed out, Gerta relied on Rachel to make her feel safe. And loved." Macie Bonaventure's eyes were like twin waterfalls. The tears were nonstop. "We tried so hard to keep it a secret. They only started manifesting in the last four years. Since then, we've had to move three times. It's almost impossible to have friends, to keep a job, when others find out. People can be so cruel."

He handed her a clean handkerchief. "For the record, I have to hear you specifically confirm that your husband had been diagnosed with multiple personality disorder. Is this correct?"

Between sniffling and wiping away the tears, she nodded and said, "The doctor treating him preferred DID, but it's the same thing."

"Can you give us this doctor's name?"

"Dr. Jane Mumsford. She specializes in this type of disorder."

Not Newhall, Sam noted, the doctor who had diagnosed Follett.

He said, "Ma'am, we have a tape, part of a *911* call around the time your husband died. There's a little girl's voice on the tape asking for someone named Rachel. I'd like to have you listen to it, see if it sounds similar to how the Gerta personality talked."

"If it'll help." She wiped her tears. "I guess there's no point in keeping it a secret now. Chris is dead. They're all dead. No one can hurt them anymore."

Sam had Tony fetch the sister. He didn't want to leave the woman alone. Macie was grieving not only for her husband, but for all the people who used to live inside him. Sam still didn't have a good handle on DID. He didn't quite believe in multiple personalities. But Macie did. And so did little Rachel. He had played a hunch and it had panned out.

How this fit in with the Carpenter was as clear as the smog draped around New York. But once in a while the sun did shine through.

The sister took Macie away, but not before giving both detectives a searing look for upsetting her again. The officers let themselves out.

"What the hell was that all about?" Tony asked when they were back in the car, headed east to the city.

"Christopher Bonaventure had Dissociative Identity Disorder. That's a fancy way of saying he had a lot of personalities inside his head."

"You mean when he talked to himself, he answered?"

"I'm not sure. I'm still looking into it. It's so damn weird."

"No argument there. But even if Bonaventure had dissocia . . . whatever, how does it matter to our case?"

"According to the files on Follett, his shrink claimed he was DID, too."

"You're shittin' me."

"It's a small thread. We've got the Carpenter on a crusade somehow related to Ray Andrew Follett, who purportedly had DID. Now we learn one of the Carpenter's victims had DID. Coincidence? I don't think so."

"How do you want to handle this?" Tony asked.

"I'd like you to play the tape over the phone to Macie Bonaventure so she can verify whether or not the voice belongs to this Gerta."

"Okay."

"While you're doing that, I'll be talking with Gillian and Calvin Moore. Both worked the Follett trial. I want their take on this. I got a gut feeling one of them knows something that could break this case wide open."

Tony raised his brow and smiled knowingly. "You mean Gillian."

Sam shook his head. "I've never met a straight-talking lawyer in my life."

"Except Stephanie."

Sam thought about how easily Stephanie had justified copying Gillian's notes. And how easily he had bought into it. "Like I said, lawyers skirt the truth. And Tony . . ."

"Yeah?"

"When you see Macie Bonaventure again, ask her if she or her husband ever knew a Jacob Miller. Dr. Jacob Miller."

"The guy on the torn business card?"

"The same."

"Sure. Why?"

"Just playing another hunch."

Chapter Fifteen

Shadowed by her bodyguard, Gillian was thoroughly flustered as she exited the elevator and headed down the hall to the courtroom, her mind mulling over her conversation with Cindy Follett, crescent and circular scars, the Carpenter, Sam, the trial, Regis. Sam.

It must have showed on her face for when Calvin caught sight of her, his eyes abruptly went saucer-wide, then just as quickly narrowed into dark beads of disapproval.

John, his assistant, coughed and looked away.

Their reactions made her stop and think. A lot of people had been looking at her strangely today, even at the hotel. She'd always thought she was fairly good at hiding her emotions. Obviously, that wasn't the case this morning. As her brother would say: suck it up.

Squaring her shoulders, Gillian raised her chin and smiled broadly. "Morning, Cal. John."

John nodded and nervously straightened his tie.

In a clipped tone bordering on being stern, Calvin asked her, "Are you all right?"

"Sure," she replied, though in truth she could still use another pot of coffee. "Why do you ask?"

His gaze swept up and down the length of her. "Except for your penchant for wearing sneakers, you're the most tasteful, conservative, monochromatic dresser I know."

She smiled at the compliment. "Thank you, Cal."

"So why, today of all days, when there's a good chance we'll start our defense, did you decide to come as Rainbow Girl?"

"What?" She looked down at her outfit and gasped. Red jacket, pale yellow blouse, blue skirt, and green sneakers. "I had no idea. I really didn't notice. I've been so preoccupied . . . I was on the phone . . . I'm so sorry, Cal."

"At least you're not wearing purple."

She hesitated, then pulled the neck of her blouse out and glanced inside at her bra. "I wouldn't take any bets on that."

Calvin was not amused. He shifted his position, using his body to shield her appearance from those passing by in the hallway. "Did something happen?" He cleared his throat. "Something, uh, last night?"

For a second, she wondered if he knew about Sam coming to see her. Or Regis spending the night. She noticed Calvin still hadn't looked her in the eye. With anyone else, she'd suspect his tonal quality and mannerisms revealed self-doubt or guilt. As far as she knew, there was no cause for either, which meant her colorful attire was the reason he couldn't look her in the face. Probably embarrassed on her behalf.

"I was on the phone with Cindy Follett this morning," she said by way of explanation.

Calvin cursed under his breath. "Don't tell me. I can guess. This has to do with Jacob Miller showing up the other night."

"That's part of it." And her confrontation with Sam last night, and Regis spending the night, and her theories about the scar on the bomber. No wonder she couldn't dress herself right. But it didn't explain Cal's anger.

"You can wear my overcoat," Calvin said.

"Thank you, no. I'll try to be inconspicuous."

Calvin raised a brow as if to question whether that was possible, given the array of colors she wore, but all he said was, "We should go in."

He began to turn away when she put a hand on his arm. It was like roping in an angry steer. He wanted to get away from her; why, she couldn't figure out. Nor did she care. She needed to settle her doubts or they would trouble her all day.

"If you don't mind, I have to ask you something first. The other night when we ran into Jacob, do you remember him mentioning Ray by name?"

Calvin whispered harshly, "Don't tell me your mind is going, too?"

"Of course not. What I mean is, do you remember him saying Ray or did he just say Follett?"

"Does it matter? Jacob doesn't know when to let go. Neither do you. Don't open old wounds, Gillian, at least not while we have work to do."

Calvin entered the courtroom, signifying the subject was closed. John offered her a shrug of sympathy, then followed their boss inside. She swallowed the criticism. Cal had every right to be annoyed. She shouldn't allow outside events to distract her from her work. It was Sam and Regis's job to find the Carpenter, not hers. Nothing was more important than this trial, she scolded herself as she slipped into the courtroom. Calvin needed her. The defendants needed her.

Stop playing amateur detective.

She ignored the stares and whispers from the gallery concerning her appearance and took her seat in the first row behind Calvin. After settling in, she glanced over at Stephanie. The prosecutor's body language revealed major irritation: a hotbed of rapid movements as she opened her briefcase, took out papers, and shut it with a smart snap. Everything she did was quick and precise. When she started tapping a pencil on the table, Gillian knew the prosecutor was on overload—lots of pent-up energy seeking release.

Whatever the cause of her foul mood, Gillian wasn't the only one to notice. Stephanie's assistant slowly inched his chair away from her, then more when she barked at him. Gillian's curiosity grew by the second. If Stephanie didn't get whatever was bothering her under control, she could lose the case. Jurors were smart. In the isolation of a courtroom, they could pick up on an attorney's emotions. Attitude played an important role in how jurors accepted testimony and evidence. So many crazy factors played into the jury's final decision, it was a wonder justice ever won out.

Everyone stood as the judge entered to begin the day's proceedings. She soon forgot about her Rainbow Girl outfit and shifted into the persona of people reader.

The medical examiner took the stand. While he answered Stephanie's questions, Gillian listened and observed. Occasionally she closed her eyes for a few seconds and concentrated on the sound of the ME's voice rather than his words. Her perception from sight, hearing, and comprehension led her to conclude that the ME believed everything he was relating. No embellishments of gruesome facts to enrage the jurors and goad them into seeking revenge on the defendants. All pretty much straightforward, which was damaging in itself.

And yet, as the testimony continued, she was surprised to hear Calvin object, then object again to elementary material. Each time it was summarily overruled by the judge, who steadily grew impatient with the defense lawyer. Even John was staring at Calvin in disbelief. Why was Cal so growly today?

Stephanie wasn't acting any better. The more Calvin objected, the more terse and surly her voice became when she asked the ME questions. Gillian wondered if they'd both taken grouch pills that morning.

Once again Calvin objected. This time Stephanie threw her hands up in exasperation. She turned to him and asked, "*What* is your problem?"

Calvin shot to his feet, mouth open to answer, when the judge called for a short recess. He ordered both attorneys to his chambers. After the three left, the gallery buzzed about the fractious behavior of the lawyers and the judge's reaction. Amidst the murmurs, Gillian heard a familiar voice say, "Excuse me."

To her dismay, Sam was making his way down the row in her direction. He stopped by the man seated next to her, flashed his shield, and told him he would have to move. "Police business."

Confronted by the shiny symbol of authority and the detective's resolute tone, the man immediately vacated his spot. Without even a glance in her direction, Sam calmly sat down, face forward, as if they were in a theater about to see a movie.

She peeked sideways at him. Dark circles shadowed his eyes. He'd cut himself shaving. Twice.

Pride told her to ignore him after what he had said last night.

For twenty long, grueling seconds she kept her mouth shut. Then she whispered out the side of her mouth, "You look like hell."

"I'm not surprised. Been there all night."

"Another bombing?"

Sam shook his head. "By the way, nice outfit. Very bright and cheerful."

She tensed. Was he being kind or subtly sarcastic? She suddenly regretted not accepting Cal's offer of his coat. Maybe she could dash back to the hotel during lunch recess and change.

She angled her notepad away from Sam. "You're here to spy on me."

"Nope."

"Guard me?"

"Nope."

"Then why are you here?"

"Just sitting."

"Shouldn't you be *just sitting* on Stephanie's side of the room?"

"I like it fine right here."

She frowned. When it came to Samson Brankowski, everything he said or did had more than one meaning. "Are you going to be here all day?" she asked.

"Maybe. It's a free country. As a citizen of this self-same country, state, county, and city, I have every right to sit here and witness the justice system."

"But you told the man who'd been sitting next to me—who was here for the same reason—that you were on police business. So why *are* you here?"

"To observe. As a cop I should keep abreast of what happens in a trial. Shh. Here comes the judge."

Stephanie, Calvin, and Judge Conway re-entered the courtroom. Right away, the ADA noticed Sam and Gillian sitting together. Sam waved one finger in greeting, then returned to looking straight ahead.

Stephanie glared at Gillian, her lips a tight, angry line of red lipstick. Gillian gulped. If looks could kill, an entirely new trial would be on the docket.

Stephanie turned away, effectively dismissing her and Sam. The trial continued. Gillian glanced at Sam out of the corner of her eye, waiting for him to do or say something— anything—that would explain his presence. Specifically, why he wanted to observe *this* judicial proceeding while seated directly beside her. He gave nothing away. He merely sat there, polite, fairly immobile, seemingly interested in everything everyone said and did, not uttering a sound. The perfect interested spectator.

It drove her crazy.

With every ounce of will power, she struggled to ignore him and concentrate on her work.

As expected, some of the jurors paled when the trauma on the victim's body was explained in blunt detail. Most shifted in their seats. She could sense a lot of people in the audience do the same. When nervous, the human body instinctually tries to ease the discomfort by expending energy. Hearing how a knife cuts through clothing and into a body was tough for most people to handle.

But not Sam. He sat there, attentive, listening, observing. In his profession, he'd probably witnessed far worse than a stabbing death. In the last few days with the Carpenter, he must have seen atrocities done to the human body that would cause any normal person to be institutionalized. In order to do his job, he apparently had learned how to turn off his feelings.

As the dreadful description of the stab wounds continued, Gillian chanced to notice the defendants. One was shifting nervously, just like most of the jury and the gallery. The other, Cesar, sat much like Sam. Calm. Still. Attentive. If Sam hadn't been sitting next to her, she might have missed the discrepancy.

She studied Cesar and was startled by what she saw.

Her pen flew across the page of her notebook. To avoid presumptions, she didn't try to categorize or analyze what she observed. She solely wrote down every mannerism, every expression, every movement that Cesar's head, mouth, hands, eyes, fingers, feet, and body made. At the same time she tried to note what the ME was saying, what questions he was asked, and the answers he gave. By the time the prosecution and Calvin had finished with him, her hand ached.

While she flexed her fingers, Sam caught her eye. It was easy to tell he wanted to ask what she had been writing. Instead, he winked and turned back to observe the next witness called to testify. After yesterday, she thought she had Sam figured out. Mean. Insensitive. Stubborn. Rigid. Implacable. Heartless. Pigheaded. Now he was an enigma. Calm and amiable. Polite and restrained. Would she ever be able to decipher his true self? The one that didn't wear a shield?

She looked down at her notes on Cesar. This, too, was an enigma, but by the time they adjourned for lunch, she was determined to have it solved.

After declaring lunch recess, Judge Conway left the bench. The spectators filed out of the courtroom. Sam watched as Gillian leaned forward and told Calvin she had to speak with him right away. She retook her seat to gather her things.

Sam hesitated, then put a hand on hers to still her movements. "Before you go, I have something to say."

She looked to where Calvin was discussing something with John. "I really need to talk to Cal."

"It won't take long. I promise."

By the look Gillian gave him, she didn't put much stock in his promises. He couldn't blame her, not after what he had done last night.

When he first sat down next to her, she had been as prickly as a wire brush. The few times she had talked with him, her words were barbed, ready to strike if he said the wrong thing.

He'd been careful in what he said, especially when it came to her choice of clothing. Initially he wanted to ask her if the circus was in town. Almost blew that, yet she didn't seem to pick up the sarcastic edge to his compliment.

And now she was waiting for his big spiel.

All night and all morning he had been rehearsing what to say. Now, when he had the opportunity to get it off his chest, his mind went blank. *Damn. Wouldn't you know it.*

"Well?" she asked impatiently.

He wished he had Tony's gift for gab. Tony would know how to word things. Make her feel good about herself, and good about him. But Tony wasn't here, and by Gillian's anxious movements, she was ready to blow him off and sequester herself with Calvin. It was now or never. No matter how bad it sounded, he had to say it.

"Last night I read all the files I could find on Ray Andrew Follett."

At the mention of Follett's name, she stiffened. He could almost swear she had suddenly put on an invisible suit of armor. She looked down at his hand on hers, and he promptly removed it.

"I want you to hear my assessment of the Follett case."

"Detective Brankowski, you pick one hell of a time to do this."

"I know." He shrugged. "What can I say? I call 'em as I see 'em."

She lifted her chin in defense, meeting his gaze straight on. "I thought you did that last night at the hotel."

"That was my initial assessment. After going over everything, I've come to some conclusions I want you to hear."

She studied his face, The Oracle in her straining to detect whether he was going to hurt her again. Her breath was deep and shaky as she said, "Go ahead."

He took one of her hands and sandwiched it gently between both of his. "Gillian Dohr, you're a good person. Great at what you do. In all honesty, if I ever get into trouble with the law, you'll be the first one I hire to be on my side."

"A compliment?" she asked with a mocking smile.

"Yeah. As I was saying, you're good at this people-reading stuff. Real good. I think deep down inside you're a good person. And I like you. So I wish I could say I forgive you for letting Ray Andrew Follett get acquitted, go free, and kill more kids, but I can't."

Pain flashed in her eyes. She tried to remove her hand but he held on tighter. *Damn.* Where was Tony when he needed him?

"The reason I can't forgive you is because you did nothing wrong. You have nothing to feel guilty about. You're not to blame. A lot of other people may be at fault over that, *but not you.*"

She looked stunned. He expected her to start crying any minute. But then he never could figure out women. Instead of getting all weepy-eyed and grateful, she got angry.

"This is a joke, right?" she asked.

"Uh-uh. I really mean it. From what I read, what you had to work with, Follett wasn't your fault."

She continued to stare at him in disbelief. "But Regis—"

"Regis is an asshole, pardon my French. I saw some stuff in the files he should have picked up on but didn't. If you want, blame him. He had more control over the evidence than you did. I'll tell you this: if Stephanie had been the one prosecuting Follett, she would have gotten a conviction."

Women. He expected Gillian to get angry when he started dissing her boyfriend, but now tears were coming to her eyes, and she was smiling at him.

She placed her other hand on top of his. Her touch was warm and welcoming, and her milk chocolate eyes practically melted as she looked at him. "For years I've been asking people to forgive me. I haven't even been able to forgive myself—not fully. But you . . . you, Samson Brankowski, are the first person ever to say I didn't need to. Oh, Sam, I could kiss you."

Okay, now *that* he had expected. Most women do kiss or hug when a guy apologizes, and though he never actually said the word apologize, it was the results that mattered. Right now, Gillian Dohr had never looked happier.

He was getting ready to finally discover just how great it felt to have Gillian's lips on his mouth when he heard Calvin cough irritably from behind him.

Gillian looked over his head at Calvin. If her frown was any indication, she seemed as annoyed by the interruption as he was. And that made him feel happy. Invincible. Special. He started wondering how long he could keep her in Manhattan.

"Gillian," Calvin said with insistence.

"It's okay," Sam told her as he removed his hands from hers. "I'll meet you out in the hall when you're done."

She nodded in agreement, and he went outside to wait. After several minutes, her bodyguard came out without her. Sam opened the door and peeked inside. The courtroom was relatively empty: only Gillian, Calvin, and his assistant. Something was going down. She was arguing fiercely in hushed tones with Calvin, talking with her hands and pointing to the pile of notes she had written during that sudden burst of energy.

Though curious, one of the promises he had secretly made to Gillian last night as he read the Follett case files was to stop intruding in her work. He had never thought of himself as a pillar of patience, but something told him Gillian Dohr was worth cultivating that particular virtue.

He closed the door and waited with the guard. When John came out looking like a schoolboy who had just come from the principal's office, he knew trouble was brewing. He must have missed something during the court session. But Gillian hadn't. He was itching to find out what, but if he had any hope of maintaining a shred of neutrality about this trial when around Gillian, he dare not ask what was going on.

"Calvin, you've got to try Cesar and Ricardo separately," Gillian insisted. "It's only fair."

"I'm not paid to be fair," Calvin replied. "I was hired to defend both men equally."

"But only Cesar may be guilty of murder. Ricardo isn't."

"I don't know that for sure."

"I do." Calvin stared her down like an angry bull, and she wavered. "Well, I'm pretty sure. Almost sure."

"Gillian, I'm not going to sacrifice one of my clients so the other one can receive a lighter sentence."

"But if only one committed murder, the other shouldn't have to risk the same conviction."

"From my perspective, both are guilty or both are innocent. My entire strategy is based upon that premise. I cannot . . ." he paused as her eyes widened in disbelief that he really couldn't do what she was asking. Acting resentful that he suddenly had to defend himself against one of his own team members, he said firmly, "I will not revise my gameplan because of conjecture."

"But—"

"I *never* ask my clients if they committed the crime they're accused of. If the prosecution can't prove their guilt, then they deserve to go free."

"Even if they *are* guilty?"

"That's for the system to decide, not me."

"What about the victim? What about justice?"

"If my clients are found guilty when they're innocent, they become victims, too. The judge and the jury are responsible for justice. I'm not." He stepped closer and said in a stern voice, "You have suspicions. A theory. There's no physical proof Cesar committed premeditated murder."

"In my expert opinion, he did."

"You keep that to yourself. You're not working for the other side, you're working for me."

"I don't believe this. You're willing to risk both of them going to prison when you know there's a strong chance only one committed murder?"

"The jury is already doubting the prosecution's case. We have an excellent chance of winning. There's no witness to the crime, the weapon was never recovered, and traces of blood can be indicative of assault but not necessarily of murder." He snorted a laugh of certain triumph. "The most our clients will receive is two years for aggravated robbery."

Chance. Winning. As if the trial was merely a chess game.

Disgusted, she asked. "What if you do win? In two years, probably less with probation and over-crowded prisons, Cesar will be back on the streets, ready to kill again. Can you live with that on your conscience?"

Calvin looked away. After a long drag of air, he replied coldly, "Subsequent to Ray Andrew Follett, I can live with anything. So should you." He turned back around and looked down at her. "It's time you came to terms with the real world, Gillian. This isn't another case of releasing a serial killer onto an unsuspecting populace. Cesar is bad news, a repeat criminal—everyone knows that. Even the Puerto Rican Justice trustees. If he survives prison, he'll get his due. My job is to win him the lightest sentence possible. Your job is to help me accomplish that."

She opened her mouth to protest, but Calvin cut her off. "I don't want to hear anymore about what our clients might have done based solely on their reactions to someone's testimony. You are not to look at them again during this trial, you understand me? They're not your concern. You just concentrate on the jurors and the witnesses. I'll handle my clients. End of discussion."

Gillian fumed in exasperation. Not a gracious loser, she headed for the door, but stopped midway when Calvin called out to her.

"Gillian, if Stephanie London gets wind of this, even a rumor of what you're thinking, I'll ask for a mistrial, a change of venue, and I'll do this all over again but the next time without you. And I'll win. Don't make me regret giving you a chance. You don't want to go back to barely making a living on that ranch of yours. You used to be the best. Could be again. Loyalty and discretion are paramount in this business. Remember that."

Loyalty without conscience. Discretion without truth. Calvin made her out to be a fool for believing everyone's allegiance should be to justice. Alice Through the Looking

Glass, and the judicial system had become the Mad Hatter's party. She'd have to deal with it, but right now she didn't know how.

She rushed out of the courtroom, barely noticing Sam and John off to the side. In no mood to talk with anyone, she headed directly to the elevators, her bodyguard following in her angry wake. The elevator arrived, and she got in, her thoughts fast and furious, all of them aimed at Calvin. In three years' time he had lost his high ideals. He'd stopped fighting the system and become someone who could justify anything with the right words. My God, hadn't he learned anything from Ray Follett?

Chills crept up her spine. She had repeated the bomber's question. Again.

Her head drooped in defeat. It seemed Ray Follett would haunt her life forever.

And yet, a bright spot existed in this gloomy day. Sam had said what happened with Ray wasn't her fault. She shouldn't feel guilty. He was right. But as long as the Carpenter was free, people would keep dying. If she could help put a stop to him, it would end whatever obligation she felt towards Ray.

Her mind returned to the question she'd asked Cal. Last night, had Jacob said Ray Follett or Follett? All of a sudden it seemed imperative to know exactly what Jacob Miller had said. In spite of Cindy's opinion of her stepbrothers, Gillian couldn't help but wonder if they were somehow involved with the Carpenter. Or whether one of them *was* the Carpenter.

She had to talk with Jacob, but phoning him was out of the question. Michelle had an unlisted number. She got a new one every year, thanks to all the people Jacob gave the number to. In his zeal for knowledge, he could stir up more trouble than a hornet's nest. But then, even if she reached Michelle, it didn't mean the woman would let her talk to Jacob.

When they got down to the lobby, she sent an email to Jacob, asking to meet ASAP. She kept her phone out, hoping this was the time of day when Michelle gave him access to the outside world. It was a long shot. When she was first contacted by Jacob three years ago, he was only online in the early morning, and then only twice a week.

Seeing him so late the other night had been quite a shock, and she wondered whether Michelle had altered his schedule. Michelle and Jacob's relationship was unusually antagonistic, to say the least.

In the lobby, she waited off to the side for Calvin. He would expect her to review the morning's proceedings over lunch. Her most important observation had already been rejected. Why bother with the rest? She glanced at her watch. Plenty of time to skip lunch and change her clothes. At least Calvin would appreciate that.

Her phone chimed. A message from Jacob. Wow. That was quick.

It was also brief.

Meet you at Hackers Coffee Slop ASAP. Dr. Jacob Miller.

"Hackers Coffee Slop?"

Her bodyguard tapped her on the shoulder and said, "I know where it is."

"You do?" She studied him in mild astonishment. His disciplined physique didn't fit the stereotype of most computer geeks. She easily surmised he spent an average of twelve hours a week in a gym. "What? You busted someone there?"

He laughed easily, not at all offended by her assumption. "Actually, it's a great hang out. Good food and smart women. A neutral, safe site for dates."

She glanced at her watch. "How far is it?"

"A few blocks."

What the hell. In all honesty, she didn't want to see Calvin until she had cooled off. Everyone in court had already seen her outfit. And she really needed to talk with Jacob.

"Let's go," she said. "We'll have lunch there. My treat."

* * *

Gillian had completely ignored Sam when she rushed out of the courtroom to the elevators. It had bothered him, but he also knew when an angry person needed space—and Gillian had definitely been upset about something.

But when Calvin came out a few minutes later, took one look at Sam and dismissed his presence with a contemptuous frown, the last of Sam's patience evaporated. He quickly caught up with the lawyer and matched his stride. "I need to talk with you."

"Detective, you couldn't have picked a worse time."

"That's all right. This won't take long."

"Perhaps I was too subtle. Let me put it this way. I need to consult with my assistant and Gillian before court reconvenes this afternoon. If you want to talk to me, it'll have to wait until court is recessed for the day."

Sam blocked his path. "Maybe *I* was the one who was too subtle. Let me rephrase. Either we talk now, and I mean now, or I take you down to the station and we talk there."

"You can't be serious."

"Try me. I believe you have information that may be connected to the bombings. That gives my needs top priority over yours. So either we waste valuable time while I haul your ass in for interrogation, or we act civilized and have a friendly chat right here and now. It's your call."

Calvin gritted his teeth. "Very well. Though what I may know about the bombings is beyond me."

"Do you believe Ray Andrew Follett had a dissociative identity or multiple personality disorder?"

"Follett." Calvin Moore growled the name, his lips distorted with undisguised distaste. "What does he have to do with the bombings?"

"That's for me to decide. Just answer the question. Was Follett MPD/DID?"

Calvin shifted uncomfortably. He glanced at his assistant. "John, why don't you and Gillian wait for me downstairs? This should only take a moment."

John stared at his boss in dismay. "Gillian already left."

"What? Where did she go?"

"She didn't say."

"Damn her." Calvin rubbed his hand over his mouth in irritation. "All right. I'll meet you downstairs in a few."

Sam was itching to know what had gone on between Gillian and Calvin that would make her walk out on him, but that could wait until later. As soon as John left, Sam asked Calvin again, "Was Follett DID/MPD?"

The attorney's posture-perfect shoulders drooped. With a tired sigh, he put his briefcase down and leaned against the wall. "Dr. Newhall thought so. He wanted to testify to the fact but my boss negated it. Not pertinent, he said. Thought he could win without having Ray sent to a mental institution. DID was our backup plan. If the jury was leaning toward guilty, the DID classification might keep Ray out of prison. Definitely prevent the death penalty. Nowadays we don't execute the mentally ill. Except Texas.

"Then again, if Dr. Newhall had testified that Ray might have MPD/DID, the prosecution could have used it to refute the irrefutable evidence from witnesses to one of the kidnappings who claimed a woman took the child. Not a man disguised as a woman, but definitely a woman. If the jury found out Ray had a female alter who was doing the killing, the prosecution might have been able to get a conviction.

"Or not. As you know, there are two elements of a crime that needs to be present in order for a person to be found guilty: *mens rea* and *actus reus*."

Sam nodded. "A guilty mind and a guilty act."

"Correct. If Ray Follett had DID, his body might have been guilty of the act, but *his* mind might have been innocent. Only the alter accused of the crime would have *mens rea*, which would absolve Ray of any criminal responsibility."

"No shit." He scratched his head. "So, did you think Follett was DID?"

"No."

Sam believed him. Until Calvin stared off to the side as if remembering something. Sam asked, "What happened that made you suspect Follett might have another personality or two lurking inside?"

Calvin swallowed. "During one of the pretrial interviews, we were checking the details of Ray's background, going over where he was at the times of the killings, searching for character witnesses and alibis. Tedious work.

"I was giving Ray a cup of coffee when I accidentally spilled some on his hand. He went ballistic. Shocked the hell out of me. Until then he had been such a mild-mannered guy. But here he was, face visibly dark with anger, contorted into features that made him look almost unrecognizable, like a different person altogether, and using language typical of the worst hoods in the city. He screamed at me, accusing me of deliberately burning him, and threatened to get even. This from a guy who grew up in the Midwest and worked as a forest ranger. It took several minutes before he calmed down and was back to being himself.

"I think he was as surprised as we were by his outburst. To make sure he didn't have a repeat performance during the trial, especially in front of the jury, my boss called in Dr. Newhall to do an evaluation, mostly to provide a prescription. If need be, we'd tranquilize him during his court appearances to keep him calm."

"Is that when Newhall discovered Follett was MPD/DID, when he did the evaluation?"

Calvin nodded.

"One more thing. Who all knew Follett might be MPD?"

"Me. My boss. Dr. Newhall, of course. Gillian. And Ray, though at first he refused to believe it."

"What about the prosecution or the judge?"

"Since we never had to use it to our advantage, Newhall insisted it be kept under doctor/patient confidentiality."

"So no one outside the defense team knew? It never leaked out? Not even to the jury?"

Calvin shook his head. "We kept it quiet even after the verdict. Ray insisted. He thought revealing it might ruin his chance for a normal life after the trial was over." He reached down for his briefcase. "You mind telling me what this has to do with the Carpenter?"

Sam's phone vibrated. He looked at the display. It was from Tony.

Possible bomb. Hackers Coffee Slop. Meet u there.

Chapter Sixteen

The street in front of the Hackers Coffee Slop looked dangerously normal for a Manhattan lunchtime, crowded with traffic, the sidewalks on either side a fluid river of pedestrians. A car honked. Then another and another. Someone yelled for a cab and music drifted out of a storefront. A careworn panhandler asking for money was steadfastly ignored while a chubby, gray-haired granny peddling watches from an assortment attached in rows inside her fashionable jacket was able to haggle money from customers.

From across the way, Sam took a long, hard look at the coffee shop. People were flowing in and out of the Internet eatery, oblivious to the fact that somewhere inside a man was holding a bomb. By now the ATF or FBI should have cleared the street and sidewalks and evacuated the surrounding businesses. After yesterday's bombing at Port Authority, Sam could easily picture everyone in sight being torn to shreds by nails, glass, and debris. His hands clenched. Any second it could happen and yet no one was doing anything.

He scanned the area. At the far corner, barely in view behind a building, he spotted Tach 3, the NYPD's white motorhome used as a clandestine command post, unmarked except for a blue stripe. He hurried to it. Tony was outside, leaning against the vehicle, waiting for him.

"What gives?" Sam asked, angling his head back toward the Hackers Coffee Slop.

"From the bread crumbs the Feds drop my way," Tony said, "they're afraid the creep handing out the bombs is in the area. If the Carpenter sees traffic being detoured and people pulled off the sidewalks, he'll get wise to us and set off the bomb. If he's not in the immediate vicinity, he could still find out soon as the media blabs that we've cordoned off the area."

Sam nodded glumly. "Logical. Practical. But you gotta wonder if the Feds would do the same if their own family members were walking by the Slop right now."

"What do you expect from out-of-towners?"

"Always easier to put strangers at risk than people in your own hometown. Remember that if you ever move the family to Jersey."

Tony snorted in agreement. "Speaking of Jersey, Christopher Bonaventure's widow said the voice on the 911 tape sounded a lot like that Gerta personality. Actually started crying when she heard it, almost as if she had lost a daughter in addition to her husband. Spooky, huh?"

"You got that right."

"Forensics says the redial on the phone you found was to 911. Confirms what you were thinking, that Bonaventure was calling for help."

"Yeah." He glanced at the restaurant. "So, how come the Carpenter didn't explode the bomb when the caddie called for help this time?"

"Hackers Coffee Slop has a secure Wi-Fi for its overachieving caffeine addicts. The guy with the bomb, Runyon McCullogh, is on a laptop. Contacted NYPD's website, texting pleas for help, asking how we're going to save him, warning his wife will sue the city if we don't."

"Did the Carpenter threaten the caddie's family like he did with Walgood?" Sam asked.

"Yeah. McCullogh has a wife and four kids. Already have units at her place of work and at the school and day care. No sign of a gunman."

"I'll lay odds there isn't one. Just the threat is enough to make the caddies do what they're told."

Tony stared grimly up the street at the Slop. "The guy keeps texting that he loves his wife and kids, his mom and dad, and will do anything to live. Trouble is the Feds aren't sure how to handle it. Lieutenant Winslow is over at their command post." Tony jerked a thumb over his shoulder to a long black truck parked down the next street. "He's arguing like crazy with them about what to do. If the Carpenter sees someone in protective padding enter the Hackers Coffee Slop, he'll figure out real fast what's going down and set the bomb off. If he sees a bunch of us going through all the surrounding buildings, searching for him, he might blow the bomb as a distraction so he can get away in the confusion."

Sam grumbled. Knowing the Feds, they already had a body bag waiting for Runyon McCullogh. The poor guy was dead; time just needed to catch up with the fact. And yet something had to be done.

"When did the caddie get the bomb?" he asked.

Tony looked at his watch. "Coming up on ten minutes."

He broke out in a cold sweat. "Regis says most of these go off within fifteen minutes of receipt."

"Or less."

"Shit. We're almost out of time." He looked up and down the streets. He could see the Fed's bomb unit in the guise of a dark panel truck parked a block away. "Where's *our* bomb unit?"

"In the alley to your left."

He strode quickly in the direction of Tony's thumb.

Tony matched his pace. "I know that look in your eye. You're planning something really stupid."

"Asshole stupid," Sam replied, but his resolve remained firm.

He climbed into the bomb unit's truck and made his way through the cramped quarters to the commander. Sam told him his plan, then volunteered to do it over the commander's objections and the objections of all the explosive experts who thought he had a death wish.

He insisted. They refused, but he refused to give up. "May I remind you that the Feds—who make twice as much as we do—are sitting on their asses while a New Yorker begs for help? They're just waiting for him to be blown up so they can collect evidence. That's all he is to them. Not a man. Not a husband. Not a father. Not someone's son. Only forensic evidence. As a New York City officer I have the right to throw my life away to save a fellow New Yorker."

Appealing to someone's humanity was always a great tactic for winning arguments. So were two 50-yard-line tickets to the first home game of the Giants. A minute later, Sam exited the truck with a laptop and a small gym bag. He headed for the Hackers Coffee Slop.

Tony caught up with him.

"You don't have to do this," Sam told his partner without breaking stride. "You've got a wife and kids."

"And an excellent pension and life insurance," Tony added. "We've been partners a long time. You're family."

"Not family enough to need a babysitter. Get out of here."

"Hey, I wouldn't dream of babysitting you. I'm back-up. Besides, if this works, you'll be right next to the bomb all the way. I'm just your fuckin' door-holder."

"Remind me to tip you if I live through this."

They momentarily split apart to go around the woman hawking watches. When they got back together, Tony whispered, "Spilling coffee in the guy's lap as a diversion while you grab the bomb and toss it in a bag padded with a couple of bullet-proof vests is pretty lame."

"Agreed. But better than what the Feds are doing."

"No argument there. Plus Gillian isn't around to do a strip tease," Tony added with a knowing smirk.

"Thank heaven for small favors." The last thing he needed was to put another person at risk.

As they approached the Wi-Fi bistro, he could practically hear all the Feds cursing to high heaven when their spotters relayed his and Tony's appearance. Probably shittin' in their pants. He grinned at the thought.

He reached for the doorknob, and his hand slipped off. His palms were sweaty, his armpits soaked, and he had to force himself not to grit his teeth or he'd soon have the added distraction of a raging headache.

He rubbed his hand on his pants and tried again. He opened the door and stepped inside. Mimicking casualness, he paused to read a menu tacked up on the wall . . . and heard his worst nightmare.

Cockroaches.

The multitude of fingers softly click click clicking laptop keys sounded too much like the cockroaches skittering in the walls of the filthy apartment where he had grown up. The bad memories unlocked from his childhood made his skin crawl. He shuddered.

Tony walked on by, talked with a waiter, then headed for the back of the place. Out the corner of his eye, Sam kept track of his movements until Tony disappeared from view in the direction of the back door. Then he turned to survey the interior.

They say computers don't have a smell to them. But they do. The bitter scent of coffee barely competed with stink given off by the warm plastic casings heated with the information running through the electronics.

His lips curled in distaste. He hated the place. It was cold and impersonal. Not a place he wanted to die in.

Long, low counters lined the perimeter of the front half of the room. People sat with their backs to the room, for the most part ignoring everyone else, facing the pale orange walls, or, more precisely, facing their opened laptops and tablets.

A four-foot-high wall ran through the center of the room, with a counter along its length on opposing sides, providing more room for people who had the compulsive need to be online while eating or drinking. Wait staff shuttled back and forth, filling cups, taking orders, prudently knowing who to stop and chat with and who to leave alone with their tech.

The back of the store had booths with tables deep enough to hold two laptops, and wide enough to position laptops back to back. He was amazed at the nearest group of four, all working keyboards while conversing with each other and occasionally gulping their coffee. He decided that if this was the future of socializing, he was leaving the country. Perhaps the owner agreed. On all the walls, just above the height of the laptop monitors, a twelve-inch-high band of mirrored tiles encircled the place. The patrons may have their backs to each other, but a simple glance up forced them to at least acknowledge all the other backs.

As indicated in the man's desperate emails, Sam found the Runyon McCullogh at the far counter, two chairs away from the front windows.

Must be a requirement of the bomber, he concluded. The victim at Starbucks had been near a window. Either the Carpenter was in the area and liked to have an unrestricted view of the caddie, or the windows afforded better reception to the carrier's microphone.

He noted the glass panes were not as wide and expansive as the ones at the Starbucks, but if the bomb went off, the shards would be just as deadly. He checked his watch. Coming up on fourteen minutes since the bomb was handed over. Close to the red zone. He'd have to act fast, always aware the Carpenter might be watching, if not listening.

Sam sat at the counter next to Runyon. He casually put the sports bag on the floor between them, unzipped it, then placed a laptop on the counter and opened it.

Runyon glanced at him without turning his head, using the mirror on the wall to acknowledge his presence. His eyes were wide and fearful, his forehead dripping with sweat. Death stalked him in the hand hidden within his sports jacket. The bomb.

"How's the food here?" Sam asked.

Runyon didn't answer. His frightened gaze returned to the laptop. He typed furiously.

Sam noted the empty counter. Runyon hadn't ordered anything to drink. *Nuts.*

"I love sexting," Sam said. "Great way to reach out and touch someone."

Their eyes met in the mirror. Sam winked, and a sparkle of hope brightened Runyon's face. His laptop pinged softly to signal an email had arrived. While Runyon opened the electronic letter, which explained what Sam was about to do and what Runyon was supposed to do in response, Sam turned and raised a hand to signal the waiter he wanted service. He ordered coffee, black. When the waiter returned, Sam took the steaming cup and sipped it, and realized the *slop* in Hackers Coffee Slop wasn't a cute misnomer but actually truth in advertising.

As he moved to put the cup on the counter near Runyon McCullogh, to *accidentally* spill the coffee onto the guy's lap, his eyes glanced up at the mirrors, checking one last time for anyone acting suspicious. A beautiful woman, seated with her back to him, was staring at him, using the mirror in front of her to look at him. Her eyes were the color of hot cocoa and full of surprise.

Gillian!

Their eyes locked, hers in curiosity, his in fear. What the hell was she doing here?

He had to get her out without alerting the Carpenter, and before she decided to try to help.

Frantic, he looked at the counter. No ketchup. No mustard.

Damn.

He bit his inner lip, then dipped his index finger in the blood, and wrote a single letter on the mirror in front of him, small enough so the Carpenter wouldn't see it if watching with binoculars from somewhere across the street but large enough for Gillian to read, understand, and leave.

At first he was going to write *C* for Carpenter or *B* for bomb but decided it might be too vague for Gillian to comprehend. Then he remembered last night and the red letters she had written on her broken mirror to signify Follett's many personalities, especially the one she thought was the killer instead of Ray. Janeane.

He wrote a small bloody *J* on the mirror and mentally yelled, "Get out of here!"

Gillian stared at the *J.*

While waiting for Jacob Miller to arrive, she'd been surprised to discover Sam seated behind her. She had just decided it couldn't be a coincidence, that for some inane reason he had followed her here, when she saw him write the red letter.

Her blood boiled.

In spite of what he had said at the courthouse, he still didn't understand. He was still playing with her emotions. How dare he mock what she had done last night! And with ketchup no less!

Furious, she grabbed her peach Italian soda and headed directly for him. His face in the mirror reflected alarm. Good. It's about time someone put the fear of God into him.

"You bastard," she said. "I believed you. Everything you said, I believed. And now you do this. How could you be so cruel?" She chucked the contents of her glass at him.

Sam ducked. The majority of the drink splashed over his head and onto the man next to him.

"Look what you did to my laptop!" the man yelled, getting

to his feet. "It's all sticky!"

Mortified by what she had done, she quickly grabbed napkins from a nearby dispenser to sop up the liquid. "I'm sorry. It was an accident. I was aiming at the jerk next to you." She handed the man half the napkins. "Here, let me help you clean it up."

"Don't bother," the man snarled. "You careless, bitless bitch! It's all shorted out! You're going to pay for this, you stupid Andorian sow!"

The man sounded angry, and his wild, menacing gestures signified anger, but his facial features lacked sincerity. Something here didn't make sense. But she didn't have time to figure it out as he stepped towards her. He was a big man. A tall man. As he continued to rail against her alien animal parentage and threaten to send her into a parallel universe, Gillian hoped Sam would come to her rescue. Or at least say something.

He didn't. But her bodyguard did. The federal agent grabbed the man by the arm to pull him away from her. Immediately, Sam tossed his coffee at the Fed. The agent howled as the hot liquid hit his chest, and he released his grip on the man.

In disbelief, Gillian watched as Sam swiftly shook the man's hand, then fumbled with the gym bag on the floor and zipped it shut. Leaving his laptop behind, Sam took the bag and hurried to the back of the place, yelling, "Stay there! I'll get the manager! He'll take care of these crazy people!"

Her bodyguard cursed Sam and the hot coffee soaking his shirt. Customers babbled, and the wait staff hurried to calm everyone down, but all Gillian noticed was Sam disappearing into the kitchen. Why was he going in there?

When the angry tall man with the laptop called her, "A Klingon's cold ass-wipe," she looked at him. Her mouth dropped open, completely baffled. He was smiling at her, yet he kept insulting her. Why did he look so happy, almost to the point of tears? And where had Sam gone? Why did he douse her bodyguard with hot coffee when the agent was trying to help her?

She studied the red *J* he'd written on the mirror. Of all of Ray's alters, why had Sam written Janeane's initial? Only now did she notice the letter hadn't been written with ketchup. It wasn't thick enough for ketchup. It almost looked like . . . She reached out a finger to touch it, and her hand trembled in realization. Blood.

Her eyes widened in shock. And they widened even more when she saw in the mirror the reflection of a small African-American Hasidic Jew stealing into the Hackers Coffee Slop.

In the back of the kitchen of the Slop, Tony opened the door to the alley as Sam raced past all the cooks and servers.

"Seventeen minutes" Tony yelled as Sam dashed out the door.

Sam prayed.

Not yet!

Not yet!

Please, God, not yet!

He quickly examined the alley. To his right, as planned, sat a huge, heavy round cylinder, courtesy of the NYPD bomb unit. He slam-dunked the gym bag into the protective barrel, then hit the ground, not even trying to close the lid. The bomb went off. The explosion made him and everything around him shudder violently and blew the windows facing the alley. Heat from the blast settled around him. A vaporous shroud of dust and debris smoked his surroundings. Coughing, he covered his nose and mouth. Just when he thought the worst was over, an errant nail from the bomb fell out of the sky and pierced his calf. He yelped in pain.

Tony hurried to him. From both ends of the alley, members of the bomb squad converged, shouting—or so the repeated opening and closing of their mouths indicated. His ears were still ringing from the blast. He sat on his butt, in something wet and oily and smelling of vomit and rancid fish, temporarily deaf, shaking uncontrollably from the rush of adrenaline, a nail imbedded in his leg. But he was alive.

And so was Runyon McCullogh, who now stood in the back doorway of the Hackers Coffee Slop with tears running down his cheeks. Fear gave way to gratitude as his eyes met Sam's, yet both knew why the other wasn't shouting with joy. In spite of Sam's heroics, the Carpenter was still at large. Any minute of any hour of any day, he could force another bomb on someone and start the deadly scenario all over again.

The thought was sobering, as was the strange coincidence of Gillian being present at yet another location of the Carpenter's victim.

Once again she had provided a diversion to get the bomb away from a caddie.

She'd been furious at him for making the *J* on the mirror. Must have thought he was making fun of her MPD explanation the night before. But how did she feel about him now that she knew what had been going on inside the Slop? He hoped it would heal the rift between them. Maybe she'd wrap her arms around him, proud of what he had done.

A kiss would be great. Getting laid even better.

He expected to see her in the doorway next to Runyon and the kitchen staff who had rushed outside to see what was going on. He squinted and blinked and decided the explosion must have given him a concussion. He was hallucinating. He could swear a leprechaun-sized black Hasidic Jew had just come out of the Hackers Coffee Slop.

A wave of dizziness came over him. He closed his eyes to give his mind time to calm down, and told himself there was no such thing as a black Jewish leprechaun.

When he reopened his eyes, his vision was clear, but the guy was still short, notwithstanding that stature is relative when standing next to a very tall Runyon McCullogh, who towered above everyone at six-foot nine. The munchkin gave Runyon a quick hug, then sped off as fast as his short legs could go, into the crowd forming at one end of the alley.

By now Tony crouched next to him. He patted Sam on the shoulder, lips moving, maybe asking if he was all right. Sam still couldn't hear a thing, but he plainly understood what Tony meant when his partner rolled his eyes and pointed a thumb down the other end of the alley. Sam looked. Hordes of angry Feds were stomping toward him.

He was soon surrounded by the ATF, FBI, Homeland Security, and Lieutenant Winslow; all seemed to be shouting at him—lips flapping, teeth flashing. For the second time that day he thanked God, this time for being temporarily deaf.

One thing for sure, the Carpenter wouldn't take the chance of giving the bomb to anyone else who had a computer. It might be worth the cost if everyone traveling to New York got a laptop to carry around until the Carpenter was caught. Or phones with text messaging. At least Runyon must think so.

Several members of the NYPD edged their way between the Feds to congratulate one of their own, and a flurry of helpful hands helped Sam to his feet. He wrapped one arm around Tony's shoulder to take the weight off his injured leg while fellow officers smiled and patted him on the back.

Sam nodded at whatever they were saying to him, but his thoughts were solely on one person. He strained to look around all the people surrounding him.

Where was Gillian?

Chapter Seventeen

Sam's not dead. He can't be.

Gillian raised her phone over the heads of the crowd and took a picture of the alley. She studied the small photo. It was jammed with people, mostly men, wearing jackets with ATF, FBI, Homeland Security, or NYPD on the back and front. Everyone was talking. Some were yelling. Thankfully, their body language didn't reflect grief over the death of one of their own. Yet the prospect of fighting her way through the crowd to verify Sam was all right would take time, and time was one thing she didn't have.

She had to find Jacob. The very second she noticed his reflection in the mirror inside the Hackers Coffee Slop, the bomb had gone off. Only then, only in that instant of massive sound, did it hit her that Sam had once again put his life at risk. He had taken a bomb away from the man with the laptop.

How could she have been so stupid? When Sam drew the bloody *J* on the mirror he had been trying to save her life. A red *J* meant evil, danger, beware, watch out, get away, death—everything connected to Janeane the child-killer.

In the ensuing panic of customers rushing to escape, she'd lost her bodyguard. All it took was one person yelling, "A bomb exploded!" and people turned into stampeding cattle. In spite of her efforts to get to the backdoor to see if Sam was all right, she had been herded out the front with everyone else.

"Be safe, Sam," Gillian said, and meant it with all her heart.

A pack of reporters shoved her aside as they bullied their way into the alley.

"Ouch!" Something hard and unyielding had ripped into her shoe. It scraped her little toe. She looked down. A nail stuck out of the sidewalk. From the bomb?

She freed her shoe, then wiggled and pulled the entire nail out of the concrete. When attached to the bomb, it was as lethal as a bullet. How many more were around, sticking out of sidewalks, cars, buildings . . . people?

But not in Sam. She didn't dare think about one of these being in Sam.

In case the police might need the nail as evidence, she started to put it in her pocket when the breath caught in her throat. Something was on the head of the nail.

It couldn't be.

Her hand quaked as she raised it to get a closer look. A letter was incised on the head. A *J*.

"Ohmigod!"

She looked down the alley, desperate to get to Sam and tell him about the nail. But there were too many people between them.

Now more than ever she had to get to Jacob. And she had a good idea where to start.

She limped away from the crowd, which continued to swell as more reporters, police, and firemen arrived. Helicopters buzzed overhead, adding to the uproar. She had to hike two long blocks from all the commotion before she was able to hail a cab. After giving the driver the address, she sat back, taut, determined, regretting Sam hadn't returned her gun, wishing she had her old Winchester shotgun in the gun cabinet at home.

* * *

The huge black federal mobile operations truck had been relocated to the front of the Hackers Coffee Slop. It was a lot roomier and more hi-tech than its NYPD counterpart. Plusher, too, with leather chairs and highly polished wood trim on the tables and countertops, though it could use a few deodorizing trees. A stench of sweat, fear, and panic competed with the stale odor of coffee and tobacco, though no cigars or cigarettes were evident. With the news media outside, the federal mandate to maintain a tobacco-free environment was suddenly enforced.

The EMS had already removed the nail from Sam's leg. Initially they wanted to take him to a hospital, but Sam wasn't going anywhere until he had a chance to talk to Runyon McCullogh. They'd cleaned out the wound, put a couple of butterfly bandages over the puncture to hold the skin together, and insisted he get a tetanus shot ASAP. They cautioned him to see a doctor if the wound swelled or reddened further.

He'd kept the nail, not so much as a trophy but a reminder to catch the bastard who was responsible for putting it in his leg. Like Calvin, a nail had become a memento.

As for his ears, he still couldn't hear very well, but as the minutes passed the muffled words became clearer.

Tony handed him a coffee before sitting in one of the expensive leather chairs next to him. Both looked to the front of the truck where *His Excellency* stood talking with Captain Freeman. Maybe yelling was more appropriate. Their lips opened wider than regular talking mouths. By the way Tony winced now and then, the Feds were declaring war on the NYPD. He and Tony were in a shitload of trouble.

Sam couldn't care less. He kept thinking back to how many people he had saved. One in particular—Gillian. Why the hell had she been there? And where was she now? Back at the courthouse? Hell, for all she knew, he could be laid up in ICU or on a slab in the morgue. He wanted to believe she felt something for him, but her absence roared through the ringing in his ears, telling him she didn't.

He tried to convince himself it didn't matter what she did or didn't do. But it did.

The muffled sound of two people yelling drew his attention back to his surroundings. Lieutenant Winslow and Captain Freeman were still going at it. Sam figured they couldn't be any angrier than he was. Once again he had been forced to dispose of a bomb just before it went off. What made him fume was the fact that the city was crawling with Feds who were better trained than he was on how to handle bombs, and they had chosen to back off and adopt a wait-and-see attitude.

If only he could figure out why the Carpenter kept handing out bombs.

Was it a coincidence that Gillian was once again in the vicinity of one?

As the unanswered question swirled around in his mind, his eyes took in the banks of monitors before him. Each showed a crowd of people gawking in the same direction. Agents sat in front of the monitors, watching the images and highlighting each individual face.

He asked Tony, "What are they doing?"

Tony leaned into his ear and said loudly, "During the bombing, they recorded the people outside the Hackers Coffee Slop. According to these experts, nine times out of ten a bomber will stick around to admire his work. They're feeding the face of every single person in the crowd to a computer that'll determine if any of them matches the image from the security recordings at the Port Authority bombing."

"Interesting," Sam said, though the process seemed tedious and boring. He was glad he didn't have to do it.

As he and Tony waited to be officially told they could leave, he leaned back and scanned the monitors. He was idly looking for anyone familiar when Van Decker sat down next to him.

"You sure your first name is Samson?" Van Decker asked. "I could swear it's Stupid."

"I heard that," Sam said.

"Good because that's the nicest thing you're going to be hearing for a long time." All three glanced to where Captain Freeman and Lieutenant Winslow were still arguing over who had jurisdiction over Sam's ass. "If you live that long," Van Decker added with a smirk.

"We've been in worse trouble," Tony said.

Maybe not, Sam thought. Strangely, he didn't mind a possible reprimand, demotion, or suspension. But all of them would be tough on Tony and his family. He couldn't let that happen. Somehow, he'd keep his partner safe from whatever repercussions were coming down the drain.

"Did you have a chance to talk with Runyon McCullogh?" Sam asked Regis.

"Yeah. The team's still with him, checking out his story. Why do you ask?"

"Did he say *where* the Carpenter gave him the bomb?"

"Right outside the Hackers Coffee Slop. Says the Carpenter almost seemed to be waiting for him. Came right up to him, told him to go inside and wait for a blonde in a short green dress to show up. After she took the bomb from him, he'd be free to go."

"A blonde in a short green dress? That's a new one."

Van Decker shrugged. "The caddie in Starbucks got nervous and phoned 911. Maybe the Carpenter devised the story of the blonde as a fantasy image. You know, something to look forward to, make the caddie hesitate long enough so he wouldn't call for help."

"Sounds more like the Carpenter didn't have time to come up with a convincing story. You get the feeling this bombing wasn't as well planned out?"

Van Decker nodded. "This caddie was picked right at the site instead of being sent there. No chance for the Carpenter to attach a wire under the caddie's shirt and on his chest—it would've attracted too much attention doing it directly in front of the café. He merely slipped it into the chest pocket of Runyon's shirt. Not slick at all."

Almost as if he decided to do it at the last minute." Sam glanced absently at the video displays. "He's not sticking with his original pattern of behavior."

"Like throwing the bomb in the Port Authority instead of giving it to a caddie," Van Decker said.

"All the earmarks of someone coming unglued," Tony added.

"There's another thing," Van Decker said. "The caddie's description of the Carpenter doesn't match. Not exactly. This time he's wearing a gray overcoat, with light red hair under a gray canvas hat. Didn't catch it on the P.A. tapes since they record in black and white."

"Had to get a different coat after leaving the tan one behind in the courthouse," Sam surmised. "Might have dyed his hair or is wearing a wig. But why color coordinate the hat with the coat? Guys really don't care about those things. You'd wear a tan hat with a grey coat, wouldn't you? Especially on short notice?"

Van Decker straightened the vest of his three-piece suit. "Some men like to look good all the time."

"While some don't even have to try," Tony said, adjusting his green twill jacket with mustard stains on the front.

Sam chuckled. "Yeah. Some of us are naturals."

Van Decker wasn't amused. "Not to stereotype, but he could be gay as we previously suspected."

"I'm not sure whether—Hey!" Sam bolted out of his chair and pointed to one of the monitors. "Did you see that?"

"See what?"

Sam looked at the man operating the monitor. "Can you back it up a few frames?"

The technician looked at Van Decker and waited for his assent. Only takes orders from other Feds, Sam realized.

"What are you looking for?" Van Decker asked as Sam peered closely at the monitor. He got up and moved closer. So did Tony.

Sam kept his gaze riveted on the display as the people started moving backwards one frame at a time. "I thought I was hallucinating after the bomb went off. A concussion or something. I mean, a black leprechaun? Here in Manhattan? But look." His finger touched the monitor as one person backpedaled into view. "There he is."

Tony squinted. "Looks like a Hasidic Jew. A black Hasidic Jew."

"You're right," Sam said.

"Didn't know blacks converted to Judaism," Tony said.

"Except for the Black Hebrews who believe they're descendants of a lost tribe of Israel, they don't," Van Decker said with a dismissive tone. "That's just Jacob Miller. I thought the boys scared him off the other night. Not too well, by the looks of it. Must have been following Gillian."

"Jacob Miller?" Both Sam and Tony turned to Van Decker. "You know this guy?"

"Actually, I know *her*. That isn't a man. It's a woman posing as a man. Her real name is Michelle Johnson."

"Holy saints. This gets weirder all the time," Tony said. "A black woman posing as a man posing as a Hasidic Jew. Only in New York."

"Dr. Jacob Miller is a woman?" Sam said in disbelief. "And he—she—was following Gillian, and you knew about this?"

"Happened the other night at Gillian's hotel," Van Decker said. "Gillian told her to get lost. So did the guards. Michelle, when she's Jacob, can be a real pest, but she's basically harmless."

Sam stared at the monitor, at the woman posing as a male Hasidic Jew. The effects of the bomb blast still made thinking fuzzy, difficult to concentrate for long, especially with a raging headache, but something was trying to get through. "I think I've seen him . . . her before. Yeah. Outside Gillian's hotel the other evening. He was in the shadows. I thought the guy just had a real dark tan."

Van Decker said, "That would prove my assumption that Jacob's been trailing Gillian."

"Okay, but I could swear I've seen him somewhere else, too." Sam closed his eyes, trying to get a fix on where. He remembered people crying and a lot of muffled noise in the background like now. But this time it was from his damaged ears. The other time was . . . was . . .

He opened his eyes and stared at the monitor where Jacob Miller stood frozen in front of a crowd.

"He was at Port Authority!" Sam said.

"Are you sure?" Van Decker asked.

"On the outskirts of onlookers with some other Hasidics. Only for a second—hell, the crowd kept shifting and he stood thirty yards away from where I was. But I swear I saw a black Hasidic Jew covered with dust. Could have been this Jacob-Michelle. If it was, this could break the case wide open."

"I don't see how."

"That's not too unusual for a Fed," Tony said.

Van Decker scowled at the remark, but Sam took it in stride as the prevailing attitude between locals and Feds. "Okay. Jacob's at the P.A. after the bomb went off. Could have been there during—I don't know. Today the camera catches him outside the Hackers Coffee Slop. And, after the bomb goes off and the bells are ringing in my head, I see him giving Runyon a hug. Then he takes off."

"Are you absolutely certain?" Van Decker asked. "The paramedics said you're suffering from a mild concussion. You could have imagined him in the alley."

Sam waved away his doubts. "Gillian was at the Slop. Ask her. Maybe she saw him."

At the mention of Gillian's name, Van Decker looked away. Sam saw it, and the hair rose on the back of his neck. "Where's Gillian?" he asked.

Van Decker wouldn't look at him. Sam got in his face. "Where is she?"

"I, uh, don't know. After the explosion, her guard momentarily lost track of her."

"Momentarily?" Tony looked at his watch. "The bomb exploded almost an hour ago. Crap. We left Gillian inside the courthouse for a few minutes, and you had us replaced. At least then we knew *where* she was."

Sam poked an angry finger in Van Decker's chest. "Where is she?"

"I told you, I don't know." The Fed looked more uncomfortable by the second.

"Is she back in court?"

"No. And she also hasn't returned to her hotel."

"Could the Carpenter have snatched her?"

"I doubt it." Van Decker winced under Sam's furious gaze. "It's not likely. He didn't try to snag her at the courthouse. Why would he now?"

"You said yourself this time he did things differently. Maybe that includes how he perceives Gillian. Maybe he wants to keep her up close and personal. An audience to come home to."

Van Decker firmly shook his head. "That would be a drastic change in his behavior. Too inordinate. I strongly believe he's not into kidnapping. Don't worry. I've got agents scouring the city for her. She'll turn up safe and sound in no time."

"She'd better." Sam pushed him away, angry at the Fed and worried sick about Gillian. He ran his fingers through his hair in frustration. He had been so close to her in the Slop, and now she could be anywhere: alone, scared, injured. Even dead.

No. She wasn't dead. He wasn't psychic, but he had to figure that somehow he would be able to sense if she had passed. What he did know was that she was in danger. He could feel it. And wherever she was, he wasn't there to protect her.

He had to find her, and fast.

He gestured at the bank of monitors. "Is she on any of these?"

Van Decker nodded. "There's a shot of her looking down the alley after the bomb went off." He spoke to the technician at the far end of the row who handed him a file of printouts. He leafed through them and handed one to Sam.

Gillian was balancing on tiptoe, trying to crane her head above the crowd. She was biting her bottom lip, peering intently down the alley. The one person in the curious crowd who appeared worried. About him? He'd like to think so.

When no one was looking, Sam slipped the photo inside his jacket. "What's the connection between this woman who poses as Jacob Miller and Gillian?" he asked Van Decker. "Why would she keep trying to see Gillian? And what did Gillian's guard say was the reason she decided to go the Slop of all places to have lunch?"

"Last question first. Gillian told her guard she had an appointment to meet someone at the Slop. Never said who, but he claims she got the text message over her phone. She seemed excited about it, and a bit anxious. As for Michelle, well, she's one of those schizophrenics who believe they have multiple personalities."

Sam and Tony exchanged knowing looks.

Sam asked, "You mean Dr. Jacob Miller is one of Michelle's alters?"

Van Decker seemed surprised by Sam's correct use of the term *alters*. "That's what Michelle claims."

"What's her connection to Gillian?"

"From what Gillian's told me, when Michelle is Jacob she has this insatiable curiosity about Ray Andrew Follett, what you might call a serial-killer groupie, one of thousands in this country who obsess about a killer and his victims, studying every nuance, every fact of the case and trial, consumed with an unrelenting desire to be an expert about a famous murderer. There's a guy in upstate New York who has two whole rooms of his house covered with clippings and photos of Ted Bundy and his victims. Anyway, that's why Michelle tried to see Gillian at the hotel the other night. According to the guard's report, *Jacob Miller* told Gillian he wanted to talk to her about Follett."

Sam rubbed his chin. Everything Van Decker was telling him about Michelle's obsessive behavior didn't gel with the mountain of information about MPD/DID he had found on Dr. Jacob Miller's website. The stuff there was clearly the work of a meticulous academician, not someone excessively preoccupied with a serial killer.

But then Van Decker didn't believe MPD/DID was a valid mental disorder.

To give the devil his due, up until yesterday neither did he.

"Excuse us a second." Sam took Tony aside and said to him, "I want you to call Roger T. Walgood's widow."

"And ask her if her husband had multiple personality disorder," Tony said. "I'm way ahead of you."

"Good. But, Tony, just ask if he had MPD/DID. Don't spell it out for her, okay?"

"Anything you say." Tony got out his notebook and phone and stepped a few feet away.

Sam turned to Van Decker. "I think Michelle Johnson is connected to this case. Do you have a current address or phone number on her?"

"Why? What's her connection?"

"Get me an address and number, and I'll tell you."

Van Decker looked ready to refuse. But the guilt of not knowing where Gillian was obviously weighed heavily on his mind. His shoulders sagged, and the sigh that followed was clearly audible. He said, "I'll see what I can do," and left to talk to a member of his team.

While waiting, Sam shifted around to study the video monitors on the off-chance he might spot someone else familiar in the crowd—and found himself face to face with Lieutenant Winslow. Cold fury frosted his superior's bloodshot eyes. He raised a finger and pointed it a half inch from Sam's nose.

"Don't speak," he said. "Not a word. You shut your sorry ass and do exactly as I say. You go home. You don't talk to anyone: no reporters, no photographers, no fellow officers, your dad, your brothers, your sister, NO ONE. Do I make myself clear?"

Sam opened his mouth to reply when the menacing finger zeroed in a centimeter from his nose.

"Were you going to say something, Detective Brankowski?"

Sam eased his head back away from the finger and shook it respectfully in negation.

"That's the first goddamn smart thing you've done today. Jeesuz! There's a reason we have procedures, Detective. Do you know what type of media circus is going on outside this truck? You're a shittin' hero to this city, and I don't want one. Not while this Carpenter is running lose. Heroes make people relax. They get careless, makes them an easy target 'cause they start thinking that no matter what they do, you'll come rescue them, like you did in the subway and now here. That's not going to happen anymore, is it, Detective?"

Sam shook his head.

"Because if it does, when your fifteen minutes of fame has come and gone and everyone forgets your stupid stunt today and moves on to the next person in the spotlight, I'll shove you down to high school hallway patrol until you're old enough to retire. Got it?"

Sam nodded.

"Now I've got to go out there and make everyone believe you've already gone home for the day. Calm things down. Keep this from turning into an idiotic reality show. First thing in the morning—you—in my office."

In a flurry of expletives that made even some of the Feds cringe, Lieutenant Winslow exited the truck. As the door closed, Sam could hear the media clamoring for sound bites.

After their boss left, Tony rejoined Sam. "I asked Mrs. Walgood if Roger was MPD or DID. She said, and I quote, 'No.'"

"That means he was."

"How do you figure?"

"Until today, did you know what MPD/DID was?"

"No."

"Exactly. But Mrs. Walgood didn't ask what you meant by MPD or DID, which means she knows enough about it to say no. And that means she knows, or knew, someone with it. I'm betting it was Roger."

"Seems like a long shot."

"That's why we're going to ask this latest caddie the same question. Where are they keeping him?"

"He's in the other command post."

"The Feds have two trucks like this?"

"Three if you count ATF's."

Sam and Tony headed for the door. Van Decker caught up with them. He handed Sam a slip of paper. "That's Michelle's last three known addresses."

"She moves around a lot," Tony remarked.

"Don't know if the top one is current," Van Decker said. "She no longer has a landline in her name."

Sam asked, "Can you call the super of the building at that address to verify she's still there?"

"I could, if you can convince me why I should waste one of my people's time finding out. I still don't see what this has to do with the Carpenter."

Sam crooked a finger. "Follow us."

The three exited the truck. The crowd of reporters and cameras were down the street, moving away from them while hounding Lieutenant Winslow on his way to the NYPD mobile control center. Sam, Tony, and Van Decker headed in the opposite direction and entered another converted truck. In a Plexiglas walled-off area, Runyon McCullogh was being questioned by four Feds. Outside the room, other agents were looking at his laptop, downloading every file, message, address, and graphic it contained, searching for clues as to why the Carpenter picked him to be the caddie this time.

"I'd like to talk to him alone," Sam said.

Van Decker grunted. "In your dreams."

Sam faked a hurt look. "You don't trust me. Why, because I'm a New York cop?"

"Because you're full of yourself. And because you're a New York cop."

"What if I tell you this may help us find out where Gillian is?"

"Then for sure I'm going in with you."

"Fine. Have it your way. But on one condition: you don't say a word. I do all the talking. Agreed?"

"Not on your life."

Sam stared grimly at Van Decker. "Not my life. Gillian's."

Van Decker's eyes clouded over, and he frowned. After a long pause, he nodded deeply in consent. He entered the interrogation room and asked the members of his team to grab some coffee for a few minutes. In the meantime, Sam got a notepad from a nearby desk and tore off two sheets. He wrote a question on each.

Tony read what was on them and smirked. "Neat trick. Van Decker'll be pissed."

"Hey, do unto others as they do unto you." Sam folded each sheet and palmed them. "He doesn't trust us, why should we trust him? Gotta have leverage or he won't cooperate."

Both Sam and Tony put on their best poker faces as the Feds filed out and headed for a coffee machine. Van Decker gestured to Sam that it was okay for him to enter the room.

Tony stayed outside while Sam sat down opposite Runyon. The man smiled briefly in recognition. He looked exhausted. Sam knew the only thing Runyon wanted to hear was that he could go home. It was written all over his face. Knowing the Feds, the poor guy would be here for at least another two hours.

Van Decker took a seat next to Sam, and Sam got right to the point. "Mr. McCullogh, I need you to answer two questions. The first one is personal and I regret having to ask it, but we believe someone else may be currently in danger from the same person who gave you the bomb."

He handed Runyon the first note. As he unfolded it, Sam could see Van Decker shift irritably, resentful of the silent communication between Sam and the witness.

The note read: Are you MPD/DID?

Runyon stared at the question. Then he stared at Sam. Fear and indecision racked his features. Unlike suspects who try to elude responsibility for their crimes by claiming to be MPD, it occurred to Sam that those who truly had the disorder kept their condition extremely private.

"Someone else's life is now in danger from the bomber," Sam reminded him.

"If anyone but you were asking . . ." Runyon rubbed his face with his hand. "Only because I owe you." He handed back the note. "The answer is yes, but I refuse to go into detail."

"You don't have to." Sam handed him the second folded sheet. Van Decker grumbled and shifted in his seat even more.

Apparently anticipating this question would be worse than the first, Runyon's hand trembled slightly as he opened it. Upon reading the question, the tense lines on his face softened. He looked at Sam. "Yes, I know Jacob Miller."

"Shit!" Van Decker jumped to his feet.

Sam told the Fed, "Maybe now is a good time to verify where Michelle is living."

Van Decker was already out the door and yelling at his team to do just that. In the burst of activity, Tony slipped into the room and closed the door. Sam introduced his partner to Runyon.

"The Feds are going to ask the same question," he told Runyon, "but I'd like to hear the answer first. How do you know Jacob Miller?"

"I first met him at group."

"Group?" Tony asked.

"As part of our therapy, several of us with DID get together every week to share what's been going on with us and our alters; how well we're handling sharing time without it interfering too much with our families and careers.

"On average, few DIDs are women, so right away Michelle stood out in a group of all men. The first time Jacob Miller came out—wow. What a smart guy. You'd think he was from Harvard or Princeton. The guy knows his stuff. Not only did he become our group expert on the disorder, he's now a respected national authority. His chat room is invaluable to those who live too far away from other DIDs to be able to have group therapy."

Tony said, "Forgive my ignorance, but isn't it kind of strange, at group, to be seeing this woman Michelle while some guy named Jacob is talking from her?"

"Not at all. When an alter comes forth, the person's entire body changes—features, mannerisms, voice. When Jacob talks, I don't see Michelle. It's almost like Jacob is transposed over her. It's hard to explain, but once you see it in person, you understand."

Runyon lowered his voice and leaned toward Sam and Tony. "Even now, Cynthia, my teenage alter, is begging to talk to you guys about Michelle. She loves how Michelle cornrows her hair, sometimes with beads. She wants to have the same done to our hair—like I'll ever have that done. Jeeze, I'd be fired on the spot if I came to work with cornrows."

"Cornrows?" Sam tried to picture the black Hasidic Jew he'd seen on the monitor without a hat and with thin tight braids. "How long are Michelle's cornrows?"

"Wait." Runyon's face momentarily went blank as if he was listening to someone. Then he sat up, rhythmically shook his shoulders from side to side, and brushed back his short hair as if preening in front of a mirror. His eyes sparkled, and a perky, almost feminine smile brightened his face.

"They are such a buzz," Runyon gushed in a cheery, high-pitched voice.

Sam and Tony looked at each other as if questioning whether they had just entered the Twilight Zone.

Runyon—or was it now Cynthia—continued. "Length, let's see, they go down to her shoulders." Runyon gestured gracefully with his fingers to his own shoulders. "Longer when she has extenders weaved into them. Then she pulls the sides to the back of her head with a gorgeous mother of pearl clip."

"Long cornrows," Sam said, thinking out loud. "And Jacob is short—I mean, Michelle would be classified as petite in stature, right?"

"Now you're cooking. She's a pretty little thing. Exotic high cheek bones. Wished I looked like her."

"Do you know where Michelle lives?"

"Sorry, can't help you there."

"What about where she works?"

Runyon twirled the hair by his temple as if he was trying to put some curl into the short strands. "She's got this boring job at the courthouse. A real yawner. She's gonna get a big fat ass if she stays there."

"Yes!" Sam slammed his hand down on the table.

Runyon sat back, startled. Tony, however, calmly asked Sam, "Fat asses turn you on?"

"What? No." Sam turned to Tony. "The courthouse. This Michelle. We both saw her at the courthouse the day the bomb went off. She was one of the women in the john. Remember?"

"Vaguely. Black dress?"

"That's her. I think." Sam turned back to Runyon and noticed the man looked puzzled. "Cynthia?"

"She left," Runyon said. "Doesn't like loud noises. Your hand hitting the table . . . it reminded her of something."

"Sorry," Sam said.

Runyon crossed his arms defensively, maybe even protectively of his teen-aged alter, and said, "It's all right, but don't do it again."

"Sure. No problem. I was going to ask her, or you, if you happen to have a picture of Michelle on you."

Runyon shook his head. "There might be one on file at the Institute of Many Friends."

"What's that?" Tony asked.

"The group used to meet at Michelle's apartment when we first started. But then, as Jacob began coming out more and more, well, he kind of took over, so now we meet at the Institute. Don't get me wrong. Jacob's a good guy. His heart is in the right place, but he can get demanding. Michelle has a terrible time making him stick to his scheduled time out."

"Scheduled time out?" Sam asked.

"A lot of alters feel a need to experience the world in person, not just through the eyes of the dominant personality like myself. It's hard to explain, but the thing is, unless I respect Cynthia and some of my other alters' right to manifest their own personality from time to time, they can become rebellious and sabotage my personal life—come out whenever they wish. You don't know how easily I can lose a customer if Cynthia pops up, preening in front of the client and complaining that she needs to get her nails done. But if we all agree to a schedule, then no one manifests at an inappropriate time."

Tony scratched his head. "So, that's what just happened to you?"

"Not at all. Cynthia knew the answer to your partner's question, so I allowed her to answer."

Sam glanced at Tony, amazed at what DIDs had to deal with on a daily basis.

Runyon continued. "The major exception to the schedule is stress. Or danger. Then there's no telling who may come out. Usually the one most capable of handling it, but not always."

Sam sat up, intrigued yet not certain he fully understood what Runyon had just said. "You were handed a bomb, Mr. McCullogh. That's a very stressful, dangerous situation. But you were the one I talked with. You were the one emailing the police."

"That's right. But it wasn't easy. At first Drina wanted to deal with it. She's my toughest alter, but I didn't think a biker chick could keep her head. All she wanted to do was pound on the Carpenter's face and kick him in the balls. Not the best solution when the bomber has a remote in his hand, ready to detonate the bomb if I don't do as I'm told. My other alters convinced Drina to back off and let me deal with it."

Tony said, "When you and these other alters were arguing with Drina about who was going to handle the situation, were all of you taking turns talking out loud?"

"Doesn't work that way. Besides, people would think I was nuts if I did that, which I'm not. No, everything happens inside my head. Can get a little crazy at times, especially when everyone's trying to talk at the same time, but that rarely happens. Usually just one or two talks."

Sam asked, "Is it always the tough alter who comes out when someone with DID is stressed or feels threatened?"

"Not always. Sometimes you just got to cry and let it all out. Or escape from adult responsibilities and go play for a while. Children are good at that. That's why at group we have one area with toys and coloring books. Sometimes it's good to let the kids out."

Sometimes it's not, Sam thought, remembering the tragic result of Chris Bonaventure's child-alter Gerta coming out to handle the stress of holding a bomb. Bonaventure probably thought no one would refuse to help a child. Certainly no one in their right mind would be so evil as to blow one up.

Except for the Carpenter. But then the creep probably didn't know he was killing a child when he killed Chris Bonaventure.

Sam recalled the childlike drawing Roger T. Walgood had made when pressured to tell the police what the Carpenter looked like. The stress of hours of interrogation must have forced the child alter to come out and handle things. It would explain why Walgood refused the offer of coffee and doughnuts but readily accepted a candy bar.

"Can I have the address of this Institute of Many Friends where your group now meets?" Sam asked.

Runyon took out his wallet and produced a business card with the place's address, phone and fax numbers, and email address. He handed it over. "It's a nice place. As I was saying, we used to meet at Michelle's until Jacob started taking over the group. Most of us decided to look for a more neutral setting. With Jacob's help, we got a grant and rented a small brownstone. Since then, we get funding from an anonymous philanthropist who we suspect is secretly DID. The Institute is now the leading information referral center on DID in the Northeast. Even has a twenty-four hour hotline and a chat room. Jacob runs the chat room during his scheduled time out."

Tony alerted Sam with a flick of his thumb that Van Decker was headed back to the room.

Sam quickly showed Runyon the list of addresses that Van Decker had given him. "Do you know if Michelle is living at any of these?"

"She's back at the bottom one. "

"One more thing. Do you know why Jacob was at the Hackers Coffee Slop today?"

Van Decker entered the room as Sam asked the question. Runyon looked at the FBI agent, then looked down, clearly not as comfortable discussing anything related to his disorder as he was with Sam and Tony.

"Answer the detective," Van Decker ordered him.

Runyon frowned. He nodded, more to himself, or perhaps to someone inside himself, than to anyone in the room. "Jacob asked me to meet him there on my lunch hour, which surprised me since that's not his usual scheduled time out. Said he had to warn me about something, that my life was in danger. I don't know how he knew, but he was right. After the bomb went off in the alley—thanks to you," he looked at Sam in gratitude, "Jacob showed up, gave me a hug—more of a Michelle hug than a Jacob hug—and told me to go home and stay home until the bomber was caught. That's all I know."

Van Decker asked, "Do you know Gillian Dohr?"

"Doesn't ring a bell."

"What about Roger T. Walgood?" Sam asked. "Vincent Ragino, Christopher Bonaventure, or Omar Shattalah?" All the previous caddies of the Carpenter.

"Sorry, none of them are familiar," Runyon said, though he seemed to hesitate, as if he wasn't exactly sure.

"Not even from group?"

Runyon shook his head, yet Sam could tell something was bothering him.

"What about from Jacob's chat room?"

"Been thinking about that. We don't use last names when chatting, and quite often our alters don't have last names. Sometimes they use nicknames, so it's tough to know who you're actually talking to. There is one guy named Omar, I remember that. An unusual name in my circles, kind of distinctive to know someone called Omar. But I don't know his last name."

"Any regulars in the chat room named Chris or Vince, maybe Vinnie?"

Runyon's face brightened in recognition. "Oh yeah. Vinnie. I enjoy talking to Vinnie. What a card. Always good for a laugh. And there's a Chris—from Jersey, I think he said once. Loves football. Jets fan."

As Sam and Tony nodded at each other, Van Decker flew out of his chair yelling, "Shit! Oh, shit!" He rapped repeatedly on the Plexiglas and motioned the rest of his team to hurry back inside.

"What's up?" Runyon asked Sam, clearly upset by the agent's reaction. "What'd I say?"

Sam got up, as did Tony. "Mr. McCullogh, I suggest you cooperate fully with the Feds. Tell them everything they ask, no matter how personal. And take Jacob's advice. When the Feds cut you loose, insist that one of them take you home. Then stay there until we catch the Carpenter. Hopefully, this will all be over very soon."

Sam and Tony squeezed out of the interrogation room as the Feds started cramming inside. Van Decker was explaining to his team that Runyon unwittingly knew who the Carpenter was targeting. They were about to get a crash course in Multiple Personality/Dissociative Identity Disorder.

"You don't want to stay and hear what they're going to find out from Runyon?" Tony asked.

"I'm way ahead of them," Sam replied. He flipped open his phone and tapped in the numbers on the card Runyon had given him. "I was at Jacob's website this morning. The chat room is closed. You can't get access except through Jacob. He's the key. He knows what's going on. I bet my pension he has a pretty good idea who the Carpenter is."

Finally, someone on the phone said hello. A woman's voice.

"Hi. This is Detec—" Sam stopped before he finished saying detective.

DIDs were shy. Most were probably nervous around law enforcement. He softened his voice. "I'm Sam Brankowski. I'm looking for some friends of mine who might be there. One is Gillian Dohr. The other is Michelle Johnson, sometimes known as Jacob Miller—Dr. Jacob Miller."

While Sam waited for the person on the other end to check, Tony unwrapped a stick of gum and calmly shoved it in his mouth. Tony said, "You notice every time Van Decker gets excited, that one vein on the side of his forehead starts to jump?"

"Yeah. Guy needs to learn how to handle stress."

Tony chuckled. "Maybe meditate on his navel."

"Look at them," Sam said as he watched the team fire questions at Runyon. "If they don't settle down and take it easy with him, his biker-chick alter, Drina, is going to come out and let 'em have it."

Tony laughed. "Or, if he has a child alter, the kid will start bawling. Jeeze, with all I'm learning about these DIDs, I could get a degree in psychology, huh?"

"Still seems bizarre." Sam turned his attention to the phone as the woman came back on. "They're both there? Great. No, I don't want to talk to them on the phone. In fact, don't tell them I called. I want it to be a surprise. I'll be right over. And, listen, if either one starts to leave before I get there, make up an excuse to keep them there. Why? Uh . . ."

He struggled to come up with something that sounded reasonable and at the same time wouldn't provoke suspicion. He happened to glance at Runyon, who was under constant bombardment of questions from the Feds. The tall man was actually shrinking in his chair. He remembered what Runyon had said about the Institute.

Sam lowered his voice to a meek timbre. "It's very important I talk to them there, in a *neutral setting*. Yes. Thanks."

Sam hung up. "Gillian and Jacob are at the Institute. Let's go."

Chapter Eighteen

The nail from the explosion at the Hackers Coffee Slop remained clenched in Gillian's hand as she watched the petite African-American complete her outward transformation from Jacob Miller to Michelle Johnson.

They were in the third floor restroom of the Institute of Many Friends. Michelle's alter, Jacob, was already gone by the time Gillian arrived. The multitude of dark cornrows, which had been tucked inside Jacob's flat-brimmed hat, were now neatly drawn back and fastened with a mother of pearl clip, falling in rivulets down the woman's back.

After Ray's death, Gillian had spent months talking with Jacob both on the phone and online. She could easily recognize him by his photo on the literature he'd sent, but this was the first time she had met his primary personality, Michelle.

The long black overcoat, which Jacob had worn over Michelle's black pantsuit, was now turned inside out to reveal a stylish, feminine-tailored coat in a geometric orange, black, and yellow African motif.

As Michelle folded up Jacob's collapsible hat and shoved it inside a pocket on the black inner side of the coat, Gillian pleaded again. "Please, Michelle, I have to talk with Jacob."

"Girl, I told you before, it's not going to happen." Michelle tossed the coat across one of the sinks and opened a small cosmetic bag. "He's had his time out, and then some. I've missed so much work these past few days because of him not sticking to the schedule, I'm lucky I haven't been fired."

Facing a mirror, Michelle proceeded to apply a thick layer of burnt orange lipstick to her expansive lips.

Gillian screamed silently in frustration. The moment she told Michelle that she was an acquaintance of Jacob's, an icy wall of indifference had met her request to see him.

"Michelle, I'm almost certain Jacob has important information about the Carpenter—the man who's turning people into bomb hostages in the city."

The petite woman raised a skinny eyebrow in disbelief, then shrugged and started applying mascara to her lashes.

"We have to stop the Carpenter before he kills again! Jacob can help. Why won't you let him try?"

"Why?" Michelle said, her voice rising as she pivoted to Gillian. "Why?" she said again, hands on her hips. "Because I don't care. This is *my* life. *My* body. I don't have anything to do with the bomber. He only goes after men. As long as Jacob stays inside, we have nothing to worry about. The police will catch him, eventually. It's their job. Not yours. Not mine. And certainly not Jacob's."

Michelle returned to the mirror and finished coating her lashes.

Gillian studied Michelle's reflection. At the height of her furious rebuttal, two red cuts had appeared through the dark makeup on the woman's forehead. They were barely noticeable; as if to hide their presence, several cornrows were draped over them.

"Are those stitches?" Gillian asked.

Michelle stiffened. She angled her head away and finished making up her eyes with sienna shadow. "That's none of your business." But her nervous movements said otherwise, and now Gillian detected other, scarcely noticeable scratches on her cheeks, nose, and neck.

"Were you at one of the bomb sites?" she asked.

Michelle refused to answer. Gillian smiled inwardly. She could read reactions as easily as some people read books.

"You were, weren't you?"

Michelle lowered her head, her mouth tight and unresponsive, her shoulders hunched. All indications of a guarded, defensive mode.

The cuts were fresh, Gillian noted, so not the first bombing or the one in the subway. "Were you at the courthouse bombing?"

In irritation, Michelle flung back the braids on her shoulders, a silent message that she wished to do the same with Gillian.

The gesture activated a memory, and Gillian clicked her tongue in sudden realization. "Of course. You weren't *outside*. You were *inside*. You came out of the restroom with the other women while the police were searching for the bomber. But that's not where you got injured, was it? It was somewhere else. More recent."

Michelle flinched. A muscle jerked in her jaw from clenching her teeth. A possible *yes*, yet also a defensive *no*. The woman glanced uneasily at Gillian in the mirror, the first stirrings of fear evident in her eyes.

Gillian scrutinized Michelle's face. The woman exhibited the same haunted, tired look Sam had right after the Starbucks bombing.

"My God, you were in the Starbucks when the bomb went off!"

That did it. Michelle's stiff poise cracked, crumbling away as her shoulders scrunched together. She swallowed hard, fighting back tears, while her eyes grew wide and scared.

Michelle was still traumatized by the event.

Gillian stepped closer and gently said, "You were there, weren't you?"

"Not inside." Michelle wiped her nose. "I was outside the Starbucks."

The door to the restroom opened. Lilly, the Institute's receptionist, poked her head in, her silver blonde curls bouncing merrily. "Hi, Michelle. I thought I'd find you in here changing. There's someone downstairs asking for you. Or Jacob."

At the mention of her alter, Michelle scowled. She put her hands on her hips and grumbled. "All the time Jacob."

Lilly nodded with a smile, never losing her perky demeanor. She looked at Gillian. "He asked for you, too."

"Me?" Gillian said in surprise.

"He asked to see both of you. Seems a bit anxious. And insistent. I'll tell him you'll be right down." Lilly promptly left.

"Yeah, you do that!" Michelle yelled after her. She threw the mascara into the cosmetic bag and shoved it in a pocket in the Michelle-side of her coat. "Everybody wants to see Jacob." She looked at Gillian. "You're all the same."

In a huff, Michelle exited the restroom. Gillian followed, curious as to who would know she was here. She'd just thought about checking her pockets to see if her bodyguard had secreted a tracking device on her when she noticed Michelle heading away from the elevator that would take them downstairs.

"I thought the reception area is on the first floor," she said.

Michelle ignored her and kept walking down a hall to the back of the building.

She quickly caught up. "Where are you going?"

"Not to meet another one of Jacob's friends, I'll tell you that." Michelle made straight for a rear door marked Fire Exit.

"Suppose it's important?"

"Oh, I'm sure it is. When it comes to Jacob, everything and everyone is important. Except me." Michelle pushed open the heavy metal door and stepped onto the fire escape. She started down the metal stairs, not bothering to check whether Gillian followed.

Gillian was, but she wasn't happy about it. The gash from the nail hadn't been treated yet. With every step she took, her foot hurt more. She glanced down and noticed blood seeping through the fabric of her sneaker.

Any other time she would back off from someone who didn't want her around. But the nail still grasped in her hand and the pain were constant reminders that the Carpenter was somewhere in the city, ready to hand out a nail-laden bomb. She had to convince Michelle to let her talk to Jacob.

"What is your problem?" she asked Michelle as she trailed down the stairs behind her. "Why are you so angry?"

"Who says I'm angry? Life is great. Things couldn't be better. Nothing to worry about but me, Jacob, Tisha, Lin Lin, Godfrey, Olga, and Six of Twelve. My alters. You want one of them? You can have them. All them. Especially Jacob."

Michelle reached the bottom of the stairs and headed down the alley to the street.

Undeterred, Gillian went after her. "Why don't you like Jacob?"

"No reason. Nothing at all. Why should I care if people are always asking to see him instead of me?"

Gillian limped along in dismay. How could she broker a truce between warring alters when the only one she could talk to was Michelle?

"It must be tough living in the shadow of someone like Jacob," Gillian said, hoping a few words of sympathy would placate her. "After all, he's a renowned expert on MPD/DID. A lot of people who have the disorder, and their families and doctors, must find his knowledge invaluable."

"You got that right. Everyone wants to know what *he* thinks. As if I don't exist." Michelle came to the end of the alley. She turned onto the sidewalk.

Though wincing in pain, Gillian kept up. For a petite woman, Michelle moved far and fast when she was angry. Gillian had to get her to slow down, if not stop.

"I'm beginning to understand," Gillian said. "You're jealous."

Instead of slowing, Michelle quickened her pace and gestured wildly as she spoke. "Who wouldn't be jealous of Jacob? People are always trying to contact him, leaving him messages, sending him the latest literature on MPD/DID, inviting him to conferences." Michelle rounded the corner to go up the next street, her steps as swift as ever. "He gets all the attention, while I . . . I get . . ."

"Overlooked?"

Michelle's pace slowed.

"Rejected?"

"Yeah."

"Is that why you resent him? Because he seems to be more important than you?"

Michelle slowed her steps to a walk. "I don't resent him."

"No?"

"I'm afraid of him."

Alarmed, Gillian placed hand on her shoulder. Michelle stopped.

They had circled around and were now in front of the Institute of Many Friends.

"Why are you afraid of Jacob? Is he dangerous?" She grabbed Michelle by both shoulders and studied her in concern. "Has he hurt you?"

"Not yet. But he will."

"I don't understand. He seems like such a gentle soul."

"Just another one of his glowing qualities," Michelle said, her voice low and bitter. She shook herself free of Gillian's touch. "Another reason to keep him around. While me, I'm just a frigid bitch with a mother of an attitude. No one will miss me if I'm gone."

While Michelle chewed on her bottom lip and struggled not to cry, Gillian tried to make sense of what she was hearing. "You don't mean . . ." What was the term for it? It was on the tip of her tongue.

"Integration," Michelle said with a harsh laugh. "Ironic, isn't it, me being black and all. But this is one black person who hates the idea. My therapist has already integrated two alters into my personality. As the process continues, he's going to figure out it's more important to the world that Jacob should be the last remaining personality rather than me."

Tears coursed onto her cheeks. She swiped them away, but a new batch quickly took their place. "It's not fair. I'm the dominant personality. I should be the one who remains."

Confused, Gillian tried to comprehend what she was hearing while wondering if Michelle was exaggerating the problem. "That would never happen. Would it? After all, you have a woman's body. It seems natural the other alters would assimilate into a female personality—you."

Michelle snorted and dried her face with the back of her hand. "Ever hear of a sex-change operation? Jacob could turn me physically and mentally into a man. Within a few weeks of Jacob taking over, I would cease to exist forever."

She'd be psychologically dead, Gillian realized, astounded by the possibility. No wonder Michelle was so adamant that Jacob stick to his scheduled time out. The less he interacted with the world, the greater chance she had of staying the dominant and final personality. "I had no idea."

Michelle sniffed. "Your pity is noted. But I bet you still want to talk to Jacob, don't you?"

Gillian glanced down at the nail in her hand. "I'm sorry. It's a matter of life and death."

Michelle was starting to reply—something sharp and biting by the ugly snarl of her lips—when the world suddenly exploded. In a bright flash of light, the windows on the first two floors of the Institute shattered and blew out, followed by a suffocating blast of heat that knocked Gillian and Michelle to the ground. Shards of glass, brick, and wood rained down on them.

Gillian opened her eyes and saw Michelle on the sidewalk next to her. Sparkling pieces of glass littered Michelle's tight braids. Her chin and cheek were scraped and bleeding from hitting the sidewalk.

Gillian coughed from the dust in the air and asked, "Are you okay?"

Michelle wheezed and winced in pain as she raised her head. "What happened?" Smoke seeped out of the broken windows. Flames could be seen inside the structure, growing in intensity. "A gas leak?"

She met Gillian's knowing gaze and shook her head fiercely. "No! Not a bomb! Not here! This is the one place we all feel safe!"

Gillian got to her feet. Ignoring her own scrapes and bruises, she helped Michelle up. "Lilly said the man who wanted to see us seemed anxious."

"Oh, no! Lilly!" Michelle staggered to the front stone steps of the charred, flaming building. At the same time someone down the street screamed. Not a scream of pain or horror, Gillian realized. A cry of rage.

From down the street, a man stomped toward the Institute, his hands raised in fury. Though camouflaged in a grey overcoat and hat and reddish hair, she'd know him anywhere. The Carpenter.

She stood transfixed, amazed he had the hubris to confront them right in front of his latest massacre.

He reached into a bulging pocket.

Ohmigod! Another bomb!

Gillian raced to Michelle, who was picking her way through the debris on the stairs. She grabbed her arm. "We have to get out of here!"

"No way! These are my friends! I have to help them!"

Michelle tried to shake her off. Gillian refused to let go. "The Carpenter—the bomber—he's here! He's got another bomb!"

Michelle looked at her as if she were crazy. Gillian yanked her around and frantically pointed to the man hurrying up the street with something in his hand. Michelle peered at him—and froze.

Gillian swore. All the feistiness on Michelle's face was gone, replaced by a blank stare. The alters must be trying to decide who would be in control to face the oncoming threat.

"We don't have time for this." She hauled Michelle down the stairs and hustled her to the street. Michelle didn't resist, but she also didn't move fast enough to suit Gillian. If she kept dragging her feet, they'd never escape.

Barely twenty yards away, the Carpenter stopped and raged. "You bitches! I've had it with you—both of you! You keep ruining everything, but you won't get away this time!"

If she was alone, she could easily outrace the pudgy bomber. But with Michelle's present state of mind, running away was not an option.

She glanced around. Cars had stopped on the street. Some of the drivers were outside, gaping at the wrecked and smoking building. From neighboring brownstones, people poured out while others peered out of upper floor windows to see what had happened, some taking pictures with their phones.

Her first thought was to ask for help. But in the Carpenter's crazed obsession to get them, he was capable of anything. Anyone coming to their aid could easily die along with them. She wasn't going to let that happen. Enough people had already died because of him.

Instead, she pulled Michelle to the nearest car. The driver stood outside, reporting on his phone to a local station about what was going on. She eyed him with contempt. He should be running inside the Institute and taking out the wounded before the fire spread, not grabbing attention for himself.

She knew his type. All talk. Doesn't like to get personally involved. Avoids confrontations except for a few verbal ones.

She boldly reached around him and unlocked the rear passenger door. While continuing his on-the-spot reporting, he watched her with a dumbfounded look on his face as she opened the back door and shoved Michelle inside.

Michelle started whimpering in a little girl's voice. "No! No! I want to go home! I want to go home!"

Gillian shut the door, then pushed the driver out of the way so she could get in the front seat.

The driver grabbed her arm. "Hey, what do you think you're doing?"

She was still holding the nail. She pointed it straight at him like a dagger and said firmly in a deep, no-nonsense voice she had learned from her brothers, "Back off. I'm borrowing your car. You want to make something of it?"

He stared at the nail, then at the fierce determination in her eyes. He backed away.

She got in, slammed the door shut, revved the engine once, and put it in drive. "Put on your seatbelt, Michelle."

She held her breath, aimed the car straight at the Carpenter, and pushed the pedal to the floor. The tires squealed. The car sped forward. She was going to run over—kill—another human being. As much as she wanted to close her eyes at the last moment, she kept them opened, focused.

The Carpenter looked shocked. Then terrified. He panicked and threw the bomb at the approaching car. The last thing she heard before it exploded was the owner of the car yelling into his phone, "You're not going to believe what just happened! Some crazy bitch just stole my Lexus!"

Chapter Nineteen

Every time Sam unzipped a body bag, he held his breath and tightened his gut before looking at the face inside. He closed his eyes. A woman. A woman with silver blonde curls. Not Gillian.

He zipped the bag closed and exhaled a long, shaky breath. Not Gillian. Not yet.

His gaze drifted to the other black bags lying like garbage on the sidewalk, waiting to be hauled away.

Four down, two to go.

With each one he opened, his hands shook more.

Ignoring the pain in his calf, he stood up and moved to the next bag. He squatted beside it and opened the zipper. Oh, God! This was the worst one yet. An old man, the front of his body scorched, cruelly transformed into a human pin cushion. At least a dozen nails pierced his stomach and face. And the teddy bear.

Emotions normally kept fastened and secured while on the job, unraveled at the sight of the bear.

Since he first arrived at the Institute of Many Friends, he had been holding his own against the outrage building. But the bear—the small brown teddy bear held in a death grip to the man's chest—threatened to let loose all the feelings a cop isn't supposed to show in public. His eyes burned as he strained to fight back the tears. Even the bear hadn't been spared.

Someone placed a hand on Sam's tense shoulder. "That's Benny."

Sam looked up.

An elderly man stood by his side. Tears flowed unchecked down his soot-covered face. With his gaze fixed on the body, he said, "Jay Silverstone was his given name. But when he was Benny, he always had a bear with him." The man turned his sad gray eyes on Sam and asked, "What do you think? If an alter is manifesting when a person dies, does the alter go to heaven or the dominant personality?"

Sam zipped shut the bag and stood. "Maybe they all go together. A group thing."

"That would mean each alter has its own soul. We could start a whole new religion on that theory." The man tried to laugh at the absurd possibility but instead dissolved into a torrent of sobs.

Sam took him in his arms and held him . . . and let the man cry. He wasn't one to show compassion on the job. It interfered too much with his perspective. But he'd seen too much death during the last few days, been at too many bombings, not to offer a crumb of comfort. Especially now that it was personal.

He glanced over the man's shoulder at the last body bag and pleaded to the universe, God, whoever was in charge, *Please, don't let it be Gillian.* She'd yet to be accounted for, but he knew she had been here. What was left of the sign-in sheet for visitors and guests still bore her name.

He caught the attention of a paramedic, who gently took charge of the weeping man. With infinite care, she led him around the firemen putting away their equipment, and took him to a nearby ambulance where some of the wounded were being treated. The most severely injured were already in transit to hospitals. Two ambulances were getting ready to leave, and two more were just arriving.

Six had died inside the Institute. One outside. The caddie was still being scraped off the floor, walls, and ceiling. All the king's horses and all the king's men would never be able to put him back together again. The bomb had been especially big and nasty, enwrapped with at least a triple layer of nails. How could anyone be so vicious?

He glanced sidelong at the last body bag. Suddenly, he couldn't breathe, couldn't swallow, couldn't move. He didn't want to look in the last bag. He'd give anything not to.

He wanted to pound his fists into the Carpenter's face. Beat him until he was a quivering mass of bloody flesh that no one would recognize as being human.

He wanted to scream, "IT'S NOT FAIR!"

The bag waited. Insistent. Unyielding. Pitiless.

It took all his strength to step toward it. His heart throbbed madly as he lowered himself next to it and reached for the zipper. Blood pulsed in his ears, and his breath came in gasps.

He grabbed the zipper. Tony reached down and placed a steady hand on his trembling fingers. "Don't," Tony said.

Sam stared at the bag. "I have to."

"You don't. She's not in there."

His gaze flew up to Tony's. "How do you know?"

"Because someone fitting her description was seen driving away." Tony rocked back on his heels and smiled. "She's not dead."

The weight on Sam's heart lifted. He felt like shouting with joy.

"But she might as well be," Tony added. "According to Officer Lahey, she's a suspect wanted for, among other things, attempted murder—"

"What?" Sam said.

"Kidnapping, carjacking, assaulting the driver with a deadly weapon—a nail, no less." Tony looked at his notes and shook his head. "At least she's got good taste. Stole a Lexus. Four door. Leased. This year's model."

"I don't believe it. Gillian did all that?"

"Better face it. You're in love with a wanted woman."

Sam stared at his partner as if he had just calmly informed him that he was from the planet Mars. "Wait a minute. Who said anything about love?"

"The look on your face when I told you she wasn't dead. The stars in your eyes every time you see her. Or talk about her. You got it bad."

"You're dreaming."

"Maybe. But you've got bigger problems. As soon as someone attaches a name to her description and word gets around that The Oracle has an all points bulletin out on her, every cop in the five Burroughs is going to be after her. There'll be bragging rights as to who gets to nail her hide to the wall."

Sam winced. Tony's expression was painfully appropriate. Follett had nailed children to walls. The Carpenter used nails to rip people's flesh. Now Gillian was marked. If caught by the wrong cops, she'd be roughed up on the way to jail. Maybe even afterwards. Some cops were notorious for getting even for imagined, and not so imagined, wrongs.

Fear for her safety had Sam examining his surroundings with renewed energy. "What the hell happened here?" Sam asked Tony. "Kidnapping? Attempted murder?"

"Let me show you something."

"Wait." He looked at the last body bag. "No one deserves to go unnoticed."

He reached over and unzipped the bag. He stared down at the lifeless brown eyes staring back at him. A young woman with a nail in her neck, clothes drenched in blood.

He would have liked to have told the person he was sorry. But he wasn't. He was too grateful Gillian wasn't in the bag. He could only nod in acknowledgment of her existence. A victim whose silence asked for justice. Another face to haunt his nightmares.

He shut the bag. Tony led him to where police barricades had been set in a circle on the street a few feet from the sidewalk.

"Is that what I think it is?" Sam asked.

"A bomb crater." Tony's index finger circled the perimeter. "See the nails embedded in the bottom and sides of the cavity? Not as big of a bomb as the one that went off in the Institute. More like the one you had in the subway. Nails make devilish shrapnel. Four of the injured over there in the ambulance are linked to this bomb."

Sam studied the outskirts of the crater. "Where's the blood from the person who was holding this one?"

"Isn't any. Witnesses claim this one was thrown at the silver Lexus Gillian stole. Specifically, when she tried to run down a man in a gray overcoat and hat."

"You're joking." Sam didn't know whether to laugh or swear. He studied the street. Sure enough, he could see acceleration marks from tires headed directly for where the second bomb went off. "She went after the Carpenter! What a crazy thing to do!"

"Gutsy," Tony added. "She didn't get him—swerved when the bomb exploded—but it appears the car caught a good portion of the blast. And the nails." He pointed to the brownstones on the other side of the street. "With all the people standing around and looking out the windows after the first bomb went off in the Institute, no one on that side of the street got nailed—literally. The car blocked the force of the explosion."

Sam grinned in admiration of how many lives she must have saved. Gillian Dohr was full of surprises.

Or desperate.

"She saw him coming," he speculated. "After the bomb went off inside, she's out here and sees the Carpenter. Maybe sees he has another bomb. Like in the subway, she can't stand aside and do nothing. So she borrows the nearest car—"

"Steals it," Tony amended.

"Commandeers it to save lives and stop the Carpenter from getting away." Sam smiled. Van Decker was wrong. Gillian wasn't suicidal. If anything, she was far too heroic.

"So, if she's so altruistic," Tony said, "why not stay? She fled the scene."

"Maybe she panicked after the second bomb went off. High-tailed it out of here. What civilian wouldn't?"

He could see it in Tony's eyes. Gillian wouldn't. She'd face the Carpenter head-on—over and over again—until only one of them was left standing. Then why . . . ?

He snapped his fingers. "Who did Gillian kidnap?"

Tony grinned. "Wondering when you'd ask. Bet you already got that figured out. A small black woman with lots of long cornrows."

"Jacob's Michelle Johnson."

"The driver of the Lexus says she kept whimpering the whole time Gillian forced her into the car. 'No. No. I want to go home.' Stuff like that."

He scratched his head, thinking. "That's four places now that Jacob/Michelle has been when a bomb went off."

"And four places Gillian has also been," Tony said. "You get the feeling one of them is the target? And the caddies are secondary targets."

"It's starting to look that way."

A deep, ostentatious horn sounded from up the block. Sam and Tony turned to look. Both groaned in recognition. One of the federal command post trucks was headed their way, trying to get past the local police cars that had blocked off the street at the corners. The driver kept blowing its horn until the grating sound had the desired effect. One of the police cars moved so the truck could park closer to the scene.

"Finally got their fill of the Hackers Coffee Slop," Tony remarked.

"Or decided it was safe to venture into Brooklyn," Sam said.

"Before they take over, let me show you one last thing. Forensics already took a sample, but the Feds don't need to know that." Tony led him to the nearby sidewalk. A small area was delineated to prevent anyone from stepping on it.

Sam assessed the six red marks. "Blood spots."

"Yeah. The thing is none of the injured treated by the EMS were anywhere near this area."

He looked at the blood. Then at the crater in the street. Then at the tire marks. All made a straight line. He drew back his lips in a grin. "Damn. You think this is the Carpenter's blood?"

"The odds would make a bookie cry."

From a pocket, Sam dug out the nail that had been in his calf. He held it up. "I hope he got one of these in him. I hope he bleeds to death, internally, where it hurts the most. But just in case—"

"I know. Alert all area hospitals and clinics to be on the lookout for a man with a wound made by shrapnel or a nail." Tony went to their car.

Sam couldn't help but keep grinning. Finally, the Carpenter got a taste of his own medicine.

That's when he saw it for the first time. He'd been so busy getting treated by the EMS and dealing with the aftermath of his heroics at the Slop that he hadn't bothered to take a good look at the nail. He squinted, not sure what he was seeing. Was that a *J* scratched into its head?

Yeah. Then again, it could be an incidental scratch from when the bomb went off.

He ran to a nearby ambulance and asked for one of their latex gloves, then went to the crater in the street. With his Spyderco serrated edge knife, he dug out the nearest nail and picked it up with the glove. The head was damaged. Scanning the nails in the crater, he determined all the heads were damaged, mangled from the force and the heat of the bomb going off right on the street. He needed a look at a nail that hadn't been disfigured.

The solution was easy, yet difficult. With a deep sigh of regret, he headed for the body bags. He opened the one with the man holding the teddy bear. Benny. Using the glove, he gently, respectfully, extracted one of the nails from the bear. He looked at the head of the nail and swore. Another *J*. He pocketed both nails. "Thanks, Benny." He closed the bag and got up.

Tony returned. He looked over Sam's shoulder. "Van Decker is marching this way with an army of Feds."

"Good. I want to talk to him. He's been jerking us around, withholding an important piece of information from the case."

"About time you let him have it. Oh, crap! The Lieutenant's car just pulled up next to the Fed's command truck. Aren't you supposed to be home for the rest of the day?"

"Shit!" As much as Sam needed to talk to Van Decker, he couldn't let their boss catch him still working or he'd be taken off the case permanently. "Let's get out of here!" He and Tony dashed to their car.

"Where to now?" Tony asked as Sam got behind the wheel.

"I want to take a look at Van Decker's boards. Make sure I've got a goddamn good reason to be mad at him."

"You need a reason?" Tony asked with an amused smile.

Sam drove the rest of the way in silence, thinking about the *J* on the nails and wondering where Gillian was. When he got to the federal building, he double-parked and had Tony stay in the car to keep tabs on the radio. Upstairs, he went to the boards where the profiler categorized clues from the Carpenter case. He snatched the clear plastic bag with a nail from the very first bomb and turned it around until he could see the head.

A *J*.

Furious, he jammed the nail into the middle of Regis's desk. "You fuckin' bastard! If Gillian dies because you withheld information, I'll make you pay! Fuck!"

When he got back to the car, Tony had news for him. "They found the Lexus three blocks away from the Institute."

"And Gillian?"

Tony shook his head. "Nothing on Jacob-Michelle either. I've got calls in to see if a cabbie picked them up in the area. The car's in pretty bad shape. Couple of nails in the tires, broken side windows, nails in the doors. And blood on the inside. Not much," Tony quickly added as Sam glanced worriedly at him. "Some smudges on the pedals and some on the steering wheel. They're running the prints."

"She's injured," Sam said in a low, tense voice.

"Could be minor," Tony said. "Probably touched the wound with her hand, got some blood on her fingers, then touched the steering wheel before she had time to clean 'em off."

"Where is she now? Where would she go?"

Tony shrugged. "With Michelle in tow, maybe back to Michelle's place."

He shook his head. "The Feds have it staked out. If they show up there or at Gillian's hotel room, we'll hear about it. But I don't think she'd go to either place. Too well known. Can't risk the Carpenter looking for them there. If he's hurt, he's pissed. He's going to want to get even with her for trying to run him down. No, she's going to go someplace safe."

"Why not just turn herself in? Ask for police protection."

"To cops? The Oracle asking cops for help?"

"Yeah, right. Bad idea." Tony frowned. "Now what?"

He told Tony about the *J*s on the nails. Between a flurry of cuss words, Tony said, "Told you. Never trust a Fed. Never trust a Fed. Gillian can't trust them, either."

Sam nodded. "Only one person left who she can trust."

Tony smiled. "You."

He shook his head. "Calvin Moore."

Chapter Twenty

From out in the hall, Sam and Tony peeked into the courtroom. Neither Gillian or Michelle were inside. Calvin had just finished questioning a witness for the defense, and Stephanie was getting ready to cross-examine. Knowing her, she'd have at least a half-hour worth of questions.

Sam wasn't sure they had thirty minutes to spare before court recessed. Gillian and Michelle were on the run, and Gillian was injured. How badly, he could only guess. He had to find her before the Carpenter did.

He closed the courtroom door and turned to his partner. "None of the files on Follett mentions whether anything was inscribed in the nails used on the children. Because of Lieutenant Winslow, I can't get to Van Decker and ask him if any of the nails had a *J* on them. And the Fed's not answering his voice mail—at least not any from me." He stared at the doors to the courtroom. "Calvin Moore has a nail in his wallet from the Follett case. I need to find out if it has a *J* on it. But you know Judge Conway. Whoever disturbs the sanctity of his court will be found in contempt."

He glanced at Tony, uncomfortable with what he was about to ask his partner to do. "The thing is, whoever goes in there to talk to Calvin won't be able to keep looking for Gillian."

Tony waved a hand through the air as if he was brushing away a pesky fly. "Are you asking for a volunteer? No sweat.

I've been putting on a little weight lately." He patted his belly. "A night away from my wife's cooking will do me good."

"You know if there was any other way, I wouldn't hesitate to do it myself."

"Don't go gettin' mushy on me. We ain't married, and you've got a fugitive to find. And I don't mean the Carpenter."

"Thanks." Sam handed him a nail. "If Calvin refuses to cooperate, show him that."

Sam stood just inside the courtroom as Tony strolled down the aisle toward the lawyer. From the day he joined the force, Tony had cultivated a low profile. His unassuming air made witnesses and snitches tell him things they wouldn't tell anyone else. When undercover, it made him practically invisible—an everyman who could melt into a crowd. His real personality was known only to Sam, Tony's wife and kids, and his parents. So Sam wasn't surprised when nobody paid much attention as he approached the defense area. But when Tony boldly walked in front of the defense table, Sam slapped his own forehead.

Tony could have slipped in behind Calvin, tapped him on the shoulder, and explained what he wanted and why. True, the punishment for interfering in the court's business would have been the same. And maybe that's why Tony was doing it this way. He was an officer of the law, about to butt heads with a judge of the law. Equals. But since judges tend to think of themselves as superior, Tony probably decided to drive the point home.

Sucking in his gut, Tony flashed his shield in front of Calvin Moore's face and stated, "I'm Detective Torelli, homicide. I have reason to believe you possess a vital piece of evidence relevant to the Carpenter case. I need to see the nail in your wallet."

Calvin looked up at Tony in bewilderment. "What?" With hands raised in a gesture of confused innocence, he looked to the judge. "What's going on?"

From the bench, Judge Conway cleared his throat and called for order. "Officer, I demand an explanation."

Tony looked over his shoulder and waved a perfunctory finger at the judge. "In a minute, your honor."

Taken aback, the outraged judge spluttered and coughed and looked at his court clerk to see if she was incensed as he was. She rolled her eyes and wagged her head as if she was mutually offended by the improper conduct. The judge grunted in agreement. He banged his gavel and ordered the bailiff to escort the detective out of his courtroom.

Tony ignored both and turned his full attention on Calvin. "Mr. Moore, I don't have much time, so I'll only say this once. Gillian Dohr is missing. Sam and I believe she has one of these," he held up the nail, "embedded in her. If there's any chance of helping her, I need to see *your* nail now."

Sam gave the lawyer points for acting swiftly. As the judge angrily decreed Tony in contempt of court and ordered him removed and jailed, Calvin got out his wallet and produced the nail. Tony took it, looked at the head, then raised his thumb to Sam and nodded.

Tony handed the nail back to Calvin. He turned to the judge and said, "Forgive the intrusion, your honor. I meant no disrespect," then allowed the bailiff to carry out the judge's decree. He was led away, head high, demeanor equal to the judge, eliciting respect from everyone present.

The audience murmured, speculating as to what had just happened, but were immediately silenced by Judge Conway. To restore the integrity of his courtroom, and his pride, he sternly reminded everyone of the proper decorum when court is in session. But for all his posturing and admonishing speech, he was momentarily ignored by Calvin and Stephanie. Both had turned to look at Sam. Stephanie seemed curiously amused by Tony's antics and Sam's presence. Calvin appeared worried. He hesitated, as if not sure whether to stay or whether to leave with Sam and help him find Gillian. He glanced at his clients. With an expression teetering on guilt, he turned his back on Sam.

Calvin had made his decision. As Stephanie would say, "Priorities, Sam. Priorities."

They had theirs. He had his.

Before the judge realized he had been in on Tony's escapade and was sent to jail along with him, Sam promptly slipped away.

Sam drove to the station, thinking hard and fast. The inscribed letter on Follett's nails was a secret, but the Carpenter, who was supposedly passing out bombs on Follett's behalf, knew about the *J*. Since it never came out during Follett's trial, it meant only the investigating officers and FBI agents knew about the *J*s, and those the police had sent a nail to after Follett was killed: Gillian, Calvin, Follett's psychiatrist Newhall, and the lead attorney Jackson.

Could one of them be the Carpenter? Or had Follett had an accomplice no one knew about?

Either assumption sent chills up his spine.

And how was Michelle Johnson's alter Jacob Miller involved?

Could he be the Carpenter's target? Could it be related to the defense team's premise that Ray Andrew Follett had Multiple Personality/Dissociative Identity Disorder? It was starting to look like all the caddies had MPD/DID. What was the Carpenter's motivation for going after MPD/DIDs to carry his bombs? And why only MPD/DIDs who were men?

Who was the Carpenter's primary target?

Not Gillian. The Carpenter could have gotten to her any time during the past three years while she was living unprotected in Wyoming. He also could have killed her while alone with her in the courthouse.

No, his objective wasn't Gillian. Which brought his thoughts back to Michelle Johnson/Jacob Miller. One of them could be the target, but which one: Michelle the woman or Jacob the male alter? The latter would fit the MO of the caddies, but it still didn't answer the question why. What was the Carpenter's grudge against MPD/DIDs? And why take it out on those who lived in or near New York City?

The questions buzzed like a swarm of killer bees, stinging him with inconsistencies. He had to figure it all out before the Carpenter struck again.

When he got to the station, he made sure Lieutenant Winslow was nowhere around, then hurried to his desk. He called cab companies, checking if a taxi picked up two women—one white, one black—in the vicinity of the abandoned Lexus. He got lucky with the fourth company. The cabbie drove them all the way to Jersey, no less. To Newark Airport. Sam grunted in relief. They had gotten out of town on a plane. A fast, clean getaway.

"Which airline did he drop them off?" Sam asked.

While the dispatcher contacted the cabbie, Sam impatiently drummed his pen on the desk. He stopped in mid-stroke. Among the background noise of the police station, he'd heard someone mention Lieutenant Winslow's name.

No, not mention. Address him. Winslow was here.

Sam drummed the pen faster. "Come on, come on," he urged the dispatcher. He had to get out of the station before *His Excellency* saw him.

The dispatcher relayed the information.

"Are you sure?" Sam asked. "Will you repeat that?"

"Detective Brankowski!"

Under the wrathful gaze of Lieutenant Winslow, Sam thanked the dispatcher and ended the call. "I can explain," Sam told his superior.

"In my office, *now!*"

There are two occasions when the entire station is seized with silence: the death of a fellow officer and being bulldozed into Lieutenant Winslow's office. As Sam led the way, he could feel the sympathy flow from the other detectives, everyone sorry for him yet grateful they weren't in his shoes.

Inside the lieutenant's office, Sam remained standing as Winslow plopped down heavily into his cushioned chair. Not one to waste time, the lieutenant started right in. "You're not home."

"No, sir."

"I ordered you to go home."

"Yes, sir."

"I've been informed you were at the double bombing at the Institute of Many Friends."

"Yes, sir."

"I've also been informed that your partner, Detective Torelli, is currently in jail in contempt of court."

"Yes, sir."

"I understand Gillian Dohr is missing."

"Yes, sir."

"And that she stole a vehicle, kidnapped a woman, and almost ran down a pedestrian."

"That would be the Carpenter, sir."

"Excuse me?"

"The man she tried to run down, I believe it was the bomber, sir."

The lieutenant raised his bushy eyebrows.

"If I may explain, sir—"

"No, you may not. You disobeyed a direct order. I won't tolerate insubordination, not on my watch and not from one of my officers. I'm taking you and Detective Torelli off this assignment and giving it to Detective Richardson."

"But, sir—"

"As for you, you're on suspension for a week. And your partner for two days, after he gets out of jail, for going along with you."

"Sir, if I may explain about Tony and—"

"Zip it, detective. Give me your shield and your gun."

Sam had often daydreamed about turning in his shield and gun while telling *His Excellency* what he could do with them. Usually, he was angry or frustrated about some case. Or tired. Real tired, to the point he wondered what had ever made him want to be a police officer.

But to actually turn in his shield and weapon, not in anger or depression, but calmly, knowing it was the right thing to do . . . it had never occurred to him it would happen this way.

He handed over his shield, checked his gun to make sure the chamber was empty before putting it on the desk—and felt like he had just handed over a huge chunk of his soul.

Lieutenant Winslow settled back and said, "I just want one more thing from you and then I don't want to see you, hear you, or smell you around here for one whole week. One week. You got that, Detective Brankowski?"

"Yes, sir."

"Good. Now, do you know where Gillian Dohr is?"

"No, sir."

Lieutenant Winslow shoved his lips from one side of his face to the other then dropped them into a frown deep enough to rival the Grand Canyon. "I thought I told you to stay close to her," he growled.

"Yes, sir."

"Then you should have a good idea where she might be."

Sam hesitated. "Sir, as bad as The Oracle's reputation is, Gillian Dohr is a woman. And because she's a woman, every time I think I got her figured out, she says or does something that has me back at square one. She changes her mind like the wind. You're married. You know what it's like."

The lieutenant grumbled in agreement.

"And now she's got another woman with her. I don't know any man who can figure out what one woman's thinking, let alone two."

The lieutenant shifted in his chair and grunted. He rolled his tongue around in his mouth and mumbled something about his wife and her sister. He looked at Sam. "One week."

"Yes, sir. I'm already gone." The notches on the desk that marked the deaths of fellow officers caught his eye. No way was he gonna let the Carpenter add him to the row. As for Tony. . . Tony had been wrong. Partners *were* married to each other. Thanks to Judge Conway's *trial separation*, Tony was safely in jail, then suspended for a couple of days. With any luck, he'd be nowhere nearby when the Carpenter took his final bow.

As Sam headed for his desk, the unspoken questions in everyone's eyes asked, "Is it true? Are you suspended?" No one dared speak, not with the lieutenant watching through the windows of his office.

Sam rummaged through drawers. A few items pertaining to ongoing cases he put on Tony's desk. When he got to the street, he hailed a cab and kept it waiting at his apartment as he went inside. He packed an overnight bag, got out his spare gun and put it in his shoulder holster, then spent several anxious minutes searching his junk drawer for the permit to carry a concealed weapon on a plane. Without his shield, he'd need it.

En route to LaGuardia Airport, he called a reporter for the *Times* who Sam owed a favor for leaking information on a case that almost got a witness killed.

"Chuck? Sam Brankowski here. Listen, you know this Carpenter case? Yeah. Hot stuff. Got a source who says two of his targets recently fled the metro area. Yeah, the ones he sends the bombs to. Yeah, there is a method to his madness. Their names? Can't tell you. But I will say they were injured in the last attack but are currently safe and sound, headed south to hide out until the Feds get around to catching the bomber. How far south? Maybe Florida. No, I don't know what part of

Florida. No, you can't call me back if you have more questions. Yeah. Bye."

Sam tucked away his phone. The misinformation should take care of the Carpenter for a while.

He made small talk with the cabbie: the weather, the bombings, who would win the pennant, and how long it'd been since the driver left Bangladesh. Sam learned a lot about the guy's country on the way to the airport. By the time he was giving the guy a tip, Sam knew he was never going to visit Bangladesh. Sounded like a billion people living in a trash compactor.

Finding a flight to his destination was relatively easy, but it took him a bit longer to get through security with his gun. Without his shiny, official-looking shield, a flimsy sheet of paper seemed, well, a flimsy reason to allow a person to tote a gun on a plane. But eventually he got through and made the plane on time.

Take-offs never excited him much. Working the streets of New York seemed infinitely more dangerous in comparison. He was tempted to sleep, but his thoughts were too full of Gillian.

As the jet climbed high over the state of Pennsylvania, he could just make out the strip of Interstate 80 bisecting the state before it was lost below the clouds. Somewhere along that tiny, manmade line were Gillian and Michelle.

The cabbie who had picked them up after they abandoned the Lexus reported he'd dropped them off at Newark Airport—not at an airline but at Streamline Car Rental. Instead of flying away they had decided to drive. Why was anyone's guess. But Sam knew with certainty where Gillian was headed. It had been in Calvin's guilt-ridden gaze when he decided the trial was more important than safeguarding her life. With a friend like that, it was a good thing Gillian had taken matters into her own hands and escaped to where she had sought shelter once before.

He took out the photo he'd snatched from the Feds and studied Gillian's anxious face as she peered down the alley of the Hackers Coffee Slop. He ran one finger over her cheek.

She was going home to Wyoming. And he was going to be there when she arrived.

Chapter Twenty-One

With coffee, energy drinks, and a steady supply of crackers to munch on whenever she got sleepy, Gillian was able to drive straight through to Wyoming in less than two days. All in all, a noteworthy accomplishment, considering who she had with her.

If Michelle thought she had an attitude problem, she should get a look at herself when she was Six of Twelve. Nothing in the world came close to dealing with an alter who thought she was half human, half machine. When Six first appeared, she immediately demanded to "exit the primitive, polluting, combustion-powered land conveyance" so she could signal her celestial ship, which she had inexplicably misplaced while exploring the universe.

Talking with someone who inundated her speech with alliteration was tough enough. Convincing her not to get out of the moving vehicle was another matter. Only when she reminded Six there weren't any cyborg repair shops on Earth if she got hit by another primitive, polluting, combustion-powered land conveyance, did Six acquiesce and stop trying to get out of the car.

Of course, being from a high tech world, Six didn't know how to drive something as simple as a car. Neither did Michelle. Because of New York's mass transit system, she had never needed to learn.

Tisha, the shy teen, couldn't drive either. Lin Lin claimed to be five, so Gillian never allowed her to take the wheel, whereas Godfrey, a fortyish uncle-type said he could but didn't know how to drive without a clutch, so in the end Gillian did all the driving.

Stopping for sleep had been out of the question. The emotional trauma of the bombings at the Institute of Many Friends had messed up Michelle's scheduled outing for her alters. They appeared for minutes or hours at a time, without any noticeable rhyme or reason.

Except for Six of Twelve. She generally showed up during the night, happily pointing out stars and constellations, reminiscing about the planets she had visited and which quadrant of the galaxy she missed most, claiming it was "in the stars" that she would be leaving soon.

Six hated Earth, especially the planet's "disgusting tradition of tactile transferral of fluids during primitive propagation."

When Gillian mentioned Six's comment to Michelle, Godfrey had suddenly come out to clarify everyone's relational significance. He confided that their psychologist believed Six was created as someone who could find a logical solution to avoiding situations where sex might be expected, and who believed violent resistance was a viable option when forced.

Someone who fought back when Michelle wouldn't. Or couldn't.

The one alter Gillian had wanted to talk to never appeared. Jacob Miller. The others blamed him for the danger they were in. As punishment, he was not allowed *out*. Trying to convince the others that Jacob might hold the key to their safety was like telling a priest sin was good for the soul. Jacob was in mental limbo.

In some ways, Gillian understood their trauma. A few days ago, she never would have believed herself capable of deliberately trying to run down another human being. Her memory of it, the single-mindedness of her emotions and intent, seemed to belong to someone else. When the Carpenter threw the bomb at the car, she had instinctively swerved. At the last second she had wanted to live more than she had wanted to kill him.

After that, preserving her own life and Michelle's seemed paramount. New York was no longer safe even with bodyguards. The nail which had grazed her arm when the bomb exploded made that perfectly clear.

Unfortunately, they hadn't been able to take a plane.

Tisha the teen hated flying. When they arrived at the airport, scared little Lin Lin—the alter who appeared after Michelle saw the Carpenter with a bomb—withdrew, and Michelle came out just in time to reveal Tisha might go into hysterics if they boarded a plane. Undoubtedly it would make the news and alert the Carpenter as to where they were headed.

Taking a train or bus could also turn disastrous if one or more of the alters manifested and caused trouble. A car became their best option. While at the rental place, Gillian managed to hide the seeping blood on her arm with a scarf Michelle kept in the cavernous pockets of her coat. Even now, with the lights of Cheyenne forming a halo in the midnight sky ahead, she could feel the blood-soaked bandages on her left arm, warm and wet, in need of changing again.

She thought about stopping by the emergency room before heading out to the ranch. But there'd be all those questions to answer: how did it happen, where, when. And she couldn't risk an alter manifesting. Since it was night, Six of Twelve had a good chance of showing up. She didn't need Six telling the ER doctor how primitive the facilities were.

She'd wait until morning to get treated.

An alter named Olga was prattling on in lilting Norwegian or Swedish—Gillian couldn't tell which—when she exited Interstate 80.

"Olga, I'd like to speak with Michelle." Sometimes the simple request worked, and Michelle came forward and took control. Sometimes it didn't, as when Six tried to get out of the car before she had time to pull over and stop.

This time it worked. Olga stared straight ahead, jerked slightly, and then Michelle's voice asked, "Where are we?"

"About twenty miles from the ranch. You'll like it. Lots of room to roam. Lots of privacy. Safe."

Michelle hissed in disbelief. "How can you promise it'll be safe?"

"My brother, Wyatt, is a deputy sheriff. He'll be there. Probably be madder than hell when I show up in the middle of the night, but he's good at what he does, a crack shot with both rifle and pistol, and I'm almost as good. We'll have a better chance waiting here for the authorities to arrest the Carpenter than anywhere else."

Michelle wrapped her arms around herself. Was she cold or scared? Was it even Michelle?

"Is that you, Six?" Gillian asked.

"Still me," Michelle said. "It's so dark out here. No cars. No street lights. No buildings. How can you stand it?"

She chuckled. "For me, this is normal. It's how the world should be, not all congested and crowded and lit up at night like a mall. When the moon is full, it's almost as bright as a cloudy day."

Michelle hugged herself tighter. "Yeah, well, in the city you learn real fast not to walk in the shadows. This is all shadow. Anyone could sneak up on you without you even knowing it."

"True, but I have the same advantage. If it's dark enough to conceal an attacker, it's dark enough to hide me. Plus I have the upper hand. I know the terrain. We'll be fine. No one is going to sneak up on us. You'll see."

"I still don't like it," Michelle whined. "There's no one else here."

"Sure there is. See that light over there?" She pointed off to the right at a distant yard light, which looked like a star on Earth. "That's the McGuire place: Tom and Mary, her parents, and four kids. Tom's ex-Navy. And over there," she gestured up ahead and to the left, "is the Terling place. Joe and Ann, two kids, plus Greg their hired hand. There are people all over the place. You just need to know where to look." She turned onto a side road and moaned.

"Your arm's getting worse," Michelle said in concern. "I don't understand why it's still bleeding. The nail only grazed it."

"It's all right. I'm just tired."

Michelle softened her voice. "All of us are very grateful for what you've done the last two days, you know, to keep us from getting killed."

"All of you? You mean you talk to each other inside your head?"

"Sort of. But not all. I don't know Norwegian, but Tisha claims she does, so she translates what Olga says."

"Does Olga really know Norwegian or does she fake it?"

"Oh, she speaks it, all right, though I'm not sure how. I can't speak or understand a word of it. My psychologist taped Olga during a session, then played it for a teacher at NYU who's from Norway. It's actual Norwegian."

Gillian shifted uneasily. For the life of her, she couldn't get a grasp on how such a thing was possible. "So, right now, while you and I are talking, the others are listening?"

"Sort of. Some are making comments to me about what you're saying. Some are talking to each other about what we're talking about. It's nerve-wracking. I'm always having to tell them to shut up so I can concentrate on what's being said out here."

"Must be like having someone whisper in your ear while you're trying to talk."

"More like a different person whispering in each ear." Michelle shrugged. "Most of the time they all stay quiet."

"What about Jacob? Does he listen or does he whisper?"

"Neither. He's one of those alters that remains distinct and apart, though he tells our therapist it's *my* choice, not his. Sometimes he leaves me written messages, but to discourage him I tear them up without reading them."

"You tear them up? Ohmigod! What if all this time Jacob was leaving you notes about the Carpenter? Maybe that's why he risked coming to the hotel to warn me. Because you weren't reading his messages."

"You don't know that." Michelle gestured angrily with her hands. "Nobody knows Jacob like I do. He's a know-it-all busybody who doesn't know when to butt out. He's such a pest."

Gillian nodded in agreement. "I know what you mean, though I have to admit he was a big help after Ray died." She glanced over at Michelle. "You do know about Ray Follett, don't you?"

"Never heard of him."

Gillian glanced at her in amazement. "Don't you read the paper or watch the news?"

"Honey, I've got enough going on in my own life without wasting time learning about what's happening to someone else. Leave me alone, and I'll leave you alone, that's my motto."

"That's a very interesting philosophy you have."

"It works for me."

"I guess I have no right to judge. After Ray died, I spent over three years holed up on the ranch, licking my wounds so to speak."

"So who was this Ray? A boyfriend?"

"An accused serial killer tentatively diagnosed with MPD/DID. Ray didn't seem to have a mean bone in his body.

His psychologist theorized one of his alters might have been the actual killer."

"No shit? And here I thought my group was a handful. I don't know what I would do if I found out one of mine was a murderer."

"Makes Jacob seem tame, huh?"

"Maybe," Michelle said grudgingly. "What does Ray Follett have to do with me or Jacob?"

"Jacob helped me understand how one of Ray's alters might have committed the crimes without Ray being aware of it. At first I didn't know Jacob was one of your alters. From his website and emails, I assumed he was a professor; he seemed such an expert on the subject. After a few months he started telling me more and more about himself, about you and the other alters. I decided I had enough info and didn't want to discuss it further, but he kept after me. Sent me emails for up to two years afterwards."

"Did you keep reading the emails?" Michelle asked.

"At first, to be polite. After a while I just deleted them unread."

"And you criticized me for not reading all his notes?"

"Sorry. Guess I'm just as bad."

"Nothing bad about it." Michelle laughed dryly. "When it comes to Jacob, less is still too much. Welcome to my world, girl."

The car rumbled across a cattle guard.

"Welcome to mine," Gillian said. "The Dohr-Chester Ranch, or, as the brand indicates, the Rocking D and Lazy C. Producers of purebred Black Angus, and organic chicken eggs on the side."

A pole light chased away the dark from the front yard of the house and the parking area. Lights were on inside the white two-story house. Two dogs came racing forward to meet the car, both barking.

Gillian pulled up next to Wyatt's white SUV with brown and gold sheriff markings. An unfamiliar red Honda with Colorado plates was parked on the other side. The family's blue minivan was absent; Susan and the children were still in hiding. Gillian's own car was parked in the open garage along with the four-wheeler and the clunky old Ram pickup used for chores.

As she opened the door and the dogs got a whiff of her familiar scent, they quieted down, tails wagging happily. They hurried to the other side of the car. Michelle kept the door closed.

"Ugly monsters," Michelle said. "They're looking at me like I'm a midnight snack."

"That's Satin and Scrounger," Gillian said as she slowly got out of the car, stiff from all the driving, her arm throbbing. "They won't bite. Satin's more cautious than Scrounger, but then Blue Heelers usually are. Consider them extra protection. No one can sneak up on—"

Gillian halted in midsentence as two men came rushing out of the house. She recognized Wyatt right away. He stood on the porch, frowning, angry as all get out at her, no doubt because she hadn't risked calling to let him know she was all right. She'd been afraid Regis or someone might tap the phone and prevent her from reaching home.

The other man didn't stop. He practically flew off the porch.

Sam!

She blinked in surprise and smiled. Sam! Here in Wyoming!

"Gillian!" Sam said. "Thank God you're all right!"

He grabbed her arms to draw her close. At his touch she groaned and winced in pain. Immediately, he let go. His hand came away wet. Red.

"You're bleeding!" He turned to Wyatt. "She's hurt bad!"

"It looks worse than it is," she tried to explain, but Wyatt was already at her side, worry etched on his face, eyeing her as if she was about to die. She glanced at Sam. He had the same stricken look on his face.

"Let's get you inside," Wyatt said. He wrapped an arm around her and started her toward the house.

"I'm all right," she said, though she didn't resist. "I'm just really tired. And Michelle. She's still in the car."

"I'll get her," Sam said, though he hated to let Gillian out of his sight even for a second. He'd come too far to lose her again.

Satin and Scrounger didn't pay much attention to him as he reached for the passenger door. He had been here for over a day, and they no longer considered him a threat. "Get away. Go chase some chickens or whatever you chase around here."

Tails wagging, they kept their distance and waited to see who was still in the car.

He tried to open the door, but it was locked. The woman inside firmly shook her head NO. He cursed under his breath. He ached to be with Gillian, but she would never forgive him if he didn't take care of her passenger first.

"Michelle Johnson, I'm Detective Samson Brankowski of the New York Police Department. Please open the door, and I'll escort you to the house."

"I don't like dogs."

"No problem. I'll make sure they leave you alone."

She eyed the dogs warily. "You promise?"

With a winning smile and a genial voice, Sam slathered on the charm. "I'm here to protect you."

"Yeah. As if I ever believed that from a cop."

Sam tried not to growl. "It's okay. They just want to make your acquaintance. I hear they do it with everyone. Makes 'em great guard dogs. No one gets in without their permission."

Michelle frowned, clearly not liking the situation, yet she slowly got out of the car, tense, ready to throw herself back in if the dogs attacked. Scrounger, the golden retriever, stepped forward. He wagged his tail expectantly and sniffed Michelle, his huge wet tongue dripping in excitement. He glanced from her to Sam then back to her as if to say, "Come on, let's play." But as the seconds passed and no one even tried to scratch him behind the ears, he turned and ran away to find something more interesting to do.

Satin, though, took a sniff and growled. Michelle spun toward the car but Sam grabbed her arm and held her fast.

"Don't move," he told her. "Never turn your back on a scared animal."

"He's not scared," Michelle said, her voice trembling. "I'm the one who's scared. Look at those teeth."

Satin's lips were pulled back into a snarl. The hair on the back of the dog stood straight up, sensing something about Michelle she didn't like. Or something about her alters. Could the dog be detecting a personality in Michelle that it found threatening?

Taking his cue from when he and Tony had worked a homicide in the fashion industry a few months back, he told Michelle, "You know, you've got great skin tone. And the way you've done your hair—the braids really bring out your cheekbones. Have you ever thought about a modeling career?"

The compliments caught her by surprise. A smile broke through her frown, and her fingers reached up and shyly touched her hair.

Sam glanced at Satin. The dog's mouth slowly closed, and the hair on her back lowered. She took one last sniff, then walked away to where the other dog had disappeared into the night.

"Come on," Sam said. "Let's get inside before she changes her mind and comes back. Got any luggage?"

Michelle grabbed a small plastic bag. "We've been traveling light."

The lingering fear in her eyes was unmistakable. It mirrored his own horrible memory of the bombings at the Institute of Many Friends.

"I'll protect you," he reminded her. Determination deepened his voice. "With my life, if it comes down to it."

"I'm going to hold you to that," Michelle said, and together they headed for the house.

Inside, Gillian sat at the kitchen table. Wyatt, with his buzz cut hair style and square jaw, looked like a marine ready to do field surgery. He had a first aid kit open and was sorting through all the items he might need. Sam moved to help, but Michelle tugged at his sleeve.

"I gotta pee. Where's the john?"

Reminding himself that patience was a virtue, though around Michelle it was elevated to a miracle, Sam showed her the main floor bathroom. He waited until he heard Michelle lock the door, then hurried back to the kitchen. Wyatt was easing Gillian out of her jacket. The bandage on her arm and half the sleeve of her yellow blouse was soaked bright red with blood.

"I'm going to have to cut the sleeve off," Wyatt told her. He grabbed a pair of scissors.

Sam dragged over a chair and sat next to her. He tenderly took her hand in both of his, distracting her from what Wyatt was about to do. He studied her face, still marveling she was here and in one piece.

Gillian sat in a daze, obviously coming off a caffeine high. Sleepy-eyed, with a huge silly smile on her face, she gazed steadily at Sam. "You're here. You're really here." She barely moved as Wyatt cut away the sleeve and slowly peeled it off her bloody skin. "Why are you here?"

"He showed up last night," Wyatt said. "Claimed to be *The Oracle*'s guardian angel, here to protect you. Not that I believed him."

"Made me sleep in my rental car the first night," Sam added.

"Didn't even have a badge, though he claimed to be a detective with NYPD. Found out he lied about that."

Confusion clouded her eyes as Gillian looked from one to the other. "But he is."

"Nope," Wyatt said. "Checked out his story the next morning. He got suspended. Has this thing about not following orders."

Gillian stared at Sam in alarm.

"I had my reasons," Sam said. "It's a long story. We—"

"Am I supposed to sleep on the couch," Michelle interrupted with a yawn, "or do you have an extra bed around here?"

Sam grumbled, about to tell Michelle she could wait until they were finished with Gillian, when Gillian squeezed his hand.

"Don't," she whispered. "In a lot of ways, the ride out here was tougher on her than me. Cut her some slack, all right?"

Sam nodded, yet understood why Satin had growled at Michelle.

"If you don't mind taking over," Wyatt told Sam, "I'll show my latest *guest* to her room."

While Wyatt took Michelle upstairs, Sam finished washing the blood off Gillian's arm.

"Ow!" she shrieked as Sam cleaned the cut.

"Sorry, but I want to make sure there's no infection. This doesn't look deep, but it's still bleeding. Hold on. Let me get a better look. This may hurt."

She clenched her teeth as Sam poked around with tweezers, and shrieked as he dug deeper.

"There." Smiling with pride, he held up the tweezers in front of her. "Had a piece of glass wedged into your flesh, keeping the wound from clotting. I don't think you need stitches, but you should get a tetanus shot."

"Anything you say, doctor."

"I just call 'em as I see 'em. Right now I see someone suffering from loss of blood, exhaustion, and probably way too much coffee. Your speech is slurred, and you sound a bit silly."

"You try driving two thousand miles with six other people—all in the same body, one of whom is from outer space—and you won't be sounding so good either. By the way, you've got the cutest dimples in your cheeks when you smile. Anyone ever tell you how sexy it makes you look?"

"You just did, but I think you're going to regret it in the morning. Hold still, this may hurt." He dabbed the cut with antiseptic, then applied a bandage. "How's that?"

"Feels better already. Before I forget, I want to show you something." She fumbled around in the pocket of her jacket and took out a nail. "I found this outside the alley near the Hackers Coffee Slop. I wanted to show it to you, but there were so many people. And then at the Institute . . ." She swallowed hard. "Oh, Sam, it was awful. All those people inside."

She scrunched her eyes in misery, making Sam wish, as he had wished a hundred times in the past two days, that he had been there with her when the bombs went off. But he hadn't.

He reached into his pocket and pulled out a nail. "Like this? Nasty bugger. Hurt like hell."

She stared at his nail. Tears filled her eyes. "Oh, Sam. The bomb at the Hackers Coffee Slop. You were injured. Where?" Her eyes rapidly searched his body for any sign of a bandage. "I'm so sorry. I didn't know. I thought when you made the *J* on the mirror that you were just rubbing it in about Ray and me, making fun of us. All along you were trying to save me and that man you took the bomb from and all the people in the place." The tears flowed unchecked. "You saved all of us. How could I have been so stupid? I'm so sorry."

Sam took her in his arms and held her close while she sobbed uncontrollably. He tried to get her to stop but she kept crying.

"It's okay," he murmured. "Everything's all right. You're fine. I'm fine. It's in the past. What matters is we're all safe, and almost sound."

"What's going on?" Wyatt had returned. As his sister continued to cry, he looked at Sam as if he was about to hit him. "I knew it was a mistake letting you stay. What did you do to her?"

Great. Crying woman. Angry brother. What more could go wrong?

"I didn't do a thing." Sam told him. "For five days she's had the Carpenter blowing up people around her. This is the first chance she's had to unwind and stop worrying about everyone and everything. You know women, they have to cry to feel better. Why don't you finish checking her over and then we can get her to bed. She's way overdue for some serious sleep."

Remembering the blood on the pedals of the stolen Lexus, Sam sat her back down and told Wyatt to check her feet. With her head resting on Sam's shoulder and his arm around her, Gillian dozed while Wyatt took off her shoes and found the scrape on her small toe. He cleaned and bandaged it.

"Time for bed, sis," Wyatt said.

Sam gently shook her shoulder. She barely stirred. Between the two of them, they managed to get her upstairs. At the door to her bedroom, Wyatt stared hard at Sam and said, "I'll take her from here. Go on to bed."

Sam didn't argue. To Wyatt, he was as much of a stranger as Michelle.

Sam headed down the hall. He stopped before the room usually occupied by Wyatt's young daughter Katie. A droning snore from the other side of the door indicated Michelle was already asleep. He entered the bedroom across from it and slipped into the bottom of a pair of bunk beds belonging to

Wyatt's sons. Sitting cross-legged, he pulled out two nails from his pocket. One had been removed from his calf. The other he had eased out of Gillian's exhausted hand. He looked at the heads and frowned. Both had a *J* on them.

Why a *J*? In memory of Janeane, Ray's alter who Gillian thought was responsible for the deaths of all those children? Could it really be that simple?

After a few hours of sleep, Sam was downstairs at the crack of dawn, his circadian clock still set on East Coast time. In the kitchen, Wyatt was making a fresh pot of coffee. From the looks of him, he had been up all night. Like Sam, he wore a gun, but Wyatt's was on his hip in a belt holster.

"I'll stand watch while you get some sleep," Sam said.

Wyatt threw on a jacket. "I'll take you up on that as soon as I get back." He grabbed two metal buckets from the pantry and left the house. Sam could hear the dogs yelping in greeting and Wyatt's voice responding in kind. A rooster crowed in the distance, and what may have been a cow bellowed from the direction of the barn.

Sam shook his head. So unlike life in New York where the inhabitants woke to the rumbling of garbage trucks, emergency sirens, and taxis honking. Animal noises were the norm here, not manmade sounds. It was like being on a different planet. A sober reminder that he and Gillian came from opposite backgrounds.

He'd just poured himself a cup of coffee when Michelle shuffled into the kitchen in a bathrobe ten inches too long for her petite size and demanded a cup. Figuring she also suffered from a two-hour time zone difference, he ignored her gruffness and served it. He offered to fix her breakfast—bacon and eggs were in the refrigerator—but when she noticed that the shells of some of the eggs he took out were brown, blue, green, or mottled, she scrunched up her nose and ordered cereal and toast.

He placed a small bowl on the table before her and three boxes of cereal he had found in a cupboard. She chose the one with colorful sweetened oat rings.

"Goat's milk or cow?" he asked.

"Don't you go giving me anything but milk that comes from a store," she replied. "I'm not into that natural stuff. It's not healthy for you."

"Yes, ma'am," he said with a smile. He wasn't going to let anything or anyone upset his good mood. Gillian was in the house, sleeping and secure, far away from New York, the Carpenter, and Regis Van Decker. That's all that mattered.

Suspecting Gillian would sleep in, he set about making a hearty breakfast for himself and Wyatt. When Wyatt returned with two pails of milk, there were scrambled eggs, bacon, and buttered toast waiting on the table.

Wyatt eyed the breakfast with surprise and satisfaction. "Thanks," he told Sam as he put the buckets on the counter. He hung his jacket on a hook by the door and started to sit at the table when Michelle spoke up.

"Where do I shower? Down here or upstairs? You got any clothes I can wear? Something that fits better than this robe is what I'm thinking."

Wyatt looked at her, then at the hot meal in front of him. He picked up a fork and said in a tired voice, "Hold your horses and I'll see what I can do."

Michelle frowned. With a "humph," she leaned back in her chair and crossed her arms. The more she stared, the slower Wyatt ate. Sam decided it was too early in the morning for war to break out.

He set his fork down. "You go on and eat," he told Wyatt. "I'll take care of her."

Upstairs, while Michelle complained about the family's choice of shampoos, Sam slipped into Wyatt's bedroom and rummaged for clothes. Chances were Wyatt would have a fit when he caught sight of the prickly New Yorker in his wife's outfit, but drastic times called for drastic measures.

He handed Michelle an assortment of lingerie and clothes to wear. Even as she was saying, "You've got to be kidding. I wouldn't be caught dead in these," a sharp comeback hovered on the tip of his tongue. He was dying to tell her what he really thought, but he had promised Gillian to lay off, and he would. But he could only take so much. He turned and left.

Wyatt was pouring milk from the buckets into two large plastic pitchers, one labeled "goat," when Sam returned. The unmarked one was for the cow's milk. Sam grabbed the pot of coffee and poured them both a second cup.

"Abrasive, isn't she?" Sam said, referring to Michelle.

"Badgers are tame compared to her."

"I'll take your word on that."

Wyatt put the pitchers in the refrigerator. "Then why are you being so nice?"

"From what little I've learned about people with multiple personalities, their alters usually manifest around strangers only when they feel extremely threatened or relatively safe. You've got a good handle on being a roughneck. I'm working on easygoing. Everyone's friend."

"Good cop, bad cop," Wyatt said as he cleaned the pails, then set them in the pantry.

Sam nodded. "I need to talk with Jacob Miller about the bomber. Can't do that unless he feels safe enough to come out."

"Even with everything you told me yesterday, it still sounds freaky." Wyatt put his dishes in the dishwasher. "I'm going to bed. Wake me when Gillian gets up. Or if anyone comes." As he headed up the stairs, Sam heard him grumble, "I swear, if any else shows up from New York, I'm gonna start charging rent."

Sam chuckled, realizing Wyatt's bark was worse than his bite. He cleared away the breakfast dishes, but when he grabbed Michelle's cereal bowl, he froze. The back of his neck tingled as he looked inside the bowl.

Some of the colorful oat rings had been left in the bottom, forming the letter *J*.

Chapter Twenty-Two

The morning was eerily calm.

Gillian and Wyatt slept. Michelle watched TV, mostly talk shows and shopping networks. The satellite system was the only thing she didn't complain about. She refused to go outdoors; the barnyard odors and the dogs kept her couched inside.

The one time Sam asked to talk to Jacob, Michelle abruptly went upstairs to take a nap. A half hour later she came down to watch more TV with a warning glance at Sam not to bring up Jacob's name again. But like a bloodhound on a scent, he refused to give up. The rank of detective had been earned by being relentless A refusal just meant he'd have to get what he wanted from a different direction.

He'd already called Tony. His partner was out of jail and madder than hell at him for disappearing to Wyoming. New York City had been pretty quiet the last two days. Nurses at area hospitals were threatening to strike if they didn't get better pay and fewer hours, the smog was gone, blue sky and sunshine were plentiful, cab companies wanted to raise their fares, and no bombings.

His "leak" to the reporter about the Carpenter's targets skipping town must have worked. Or the Carpenter was more severely injured from the last bombing than anyone thought. Time would tell.

Michelle was on her third Dr. Pepper of the morning and asking, "When's lunch served around here?" when Wyatt tramped downstairs. Almost at the same time, a news bulletin popped up on TV. A bombing in Pittsburgh. No dead, but three were injured, all by shrapnel—nails, to be specific. Sam would lay odds they all had a "J" on them.

"He's on the move," Wyatt said.

"And headed this way."

Wyatt scowled. "Won't know that for sure until he strikes again."

Sam followed up on what they both were thinking. "How long would it take to drive from Pittsburgh to here?"

"I'd say a day."

"Longer if he decides to set off more bombs along the way."

"As I said, we won't know that for sure until he hits again." But the shadow that crossed his features said he already knew, and with a heavy tread, Wyatt went into the kitchen.

The talk show resumed in progress. Michelle muttered, "Finally. Hope I didn't miss much," and settled back to watch, but Sam noticed she was biting her fingernails.

He felt uneasy. The Carpenter should have been headed for Florida, following the false lead in the newspaper story. How did he know Gillian and Michelle were here? No one knew except Wyatt, Gillian, Michelle, and Tony.

He asked Michelle, "Have you called anyone since you left New York?"

"Are you crazy? How stupid do you think I am? 'Course I haven't."

"What about your alters?"

She glanced back at the TV and her voice lost its hostile edge. "Not that I know of."

"But you can't be sure."

"Pretty sure. Ask Gillian. She never let us out of her sight." Michelle gave the TV her full attention, her way of saying she wasn't going to discuss it any further.

His instincts said Michelle was telling the truth. But he would check with Gillian later, just to be sure. As for Tony, Sam had only told him this morning where they were.

Then there was Wyatt. The guy dealt with facts, not assumptions. He hadn't believed Gillian was coming here until she actually showed up last night. So how had the Carpenter known where Gillian would take Michelle?

Sam knew because he had gotten to know her. Knew her past, knew how she thought. The logical answer was the Carpenter knew her, too. But how? And from where? When?

He ground his teeth, trying to figure it out. Something was missing, some piece of information that would finally make sense of out it all. In the meantime, he hoped the Carpenter wouldn't get this far without being caught. But with the Feds after him, nothing was certain. Might be a good idea to have Wyatt show him around the place, plan for contingencies in case the Carpenter appeared on their doorstep.

His gaze traveled around the room, assessing weaknesses. Maybe they should board up the windows. The interior walls seemed strong and sturdy, covered with family photos. A large family portrait above Michelle's head depicted two middle-aged parents, a young, carefree teen-aged Gillian, and three teen-aged boys.

Hold on. Gillian had two brothers: Wyatt and Cody.

He scanned the other pictures. Almost half had the unknown boy.

Michelle said, "I'm hungry. When are we gonna eat?"

He ignored her and headed for the kitchen. Wyatt was drinking a glass of milk and looking out the window to where the vehicles were parked. More specifically, to where the road entered their place. A blue pickup was driving past on the county road, its tires kicking up dirt like a smoke signal from the days of the Old West.

"Anyone you know?" Sam asked as the trail of dust followed the vehicle even after the pickup disappeared from view.

"Jenny Murdock, on her way to the weekly Happy Helpers meeting. A little late, that's probably why she's going faster than she should."

"You must know everyone out here."

"Them and their vehicles."

"In the living room, I noticed there's another kid in some of the family photos. A boy. Is he a relative?"

Wyatt took another swig and left the question unanswered, which only piqued Sam's interest.

"A friend of the family?" he asked.

Wyatt stared out the window.

"A stranger who happened to show up when photos were being taken? A ghost not camera shy? Maybe a black sheep of the family? Might as well answer. I can keep this up for hours if I have to."

"Always the cop," Wyatt said evenly. He glanced at Sam, sizing him up. "If you're as good as I am, you won't let it drop until your curiosity stops crawlin'." He drained the last of the milk, then took his time rinsing out the glass before putting it in the dishwasher. "His name's Jayson Spelling. He's the reason I became a deputy sheriff and Gillian became The Oracle."

"When's lunch?" Michelle yelled from the living room. "I'm starving!"

Wyatt shook his head in irritation. He said to Sam, "Come outside. I want to show you something." He glanced at the gun in Sam's shoulder holster and added, "First, let's get you better armed."

Wyatt went to the bookcase in the living room and took down *War and Peace* from the top shelf. He reached in a small, hollowed-out cavity among the pages and removed a key, then re-shelved the book and headed for the back hallway. Sam followed. In the mud room by the back door, Wyatt unlocked a five-foot-tall metal gun cabinet.

Wyatt said, "A pistol means he's close enough to use a bomb. A rifle means he's dead before he can."

"Agreed," Sam said. "Having witnessed what his bombs can do, I'd rather take out the bastard from a safe distance."

Wyatt's hand slid over several shotguns before settling on a Winchester rifle, which he handed to Sam. Another rifle, a Remington, he chose for himself. In a small recess inside the top lip of the cabinet, he fished out a small key, which he used to unlock one of two metal ammunition boxes on the top shelf of the cabinet. He gave Sam a box of bullets for his rifle, and pocketed another after loading his own gun.

He replaced the ammo key, then locked the gun cabinet. They returned to the living room. Wyatt took down *War and Peace* and was opening it to re-hide the key when he noticed Michelle watching him.

"I don't trust her," he whispered to Sam.

"Once again, we agree."

Wyatt looked around the living room. A knowing smile tugged one corner of his mouth, and he headed to the kitchen. Sam stayed in the living room but shifted his position enough so he could make sure Michelle wasn't noticing where Wyatt hid the key. He smirked. Gillian's brother put it under the milk pitcher labeled goat. Even starving, Michelle would never touch the stuff.

"Remind me to tell Gillian where it's at," Wyatt told him. He grabbed his jacket, tossed Sam his, and said to Michelle, "We'll be right back." They went outside, taking the rifles with them.

They headed for the multi-vehicle garage. The two ranch dogs came running, tails wagging, mouths grinning, eager for something to do. Wyatt followed a well-worn path that circled around to the backside of the garage.

Sam staggered to a halt, eyes wide, mouth ajar. He stared in surprise and amazement. Not in a million years would he have expected to see this on a ranch.

Before him was a large area of grass, fenced in with chicken wire. Chickens and some strange-looking black and grey fowl strutted around inside, pecking the ground for any tidbits to eat. A very tranquil, domestic setting except for the three ten-foot-high gold pyramids within the fence.

"Pyramids?" Sam uttered in disbelief.

"Actually, they're chicken coops," Wyatt said, keeping a straight face. "The first two are. The smaller one in back, which replicates the one for Menkaure, is where we keep the feed. The originals at Giza supposedly were laid out to imitate the stars of Orion's belt. This is the same alignment."

"Why?"

"To maintain the historical accuracy of the original site."

"No, I mean why build this just for chickens?"

"You'll have to ask Gillian that."

"She built these?" He looked at Wyatt, and remembered how Gillian had admired the woodwork in the sports bar after the subway bombing. From the moment he had met her, nothing about his life had been the same. His simplistic black-and-white perspective of the world was gone. And what he was looking at proved it. "She's a carpenter?"

Wyatt nodded. With a mercurial smile that indicated he understood Sam's confusion, he opened the gate. "Want a closer look?"

"You bet." He entered the enclosure and circled each pyramid in turn, marveling at what might have spurred Gillian to construct such oddities. The man-sized doors on the coops were open to the warm day. A quick peek inside revealed the structures were wood-framed and wood-sided, with shelves of nests layered in rows on the inside slope of three of the walls. Like the exterior, the inside was painted gold.

On the outside, the oblique sides were scored to resemble thousand of stone blocks. He ran his hand along the slope of one of the walls.

"Everybody who sees them has to touch them," Wyatt said. "Don't know why." His hand rubbed along the side of one, too. "Guess it's because it's so different from what we're used to. As for that New Agey thing about pyramid power, well, to tell you the truth, since the chickens have been using these, production is up. And we get more than the average number of double yolks."

Sam stroked the side of one pyramid a few more times, pleased by the sensation though he couldn't say why. His hand stilled. He looked at Wyatt. "What does all of this have to do with Jayson Spelling?"

"Maybe I should answer that."

Both men turned to see Gillian standing at the gate. She wore denim jeans, a light blue t-shirt, denim jacket, even denim-colored cowboy boots. Her propensity for monochromatic dressing included life at home. Sam easily pictured her in denim-colored bra and panties, and the thought made him feel like he was on fire. Tony was right. He had it bad.

"I made dinner, Wyatt. Why don't you go on in and have some while I talk with Sam."

Wyatt patted his sister on the shoulder, then headed for the house, accompanied by the dogs. Sam and Gillian kept silent until the house's screen door banged shut.

"How're you doing?" Sam asked.

"I have a terrible headache from caffeine withdrawal, and my body is still on New York time, but I'm all right."

"And the arm?"

"Better. But I probably should get a tetanus shot."

"I'll go with you. I'm supposed to get one, too."

Gillian's brown eyes darkened with concern. She scanned his body, looking for a wound. "Where did you get hit?"

"In the calf. Stings, but it's nothing compared to being shot, or so I'm told."

She shook her head. "I'm sorry about the Hackers Coffee Slop. I misunderstood about the *J*. After the bomb went off, there were so many people in the alley I couldn't get to you." Her eyes seemed to ask for forgiveness. "And I had to find Jacob. We were supposed to get together at lunch."

"Yeah, I wanted to ask you about that. What made you want to see him?"

"He came to my hotel one night, trying to warn me about Follett. I assumed he was talking about Ray, but then I got to thinking that maybe he was talking about another Follett. Maybe one of Ray's brothers. I thought it might have a connection to the Carpenter, so I sent Jacob an email asking to meet. We never had a chance to talk. He arrived right after you took the bomb outside."

"Our timing has been off throughout this whole case." He kicked a clod of dirt in frustration. "I tried to get Michelle to let me question Jacob. Sheesh. Talk about an ice queen. Acted like I was asking for the moon."

"Jacob's in isolation for putting all the alters in danger. There's no telling when they'll let him out." She glanced at the rifle in his hand. "I heard about the bombing in Pittsburgh. He knows we're here, doesn't he?"

"It's possible. Was Michelle ever out of your sight long enough to make a phone call?"

"Uh-uh. With her alters making guest appearances, I couldn't take the chance."

He glanced at the pyramid chicken coops. "So, who is Jayson Spelling?"

She stared down at her feet. "Jayson was a foster child who lived with us for over eight years. He was ten when he first arrived, fragile, defensive, but in time it was like having a third brother." She smiled and looked at Sam. "He could be ornery and sweet, thoughtful, mischievous, rebellious at times, but also protective. What teenager isn't? A good kid from bad parents, in need of a good home or else he'd go bad, too.

"Everything went well until his senior year. Candy, a girl he was sweet on, accused him of rape. Of course, it didn't help that Candy waited a full week before reporting it. The allegation tore the school and the community in half. Emotions ran high. Seemed like you either believed one or the other—definitely no middle ground.

"I was very naive back then. With no DNA to analyze and some bruising that should have been easily refuted, I believed Jayson would be free by the end of the trial. What I didn't realize was how potent words could be. In closing remarks, the prosecution talked about what a fine upbringing Candy had, while adding some sly remarks about Jayson's questionable parentage."

Gillian shoved her hands in her pockets. Her feet shifted restlessly, and she swallowed several times before continuing. "The jury found him guilty. I couldn't believe it. Mom cried, my brothers shouted angrily, while my dad and the lawyer agreed to appeal the conviction. And me, well, even back then I was headstrong. I slipped out of the courtroom and went to where the jurors would sneak out. I had to know what made them believe Jayson could do such a thing.

"I waited. When they appeared, most didn't look happy. Some put their heads down when they walked by. I knew one woman; she had bought eggs from us. I asked her point blank what made her think Jayson was guilty. Before she could answer, the foreman came out. He looked me straight in the eye and told me the apple never falls far from the tree, which meant Jayson was guilty because his dad had been sexually abusive. Like father, like son.

"I told my dad and Jayson's lawyer what I'd heard. The lawyer said it might help, and I went home feeling good. We would appeal, tell the judge what the foreman had said and maybe get a mistrial. I was so excited, so hopeful, I could hardly sleep. I was still awake when the phone rang." Gillian closed her eyes and hugged herself.

"After all these years, I can still hear my mom screaming. The house was filled with her screams. When I got to my parents' room, my brothers were there. Wyatt was pounding his head against the wall, Cody was crying. Dad had his arms wrapped around Mom, trying to get her to stop screaming. Jayson had hanged himself in his cell. The fragile boy who had come to live with us eight years ago must have resurfaced. Maybe he couldn't handle the thought of being locked up for years to come. Maybe he feared being abused in prison like he'd been abused by his father. We'll never know."

Sam dragged in a breath and let it out. "That explains why you took it so personal when you heard Roger Walgood had committed suicide in his cell." He took her in his arms and held her close. "Damn. If I remember correctly, I was pretty crude when I broke the news."

She nodded in misery, fighting back the tears.

Gently, he leaned her head against his shoulder and kissed the top of her head.

"With Jayson dead," she murmured, "an appeals court never had a chance to decide whether he was guilty based on the evidence and not on the prejudice of the jury."

Gillian heaved a sigh. "In the end, it didn't matter. Less than a year later, Candy was raped and beaten at college. DNA proved her high school sweetheart was guilty. At trial, she claimed he was the one who had raped her in high school, not Jayson. She'd accused Jayson because her boyfriend threatened to kill her if she told her parents who really assaulted her. Most people will believe foster kids are guilty of just about anything. Jayson was an easy target."

"I'm sorry," Sam said.

Gillian got out a blue bandana from a back pocket and wiped her eyes.

"What does this have to do with pyramid chicken coops?"

Gillian managed a dry laugh, and a light smile broke through the tragic memories. "Therapy. Everyone deals with grief in their own way. Mom read the Bible cover to cover. Dad and my brothers went out on the north range and shot fifty boxes of shells—never did hear what they were shooting at. As for me, I couldn't forget how Jayson had planned on going to college to be an Egyptologist. Combine that with the fact our chicken coop was in bad shape and needed to be replaced and voila." She gestured to the pyramids. "Egypt in Wyoming."

"In memory of Jayson," Sam said.

"They're to remind me never to give up. To always seek the truth. Like the pyramids, truth stands the test of time, no matter how much it may be covered up with lies and innuendoes. If Jayson hadn't given up, he would have been freed."

She eased out of his embrace and started walking in the direction of the barn. "Come on," she said, beckoning him to follow with a wave of her hand. "I'll show you what I built after Ray died. If you liked the pyramids, you'll love this."

Rifle in hand, he quickly caught up to her, his thoughts heavy with anticipation. Ray had been the love of her life. He, or one of his alters, had also been a serial killer. After seeing the chicken coops, Sam couldn't even guess what she had built to get over the pain of losing someone she had both loved and hated.

They neared the barn, and the dogs came running. Scrounger barked and scratched at the closed doors to the large structure. He barked again and looked at Gillian. Satin circled the other dog, sniffing the ground, then barked as well.

"What's with them?" he asked.

"Vermin. They like hanging out in the barn. We also keep oats for the horses in there. Scrounger loves oats. Sometimes I get the feeling he thinks he's a horse." She and Sam kept walking. "Let's go, you two. This way."

The dogs ran ahead as they skirted the corral on the other side of the barn. A satin brown quarter horse stuck his head over the fence to watch as they headed into a small orchard of cherry and apple trees in bloom.

"In memory of Jayson," Gillian said as they strolled along, "I became a people reader and jury consultant. I make sure juries are as impartial as possible so no one else who's innocent gets wrongly convicted." Her voice turned low, laden with emotion. "So no one ever loses hope."

"I understand," Sam said.

She tilted her head and looked at him, and smiled. "Yes, I think you finally do." She took his hand in hers and squeezed it gently. "Now I know you're going to like this."

They continued through the rows of fruit trees, the sun warming them. He liked the feel of her hand in his, tender and undemanding. New York seemed far away.

He asked, "Do you like living here with your brother and his family?"

"Actually, they live with me."

He raised his brow in surprise. "You own this place? All of it?"

"It's a family ranch, jointly owned. As long as someone is here to work the place, the others can come and go as they please. Except for branding time. Then everyone has to help out."

"You never worry about interfering with Wyatt and his wife? You know, not giving them time alone."

Gillian shook her head. "After Mom died, I stayed on to help manage the place with my dad. By then Cody was in Oregon with his wife, and Wyatt was newly married, living in Cheyenne. When Dad died, Wyatt already had two kids with a third on the way. He and Susan liked the idea of raising kids away from the city and asked if they could come out."

"Cheyenne only has about 60,000 people. You call that a city?"

Gillian laughed. "In Wyoming, that's huge, but still too big for Wyatt and Susan. I was glad to have the company and the help with chores. My career was taking off and someone had to watch the place when I was gone. As for Wyatt, he and Susan have a built-in babysitter. Things even out. And it's always nice to have children around."

"Do you ever think about having children of your own?" he asked, then immediately wished he hadn't. He didn't even know where the question had come from. It just popped out of his mouth.

She eyed him carefully, as if trying to figure out what he was really asking. "There are times. What about you?"

"With my ex-wife, it never entered my head."

"And with Stephanie?"

"A solid no. Which is good, since we recently broke up."

This time it was Gillian who raised her brow in surprise. "Trouble in paradise?"

Sam looked around. "I'd say you have your own version of Eden going on right here."

Their eyes met. Gillian licked her bottom lip, then looked away. He would give a month's pay to know what she was thinking.

They left the fruit orchard behind, exiting through a break in a natural fence of raspberry bushes, and stopped on a rutted dirt road that circled around the far side of the orchard back to the barn and corrals. She let go of his hand as he stared across the road at the white, columned structure which seemed as out of place here as the pyramids.

"Is that what I think it is?" Sam asked.

"If you're thinking of a farrowing shed for pigs, then I'd say you're correct."

"Farrowing?"

"A maternity ward for sows."

"A pig barn?" He laughed, a good deep-in-the-belly laugh. "Gillian Dohr, you have a wicked sense of humor." He laughed again. Before him stood a twelve-foot-tall replica of the Capitol. "You don't think someone might consider this disrespectful or unpatriotic?"

"Nah. With all the pork that comes out of Congress, it seemed more than appropriate. I'll take you inside. It's not in use right now. We have a few pigs penned up behind it, one for butchering and the other two for my nephews' 4-H projects. When the boys get older and into FFA, they'll be breeding pigs like crazy. By then I should be done."

Gillian opened a door that covered the facade of the central entryway of the Capitol. Sam noted the exterior detail of tiny windows and columns carved into the door and outside walls. Must have taken a mountain of patience to do it. Three years worth, he remembered.

The dogs stayed outside, nosing around the perimeter of the building.

Gillian turned on an overhead bare bulb. She gestured to the right. "The south wing is done and ready to go." In the eight-foot-tall rectangular wing, Sam noticed two small stalls, each with water and feed troughs.

She pointed in the other direction. "I'm still working on the north wing."

In the other half of the building, Sam noted the walls and roof were done, but only one of the two stalls were finished. Nearby was a worktable with pneumatic tools, a saw, and assorted nails, screws, and other woodworking material. He picked up a large, heavy orange cordless nailer. "Every tool lover's dream."

"It can spit out a thousand nails an hour."

"Sometimes I wish my gun could do the same." He put it down.

At the back of the building, she opened the top of a Dutch door. She leaned on the bottom half and looked out. He joined

her. Three white pigs with black markings came toward them
in a fenced-in pigpen. Their large pink noses rose up, sniffing
to see if they were getting fed. Gillian scratched one on its
head and said, "I'll bring you scraps tonight."

When it was obvious they weren't going to get any food,
they snorted and ambled back to one corner of the yard where
they lay in the shade of a blue spruce.

"I can understand the pyramids," he said, "but for the life
of me I don't see the connection between this and Ray
Follett."

Gillian watched the pigs for a long time before answering.
"Some zoologists think pigs are more intelligent than dogs,
but most people treat them as stupid. Pigs need to roll around
in the mud to stay cool in the summer, which makes people
assume pigs are dirty when actually they try to keep
themselves and their surroundings clean. You see the
pattern?"

"People see what they expect to see, which isn't always the
truth."

"And then there's Congress. People elect them, they're
supposed to be working for us, they're our employees, and yet
after they go to Washington, they vote themselves better
wages, better health care, and better pensions than the people
they're working for. They start to think they're better than the
people who voted for them."

"The hypocrisy of good intentions," Sam said.

"The many faces of power and politics. Like the many faces
of someone with multiple personality disorder."

Sam nodded in comprehension.

"Are you hungry?" Gillian asked. "We should go back
before Wyatt and Michelle eat all the food. Then we can take a
quick trip into town and have my arm looked at."

"And tetanus shots," he added as he closed the top half of
the Dutch door. They headed for the front entrance. He was
about to pass through the doorway when he noticed a nail on

the wall off to the side, holding a bucket by its handle. Its head had a *J* inscribed in it.

A shiver shot up his spine. "Is this the nail sent to you anonymously after Ray died?"

Gillian looked at him in surprise. "How did you know about that?"

"Calvin. Do you know he keeps his in his wallet?"

"No, I didn't think it bothered him as much as it does me. But then I leave mine here when I go out into the world while he takes his piece of hell along with him." She turned off the light and exited the building with Sam. "He has more feelings than I give him credit for," she added. "I wonder how the trial is going?"

"I heard on the news this morning that the jury is still deliberating."

Gillian nodded. "Good. We worked hard to pick jurors who would take their time and think things through."

He looked back at the ostentatious pig shed, remembering one particular nail inside. "Gillian, you must have seen the evidence during the Follett trial. Did the nails all have *J*s on them?"

"They were plain. Only the ones used in the killings after the trial were marked."

"Did anyone question that? Think it strange Ray would suddenly inscribe the nails?"

Gillian raised her hands in the air, bristling with resentment. "*Ray* didn't put the *J*s on the nails. *Janeane did.* She's the killer."

Sam looked at her—feisty, spirited, ready to go the distance to defend someone she had loved regardless of the fact that he was dead. Sam couldn't help but wonder what it would be like to have a woman like her love him. "Sorry. You're right. I gotta remember not to use the name of the dominant personality to refer to them all."

She lowered her hands, accepting his apology, but her eyes still looked feisty.

"What I meant was, did anyone have an explanation for why the Js suddenly showed up?"

"Regis doesn't believe in MPD, so he thought it was simply hubris: Ray feeling cocky after being acquitted, thinking himself invulnerable, daring anyone to catch him by flaunting an identifying mark. Regis thought the J signified Jesus. Ray's stepfather used to drive nails in the palm of Ray's hands every year on Good Friday to teach him that pain and suffering were sanctified—obedience mandatory."

Sam spat out of the side of his mouth in disgust. "Ray's stepfather was a monster."

Gillian nodded sadly in agreement. "I think Janeane copied the stepfather's ritual to kill the children."

"So you agree with Regis. The Js on the nails are a product of Ray's warped religious upbringing."

She shook her head. "I lean more toward the psychiatrist's theory. It wasn't Ray who was feeling bold after he was acquitted. It was Janeane. She put her initial on the nails to thumb her nose at anyone who would try to convict her again. That or leaving her mark would force the world to recognize her existence as a distinct individual separate from Ray."

"Ironic since few know she ever existed."

"Only because some cops took the law into their own hands and killed Ray before the truth came out. And that, Sam, my favorite officer of the law, is the final reason I built a pig shed after Ray died and then put the nail in it."

Puzzled, Sam tilted his head.

"In what profession are people referred to as pigs?" She spun on her heel and headed back to the orchard.

Sam stayed behind, momentarily stunned. Just when he thought he had her figured out, she threw him a curve ball. He should be furious at her for the belittling reference to his profession. But he wasn't. He finally realized how much rage she'd had after what happened to Ray.

Good thing she decided to funnel all that negativity into building things. Might also be a good thing that she wasn't independently wealthy. With heavy equipment at her beck and call, this place might be surrounded with a full-scale model of Stonehenge or the Taj Mahal.

He jogged to catch up. "You've got a unique way of dealing with stress."

Gillian shrugged indifferently. "Building small mock-ups is good therapy. Keeps me busy. Can't strangle anyone if I've got a gas-powered hammer in my hand, shooting nails into lumber."

Like the Carpenter shoots nails into people with his bombs, he thought. A damning coincidence.

They stepped through the break in the raspberry bushes and entered the fruit orchard. The dogs reappeared from their wanderings and headed back in the direction of the house, barking occasionally as they disappeared from sight.

"What about Wyatt?" Sam asked. "He said because of Jayson, you became The Oracle. But he also said Jayson's the reason he became a deputy sheriff. Seems like you two are on opposite sides of the same coin."

"From my brother's perspective, Jayson never should have been arrested, let alone tried for rape. He put the blame on shoddy police work. A more thorough investigation would have uncovered Candy's abusive boyfriend. Instead, like a lot of cops, they got myopic. They picked the most likely suspect—Jayson—and spent all their time digging up evidence, trying to build a case around him. Wyatt decided there should be better people in law enforcement, the kind who look in all directions. So he became one himself."

He opened his mouth but she wagged a finger at him. "If you're going to tell me about how heavy your caseload is and how understaffed and underbudgeted police departments are,

don't. I've heard it all. Maybe your unions should work on
that instead of soaking you guys for dues."

"Yes, ma'am." He playfully saluted her.

She smiled sheepishly in embarrassment. "Sorry. Once in a
while my fire and brimstone speech escapes."

"I wouldn't have you any other way."

She halted under an apple tree whose branches were filled
with soft white blossoms. With a steady warmth in her eyes
and a slight smile on her lips, she studied him. "Samson
Brankowski, are you flirting with me?"

He leaned the rifle against the tree. "Telling me how sexy I
looked last night, that's flirting." He moved closer and
lowered his mouth to hers. "This is seduction."

It was perfect. He had her alone, in the right mood, or so
he thought until she halted the approaching kiss with a lone
but determined finger placed lightly on his lips.

"Hold it," she said. "Before this goes any further, there's
something I need to know. Why are you here? Somewhere last
night in the fog of sleep deprivation, I think I heard Wyatt say
you're on suspension. Is that true?"

He studied the lips he had been so close to tasting and
stifled the frustration lodged in his throat. Women were such
verbal animals. Even when it came to sex, they had to talk
everything out. Never could just get right to it.

Knowing he wouldn't be able to get near those sexy lips
without answering her, he handcuffed himself to patience and
said, "Yeah, I'm on suspension. Me and the Lieutenant had a
major disagreement. One of us had to give. Figured it might
as well be me."

"Just like that? One day you're a dedicated cop, the next
day you're on forced vacation? Uh-uh. Nothing is that simple
with you. Come on, Sam, spit it out. What really happened?"

"A woman I know stole a vehicle and tried to assault
someone with the same said vehicle." She opened her mouth
to speak but he held up his hand to stop her. "I know, I know.

You had good cause. But that's usually for a judge to determine. Until you turn yourself in, you're a fugitive. As a cop I was obligated to report your whereabouts so you could be apprehended and returned to New York. Given the circumstances, the last thing you needed—besides the Carpenter on your tail—was a bunch of cops and Feds coming after you. So I made such a jerk of myself, the Lieutenant couldn't help but get me out of his sight."

"Oh, Sam," she murmured. "I can't believe you did that for me." She touched his cheek, her lips parting in invitation, gaze steaming with gratitude at what he had sacrificed for her.

He couldn't resist. Aroused, he reached for her, knowing the time was ripe for him to discover if the color of her bra really did match the rest of her clothes, and was disappointed when she suddenly drew back.

"So why did you decide to come here?" she asked, her voice irritatingly patient, as if they had nothing better to do but chat.

He grumbled silently. She still needed to get everything worked out in her mind, fill in all the blanks until there was nothing left to talk about, nothing left to do but accept the fact that he wanted her and she wanted him.

"I came for two reasons. First, I figured when the Lieutenant got to cooling off, he might realize I really did know where you were. He's not the type you want to be around when angry. Doesn't have a constructive outlet like you do."

She grinned at the compliment. "And the second reason?"

"I decided you and Michelle wouldn't be safe until the Carpenter was caught. Figured I could explore the perks of being your bodyguard. Now can I seduce you?"

He didn't wait for her to answer. He gathered her in his arms and lowered his mouth, his eyes open, watching her, wondering how she would react to a "pig" kissing her. He captured her mouth and was amazed when she closed her

eyes and opened her lips to take him in. Oh, yeah. This was
paradise.

Careful of her injured arm, he held her tighter, lengthening
the kiss, sliding his mouth back and forth against hers,
savoring every moan she released. She pressed into him, her
lips soft and beckoning and eager, the fullness of her breasts
asking to be touched and caressed. He groaned as her hand
explored his back, inching lower, curving over his hip and
pulling him against her, spurring him on, putting wild ideas
into his head about lowering her under the tree and making
love. It was a dream come true, one he had been fantasizing
about ever since he saw her strip in the subway. And now she
was here, in his arms, making all the right moves.

But this was not a woman who would want a simple romp
in the hay. She was a smart yet compassionate woman whom
he had grudgingly come to respect. Even admire. They had
saved each other's life, and were on the verge of friendship.
Sex might ruin all that. Or make the bond growing between
them stronger and something special.

Only one way to find out.

He'd been taking a lot of chances since meeting Gillian.
Why not take the ultimate one?

As they kissed, tongue stroking tongue, tasting each other,
growing hot and excited, he slowly eased her around until he
was facing the house. *Damn.* In spite of being among the
trees, a window was still in view.

Though he didn't want to, he drew back, and immediately
missed the heat of her lips. Her eyes, glazed with desire,
looked at him, questioning why he had stopped touching her.

"We're not completely alone," Sam said, glancing at the
house.

A mischievous smile played across her lips, matching the
devilish glint in her eyes as she gestured with her head to the
barn. "Ever do it in a hayloft? Lots of nice soft straw to tumble

around in." She leaned against him and rubbed enticingly against his erection. "We can—"

Gillian blinked, and then stared off to the side as if he wasn't there.

"What's wrong?" he asked. "You okay?"

"I'm remembering something. Do you mind?" She rubbed up against him again. No emotion. No desire. As if conducting an experiment.

Not something that keeps a man turned on.

She stepped back and snapped her fingers. "Of course." Her eyes sparkled in excitement. "How could I have been so blind? It was there all along." She looked at him. "I've got to call Regis."

"Regis?" he said in disbelief as she took off at a run, straight for the house. Rubbing against him brought thoughts of Regis? Seconds ago, paradise had been in his grasp, his for the taking. And now she was running to get in touch with that bastard Regis Van Decker.

Sam looked up at the apple tree, expecting to see a snake. What had he done wrong?

Dejected, he grabbed the rifle and followed her to the house, feeling like he had just been kicked in the balls.

Chapter Twenty-Three

As Sam opened the screen door, he noticed a maroon car parked next to the rental Gillian had driven from New York. Wyoming plates with the local county number 2, Laramie County, on them. Probably a neighbor or friend come to visit.

He entered the house and heard Gillian on the phone in the kitchen arguing with someone, insisting on speaking with Special Agent Regis Van Decker. The TV was on but Michelle and Wyatt were nowhere in sight. Neither was the person who belonged to the maroon car.

Gillian slammed the phone down. "Bureaucrats!"

"There's a car out front," he said. "Recognize it?"

Gillian craned her neck to look out the window over the kitchen sink. "That's Fred Kennedy's car. He comes over every so often to borrow tools."

She turned around and gestured to the phone. "I can't get ahold of Regis. All I get is his voice mail. The agent I just talked to in New York says he went to Pittsburgh to investigate the bombing there, but he'd leave him a message. Makes me want to scream."

"You miss him that much?" Sam slumped into a chair at the table. He was in a major funk knowing Gillian would rather talk with Regis than go to the barn with him for a roll in the hay.

"What are you talking about?" She studied him. Realization dawned in her eyes. She ruffled the wavy black hair on top of his head, and a tender smile curved her lips. "You've got it all wrong, detective. This has nothing to do with

Regis and me. This has to do with the difference between men and women."

"If what we were doing out by the apple tree is any indication, we already have that figured out."

"Not sex, Sam. Gestures."

He scrunched his forehead in confusion.

"Think about the last time you saw a man who was angry. What did he do with his hands?"

"Made a fist and acted like he wanted to hit me."

"Exactly. Now how about the last time you saw a woman who was angry at you?"

"She pointed a gun at me."

"Oh." Gillian's cheeks burned in embarrassment when she realized he was talking about her. "Think about an *unarmed* woman who's angry."

That was easy. Stephanie yelling at him to do something about the punk who had just grabbed her briefcase. "She waved her hands in the air and pointed a finger at me."

"Basically, the hands are open," Gillian said. "But the man made a fist. He closed his hand."

Sam thought back to other times he had seen men and women angry. Gillian was right. Most of the times the men made a fist. The women kept their hands open, sometimes curving the fingers like the claws of a cat, sometimes pointing a finger in accusation.

Gillian said, "When Michelle and I saw the Carpenter outside the Institute, he was furious. But he didn't shake a fist at us. His hands were raised in anger, open, fingers apart."

"You think the Carpenter is a woman?"

"When I was alone with him in the courthouse, he rubbed up against me. It made me feel so dirty, so humiliated, I didn't even want to think about it. But you forced me to analyze it physically, not emotionally. With him I felt a small lump, definitely not long and hard like you were a moment ago. It was all wrong on him. Too low and small.

"Then I remembered: one of my English teachers in high school had us switch gender roles for a play, like they did during Shakespeare's time when women weren't allowed to act, and men did both parts. To get into the male persona, she had the girls put beanbags, sandbags, marbles, anything small and heavy in our pants down by our crotch to change our center of gravity to match a man's. The boys in class had to wear straps on their chest with a little weight in them to pull their center of gravity up to match a woman's."

"And?" Sam twirled his finger in the air so she would hurry up and get to the point.

"I saw sand in the hall of the courthouse after the Carpenter took off. It was by the stairs."

His head perked up. "There was sand in the john. Not the men's. The ladies." He slapped his forehead. "The Carpenter's a chick!" He looked up at Gillian who was nodding excitedly in agreement. "She threw her overcoat in the men's room to throw us off, then raced into the ladies room and changed just before we searched. In the rush, she probably poked a hole in the bag, small enough to keep her from noticing it right away but big enough for it to start seeping sand."

"Using the sandbag gimmick might indicate she's an actress or has experience in theater."

Sam nodded. "Michelle was in the courthouse john when the Carpenter entered it. Because I was searching for a man, I wasn't paying much attention to the women, but I bet Michelle saw her. She knows what the Carpenter looks like as a woman." Sam glanced toward the living room. The TV was on, but Michelle was strangely absent.

"I'll find her," Gillian said. "You go get Wyatt. In about twelve hours or more, the Carpenter will be in the area. Wyatt can alert the sheriff and local police to be on the lookout for a woman who might be posing as a man. I'll get the description from Michelle."

"But where do I find—" he began to ask when Gillian held up a finger for him to be quiet.

"Listen," she said.

One of the dogs was barking. He went to the door. "Sounds like it's coming from the barn."

"Probably where Wyatt and Fred are. We keep a lot of tools in there."

Sam grabbed the rifle and hurried out the door. Gillian checked the bathroom and found it unoccupied. She looked in the mudroom, laundry room, then opened the door to the basement. It was dark below, no lights on. Michelle hated the dark. She closed the door and went to the stairs that led up to the bedrooms and yelled, "Michelle? I have to talk to you!"

No answer.

She hurried up the stairs. Michelle could be one stubborn bitch when she wasn't happy. Now what was bothering her?

At the top, she called out, "Michelle? Where are you?"

No answer. She headed for Katie's room, expecting to find Michelle on the bed, sulking with a long list of things to complain about. To her surprise, the room was empty.

She scratched her head, thinking. The woman had made it infinitely clear she wasn't stepping foot outside. The wide openness of their surroundings gave Michelle "the creeps." The city girl preferred being lost in a crowd or safely nestled inside a building. So where could she be?

Was she even Michelle right now?

If little Lin Lin was out, she'd be in Katie's room, playing with her niece's dolls.

So if not Lin Lin, then who?

Could Jacob have been finally let out?

No. Jacob had been desperate to talk with her. If he was out, the first thing he would do was go look for her.

Tisha the teen? Most teens love to experiment with make-up. Gillian hurried to the bathroom. Empty. She looked in Wyatt and Susan's room. Empty. The beat of her heart went up a notch as she checked her own room. Empty. Frantically she searched the entire upstairs, including the closets, but couldn't find any trace of Michelle.

Hmm. Godfrey was too polite not to answer her calls. Olga would be chattering nonstop in Norwegian. That left . . . Gillian groaned. Six of Twelve. Had to be.

Where would Six go in the house?

Michelle might hate the dark and shadows, but for Six anything resembling the nighttime sky brought comforting thoughts of home.

She hurried to the basement.

"A woman," Sam muttered to himself as he headed for the barn. "All this time, a woman. I should have known, should have seen it." Statistically, he knew most women hate a direct, physical confrontation when they orchestrate a kill. They prefer a method with the least amount of mess. Poison. Drowning. A gun. Preferably someone else holding the gun, like a hitman or an accomplice.

Bombs made a bloody mess, no doubt about it, and was usually the choice of extermination picked by men. So as a woman, the Carpenter didn't seem to fit the law of averages. But she had someone else deliver them, caddies, unwilling accomplices to assure she'd be at a safe distance when the bombs went off. So, in that respect, she did fit the statistics.

Thanks to Gillian, they were closer to catching her. Gillian was smart, no doubt about it. She'd found the one matching set of clues that indicated the bomber was a woman. But she wasn't bitchy smart like Stephanie. She was sexy, vibrant, unpredictable at times, yet also dedicated and loyal.

As he entered the barn, he couldn't help but imagine getting her in here after the Carpenter was caught, and finding out just how soft straw could be when making love. But first things first.

He scanned the interior. The barn had a musty primal, earthy scent as he walked past a row of stalls on the right. In the light from the open double doors behind him, he could make out Satin and Scrounger several yards away. Scrounger was eating grain, probably oats, out of a torn sack on the ground. Satin was . . . he paused, not sure if he was seeing right. Among the shadows, Satin was licking something on the floor—the limp, outstretched hand of someone lying on the ground, the rest of the body in a stall.

Shit!

Sam raised the rifle. Too late he saw an object swinging toward him from the right. Pain burst at the side of his head, followed by darkness.

Gillian opened the door to the basement, the only place in the house she hadn't searched. She didn't know what she would do if Michelle or one of her alters wasn't here.

She called out, "Six of Twelve? Are you down there?"

The hot water heater gently rumbled, the skittering of tiny feet meant they needed to get some mousetraps, but no human-made sound rose from the dark.

She switched on the light and slowly headed down the stairs, cautious, concerned that if Six was in the basement, there was no telling what mood she might be in. Or what she was capable of if startled. Michelle had told her Six was one of her most aggressive alters. From Ray, Gillian had learned how dangerous an alter could be.

"Six?" she called out again. "I need to talk with Michelle. Speak to me. Tell me where you are."

By the time she reached the bottom of the stairs, even the hot water heater had gone silent. Along one of the concrete walls, metal shelves held the overflow of canned goods and preserves from the pantry upstairs. Next to a sewing machine, numerous garments hung from a portable clothes rod in Susan's sewing corner. A worktable and a box full of clothes patterns were nearby, guarded by a dressmaker's dummy with a prom dress Susan was making for a friend's daughter.

The next section of the basement housed the water heater, water softener, boards, and some of Wyatt's tools for repairs around the house.

Stacks of boxes were in the next area, filled with old toys and clothes, some of which would be taken to the Salvation Army. Boxes made great building material for the imagination. She noticed her nephews' toys scattered around. From the look of things, a scene from *Star Wars* had been recreated, what with all the action figures, weaponized vehicles, and spaceships.

Spaceships?

She inched closer and peered around the boxes.

Six of Twelve sat cross-legged on the floor, encircled by an array of alien figures and space vehicles. Her eyes were closed, her hands raised, an index finger resting on each of her temples.

"Six, why didn't you answer when I called?"

Eyes closed, Six spoke in a monotone voice. "I am occupied with a critical concern. Concentration is crucial. Extinguish the incandescent bulb and exit the area."

Gillian ran her hands up and down her jeans, always nervous when dealing with this alter. She stepped closer and reminded herself to use patience yet firmness with Six.

"I'll comply, but first I need to talk with Michelle. It's very important. A matter of life and death."

"Michelle does not wish to come out."

"She doesn't?" That was strange. Michelle jealously fought to stay out for as long as possible. As often as possible. Could Six be lying?

Gillian sat down across from her, matching her posture and gestures, trying to get into Six's head by mimicking her body language. Though it seemed to be a form of meditation, the tenseness in her face indicated Six was anything but relaxed. "What are you doing?"

"I am contacting my companions on our celestial ship, urging them to speed swiftly through the solar system they are currently surveying and rescue me."

"Rescue you?" Gillian laughed dryly in disbelief and lowered her hands. "I know Michelle hates the ranch, but I thought at least you would find the animals here interesting."

With one brow cocked skeptically, Six opened an eye and looked at her.

Good, Gillian thought. Now that I have her attention, I'll throw in a little alliteration and we'll be best buds in no time. "From the perspective of a planetary zoological survey, this place is practically a gold mine. You could compile a lot of data to share with your fellow celestial companions about the domesticated animals of Earth."

Six of Twelve's other eye opened, obviously thinking about what Gillian had said. She lowered her hands to her lap. "Agreed. Perhaps at a future time this would be favorable. But for now I must continue communication."

Six raised her fingers to her temples, closed her eyes, and squinted in concentration.

"What's the rush?" Gillian asked. "Couldn't you do that later, after you let me talk to Michelle?"

Six of Twelve shook her head. "Contact is crucial. Jacob Miller observed an individual he did not like in the area of the tall structure to the north northwest of here."

"The barn? You must mean Fred." Yet she doubted a ninety-year-old would cause Michelle to switch to her defensive alter, and her voice rose in concern. "Did Jacob know who it was?"

Six tilted her head as if listening to someone. "Affirmative. Jacob Miller contacted Olga. Olga told Tisha, who translated and relayed to the rest of us the inevitable danger if we remained in this rural setting. Michelle concurred. She informed the entity Wyatt Dohr when he exited the excretory room about the inappropriate ingress of the intruder. He concurred and left to conduct an exploratory investigation. When he did not return from the structure in a reasonable amount of time, Michelle relented and agreed with my rationalization that the correct response was to seek relief by calling my celestial companions."

Gillian's heart raced in alarm. Wyatt was in the barn! Sam had just gone there to find him! "Who did Jacob see? Who's the intruder?" As far as she knew, Michelle was afraid of only one person. The Carpenter.

She thought back to her discussion with Sam about the sex of the bomber. "Is it a woman?"

"Silence!" Six squeezed her eyes shut even more in her futile efforts to contact an imaginary ship. "Concentration is crucial."

"Like hell it is. There's no time for this. I want to talk to Michelle NOW." Desperate, Gillian grabbed Six by the arm and shook her until she reopened her eyes.

There were times in Gillian's life when she knew she had walked into trouble: the rattle of a snake within arm's length of striking; the wild stare of a bull when she's too far away from the pickup to escape; Wyatt finding her on Lookout Point with the high school team's running back.

Six didn't have a rattle, and she certainly wasn't snorting in prelude to a charge, nor seething like a furious brother, but there was no mistaking the look in her eyes as Six stared at the hand grasping her arm. Gillian swallowed hard as Six's fierce gaze swept up to her face.

Now I've done it.

Chapter Twenty-Four

Sam's head pounded in excruciating pain. His vision was fuzzy, yet he could still make out Wyatt sitting across from him against the wall of the stall they were in. A gash on Wyatt's forehead was bleeding profusely, some of the blood getting into his eye, but Wyatt couldn't wipe it clean. His hands were tied behind his back, his feet tied, too. Satin lay by his legs, whimpering, the dog obviously confused by what was going on.

Join the club, Sam thought as he tried to sit up. Vertigo overwhelmed him, and he lay back down to catch his breath and quiet the queasiness in his stomach. Great. Another concussion.

Unlike Wyatt, he wasn't tied up. He reached for his shoulder holster. It was empty.

"Sorry. I screwed up," Wyatt said. "Didn't see him until it was too late."

From outside the stall, a deep voice rasped, "Shut up! I told you not to talk!"

In the gloom, a figure in a grey overcoat and hat stepped into the stall. The Carpenter pointed Sam's own gun at him. From the awkward way she held it, Sam deduced she was more proficient with bombs than pistols. Then he noticed the bandage on her hand and remembered the blood on the sidewalk at the Institute. A nail must have skewered her dominant hand. Maybe he could use that to his advantage.

Disregarding the pain and dizziness, he sat up. "Gray's not your color, lady."

The Carpenter scowled. She took off the hat and threw it at Satin. The dog backed away from it, growling. But he didn't growl at her, Sam noted. Strange. The day he arrived, both dogs growled at him for hours until they got used to his presence.

The dogs must have met her before.

"How did you know?" she asked Sam, her voice not as deep as when masquerading as a man.

He deliberately ignored the question and said, "Red hair's all wrong, too. Doesn't match your skin tone."

She pulled off the wig, releasing a mat of frizzy hair. "What gave it away?" she demanded to know. "I did everything perfect."

Again he ignored her question, trying to keep her off-balance until he could figure a way to literally throw her off-balance and get his gun back. He studied her brown hair. "Didn't I see you outside Hackers Coffee Slop?" he asked. "You were hawking watches."

She cackled with pride. "Sold three before I brought the house down."

"And on the subway with Roger Walgood?"

She grinned. "You looked right at me. But you were after a man in a satin jacket, not a woman talking on a phone."

He vaguely remembered her being in the first car. "You weren't making a call," Sam said in sudden realization. "You were listening to what was going on with Roger, making sure he behaved and did as ordered."

"Finally, a correct answer." She squatted down to his level, the gun pointed at his face. "I had to keep him under supervision; props are so unpredictable. Now, how did you know I wasn't a man?"

"You had leaky balls at the courthouse."

No laugh this time.

She frowned and stood back up. "No scene is perfect. But I bet the kiss worked."

"Nah. You couldn't even do that right. Gillian knew something was wrong with the way you Frenched her. You need practice."

"Practice?! I'll have you know no one has ever complained—man or woman. I was the best. I AM the best. I don't need practice. I've done my homework. My technique is beyond question. If Gillian can't get it on, don't blame me. Blame Ray."

"You mean Ray Andrew Follett?"

"Ray never could stay in character. I learned more from the others than from him. You don't get the Oscar playing wimps. You have to go after the hard, gritty roles: the sympathetic, abused misfits or the devilishly insane villains. The ones who kill or are killed. Nice characters don't win a thing."

Characters. Props. Oscars. Roles. The woman had ties to show business. And to Ray Andrew Follett. He puzzled over her remark that she had learned more from the others than Ray. Was she referring to his alters?

"You knew Ray had multiple personality disorder," he said. "You grew up together. You're one of his sisters, aren't you?" He thought back to all the files he'd read on Follett. One of his stepsisters was an actress. What was her name?

"You're Sonya Follett, the actress, right? And you've been going after MPD/DIDs because Ray was one. You hated Ray for ruining your career, so now you hate all DIDs. That's why you put a *J* on the nails, for your new name, Terri Joy."

"Not even close," she said with a sneer. "The man gets an F."

Sam refused to believe he could be that far off base. He remembered Gillian's lecture about the Carpenter needing to know beforehand what type of person would do as ordered. From the info Regis's team discovered, the Carpenter had practiced for almost a year with men from different socioeconomic backgrounds. Practiced until she got it right. Almost got it right. As she coldly pointed out, people can be unpredictable props. Even after a year of planning and practicing. That meant . . .

He almost chuckled out loud. Gillian was right. Cops do tend to be myopic.

The Carpenter uses show business lingo, but she also plans, practices, does her homework, and gives F's for incorrect answers.

"You're Jodi Follett, high school teacher." He'd bet a month's salary the wannabe actress taught drama or English.

Sam glanced around, trying to find a way out of the crappy situation they were in.

"Don't move, detective." Jodi tightened her grip on the gun. "Any heroics and Wyatt becomes a prop." She glared at Wyatt. "Show him."

With his hands tied behind his back, Wyatt leaned forward just enough for Sam to see an object tucked into the front of his shirt.

A bomb!

Small yet capable of blowing a hole in his chest.

Jodi cackled and fingered a remote control now in her other hand. It had five switches on it. Sam held his breath. Five bombs!

She said, "In case you're feeling sorry for him, don't. I've got one for you, too."

A finger hovered over one of the switches as she pocketed the gun and took out a bigger bomb encircled with a strip of nails. She tossed it to Sam. He caught it automatically, just like Roger T. Walgood when he caught Gillian's bra in the subway.

With the gun in one hand and the remote in the other, Jodi Follett withdrew several steps into the shadows, out of fatal range if she decided to detonate either bomb. "Here's the way we're going to do the scene," she said. "Wyatt stays here with his bomb to make sure you do as you're told. You go to the house and give yours to Jacob. Then it's up to him whether we all live happily ever after."

Sam stared at the bomb. He'd always promised himself never to be a victim. His worst nightmare had come true. *Fuck.*

The grim tight line of Wyatt's mouth, the somber look in his eyes as he stared at Sam, indicated he knew what was at stake and had already given his silent permission to offer his life to save his sister's.

Sam calmly told the Carpenter, "No. I won't do it," and tossed the bomb over his head. It landed with a soft thud in a distant stall.

Jodi Follett shrieked in disbelief.

Sometimes the only way to deal with a crazy person was to do something crazy yourself.

"Spent most of high school in detention," Sam told Wyatt. "Teachers are so predictable."

Not sure what Michelle's most belligerent alter might do to defend against an unwanted physical contact, Gillian quickly let go of Six of Twelve's arm. But she refused to back down, not with Wyatt and Sam confronting some unknown person in the barn.

"Let me make myself clear," Gillian said. Her steely voice matched the glint of warning in Six's eyes. "If you don't let me talk to Michelle right this second, I'm going to call the Air Force. I'm telling them that when your celestial ship shows up in the skies over Wyoming, they have my permission to shoot it down. Got that?"

She could see Six thinking it over.

Six of Twelve might be the alter that claimed to have no emotions, but she was in a human body chock full of them. Gillian decided to use that to her advantage.

She raised a booted foot and stepped on one of the plastic spaceships. *Crunch. Crackle.* Six flinched repeatedly as Gillian ground it into pieces. "That's what's going to happen to your companions and your ship," she told Six, "if you don't let me talk to Michelle."

Gillian removed her foot. Six stared down at the broken toy. A lone tear fell onto her cheek. Her body jerked ever so slightly, and she took a deep breath. The next voice Gillian heard was definitely Michelle's.

"That was mean. I didn't know you were such a bitch."

"I'll buy her a new one," Gillian said evenly. "Now tell me who Jacob saw go into the barn."

Michelle crossed her arms over her stomach, over the solar plexus, which occurred when people were defensive—either from dislike or fear. Gillian would lay odds it was caused by the latter.

"Who?" she asked again.

"Someone he calls Follett."

"Male or female?"

"Huh?"

"When Jacob relayed his concern to Olga, did she get the impression that it was a man or a woman named Follett?"

"How would I know? I don't speak Norwegian."

"Shit, Michelle. Stop being so difficult. This isn't the time to be jealous of your alters. Tisha knows Norwegian. Ask her."

"Oh, all right." Michelle acted as if she was listening to someone. She sighed irritably. "Female. You happy?"

Gillian ignored Michelle's blustery attitude, recognizing it as a defense mechanism for when the woman was afraid, and ran through a mental list of all the female Folletts. Ray's mom was in a nursing home, incapacitated by arthritis and in need of knee transplants. The other adult females were Cindy, Jodi, and Sonya. When she had talked to Cindy, she'd asked if her brothers were capable of being the Carpenter. It never occurred to her to ask about Jodi and Sonya. Then again, until this moment, she had never considered whether Cindy might be the Carpenter.

Cold dread slithered through her. The Carpenter was someone she knew. Someone who could figure out that she would return to the safety of the family ranch as she had done three years ago after Ray died.

A Follett who wanted to kill Michelle.

She grabbed Michelle by the hand. "Let's go. The Carpenter's here."

Michelle pulled back. "Are you nuts? We just heard this morning the Carpenter's in Pittsburgh. There's no way he could get here so fast. He's not Superman."

"I agree. But he is a she, and there are other ways to set off a bomb when you can't be there in person. Maybe a timer or something. She must have been only a few hours behind us when we left New York."

"The Carpenter's here?" Michelle's lips quivered. Her eyes turned scared and watery, and her voice reverted to that of a little girl's. "I wanna go home. I don't like this place. Take me home."

Lin Lin, the little girl alter who had appeared when they saw the Carpenter in front of the Institute of Many Friends, was now in control of Michelle's body. She slipped her hand out of Gillian's grasp and tightened into a ball on the floor. Her hands hugged the drawn up legs, head hidden against the knees. She trembled in fear. "I wanna go home. Take me home. I wanna go home."

The phone upstairs rang. Gillian looked at Lin Lin, a frightened little girl in a woman's body.

The phone rang again.

"I'll be back," Gillian said, and ran up the stairs.

Sam moved fast. While Jodi Follett ranted and raved in the shadows about having her precious bomb thrown away, he dove across the stall to Wyatt, reached in his shirt, pulled out the bomb, and threw it toward the far end of the barn.

The Carpenter went ballistic, yelling and screaming.

"Let's get out of here." He began untying Wyatt. The Carpenter had their guns, but he'd take his chances surviving a bullet rather than a bomb any day.

Wyatt muttered, "Uh-oh," followed by the sound of Jodi's menacing laugh.

Sam looked sideways and groaned. In the stall stood Scrounger, tail wagging happily. He dropped the bomb he had retrieved on the ground by his master.

"Props—always unpredictable." Jodi edged out of the shadows and pointed the gun at Sam. "New scene, detective. Take the bomb to Jacob or I'll have Scrounger do it for you."

"Go ahead and use the dog," he said through tight lips. "I'll lay odds Gillian won't play along. Living on a ranch all her life, she figures animals are expendable. She'll either call 911, arm herself, or grab Jacob and run out the back door. Maybe all of the above."

He could see her thinking it over. Multiple choice questions could be such a bitch.

As she ran through her list of options, he noticed the barrel of the gun lower ever so slightly. A little lower and he would risk a running tackle before she had time to aim and shoot.

He was getting ready to leap when the barrel suddenly rose.

"We'll go back to the original scene. You take the bomb, and we visit Jacob. But this time, instead of throwing it away, you keep it. Or else . . ."

The gun fired. Sam jumped, startled. Scrounger yelped and dropped to the ground, whimpering in pain. *She shot the dog!*

"Take the bomb or I'll shoot the brother next—in the leg, the other leg, then the arm. Get the pattern?"

"Yeah," Sam growled, not liking it. He and Wyatt deciding to die to save Gillian and Michelle had been a no-brainer.

Whether from a bullet or a bomb, he could handle his own quick death. But watching the Carpenter torture Wyatt to death with multiple wounds was another thing entirely. His gut twisted into knots. He had never felt so helpless.

As Satin crawled over to lick the blood from the other dog's wound, Sam picked up the bomb Scrounger had dropped. He saw the worried look on Wyatt's face and said, "It'll be okay." And hoped he wasn't lying.

Gillian grabbed the phone in the kitchen on the third ring. "Dohr-Chester Ranch."

"Gillian?"

"Regis! Thank God! We need help!"

"I know. The Carpenter's using timers. Found out on my way to Pittsburgh and had the plane diverted to Denver. We're just south of Cheyenne."

"You're too late. She's already here."

"She?"

"I'm almost sure it's one of the Follett girls. Maybe Cindy. She's been here before. Knows the lay of the land. She—"

Someone outside had called her name.

Sam?

She took the cordless phone to the front door and opened it. Sam was exiting the barn and walking toward the house. Gillian gasped in alarm. Even from fifty yards away, she recognized one of the Carpenter's bombs.

"Ohmigod!"

"Gillian, talk to me," Regis said over the phone. "What's going on?"

"Sam's in the yard with a bomb! Oh, Regis," she cried in despair. "Why didn't you warn us sooner?"

"I did. Didn't Wyatt tell you?"

Wyatt! Ohmigod! She stared at the barn in dismay. *Wyatt's still in the barn! Alive or dead?*

If Sam had a bomb, did Wyatt have one, too?

"I have to go," she said.

"No! Wait—"

She dropped the phone and stepped out onto the porch.

As soon as Sam saw her, he stopped. "Don't come any closer! Get out of here!" Positioned halfway between the barn and the house, he was close enough to warn her, but not enough to kill her if the Carpenter exploded the bomb. His unflinching self-sacrifice tore at her heart.

But she couldn't let him die for her, not without a fighting chance for him to live.

She noticed a figure slink out of the shadows of the barn. A woman who had ruthlessly murdered in New York and who was now bringing death to her home.

The hair was shorter than she remembered, the girth thicker by about seventy pounds, but once she knew what to look for, recognition was plain as day. It explained why she had a partial scar similar to those on Ray's body. She was from the same abusive family.

Gillian spoke her name in disgust. "Jodi Follett."

"The slow learner gets a B." Jodi raised a hand so Gillian could see the row of switches on the remote. "Tell me where Jacob is or I turn your brother into hamburger."

"She's lying," Sam said. "Only I have a bomb."

"Shut up and keep moving!" Jodi yelled. She pointed the gun directly at him.

Sam stayed where he was, feet firmly planted.

Jodi shook in frustration. "I'll kill him," she told Gillian as she raised the remote higher. "If you don't tell me where Jacob is, I'll kill your brother *and* the cop."

"If you do, you'll die, too," Gillian said, hoping the logic of the situation would save her brother's life. To her surprise, Jodi cackled in response.

"Not likely," Jodi said. "The bombs are small. Only enough to kill the person holding it."

"What about the nails? They can kill just as easily."

"True, but his body will absorb most of them." Jodi tapped her chest. "Got a Kevlar vest just in case." And yet for all her bravado, she stepped further away from Sam, back toward the barn.

"Where's Jacob?" Jodi asked.

"I haven't seen him since New York."

"You're lying! I know you're lying! I saw the two of you leave together."

Actually, she had left with Michelle, not Jacob. And yet Jodi thought of Michelle as Jacob. That might explain why she had sent a bomb to the courthouse where Michelle worked. If she killed Michelle's body, she killed the alter Jacob as well.

Gillian said, "I swear, on my brother's life, I haven't seen or spoken to Jacob since New York!"

Jodi jerked her head back, startled by the unexpected reply. She sputtered, "He's here. He has to be."

"The only one inside the house right now is a little girl." *Lin Lin.*

Jodi hesitated, confused. The hand holding the remote fell to her side. "You're lying."

"Look who's talking. Masquerading as a man, telling the men you gave the bombs to that you wouldn't kill them if they delivered the bombs to the places you picked. You had no intention of letting any of them live."

"Yes, I did. If they had just followed the script, none of them would have died."

"What script? What are you talking about?"

"All they had to do was let their prisoners out. If they couldn't do that, then taking a bomb to Jacob would suffice. Hey, it's not my fault they died. Everybody knows you get punished for not following directions."

Gillian shook her head. Jodi wasn't making any sense, and she wondered if Jodi was on drugs. Regardless, she had to get through to her, reason with her, get her to let Sam and her brother live. "So, you admit your bombs were intended for Jacob."

"Of course. That's why I came to see you in the courthouse. To get your approval, maybe your help. With everyone in the city saying bad things about me, I needed one person on my side. Of all people, I thought you would understand."

"Understand what? That you're trying to kill Jacob?"

"Of course not. What gave you that idea?"

She struggled to understand the woman's reasoning. "If Sam hadn't grabbed the bomb at the Hackers Coffee Slop and taken it out to the alley, Jacob would be dead. Isn't that what you've wanted all along?"

"Scare him to the point of death, sure. But kill him? Not unless he deserved it. You know what it's like. You loved Ray. Don't you miss him?"

The question threw her. What did her feelings for Ray have to do with sending bombs to Jacob? "There's not a week that goes by that I don't think about him."

"A week? For me it's every day. Every hour. Every minute. When Ray died, I lost my best friend. With Jacob and the others I had a chance to find someone new. Maybe someone better." Jodi took an angry step toward her. "Didn't you get the nail?"

The nail?

"You mean from your bombs?" Gillian asked.

"Hah! No wonder Ray liked you. Both of you, simpletons. Haven't you figured it out yet?" Gillian shook her head. "The nail was my gift, my memento to you from Ray's final scene."

She gasped. It couldn't be. And yet . . . "The only nail I got was after Ray died. I thought it was from the police, a hideous souvenir, a warning to get out of the business or else. Now you're telling me *you* sent it?"

Jodi's vicious smile, her flippant nod in confirmation, showed the true depths of the woman's madness.

Gillian's skin crawled in sudden realization. "It had blood on it. Your blood or Ray's?"

"It came from the props," Jodi said.

"Props?" Gillian saw Sam grimace.

"Still not seeing the big picture," Jodi told her. "Actually, everything that happened in New York is your fault. You're the one who insisted Ray see the psychiatrist after he was acquitted. Because of that quack, Janeane disappeared. Growing up, she was my best friend. We shared our deepest secrets with each other. I loved her. And then she was gone. Cut off. Imprisoned. I had to get her back. I couldn't let her die. She meant more to me than Ray."

"You never told me you knew Ray was MPD," Gillian said. "After the trial, you said it was a complete surprise."

Jodi shrugged. "I lied. Figured if you knew, you'd stop me from trying to get Janeane back."

"You've known Ray was MPD/DID since childhood?"

"Sure. Dragon hated me; none of Ray's alters liked me. Except Janeane. We got along great. Like sisters. After the trial, I tried to release her. I figured if I did exactly what she had been doing, it would draw her out. So, I created the perfect scene. It wasn't easy to get five props all at the same time, almost got caught grabbing the last one, but I wanted a big production."

Gillian's stomach churned. Her lips twisted in revulsion. "The children crucified on the walls of the bedroom, you thought of them as props?"

"What else? After I got them nailed up, I phoned Ray. Said it was an emergency and told him to come to the address. When he got there, I showed him what I had done, expecting him to approve and let Janeane out. Instead, he called me a monster." Jodi pounded her chest with a fist. "Me—a monster. After all the work I did to set Janeane free.

"He threatened me—and still Janeane refused to come out and take my side. But I'm no fool. If she was too much of a wimp to appear, then I didn't want her anymore. While Ray went to the bedroom to take the props off the walls, I decided to put an end to Janeane once and for all."

"You're the one who called the police." Gillian staggered to the side and gripped the porch railing. The horror of what had actually happened three years ago to the man she loved was too much to bear. Shaking, she covered her heart with her hands, and her eyes filled with tears. Barely able to breathe, she gasped, "You told them where to find Ray and the children."

"Ray got what he deserved."

The look of triumph on Jodi's face made her choke. Ray's evil alter had spawned a slaughtering admirer.

Heavy with sorrow, she said more to herself than Jodi, "That's why the police found Ray with blood on his hands. He was trying to save the children. He was innocent."

"He never should have been killed," Sam said.

She looked at Sam, and her heart went out to him. When he added, "Everyone deserves their day in court," she knew without a doubt that this was the one cop she could love.

"Give me Jacob!" Jodi yelled. She raised the remote, her finger on two of the switches. "Or I'll kill your brother. If I could kill my own, yours will be easy. And the cop."

"NO!" She couldn't let Sam and Wyatt die. And she couldn't hand over Michelle.

She looked at Sam and was surprised to see him smile. Just loud enough for her to hear, he said, "In the subway, remember how we got rid of Roger's bomb?"

Her mouth dropped open. He didn't mean—

Jodi inched forward and yelled, "What are you saying to her?"

Quickly, Sam said to Gillian, "On a count of two, run in the house and don't look back. One, two."

He never gave her a chance to object. In a blur of motion, he swiftly turned and lobbed the bomb toward Jodi.

Ohmigod! He's crazy! Gillian ducked into the house.

Chapter Twenty-Five

Sam ran to the closest structure, the garage.

He hadn't taken more than three steps when the bomb exploded, knocking him off his feet, making his head hurt even more—until the nails started hitting everything in the barnyard. They hurt worse.

A stabbing pain in his side indicated one had struck him in the ribs. *Damn. Not again.* He opened his eyes. He was covered in dirt, straw, and planks of wood. Gingerly, his fingers examined the side where it hurt the most. He found a nail, rigid, which meant it was lodged in a rib.

Great. Human pincushion.

Rubbing the grit from his eyes, he scanned the area. Pieces of wood were on the ground. Dirt and debris still filled the air, making it difficult to see. A lot more dust than he expected from a bomb that had been detonated in midair. Unless . . .

Through the sifting cloud of dirt, he could just make out a jagged hole in the side of the barn. *Shit!* In a panic, the bitch must have detonated both bombs. *Wyatt!*

The constant ringing in his ears from the blast kept him from hearing cries or moans from anyone, inside or out. Through the haze, he saw a figure on the ground by the barn, trying to get up, writhing in pain, gun still in her hand. Jodi. He hoped she was hurting more than he was.

Painfully, he raised his head and looked toward the house. No sign of Gillian. *God, I hope she's all right.* As for himself, he needed to be mobile before the air cleared, but he couldn't with a nail tearing at his flesh every time he moved. He grabbed onto the nail and, on a count of two, yanked it out.

Man, that hurt. Worse than the one he'd had in the calf. He dropped the nail and tried to get to his feet, but only managed to get to his knees before the throbbing in his head threatened to make him pass out. He took several deep breaths, willing himself to stay conscious, needing to get moving. He clenched his teeth and crawled toward the garage, determined to get inside before Jodi saw him.

The blast knocked Gillian down just inside the front door. At the same time, the force shook the house, cracking windows facing the barn. Dishes, pictures, and books shuddered and crashed to the floor. From the basement, Lin Lin screamed in terror, while outside, chickens squawked, horses neighed, and cattle bellowed in fright.

Her legs shaking like rubber, Gillian got to her feet and made her way to the door. The pungent odor of burning wood filled the air. Dirt and straw billowed in the yard. Broken planks and boards littered the porch; the split and splintered strips had red paint on one side. Barn red.

Wyatt!

Her gaze flew to the barn. Through the mass of dust she could make out a dark hole in the side. *Ohmigod!*

Frantically, she scanned the yard for Sam. She couldn't see him.

A shrill cry drew her attention back to the barn. In the haze, she could see a figure with a gun stumble toward the house, coughing violently from the soot and dust while intermittently yelling for Jacob. Jodi Follett.

Gillian's fear gave way to iron resolve. Her brother might be dead, God knows what had happened to Sam, but she wasn't going to let Jodi or her bombs get anywhere near Michelle. Not if she could help it. She raced to the bookcase in the living room. Shoot to kill was her intent; not a doubt in her mind to do otherwise.

Grabbing *War and Peace,* she opened it and moaned in dismay. The hidey-hole was empty. She rifled through the pages, turned the book upside down and shook it. *Damn!* The key to the gun cabinet was gone.

She looked around, assessing her options. Knives? Baseball bat?

Jodi had a gun and bombs.

Keep moving, she could hear her dad say when he taught his children how to hunt and survive. Unless camouflaged, a stationary target makes an easy kill. Every elk and deer that had ever filled their freezer with meat had been shot while standing still. Until she could think of something else, she had to get Michelle away from Jodi and hope to God Regis got here before it was too late.

She ran to the basement. Hidden among the boxes, Lin Lin, her body compressed into a tight ball, was still screaming. Gillian squatted down in front of her. Though she looked like a woman, she was actually dealing with a frightened little girl.

Struggling to sound calm and comforting, when what she really wanted to do was grab her and run, Gillian said, "Shhh. Quiet. I'm here. I'll take care of you."

Lin Lin's screaming sputtered to a stop. With tear-filled eyes, she lifted her head and looked at Gillian. Between sobs, she said, "This is a scary place. I want to go home. I don't like it here. Please, take me home."

"I can't right now, sweetie, but I will take you someplace else. Someplace safer."

The wooden floor above their heads groaned. Gillian held her breath. Either the house was still settling from the blast or Jodi was inside, walking around, hunting for Jacob.

Frantic with worry, she whispered to Lin Lin, "You have to come with me. There's not much time." She took Lin Lin's arm to hurry her along. Immediately, Lin Lin shrieked and shook free of her grasp. She scooted away, knocking boxes over as she scrambled into the corner.

Gillian studied the woman's fear-filled face, and sighed in understanding. Lin Lin was a product of child abuse. Anyone who touched her without permission was potentially a molester. "I'm sorry," she whispered. "I shouldn't have grabbed you like that, but I really need to talk with Michelle. Would you please let her out?"

Lin Lin shook her head, looking like a scared little mouse being stalked by a cat.

"All right, sweetie. If Michelle doesn't want to come out then I need to talk with Six of Twelve. Tell her I, uh, I've got news about her ship. I know when it's coming."

It was like magic. With a jerk and an exhalation of breath, Michelle's features were transformed from a scared little girl to a tough, determined alien with an unmistakable spark of curiosity in her eyes. "My ship?"

Gillian breathed a sigh of relief. "I've received word your ship is on its way. But they'll only wait a few seconds for you. We have to go now or you'll miss your ride home."

"Agreed." Six got to her feet. "Proceed."

"First, I have to warn you. There's, uh," Gillian paused. She couldn't mention Jodi, the Carpenter, or bombs. It might cause Lin Lin to reappear. "There's an alien from another planet—a hostile planet—in the house, trying to stop you from reaching your ship. She looks like a white woman with frizzy brown hair. We must be very quiet and get out of the house as fast as we can without her seeing us if we're to make it to the landing site in time. Understand?"

"Affirmative."

Six followed her up the stairs. Gillian paused at the top and strained to hear any sound that might indicate where Jodi was. She heard a familiar creak on the stairs to the bedrooms.

"Jacob?" Jodi called out. "Where are you? I've come a long way to find you." She coughed, then sputtered, clearly in pain. "I have something for you."

Gillian silently motioned for Six to follow, then hurried to the back door. She held it open and whispered to Six to run to the nearby trees for cover. As Six did as she was told, Gillian heard a cackle. The hair on the back of her neck stiffened. She looked over her shoulder.

Jodi stood down the hall by the kitchen, looking straight at her, smiling in triumph, a bomb in one hand, a gun in the other. Blood oozed from a hole in her cheek, no doubt made by a nail from the bomb Sam had tossed. A spreading splotch of blood on the thigh of her pants glistened bright red. "Jacob's with you, isn't he?"

"Go to hell, Jodi!" Gillian dashed outside, flinching as she heard a bullet thud into the doorframe. She raced to Six's hiding place behind an old oak. Heart pounding, she peered at the cars in front of the house and frowned. She told Six, "We're going to a building that looks like a small version of the Capitol in Washington, D.C. Do you know what that looks like?"

"Affirmative."

"Good. If we get separated, go there and wait inside until your ship arrives. Whatever happens, don't let the alien get you."

"Affirmative."

"Let's go."

With a tire iron in one hand and a hammer in the other, Sam peeked out from the garage. The dust cloud had cleared, enabling him to catch a glimpse of Jodi limping into the house. He hoped Gillian and Michelle weren't inside.

From where he stood, he noticed each of the cars in front of the house had at least one flat tire. Except for Fred Kennedy's. Jodi probably had the keys to that. For a split second, he wondered what had happened to the owner, and decided the answer could wait.

A quick inspection revealed all the vehicles in the garage also had a flat. Jodi had made sure no one was going to leave without her permission.

He slipped out the back of the garage, around the pyramid chicken coops, and to the back door of the barn. He heard a cow bellow, which meant his hearing was returning. His head still hurt, but the pain was manageable. The throbbing in his side was getting worse, and the warm wet blood soaking his shirt and jacket made it clear he needed to take care of the Carpenter fast before his body succumbed to shock.

The rear door of the barn had been blown ajar. He stepped inside. The confines of the structure was hazy with dirt and straw particulates. Blood, manure, and burnt straw scented the air. He headed for the stall where he had last seen Wyatt, expecting the worst. Scrounger was there, panting, whimpering in pain, but Wyatt and Satin were gone.

"Wyatt?"

"Here," a hoarse voice answered.

Sam hurried to where the second bomb had blown a hole through the wall of the barn. In the light filtering in from outside, he saw a bloodied, torn body on the ground. Too small for a person. Satin.

"Over here."

Through the blown-out side of the stall, Sam followed the voice into the next one. Wyatt was on the ground, his hands and feet untied, but bleeding from at least four new wounds on his body, at least two with nails protruding from them.

Sam hurried to his side. "What happened?"

"Went looking for the rest of our guns. Found 'em." Wyatt patted the straw next to him, and Sam saw the glint of metal. "Figured I'd have an easy shot at her, but then the bomb you chucked went off. Damn, those nails hurt."

"Tell me about it." He flicked open his jacket to show his own damage. Wyatt nodded in sympathy.

Wyatt coughed deeply, violently.

Sam eyed him in concern. "You okay?"

"Yeah. It's the dust." He coughed again, and spat a dark glob of mucus to the side. "Where's Gillian? She okay? And Jodi—dead?"

Sam shook his head. "The bitch has nine lives. Saw her go into the house. I haven't seen Gillian since the bombs went off. Thought I'd come here, check on you, and get armed."

Wyatt winced in pain. "It's okay. Gillian's a good shot."

"I'm sure she is, but did you ever tell her where you hid the key for the gun cabinet?"

Wyatt's eyes widened in sudden realization. "Shit."

He tried to get up. Sam put a firm hand on his shoulder. "Stay put. You're in no shape to move." He gathered up the guns and checked to make sure all three were still loaded. He put the handgun in his shoulder holster and handed one of the rifles to Wyatt. "Keep this in case Jodi comes back." He hefted the other rifle. "Where would Gillian go? Other than the trees and windbreaks, it's pretty wide open around here. Where would she take Michelle to hide?"

"Might try to get to one of the cars."

Sam shook his head. "All have flats."

Wyatt frowned. He thought for a long moment, then nodded to himself. "Her second home has been that pig shed. All her tools are there." He managed a painful grin. "Pretty nasty with a pneumatic hammer."

"I'll check it out."

"Almost forgot to tell you," Wyatt said. "Regis called while you and Gillian were taking a walkabout. Knows the Carpenter used a timer in Pittsburgh. He's on his way up from Denver."

"I don't think we can wait."

"Neither do I. Good hunting."

Chapter Twenty-Six

With Six of Twelve sticking close behind, Gillian sprinted through the windbreak. They dashed through the fruit orchard and into the Capitol-shaped farrowing shed. Gillian closed the door and unscrewed all the light bulbs, making sure the interior stayed as dark as possible.

"When will my ship arrive?" Six asked.

"Soon. Until then, we're going to have to hide so the hostile alien doesn't find us."

"Agreed."

At the back of the shed, Gillian opened the top half of the Dutch doors. Flat pasture as far as the eye could see. Out there they'd be easily spotted. She wasn't sure how good of a marksman Jodi was, but she didn't want to be an easy target. Alone, she could call one of the horses and ride bareback. But Michelle was a city girl who'd never been around horses, let alone knew how to ride one without a saddle.

She studied the large blue spruce, which provided shade in the corner of the pigpen. They could climb up and hide in its branches—and then be cornered if Jodi discovered them. She could pick them off with the gun or just blow the whole tree down with one of her bombs.

Jodi yelled from outside the shed. "Jacob!"

At the sound, Six looked up from where she had been inspecting the carpentry tools. "Is that the hostile alien?"

"Yes. Hide over there and don't make a sound, no matter what."

"But my celestial companions—"

"Shush," Gillian said in an anxious whisper. "I don't think they'll get here in time to save us. We're on our own."

Six disappeared deep into the shadows of the partially constructed stalls.

Gillian quickly opened the bottom portion of the Dutch doors and closed the top to keep the interior dim. She grabbed two handfuls of corn from a nearby sack and threw it around on the floor inside. She took another handful and scattered it in the open doorway to entice the pigs in, hoping their lumbering, snorting presence would discourage Jodi from making a thorough search of the interior and have her think only animals were in the shed.

Shoes crunched on the gravel outside the front door. Gillian grabbed the nearest things at hand: a simple hammer and a short-handled manure fork, and fled to the wing opposite the one Six was in. She hunkered down in the stall at the end, and tried to quiet her breathing and pounding heart. She soon heard pigs grunt as they entered the building in search of feed. One found its way to her stall, its nose snuffling along the ground, seeking the scent of corn.

Suddenly, more light entered the shed. Someone had opened the front door.

"Jaa—cob," Jodi's singsong voice called out. "Jaaa—cob."

Gillian held her breath, afraid for herself. Afraid for Michelle. Afraid of what might happen in the next few minutes.

Some of the pigs snorted and grunted, spooked by the strange woman limping into the shed. A few hurried back outside. Some, like the one near Gillian's hiding place, ignored the distraction and continued searching for food.

"Get out of my way," Jodi snarled.

Gillian heard a shot, followed by a pig squealing. Alarmed by the ruckus, the pig in the stall with Gillian grunted and hurried to escape. So did the other pigs still in the shed.

Keep moving, her dad's voice echoed in her head.

He was right. This was her chance.

Bent over, she followed the pig, hoping to appear like just another animal low to the ground scurrying amidst the shadows. Only she had a hammer in one hand and a manure fork in the other. She had the strange feeling Ray would approve if she crucified his murderous sister to the wall with the tines.

Jodi had shifted sideways, trying to keep from being knocked over by the fleeing, squealing pigs. Gillian was halfway to her—just a little further and she could stab her with the manure fork—when the distant *whump, whump, whump* of an approaching helicopter filled the air.

Six shot up from her hiding place and shouted, "My ship! My celestial companions have come to convey me home!"

Startled by Six, Jodi turned and immediately caught sight of Gillian. She aimed the gun at her. "Put that down."

Gillian threw the manure fork to the ground but kept the hammer hidden behind her body. A ripple of apprehension swept through her as Jodi smiled at Six.

"At long last, she's finally mine."

Confused, Gillian said, "I thought you wanted Jacob."

"The jailor?" Jodi laughed in disdain. "Jacob wants nothing to do with me."

"Why? Because you're so fat?"

Jodi bristled in anger. She shambled toward her and away from Six, who was looking up at the ceiling of the shed, listening to what she thought was the approach of her spacecraft.

Gillian tightened her grip on the hammer behind her back. Nothing like a little rage to throw off Jodi's aim. Just a little closer and she'd be within reach. "No wonder Jacob's been avoiding you. Have you looked in a mirror lately? You should feel right at home with the pigs."

"Shut up!" Furious, Jodi's hand shook as she pointed the gun at her. "I gained weight for my disguise. I can lose it. De Niro did. So did Hanks. It won't take long. Besides, it doesn't matter what he thinks. Only what *she* thinks."

She? "Are you talking about Michelle?"

"That scaredy-cat? What a joke. She's absolutely worthless. Another wimp infesting the world. I'm surprised Jacob hasn't exterminated her by now."

If not Michelle, then who? Lin Lin? Olga? Six?

Six.

Suddenly it all became clear: the reason why Jodi gave bombs only to middle class males with multiple personalities; the reason why she wanted above all else to threaten Jacob. He was the first MPD/DID Jodi had met after her brother's death when Jacob started doing his research on Ray. "You want Six of Twelve to take Janeane's place."

"The lady gets an A. Took you long enough to figure it out."

"All those men you gave bombs to, they were like Ray— solid middle class values, meek, loving, all with multiple personalities."

Jodi grinned. "All with someone like Janeane lurking inside, waiting for me to appreciate them, to release them from their jailors and help them stay out."

"You found them all on Jacob's website."

"In his chat rooms. It's how I knew which ones had the alters I was looking for. Janeane loved handing out death. What better way to bring out the same personality than to threaten them with death?"

The steady beat of the helicopter continued to grow louder.

"My ship!" Six cried out.

Jodi limped toward Six and smiled fondly. "God, I love her."

Gillian nodded, at last unraveling the Carpenter's tangled thinking. "If Janeane found herself with a bomb in her hand, she would have laughed and thrown it away."

"Exactly."

Gillian inched closer to Jodi. "So the microphones on the caddies weren't just to make sure they were doing as told but to listen for when the personality you wanted came out."

Jodi scowled. "But none of them did. Most reverted to their wimpiest alters, not their strongest. At the Institute, I made the mistake of showing the bomb to Michelle. Lin Lin came out. But now that's all changed. Six is already here. I don't need Jacob to lead me to her. Watch, I'll show you."

Jodi approached Six and held out the bomb. "Six, if you want to get to your ship, take this."

Six studied the bomb in the outstretched hand. Then she looked at Gillian.

Gillian shook her head in alarm. "NO! Don't touch it!"

Six looked up at the ceiling of the shed as the *whumps* grew louder. The desperate longing on her face was unmistakable. "I want to go home." She grabbed the bomb.

Immediately, Six changed. In rapid succession, her physical appearance altered. She became the scared little girl, Lin Lin; a bewildered, stodgy Godfrey; the stooped-over, eye-averting old Jacob; a frightened Michelle; a cringing teenage Tisha; and then back to Six—a calm, logical thinking alien.

"How does this work?" Six asked Jodi.

Jodi removed the remote control from a pocket and held it up for Six to see. "I can detonate it with this."

Six eyed the device in Jodi's hand. "A primitive device that uses radio waves to send instructions or coded signals."

Jodi nodded in assent. "Don't you love her?" she said to Gillian. "She's perfect."

The *whumps* from the helicopter started to recede—towards the open pasture behind the barn, Gillian surmised.

"No! Don't go!" Six's face twisted in anguish, believing the craft was leaving forever. She glared at Jodi. "This crude contrivance will not procure my passage from this primitive planet." She set the bomb on the nearby workbench, then grabbed the large orange pneumatic nailer and pointed it at Jodi. "Concede the controller."

Jodi stared at the menacing tool in Six's hand, not sure what to do.

The large orange nail gun was heavy. Having a petite woman like Michelle wielding it seemed almost comical, but from experience Gillian knew that the personality of an alter could provide strength and knowledge the dominant personality didn't have.

Six didn't even have to use two hands to keep it aimed steadily at Jodi. "Concede the controller so I can contact my ship," Six said in a flinty voice, "or I will be forced to use this concuss zat zapper on you."

"Yes!" Jodi practically jumped for joy. "She even uses nails just like Janeane! My sister! My new sister! You're finally out! Finally free! And you can stay out for as long as you want." Keeping the gun pointed at Gillian, she wrapped an arm around Six, crying and hugging her as if she was a long lost sibling.

Six remained still, seemingly unaffected by the emotional embrace. Coldly, she said, "Warning was provided. No one may impede my egress from Earth."

With cool, mechanical efficiency, Six raised the nail gun to Jodi's side and uttered, "Zzzzz." Gillian heard a pop, like a small firecracker going off. In horror she saw Jodi's body jerk once. Another "Zzzz," another popping sound, and Jodi jerked again.

Jodi dropped the gun, then the remote control. Her body slumped to the ground, and Six let her fall, keeping the nail gun pointed at her.

Gillian ran forward. "I don't understand."

Jodi was gasping for air at her feet.

Gillian looked at the nail gun, then at Six. "I can't believe you did this. It shouldn't have worked." She tried to snatch the tool away from Six but the woman refused to let go. Instead, she pointed it at her.

"That's one wicked alter."

Gillian swiveled in the direction of the voice. Sam crawled through the open bottom of the Dutch door, a gun in his hand.

Gillian smiled in relief "Sam! Of course. *You* shot her."

Sam secured the gun Jodi had dropped, then got to his feet. He kept his gun pointed down at Jodi. "How'd you know she wasn't getting nailed?" he asked Gillian.

"Pneumatic tools can be deadly as guns. With two nephews and a niece around, I keep the fuel cells that power them in the gun cabinet."

"Smart."

She moved to put her arms around him but stopped when she saw the dirt-caked blood on the side of his clothes. "Sam! You're hurt!"

"I'll be fine." He wrapped one arm around her and held her close.

"Wyatt—"

"Injured but he'll be fine, too."

"See," Jodi said between gasps while grimacing in pain. "I knew it. Someone like Janeane *is* in Jacob. Just needed death to bring her out. Did you see how great she looked? Fierce. Determined. And loving it. Just like Janeane. God, I miss her. It'll be good to see her again."

"Only in hell," Sam said.

"Doesn't matter. Anywhere, as long as we're together." With a final gasp, she passed out.

"Is she going to die?" Gillian asked Sam. "You shot her twice." Other than the wounds Jodi had gotten from the bomb, she couldn't see any new ones bleeding through the overcoat.

"Even with a bulletproof vest, getting hit with a bullet can knock the breath out of you. Getting hit with two, plus her injuries from the nails, should keep her down and out for a while. She'll live, at least long enough to stand trial." He looked at the ground. "Where's that remote?"

Gillian screwed in a light bulb overhead to provide more light. "I thought it fell over there by Six." She looked around in alarm. The nail gun was back on the bench, and Six was gone. "Where is she?"

"There." Sam pointed out the front door of the shed. Six was walking toward the barn where the helicopter could be heard powering down. She was looking at something in her hand.

"Ohmigod!" Gillian ran after her. So did Sam.

"Six!" Gillian yelled. "Put that down! Don't touch it!"

Six turned to them but kept the remote solidly in her grasp. "I want to go home. I must summon my ship."

Her eyes widened in alarm. She could see Regis and his team running from behind the barn towards them, weapons drawn, pointed at Six.

Even Sam had his gun pointed at her. As they moved nearer, he told Six, "Take it easy. Put it down, now, or I'll be forced to shoot. You can't go home if you're dead."

Gillian pleaded with her. "He's right. That thing in your hand, it won't work. It's not for summoning ships."

Six stared at her.

"Let me talk with Michelle. Or Tisha. Or Lin Lin. Jacob. Anyone. Please. They'll understand."

"They do," Six said.

Or was it Six?

Gillian looked at her, puzzled by the strangeness of the voice. While she tried to identify which alter had spoken, Six held out the control for Sam to take. As he grasped it, Six's thumb flicked the last three switches. The farrowing shed exploded, knocking everyone off their feet, littering the ground with debris.

As Sam reached over and checked to make sure Gillian was all right, he heard a sharp cry from Regis. He couldn't help but grin. A nail. Had to be a nail.

Chapter Twenty-Seven

Wyatt Dohr sat on a bench on the front porch of his home, trying to sit still with all the activity around him. He had gotten out of the hospital just yesterday, two days earlier than expected, not because he was a fast healer, but because he was "the orneriest patient" the hospital in Cheyenne had ever dealt with, or so his doctor said.

He'd promised to stay in bed for a week but had insisted on sitting outside to see their guests off. Gillian was a few yards away, walking slowly with Michelle toward the orchard. Regis, his arm finally out of the sling after being injured by a nail, was helping a female FBI agent put Michelle's suitcase and packages in the trunk of a blue sedan. She would accompany him and Michelle on the drive back to New York. The alter Tisha still refused to fly.

He tried not to chuckle—it hurt to laugh—but he did so anyway as he recalled Regis trying to convince Sam just that morning to take his place on the long drive. It was like arguing with a bale of hay. Sam had stood there, impassive, while Regis cajoled, bargained, and tried to bribe the New York detective.

For being a hotshot profiler, Regis could be as dull as a fence post when it came to matters of the heart. But at least he had the good sense not to press charges against Michelle. It was impossible to prove one of her alters didn't accidentally flip the last three switches when handing over the remote control to Sam.

Everyone had their doubts, but doubts don't get a conviction.

Susan Dohr came out on the porch with two steaming cups of coffee in her hands and her purse hanging from a strap on her shoulder. She handed one cup to her husband and asked, "Where are the boys?"

He nodded in the direction of the chicken coops. "They're with Sam, feeding the chickens."

Susan let out a whistle anyone could hear from a mile away, then yelled, "Travis! Randy!" While she waited for a response, she told Wyatt, "That was Fred Kennedy on the phone just now. Says he wants to borrow the fence post digger. Asked if you could bring it over sometime this week."

"Afraid to come here?"

"Afraid to drive. Wouldn't you if you were conked over the head, then stuffed in the trunk of your car by a killer posing as a stranded motorist?"

"If I was ninety years old like Fred, maybe."

The boys came running from around the garage. Sam strolled behind.

"Time to go visit Scrounger!" Susan yelled.

The boys whooped and hollered and raced to the family's minivan. The veterinarian wanted to keep the dog for another week to make sure Scrounger rested long enough to heal properly, but during the last visit, the boys had gotten her to shorten the stay by a day.

Chips off the old block, Wyatt thought, and he smiled.

"Is Katie going with you?" he asked.

"She's inside, wrapping a gift for Michelle. She insisted on staying to take care of you. She'll make sure you get back upstairs and in bed the moment they leave."

A chip off the old Susan block, he noted, and smiled some more.

Susan kissed him, then headed down the stairs to the car. On the way she handed Sam the other cup of coffee, which he took with a warm smile and a "Thanks." She said good-bye to Regis and got in the minivan with her sons and drove away. In the meantime, Sam reached the porch and sat on the railing, sipping the coffee.

"I'm going to miss helping your sons feed the chickens every morning," Sam told Wyatt.

"Among other things." He glanced knowingly at Sam. "I heard from my kids you and Gillian have been spending a lot of time in the barn."

Sam coughed and looked away. "Yeah. Um, we've been working on the damage. Rebuilding the broken stalls, reframing the hole in the wall."

"And testing out the straw?" He gave Sam his full attention. "I grew up here, remember? I know what barns are for. One of my sons got his start in there."

Sam took a long pull on the coffee, then looked down at his feet.

"I'm not going to ask if your intentions are honorable," Wyatt said. "You're a hell of a lot better for my sister than Regis. I'm glad she finally saw sense and told him they could only be friends. But now what? New York is your home. This is Gillian's. How the hell do you expect to compromise over that?"

"We're still working it out."

He shook his head, seeing no solution to their problem. "Long distances tend to weaken relationships."

Sam frowned. "I know."

"I'll say one more thing on the subject and then let it go. One of the deputies is planning to retire in a few months. The sheriff's department is already advertising the position. Might be good to have an outsider around to give us an idea on how things are done in other areas of the country."

Sam raised his brow in surprise.

Wyatt looked to where Regis was getting inside the sedan. "Can't wait to get rid of these Feds. Snobbish bunch."

Sam laughed. "Know what we call the FBI in New York?"

While Wyatt and Sam exchanged monikers such as Fuss-Butt Inspectors and Fat Bureau of Idiots, Gillian and Michelle wandered among the cherry trees, talking.

"I'm not as smart as Jacob," Michelle said.

"Sure you are," Gillian replied.

"Are you kidding? I barely made it out of high school, while he has a Ph.D."

"But all the knowledge he has is in *your* head. In *your* brain cells. Maybe if you quit fighting him you'll gain access to all the info he's accumulated."

Michelle stopped and looked at Gillian, her lips quirked with skepticism.

"Maybe one day when Jacob is integrated into you, you'll become Dr. Michelle Johnson, New York City's renowned expert on MPD/DID."

"Yeah, right. I'll be Super-brain overnight."

"It may not happen that fast, but with time most anything is possible—if you let it. If you let him become part of you."

Michelle scrunched her face in uncertainty. "I'll think about it. No promises there. But one thing."

"What's that?"

"I refuse to eat only kosher food. The pickles are okay, but I'm not giving up bacon and ham."

Gillian laughed. "Tell you what, next time we butcher a hog, I'll send you a side of bacon."

"Thanks. I guess I owe you a lot—all you did to keep me safe, what happened to your place, your brother getting hurt, your buildings damaged. The least I can do is let you talk."

"Talk? But I'm already—"

The transformation was immediate. Michelle turned stiff with age, her shoulders hunched slightly forward, her face drawn, with wrinkles on her forehead that Gillian could swear weren't there a few seconds ago. Michelle smacked her lips several times and cleared her throat. She no longer looked directly at Gillian but off to the side.

"It is good to finally see you again, Gillian Dohr."

She studied Michelle, marveling at the dramatic change in appearance. Even without the flat-brimmed black hat and curlicues at the temples, she could almost swear they were there. With a tentative smile, she said to Michelle's alter, "Nice to see you too, Jacob. I'm sorry I ignored your warnings at the hotel. I—"

He raised his hand and wiggled it back and forth in an effort to halt her apology. "Quite understandable, given the circumstances. None of us were thinking logically. In the end, everything worked out. The evil was stopped. Peace restored. We should all be thankful to the Almighty that more were not killed."

"Yes, including us." She paused for a moment, truly grateful that she, her brother, Sam, Jacob and Michelle and all her alters, and Fred Kennedy, were still alive.

"Do you think Jodi Follett really killed the other men out of frustration?" she asked. "That it was all a convoluted scheme to get Six of Twelve to come out and be her best friend?"

Jacob shrugged. "Through all our emails, Jodi constantly told me how much she missed Ray, when in truth she really missed Janeane. She thought I had an evil alter like her brother with whom she could become friends, maybe even lovers. Who can say how a crazy mind works? Look how long doctors have been trying to figure out whether DID is real. Many still believe Michelle makes me up, imagines I exist in order to get attention or fulfill some sexual fantasy only a Freudian psychologist could figure out. Even after mankind has explored the universe and all the oceans, we will still be trying to figure out how the mind works."

Gillian frowned in agreement. "Strange how Jodi considered the dominant personality of someone with DID to be a jailor, and all the other personalities prisoners. Since she kept trying to find you, she must have thought you were the dominant personality, not Michelle."

Jacob nodded solemnly. "She would not be the first."

Including Michelle. An ongoing problem for these two.

She looked toward the house and saw Sam talking with her brother. "There's something I've been wondering since all of this started. The bomb that went off on Broadway and 43rd, were you in its vicinity?"

"You mean the bomb Vincent Ragino was coerced into delivering to me because Jodi Follett hoped it would entice Six of Twelve to appear?" Jacob raised his hands in regret. He sighed heavily, and his face seemed to age even more, the wrinkles deepening with sadness. "I am a creature of habit. Some of it of my own doing. Some necessitated by the schedule Michelle makes me adhere to."

He patted his stomach. "My favorite bakery is near 43rd. When I have been a good boy, as Michelle puts it, she lets me have breakfast there. Unfortunately for Vincent, Michelle overslept that morning, and we were late arriving. I was half a block away when the bomb went off. With both Vincent and Jodi dead, we will never know whether he did it accidentally or she detonated it out of impatience."

"Amazing how the simplest thing like waking up late for work can alter so many lives."

"In life, it is always the small things that make the big difference."

Again, she looked over at Sam. She smiled, remembering the first time she saw him. "Would you know why Roger Walgood was told to take a bomb to Union Square?"

"That is where Michelle usually changes trains."

"And the Starbucks? The Port Authority Bus Terminal?"

"Both Michelle and Godfrey call that particular Starbucks their 'favorite haunt.' As for the Port Authority . . . I am ashamed to say I was trying to run away. By then I suspected I was the one the Carpenter was after. I thought if I left the city, the bombing would stop." He looked down at the ground. "It only made Jodi angrier. She must have been following me. Knew what I was planning to do."

"Jodi became desperate," Gillian surmised. "How stupid of her not to realize her bombs would alter everyone's routine. With you on the verge of escaping, she didn't have time to find someone with DID to bring you the bomb."

Jacob nodded. "I heard a scream from the other side of the terminal. Then I saw an object hurtling through the air toward me. She did not have a good arm—it landed short and far away. Even so, Lin Lin came out to take my place and huddled to the ground, crying. It was then, when Jodi lost sight of me, that she detonated the bomb."

"That makes sense, sort of. If Jodi couldn't stop you, she could use the bomb to stop the buses from running."

"It worked. When Lin Lin let me back out, I promised myself not to endanger so many lives again. I would stay in the city and pray for help." He shook his head repeatedly and sighed. "And yet more continued to die."

"It wasn't your fault. Jodi made that decision. As you said, how can anyone figure out a crazy person. Besides, once I realized the Carpenter was after you and Michelle, the first thing I did was get both of you out of the city."

A smile teetered on his solemn lips. "Great minds think alike."

Gillian laughed, and his smile broke through for a moment. Then he lowered his head and sighed again. "I will miss my friends: Roger, Vincent, Christopher, and Omar, and those who lost their lives at the Institute of Many Friends. All good people. And I will miss their alters as well. I would have gladly given my life to spare theirs. If only I had realized sooner the Carpenter was Jodi Follett and that she was using the others to get to me."

Gillian placed a hand on his shoulder to comfort him, but withdrew it immediately as he stiffened and moved away from her touch. She had forgotten a Hasidic Jew is polite and respectful but refrains from physical contact with the opposite sex in public, especially when not married to the other. "Sorry."

He shrugged. "It is forgotten. You meant well. Accept it. We are who we are."

"One more thing, if you don't mind. There's something that's been bothering me. The voice who spoke just before Six detonated the bombs in the pig shed with Jodi. That wasn't Six's voice. It wasn't the voice of any of Michelle's alters."

Jacob smacked his lips and nodded deeply in thought. "It would seem there is still one inside us that none of us knows about. I will consult our psychiatrist first chance I get."

She studied him. With all his expertise, could Jacob really not be aware of another alter dwelling inside Michelle?

As she looked at him, his gaze rose, and he stared directly into her eyes. "Until we meet again, the Almighty willing."

He smiled warmly. And was gone. The elderly man dissolved into Michelle's feminine stance, fluid and graceful and young, with an ever-present wariness in her eyes.

Before Michelle could resist, Gillian reached out and gave her a hug. "Thank you. That was so nice of you to do that for me and Jacob."

Michelle reluctantly hugged her back. "The others said it was the least I could do."

"But *you* did it, not them. That's what counts." She drew back and looked toward the house where a car horn was honking. "I guess they're ready to go."

"Yeah. Somehow I don't think it's going to be as much fun as the ride out here. Maybe I can get Olga to come out for a few hours. Her incessant talking should annoy the shit out of that stuffy Regis."

Gillian laughed. "I have to admit, at first I wasn't sure I liked you, but you have a wicked sense of humor. I'm really going to miss you."

Her revelation seemed to startle Michelle, and her eyes teared when Gillian added, "Do you mind if I look you up the next time I'm in New York? Maybe have dinner together?"

"You're not talking about Jacob? You want to come see me?"

"Sure."

This time it was her turn to be startled as Michelle rose up on tiptoe and threw her arms around her. "Call me."

"I will."

They headed back to the house. When they neared the porch, Katie, who had been sitting next to her dad, ran down the stairs to them. She handed Michelle an object almost a foot long, wrapped around and around with white freezer paper with yellow daisies drawn on it and a lopsided pink bow on top.

"This is for Lin Lin," Katie told Michelle. "Yesterday while we were playing dolls she told me her birthday's today and no one's ever given her a present. That didn't seem right. She can have this one, okay?"

At first Michelle looked surprised. Then she smiled warmly. "I'm sure she's going to love it. Thank you."

"You're welcome." With a huge smile on her face, the little girl ran back up onto the porch to sit next to her dad.

Wyatt told her, "You did good."

Michelle went inside to fetch the purse she had bought on a recent shopping trip into Cheyenne. When she returned, she thanked Wyatt and Sam for all they had done to help her. Regis honked the car horn, impatient to be going. She frowned. "Definitely going to introduce him to Olga."

Wyatt and Sam looked at her in confusion, but Gillian couldn't help but laugh.

She and Sam accompanied Michelle to the car to see her off. A few minutes later, their eyes were following the trail of dust as the vehicle headed south to Cheyenne and the interstate.

Sam said, "One more to go and your life can get back to normal."

For all the bravado in his tone, he seemed uncertain. She searched his face to see if he regretted leaving as much as she did. "You sure you have to go so soon? You can change your tickets and stay another day or two."

"Or three. Or four." He sighed heavily and drew her into his arms. "My suspension was up days ago." He held her close. "I'd love to spend more time here with you, but there's a backlog of cases Tony and I were working on before the Carpenter came to town."

She rested her head against him and listened to the strong beat of his heart. Being in Sam's arms, having him around all day and all night, talking with him, laughing with him, seemed to be as natural as the sun rising and setting. But then, out of the corner of her eye, she saw the last vestiges of dust from Regis's car disappear along the horizon, and she had to ask, "Are you going back to New York to tie up loose ends . . . or to return to your life there?"

"I don't know." He felt her shudder beneath his embrace. Obviously not the answer she wanted to hear. He didn't want to hurt her, but honesty was the foundation of their relationship. "I like it here. I like hearing Katie talking with her daddy on the porch, like they're doing now. I enjoy doing chores with your nephews. I like being part of your family. And I love being part of your life. But there's another life I don't know whether I can leave. I've gotta go back and see how it feels to leave you and this life behind."

She swallowed hard and looked up at him with dark chocolate eyes. "I'll miss you."

"I'm already missing you." He bent his head and kissed her for a long time. "I better go get my things. The shuttle from Cheyenne to Denver leaves in two hours."

"Enough time for one last trip to the barn?" she asked, a mischievous sparkle in her eyes.

He glanced at the porch and noticed her brother's watchful gaze. "Unfortunately, no." He wrapped one arm around her, and they started for the house. "So, what are you going to do with no one around to distract you? Start work on a new pig shed?"

"Calvin will be here later this week. He's feeling pretty good. His clients were only convicted of aggravated robbery, not murder. He wants to settle our differences. I thought it only fair to tell him in person what Jodi Follett revealed about Ray's death and the last five children to be killed."

"Maybe then he'll stop carrying the nail in his wallet. Stop holding on to the guilt."

"I hope so." She smiled lightly. "And then I'll start on the new shed."

"Will it look like the Capitol again?"

"Nope." She pulled a folded sheet of paper out the back pocket of her jeans. "Six paid me a visit last night. She drew up plans for the new shed, hoping the design would catch the interest of her celestial companions the next time they zoom by and entice them to stop and investigate—and pick her up."

She unfolded the paper and handed it to Sam. Wait for it, she told herself as his eyes widened in surprise. The grin that broke out on his face and the joyful laugh that accompanied it warmed her heart.

"You're kidding?" he said, easing into chuckles.

"In spite of its appearance, it's completely doable."

"But a spaceship as a pig shed?"

"Farrowing shed. Look here." She pointed excitedly to the drawing. "The saucer section will have pie-shaped stalls. One of the engine nacelles will be used to store feed and tools, the other straw. The top section will be the bridge. Sort of a science fiction clubhouse. My niece and nephews will love it."

Sam reached up and caressed her cheek. "You're something else, Gillian Dohr."

"I know," she answered softly, moving into his touch. "After all, I am The Oracle."

Six wanted to use the design to snare her fellow space travelers' attention, but already it had captured Sam's curiosity. Hopefully, he'd return to see its completed version, and its builder.

Six might say it's in the stars. Gillian didn't believe in astrology or space aliens, but as Sam kissed her one last time, she was certain they'd get back together. It was inevitable. Resistance futile.

Sam went to the porch to get his bag. She'd packed it that morning, clothes neatly folded. Knowing Sam, he'd shove and cram it into the overhead storage bin on the plane to make it fit, crushing the love letter she'd hidden among the clothes for him to find when he got home. A reminder of who he had left behind.

And she realized if she chose Sam, she'd better get used to being crammed into his life.

Is that what she wanted? Was he worth it?

She took a good long look at his tight butt as he stowed the bag in the back of the car.

Definitely.

Acknowledgements

Though alone at a computer for hours at a time, a writer's work is never the product of only one person. There are a lot of people who helped to hone and polish this story, all of whom I am very grateful for. They include:

Bill McCoy, Mary Hartman, and Elizabeth Durbin, who have gone on ahead but who I wish were still here to see the book in its published form;

Russell Crago, who tried to teach me how explosives work—any laws of physics broken in the story are entirely my doing;

the Alpha online critique group of the Rocky Mountain Fiction Writers, who helped with the original first chapters of the story when it was called The Oracle, while I was living in the tiny town of Wamsutter, Wyoming, over ninety miles away from a fellow writer to look over my work;

CAWG, the Cheyenne Area Writers Group, composed of Michael Shay, Mary Gillgannon, and Jeana Byrne, all wonderful writers in their respective genres, who never hesitated to tell me what worked and what didn't work;

the encouragement of contest judges who looked at my entry and kept commenting "I can't believe this isn't already published;"

to Robin D Owens and Jeana Byrne who took the time to read the entire story one last time to make sure I hadn't taken too much out when I revised and shortened it;

to Amanda Cabot for discovering a crucial mistake;

to Karen Duvall for the great looking cover and Rose Beetem for the final edits;

to Eric Roadifer and Cody Lee Francis for help with the logo;

to Sharon Mignerey, Steven Moores, Cate Rowan, and Jeff and Beth Shelby for your advice and encouragement in publishing my book.

To all of you. Thank you.

To my husband Gary, who agreed to let me write full time even though it impacted our budget. Thank you for your support and encouragement. You're the best.

About the Author

Liz Roadifer is an award-winning author, poet, and columnist. Her work has been published in newspapers, magazines, and literary journals.

Born and raised in New Jersey near New York City, she attended the University of Wyoming and fell in love with the wide-open sky, the high plains, the friendly, laidback people of Wyoming, and a certain cowboy from a ranch near Sundance. She now lives in a small town outside of Cheyenne with her husband and enjoys spending time with her sons, daughter-in-law, and three rambunctious grandchildren.

Thank you for buying my book. If you enjoyed this story, please consider posting a favorable review on book review sites such as Amazon, Barnes & Noble, and Goodreads. For independent authors like myself, good reviews help us compete with the big name publishers.

I can be reached at lizroadifer@gmail.com or my website LizRoadifer.com

CPSIA information can be obtained at www.ICGtesting.com
Printed in the USA
LVOW07s2148130515

438448LV00003B/148/P